"WHY SUCH PRETENSES TO GET AWAY FROM ME?"

As he spoke, Rock's gaze fell playfully on Beryl's angry face. Cradling her in his arms, he bent to kiss her, first tracing his tongue along the soft flesh of her bare shoulders.

Torn by warring emotions, Beryl pulled free of his sensuous touch. "I won't be fooled!" she stormed. "You're just a male opportunist—the kind that isn't happy until he has every woman around him wanting him."

Her outburst swiftly dissolved under the intimacy of his touch as he drew near her again. His probing tongue parted her trembling lips, and his hands knowingly caressed her.

Gently, he lifted her head and met her eyes firmly. "If you believe what you said, you don't know me at all. There's only one woman I want right now...."

AND NOW...

SUPERROMANCES

Worldwide Library is proud to present a
sensational new series of modern love stories—
SUPERROMANCES

Written by masters of the genre, these longer,
sensuous and dramatic novels are truly in keeping
with today's changing life-styles. Full of intriguing
conflicts, the heartaches and delights of true love,
SUPERROMANCES are absorbing stories—
satisfying and sophisticated reading that lovers
of romance fiction have long been waiting for.

SUPERROMANCES
Contemporary love stories for the woman of today!

DEBORAH JOYCE
A QUESTING HEART

A SUPERROMANCE FROM
W RLDWIDE

TORONTO · NEW YORK · LOS ANGELES · LONDON

Published April 1983

First printing February 1983

ISBN 0-373-70061-X

Printed in Canada

CHAPTER ONE

THE FIRST BRIGHT RAYS of early-morning sunlight were peeking over the jagged horizon, heralding the arrival of a new day, and from all corners of the tiny village sounds of bustling activity began to drift out into the crisp fresh dawn air. A team of mules plodded slowly down the narrow pathway that divided rows of ragged houses from a swift-flowing noisy mountain stream. The singsong cadence of the muleteer as he urged them along mingled harmoniously with the muted ringing of the bells that decorated the packs.

Beryl Bartlett opened her green eyes briefly in response to the sounds and then reached automatically to adjust her pillow more comfortably before settling down for another hour of sleep. Instead of the soft pillow she expected to find, her hand encountered rough unsanded wood, forcing her abruptly into a state of wakefulness. For a moment she lay absolutely still, a hint of confusion evident on her lovely oval face as she silently surveyed the contents of the dingy room.

Her eyes adjusted gradually to the dim light that filtered in through a solitary window. Things looked different this morning. Last night the huge cobwebs that festooned every corner of the ceiling had seemed oddly frightening, and she had wasted no time before crawling up on the narrow ledge that served as a bed. This morning she could see that the only furniture in the room was a rickety table, minus one of its spindly legs. Her own bright canvas suitcase looked out of place against the bare shabby floor.

As her glance moved to a pile of neatly packed crates behind her suitcase she felt a burst of excitement that left her heart beating faster. She wasn't at home in her luxurious bedroom in Dallas, Texas; she was in Nepal, in the legendary land of Shangri-la.

The haze of sleepiness had completely receded from her mind now, leaving her achingly aware of her cramped muscles. The narrow ledge on which she had slept, wrapped in a serviceable wool blanket, had definitely not been designed for someone who was nearly six feet tall. Her thoughts turned longingly to a cup of hot tea or coffee as she listened to the unfamiliar sounds outside her room.

Suddenly she felt a pressing need to see her surroundings again, as if to reassure herself that she was really here in Nepal. She sat up carefully, stretching her bunched muscles and shivering slightly as the blanket dropped from her shoulders and she felt a rush of chill morning air against her skin. Jade green pajamas clung softly to the soft curves of her figure as she stood up and walked over to the tiny window set high in the rough wall.

Far out on the horizon were the glacier-covered lofty peaks of the Himalayan Range, rising into the clouds with majestic splendor. On distant mountainsides, snowfields of faint pink were illuminated by the rising sun, while deep ravines lay buried in purplish black shadows. Here and there faint misty rays of sun passed diagonally across the meadows, reflections from the steep snow peaks.

From this side of the room she couldn't see the rest of the village, but the air was filled with snatches of conversation and the clattering of dishes and pans that indicated breakfast was under way.

She doubted that anyone would offer her breakfast. The villagers had stared at her in silence the evening before as the pilot of the small aircraft that had flown to this remote place led her to the one-room hut. Her thick wavy blond hair and the regal carriage of her tall slim body had seemed to mesmerize the silent crowd of men, women and children who gathered to watch the plane's arrival. She wasn't quite certain why they were so unfriendly. Didn't they see a lot of foreigners here? After all, many mountaineering expeditions trekked through this area.

As a faint, unidentifiable but appetizing odor began to drift into the room, Beryl forced herself to ignore the pangs of hunger that were beginning to assail her. There had been no dinner the previous night, either, and she suddenly realized that it was close to twenty-four hours since she'd eaten her last meal.

Her gaze focused once more on the glittering panorama before her, and she caught her breath in a gasp of pure ecstasy. She took a deep breath of the cool air, fragrantly scented by the pines and rhododendrons that dotted the meadow before her. It was unbelievable; this land of mystery and spectacular scenery seemed to be beckoning to her, drawing her onward to inevitable adventure.

It was exactly one week ago that her twin brother had become ill—on the very day he was supposed to leave to join a mountaineering expedition. Before she'd quite known what was happening, Beryl had found herself on a flight to Nepal, accompanying the supplies Brad had been carefully organizing for more than a year, supplies that were vitally needed by the mountain-climbing team that hoped to scale Mount Everest.

"The group has to have that equipment," Brad had told her when she'd visited him in the hospital before she left. "They're not going to believe that I'm being stopped by a stupid thing like appendicitis," he'd added despairingly.

"Just be thankful it wasn't anything more serious," their mother had chimed in. And Beryl had to agree; she'd been secretly a little relieved that her twin brother wouldn't be able to join the expedition. They had always been close, and she hadn't liked the stories she'd heard about the leader of the expedition, Rock Rawlings. He seemed to thrive on danger, urging those who trekked with him to challenge themselves to the limit.

"I'm not sure Beryl should go over there by herself," her mother had continued. "Are you certain it's absolutely necessary?"

"Don't worry." Brad had patted her hand reassuringly. "Beryl can take care of herself; she's a big girl now."

"Yes, she is big all right," their mother had agreed thoughtfully, gazing disapprovingly up at Beryl as if it were her fault that she had turned out to be nearly six feet tall. The twins had inherited their father's

height—a fact Monica Bartlett found endearing in
Brad but deplorable in Beryl.

"Now, mother, would it make things any better if
I told you that Rock Rawlings is a bachelor and he is
a lot taller than Beryl?" Brad had teased. "And
besides, he's a university professor with a doctorate
in physiology."

"Really?"

Beryl had groaned inwardly as she saw how her
mother's interest perked up at the mention of an
eligible bachelor. Her single status at twenty-three
was a constant affront to her society-conscious
mother.

She'd hurriedly changed the subject, and they
spent the rest of the visit discussing their father's bid
for a seat in the Texas senate. Her mother had worried that it didn't look right for the daughter of a
political candidate to go running around the world
on her own. She'd launched into a lecture on proper
social behavior, which caused Beryl and Brad to grin
at each other behind her back. But underneath that
smile Beryl had felt a spark of resentment tinged with
pain. It seemed there was no way to please her
parents without giving in to their desires that she
make marriage her primary goal.

Beryl had arrived in Katmandu, the capital city of
Nepal, early the previous morning. A representative
from the American Embassy had greeted her with the
news that Rock Rawlings had already left with his
team, leaving instructions for Brad to meet them in
the small village of Lukla. Obviously Rock hadn't
received the messages they had sent about Brad's illness.

After a brief consultation with the embassy official, a charter flight had been arranged, and with scarcely any time to catch more than a glimpse of the old capital, Beryl had flown to the village with Brad's supplies.

She glanced out of the window again, attempting to judge the time. Her watch had stopped hours ago, and even if it were still running it wouldn't be correct, since she had crossed several time zones during her long overseas flight.

It still appeared to be very early; just after dawn, in fact. She flipped open the locks on her suitcase and rummaged through an assortment of clothes before pulling out a pair of jeans and a cable-knit beige sweater. The sight of a pair of heavy sensible hiking boots she'd purchased right before leaving Dallas sent a wave of irritation through her.

She pulled them out and stared down at them, seeing them as a symbol of everything that was wrong with her life right now. Not that the boots were the problem; they were perfectly suited to their purpose. The problem was her mother's aversion to them. To be absolutely honest, it went much deeper than that. The crux of the matter was that she was living at home once again, under the domination of her mother and father, and it was all her own fault.

A little more than a year ago she'd been free, living in her own apartment and working as assistant editor of an oil company's employee newsletter in Dallas. It had been her first attempt to break the stranglehold of the powerful Bartlett family—and it had ended disastrously, sending her home in defeat.

How had she let it all happen? She'd had plenty of

spunk when she announced to her dad that she'd taken the job and was moving out. At first there had been the usual stormy scene, and then he had tried cajoling her, trying to point out that none of the young ladies of their social set left home before marriage. But when he finally recognized her determination, he'd even shown a little grudging respect for her fierce need for independence.

Those had been days of excitement and enthusiasm when she'd felt there was no obstacle too big to stand in the way of her dreams. And then had come Paul....

Shrugging her shoulders impatiently, Beryl forced thoughts of Paul Selleck out of her mind. As her gaze fell once again on her boots, she remembered Monica's horrified outburst when she'd seen Beryl packing them in her bag. She had demanded to know why Beryl was taking them with her.

"I might get a chance to do a little hiking myself," Beryl had said defiantly. Her mother's only answer had been a shrug of her elegant silk-clad shoulders.

A quick survey of the room showed Beryl there was no hope of a shower. One lone cracked pitcher sitting on the table was the only amenity, and it was bone-dry.

When would Rock arrive? Would he come himself or would he send one of the other team members? She would probably have quite a long wait. The pilot had been vague about what time he planned to leave the next day, and Beryl hadn't been able to understand much of his broken English. He would wait with his plane, he'd told her. When she was ready to go she could find him.

After deliberating for a few moments she decided that there was no reason to get dressed in a hurry. She might as well go ahead with her usual morning exercise routine. It took a few moments of careful stretching and warm-up exercises before her muscles felt relaxed enough to move into the more demanding calisthenics she did every morning. The long hours on the plane and her cramped sleeping quarters had left her a little stiff and sore.

It was really too bad she couldn't go outside and do some jogging. The beautiful backdrop of the mountain ranges and the exhilarating fresh air would be the perfect antidote to her nervous anticipation over meeting Rock Rawlings.

Would he be upset that she had brought the supplies in Brad's place? But really, there hadn't been any other choice. With flight schedules into the tiny kingdom so undependable, they hadn't dared risk sending the boxes by themselves. The hardware and ropes packed in those crates were vitally necessary if the group hoped to reach the top of Mount Everest.

For a moment she let herself dream about how exciting it would be to scale a mountain. What was it Brad had said—that the climb was a way of challenging your physical and mental abilities to the limit? Brad had participated in one of the Rawlings expeditions several years before, and from then on he'd thought of little else. Beryl couldn't help thinking it was not only the actual experience of climbing but also the chance to follow the inspiring example of Rock Rawlings that motivated him.

As always the physical exercise left her feeling alert and happy. That was why she had started jogging in the first place: she'd needed an outlet, a way of escape from her bitter memories of Paul and from her mother's constant chatter about clothes, social events and eligible men once she'd returned home.

Her work as a speech writer on her father's campaign wasn't enough to keep her busy. It still left too much time for berating herself mentally. Jogging had been her lifesaver, leaving her exhausted enough to sleep soundly each night.

After only a few months of serious running, Beryl had found herself involved in local marathon races, and just a month ago she'd placed high in a statewide competition. Her photo had appeared in a Dallas newspaper, showing her looking flushed and tired and dirty as she crossed the finish line. A rueful smile filtered across her face as she remembered the way her mother had carried on about that.

After finishing her exercises Beryl sat on the floor for several minutes, soaking up the warmth of the sunlight that was beginning to flood the room as the sun rose higher in the sky. Her spirits rose, too, and she realized it was time she got dressed and went in search of some breakfast.

She stood up, reaching for her jeans and sweater, and began to unbutton the pajama top. As always, she fought off a lingering sense of dissatisfaction with herself as she surveyed her figure, seeing only the extra inches of height and totally failing to appreciate her slim graceful arms and legs, delicately tanned to a soft golden shade. Her conscientious exercise had smoothed her shapely figure into willowy curves and her skin had the beautiful glow that reflects a healthy body.

A sudden commotion outside the building startled her as heavy footsteps sounded on the gravel pathway in front of the door.

"Bartlett! Are you planning on sleeping all day?" a sudden harsh voice bellowed through the flimsy door on the other side of the room. The tranquillity of the morning was shattered in an instant as Beryl felt a wave of apprehension course through her. Before she could answer, the door was flung open and she found herself confronting the imposing frame of a man who was obviously as startled as she was. For a moment they stared at each other without speaking.

Beryl dropped a swift glance down at her open pajama top and then reached frantically for her sweater, trying ineffectually to cover the exposed curve of her soft full breasts. A slow tide of warmth crept up her neck as the man continued to stare at her, his dark penetrating eyes tracing the length of her body. The slashing line of his brows deepened the intensity of his gaze, stripping away her customary poise and leaving her trembling and slightly breathless.

"Where's Brad?" he asked abruptly, his deep husky voice breaking the silence between them.

"He's in the hospital," she answered, frowning slightly as she heard the tremor that had crept into her voice. "I'm his sister, Beryl. You must be—"

"Where are the supplies?" he cut in sharply.

Beryl pointed at the stacked boxes without speaking. He turned away for a moment, lifting the lid of the top box. She watched him warily, noting the rugged contours of his face, the unruly thickness of his dark hair. His green plaid wool shirt was open slightly at the neck, emphasizing the deep burnished copper of his tan. A pair of worn faded corduroy jeans molded the length of his legs, outlining the powerful muscles of his thighs. He was tall, very tall, and he carried his height with a lean easy grace that showed no signs of apology for the fact that he must tower over most of the men he met.

He turned back to face her abruptly, catching her in the act of carefully assessing him. A brief smile flitted across his face, almost as if he were amused at her obvious curiosity. Her face flamed with color and she glanced away angrily.

"I'm Rock Rawlings," he told her, and this time Beryl was certain his voice was tinged with humor.

"Brad's really sorry he couldn't come," she said stiffly, clutching frantically at her sweater, which seemed to be shrinking under his piercing gaze.

His look was suddenly unreadable, the dark unfathomable eyes losing their amusement and looking almost coal black in the shadowy light near the half-open door. "He's not seriously ill, I hope?"

"Not really," Beryl assured him. "A case of appendicitis."

"So he sent you with the supplies," Rock said after a long pause, during which Beryl felt sure her heart was pounding so loudly that it was audible in the quiet room. His voice had taken on a cool remote quality that seemed to indicate he didn't need any further explanations from her.

"Now that you're here, I suppose I can go back to Katmandu," she told him with an attempt at friendliness. She smiled tentatively. "I'm hoping to do a little sight-seeing before returning to Texas.''

"I'd like to see how you're going to do that.''
This time there was no mistaking the curtness of his
voice.

Beryl scanned his face nervously, noting the
closed, shuttered watchfulness of his eyes. She
moistened her lips carefully before saying, "I hired a
plane. The pilot is waiting to take me back this morning, as soon as I've delivered the supplies.''

"Correction: the pilot *was* here. I've just sent him
back to Katmandu with one of my porters who needed to be taken to the hospital. I was expecting to find
Brad here.'' The clipped precise tones showed no
trace of emotion, and it was a moment before the full
impact of his words hit her.

"You mean I'm stuck here?'' she finally managed
to choke out.

"It looks that way, doesn't it?'' His lips com-
pressed in a forbidding line and he glared harshly at
her. "This isn't Texas, you know. There are no taxis,
no buses, no trains and no regular planes out of this
village.''

Beryl suddenly felt a wave of nausea wash over
her. She tried to ignore the fact that her knees were
feeling decidedly shaky, but Rock's steady gaze
missed nothing.

"You're not going to faint on me, are you?'' he
asked shortly. "At least, if you are please have a seat
first, because I don't particularly relish having to
catch you.''

Beryl felt a flash of resentment at the callousness
of his tone, but the sudden rash of spots before her
eyes made her walk unsteadily back to the ledge

where she had spent the night. She sat down and tried to think clearly about her situation, but her mind refused to cooperate.

"When did you last eat?" A note of grudging concern had crept into Rock's voice, dissolving Beryl's last thread of composure.

"I'm not sure," she said weakly. "Yesterday, I think."

With a muttered oath Rock turned and walked decisively out of the room, slamming the door behind him. His firm measured steps gradually disappeared and Beryl felt a surge of acute panic. She jumped up quickly and jerked off the pajamas with shaking fingers before pulling on the close-fitting jeans.

As she shrugged into the bulky sweater and tied the laces of her hiking boots, her numb mind tried to sort out why this arrogant man had affected her so. His rude greeting and obvious displeasure over seeing her there weren't the only reasons. For some strange reason he was reminding her of Paul.

Perhaps it was because her first meeting with Paul had been stormy, too. She remembered how he had swept into her life unexpectedly, barging into her office at Lone Star Oil and demanding to know who had written the article about his department without his permission.

But the resemblance between the two men stopped there. Paul was blond and slender, while this man was massive and dark. And Paul had valid reasons for being angry, while Rock had shown total ingratitude for her long tiring trip to bring him these supplies.

It must be that her mind was playing tricks on her,

she decided, hurrying over to the door to swing it open and look outside. Rock was coming back toward the little hut carrying a thick white pitcher. He was followed by an old woman dressed in a colorful skirt and a black shawl, bearing a plate and a battered tin mug.

Beryl backed into the room and waited while they entered, her stomach knotting with hunger as she caught a whiff of some delicious odor. She grasped the mug gratefully when the woman handed it to her, attempting to smile her thanks.

The tea was slightly bitter, but the warmth felt wonderful as she gulped it down quickly. Over the rim of the mug her eyes met Rock's sharp gaze. Her glance moved again to the Nepalese woman who was standing uncertainly near the door. Beryl walked toward her, handed her the mug and smiled.

With a sudden flash of her colorful skirt, the woman turned and fled from the room. Beryl stood gazing after her disappearing back; then she whirled and asked in a shocked whisper, "What on earth did I do to offend her?"

Rock's hearty laugh rang out in the silence, causing her to flush with annoyance. "The villagers all think you're some kind of goddess. They've never seen a woman so tall." His glance mocked her as he traced her length with a flick of his dark eyes. "You are tall, aren't you?" He laughed again.

Beryl felt a surge of sudden resentment. "How dare you make fun of me! I didn't grow this way deliberately," she snapped.

His eyes clouded with a momentary regret. In a kinder tone he urged, "You need to eat. Come over here and sit down." He lowered his own tall frame onto the narrow ledge where she had slept and patted the empty space next to him. "Bring that plate over here and eat."

After a brief hesitation, Beryl grabbed the plate and fork and settled down beside him. The plate contained a mixture of chicken and vegetables in a thick heavily spiced gravy, which she ate quickly under Rock's watchful gaze.

The meal revived her earlier optimism, and after they had sat in thick silence for a while she said, "I'm sure there's some way I can get back to Katmandu."

"If you're thinking of walking, I wouldn't suggest it. There are hundreds of miles between us and the city. Besides, my team has to start off this week. We can't afford any more delays or we'll be caught by the monsoons. There's no way I can spare one of my guides to take you back." A frown creased his forehead as he spoke, and he startled her by leaping up and smacking one fist against the narrow ledge. "Damn," he muttered. "There's nothing I need less right now than some woman holding up the whole expedition!"

The seething resentment Beryl had been feeling ever since his reference to her height surged to the surface. "You don't have to worry about me! I can take care of myself. Just go on and leave me here." Her voice was shaking with rage.

He gave her another cool assessing glance before reaching out and gripping her shoulder. Pushing her gently back down on the ledge, he said in a kinder tone, "Okay, just calm down. I have no intention of leaving you here. Besides the fact that I don't make a practice of deserting stranded women, I also happen to consider Brad one of my best friends. There's no way I'd let anything happen to his sister.''

Raking one hand impatiently through his hair, he shifted away and looked out of the window. "You realize there's only one thing that can be done," he said at length. "You'll have to accompany us as far as base camp. I hope I can hire enough extra Sherpas to rig up some kind of chariot to hold between poles and carry you."

Furious over what she considered a crude attempt to cast slurs on her size, she gasped, "That won't be necessary."

"You're not trying to say you can hike through this rugged terrain, are you?"

"I am." She tilted her chin upward in defiance.

He glared at her, a mixture of anger and impatience playing across the smooth planes of his face. "I'm tempted to let you kill yourself," he said finally. "A stubborn fool like you deserves nothing better."

"You do that," she answered with apparent calm. "You let me sink or swim, but I may fool you and not die as easily as you think. How far is base camp?"

"More than a hundred miles, through what is probably the most rugged terrain in the world. With extremes of temperature that are unbelievable. And let's not forget the insects and the wild animals." Each word was uttered forcefully, in emphasis of what he considered to be her total ignorance.

"The only thing that might bother me is the altitude, but I think I can adjust to that," she said firmly. "And what are you going to do when we get to base camp? Shove me off a cliff?"

He glanced at her sharply, impatience warring with a trace of amusement on his face. "Don't tempt me." He turned thoughtfully toward the window again. "There's a rescue station where you can wait. A safe party is bound to come by and let you tag along with them."

"How many days will it take?" she asked, ignoring his gibes. Suddenly she wished she had listened more carefully when Brad had discussed his itinerary in Dallas.

"*Weeks* is more like it. It's not flat Texas land." Rock's harsh voice grated in her ears. "If we're lucky and everything goes perfectly it will take nearly three weeks in. Then, depending on how long you have to wait before a party is returning, you'll have another three weeks or so. Most of the teams have trucks hired to pick them up here on the return trip."

A faint sense of foreboding assailed her as she tried to think about what her family's reaction would be. Both her social and work calendars had been crammed full when she left. "How will my parents know where I am?"

"We'll see if we can get a message passed back with some of the local people to the embassy in Katmandu. That's the best I can do." He stared at her unseeingly, his face worried and angry.

Letting her eyes linger on his square jawline and the dark hair that looked as if it had been blown by the wind whistling through the mountain passes, Beryl realized he was offering her the only alternative. She shivered with apprehension. There was something in his appearance that made her remember the feeling she had experienced looking at the rugged spines of the Himalayas. Something primitive and untamed that defied description.

"There's only one problem," he continued, the intensity of his husky tone startling her. "Sleeping quarters."

"I have all of Brad's things with me," she returned swiftly.

"I wasn't referring to a sleeping bag; the team sleeps in two-man tents."

"Aren't there any other women?" Beryl remembered Brad's mentioning some women who had been accepted on the team.

"Two, and they're already sharing a tent. Brad was my tentmate, so that leaves us in the same quarters."

"The same tent?" she echoed shrilly.

He shrugged his shoulders. "It looks that way, doesn't it?"

"But that's impossible. What will everyone else think?"

"Don't be so puritanical. What does it matter what anyone else thinks?" Rock's probing gaze left her defenseless as he continued, "Of course, everyone will assume we're lovers. Does that bother you?"

His mocking tones made Beryl clamp her lips together in exasperation. She sat thoughtfully, weighing her words, before suggesting, "Why don't we take turns sleeping outside?"

Rock laughed harshly, shaking his head ruefully at her ignorance. "One night out in the open and you'd be begging to share my tent. And, let me assure you,

I have no intention of giving up my warm bed in the tent.''

Beryl fixed her gaze obstinately on the floor. Was there more behind Rock's words than the practical arrangement he was suggesting?

After a few moments he added, ''The best solution is for us to act as if we're interested in each other. If we appear matter-of-fact about the whole situation, no one else will give it any thought. Everyone knows Brad and I are friends; it won't take much for the group to believe that we're continuing an already established relationship.''

A knot of protest had formed in her throat, but she was unable to contradict the cool logic of his words. As he said, what other solution was there? She felt a shiver of fear at the mere thought of having to sleep outside alone.

No, the only choice was to do as he proposed; they would share the tent calmly and she would keep her silly emotions under control. There was no reason to act panic-stricken over the idea of camping out with a man. If she viewed him objectively, joined in the team and treated him as an equal, they should get through this episode with no problems.

''Okay,'' she agreed faintly. ''As you say, that's the sensible way to handle it.''

With a swift gesture of impatience he wheeled around toward the door and glanced at the luminous dial of his waterproof watch. ''I've got to round up my porters and get them started with these crates. As soon as they've cleared out of here, you'd better get some more rest.''

He gestured toward the pitcher he had brought in

earlier. "There's water in there. Those are the only amenities I can offer you for cleaning up. But you'll have to get used to going without the comforts of home."

Pulling the door open decisively he continued, "We'll leave this afternoon to join the rest of the team. I'll have one of the village women bring you some lunch." He smiled over at her then. "Maybe you'd better be sitting down when they arrive, so you don't frighten them off." And with that parting shot he pulled the door shut behind him.

For a moment Beryl didn't know whether to laugh or cry. She had wanted to do a little hiking in these magnificent hills, but it looked as if she might have got more than she bargained for. She walked restlessly around the room several times before the view from the window drew her attention once more.

Looking off into the distance she tried to determine which direction they would take to the base camp. Katmandu lay in the opposite direction. The words of a poem long forgotten slipped softly from her lips as she felt a surge of excitement over the coming trek. "And the wildest dreams of Kew are the facts of Katmandu...."

What were her wildest dreams? She glanced down, smiling ruefully as she remembered all the years she had longed to be small, dainty and petite, tired of hearing the same inane comments about her height from people who felt compelled to mention it, as though she had never noticed it herself. But she had learned to live with that now, realizing it would be stupid to use her height as an excuse in life, finding instead that her size had its own rewards.

No, her wildest dreams no longer included being miraculously made shorter. And they were no longer centered on bringing credit to her family. To do that she would have to marry someone they chose, someone who satisfied her mother's requirements, and she doubted if that were really possible.

She hadn't ruled out marriage, though. She still dreamed of falling in love, of sharing life with a man who returned her feelings and respected her as an individual, a man who desired her for more than the Bartletts' wealth and prominent family name.

It seemed incredible to her now that she had thought Paul was that man. After that first meeting, when she'd apologized for not consulting him about the article she had written, he had calmed down and asked her out to dinner. She still comforted herself with the thought that he hadn't known her name at that time. Or had he?

For several months they had dated sporadically, since his work took him on frequent business trips. She hadn't made any demands on him, enjoying his company, not getting upset when he disappeared and then reappeared without notice.

The first problems had started when she introduced him to Brad. Her brother's antipathy had been obvious from the beginning, and the antagonism between the two men became intense. Paul had explained it away, insisting that twins were closer than most brothers and sisters and that it was only a natural jealousy Brad was feeling over Beryl's sudden interest in someone else.

Beryl knew now that she'd been only too eager to accept Paul's rationalizations. She'd been too infatuated to see any of the warning signals that something was wrong, too blind to see Paul's glaring lack of consideration for her, too stubborn to listen to even her closest friends.

At least, she consoled herself, she'd been reluctant for their lovemaking to go too far. But as Paul became more and more persistent she had given in at last, fearing she might lose him, and agreed to a weekend in Acapulco.

Beryl whirled away from the window, putting a sudden stop to thoughts of Paul. This was no time to be dredging up bitter painful memories. She no longer fooled herself that she had ever been in love with him. Only her pride had been demolished, and in its place was a fierce determination never to let any man play her for a fool again.

She was tired of the helping role she'd slipped into early in life: helping her father's rise to fame by never doing anything to cause him a moment's worry; helping her mother's social status by learning all the social graces. She had even been overshadowed by Brad, standing on the sidelines as he won awards for his athletic skills.

But here in this enchanted country she felt as if anything were possible. It appeared that she was being given a chance to find out if she had it in her to do something difficult, to set a goal for herself and reach it no matter what the cost.

She could win secret satisfaction from having made the effort to reach base camp on an equal footing with the others in the group. She would keep a record of all the unusual sights and smells and sounds along the trail and try writing an article for a travel magazine when she returned. She was through limiting herself in life.

Squaring her shoulders with determination, she went quickly over to the narrow ledge and lay down. Rock had been right about one thing: now was the time to get some rest. She had a feeling that the next few weeks were going to be the greatest challenge of her life.

CHAPTER TWO

THE VILLAGE HAD COME TO LIFE as afternoon shadows, reflections of the distant mountain peaks, lengthened across the meadows. Wordlessly Rock motioned for Beryl to follow him down the narrow path edging the turbulent stream. Walking beside him, she was able to look around at the small settlement, which had seemed faintly sinister the day before. She felt strangely disturbed as she noted the abject poverty of the villagers and their thin children, listless dogs and scrawny chickens.

"It's so sad," she murmured, her eyes darkening with compassion. "Is all of Nepal like this?"

Rock stopped abruptly and gazed at her, his probing eyes intense and flickering with some answering emotion. "Not all of the villages are this poor, but poverty is a reality in this part of the world."

His hand lightly gripped her shoulder as he swiveled her around to face the opposite direction. "Look at that, Beryl," he commanded. "That's the beauty of Nepal."

High above the shabby village she saw a luminous whiteness shining as if suspended in space. "Mount Everest?" she whispered.

"No, only a glacier in the foothills. Beautiful, isn't it? Each hour of the night, each night of the month, the glaciers take on different faces." His grip tightened reassuringly through the bulky knit sweater covering her shoulders. "When things get too much for you over here, look up."

Beryl turned her face slightly toward his, meeting his disturbing expressive eyes. Behind him the sky was aglow with crimson warmth as the sun reached the crest of the jagged peaks. Rock's burnished skin, darkening to bronze in the evening light, was etched in sharp contrast to the slate gray rocks around him.

A tiny shiver danced restlessly along her nerves as she saw how the lengthening shadows emphasized the chiseled features of his face. His deep-set eyes were fixed in tranquil concentration on the distant sunset. She felt a sense of hollow disappointment as he dropped his hand and strode on, not checking to see if she kept pace with him.

Night came without warning. A flock of white birds—egrets, from what Beryl could see of them—winged their way back and forth overhead. As she followed the narrow grass path several steps behind Rock, his broad back offered her a sense of reassurance that amazed her. But was it really so strange? In the ever darkening silence around them, he was her only link with security.

As they walked along silently she was able to study him, appreciating the effortless manner in which he walked. He looked to be in his early thirties, a powerful confident man who seemed oddly at home in this mysterious world. It was hard to imagine him as a professor, surrounded by the bare walls of a lecture hall, poring over exam papers and dusty textbooks.

As they came to a curve in the trail, she caught a

glimpse of the flickering lights of a camp fire blazing in the distance, and its glowing warmth seemed to attract her with a compelling magnetism. The light acted as a friendly guide, sending long piercing shadows into the hushed darkness. The group of people huddled around the fire was distinguishable more by the cheery sounds of camaraderie and laughter than by the blurry silhouettes against the light.

Beryl felt her pace quickening as the light of the fire made her more sure of her steps. A hearty peal of laughter echoed through the pines; so intent was the group on their conversation that Rock and she were able to walk to the edge of the circle without being noticed. Beryl stayed in the shadows, close behind him, watching as he called out a cheerful greeting.

A pleasant, friendly faced man who was leaning back against a fallen log returned the greeting and asked, "Rock, who was the strange creature the villagers said was waiting for you?"

"A great surprise!" Rock draped one arm casually around Beryl's waist, pulling her against him and introducing her by name before adding, "Beryl and I are...." He paused. "What is it called these days?"

"Your significant other?" suggested a woman's voice laced with sarcasm.

"I like that," Rock returned, his arm tightening around Beryl's waist, forcing her to lean against his firm chest. "Meet my significant other."

Beryl flashed an indignant glance upward at Rock, twisting her body away from him. There hadn't been any need to blare out an announcement of their relationship to the group the moment she arrived.

"Bartlett?" the first man was asking. "Any relationship to Brad?"

"His sister; Brad had an emergency appendectomy last week," Rock replied. The murmur of sympathy that swept the group warmed Beryl; it was clear these people had a genuine affection for her brother.

Her glow lasted only seconds before Rock's next words sent a ripple of shock along her veins. "Beryl got this wild idea to use his ticket and come see me. If I weren't so happy to have her here with me, I'd be tempted to spank her."

Rock kept a strong arm firmly around her as Beryl struggled ineffectually to get away from him. Resentment over his patronizing attitude boiled inside her, and she opened her mouth to tell him so. But the words of protest died away as she met the warning glance he threw in her direction.

"Is she going to climb with us?" There was a querulous note in the voice of the woman who continued dominating the conversation.

"No, she'll be with us as far as base camp. Then she'll have to join a group going out," Rock explained.

Beryl sensed the relief in the other woman's voice as she said, "I'm glad you're not going to let your love life endanger us in any way."

"You know me better than that." Rock's firm decisive tone added a note of finality to his statement. He prodded Beryl forward into the circle of people. "Beryl, I'd like you to meet the team members you've been hearing so much about. This is Jane Lansing. She's a professor in the geography department at the university where I teach."

Jane's chin was thrust forward defiantly as she scanned the newcomer with cold eyes. She nodded brusquely in response to Beryl's polite greeting, then turned to Rock. "Do you want me to send a message back to Fran so she'll know Beryl's here? She might want to mention it in the first progress report."

"I'll keep her informed whenever I think it's necessary," Rock snapped.

Beryl felt caught between a current of anger as she glanced first at Rock and then at Jane. To ease the tension she said, "Brad has mentioned you to me, Jane. I believe he made another trek with you."

Jane tossed back her windblown dark hair and smiled at the mention of Brad's name. "He's a great climber. We're all going to miss him."

"And this is Susan White, our team physician," Rock's smooth tones returned. "She's a professor in the cardiology department, besides being one of the best climbers I've ever had the privilege of leading."

Susan's smile was friendlier, lighting up china-blue eyes in a rounded face framed by curly brown hair. "That's great praise coming from you, Rock," she said huskily. "Welcome aboard, Beryl. I hope you're healthy, because I don't want to spend much time tending sick people on this trip. Have you climbed in high altitudes?"

Rock answered before Beryl could open her mouth. "We're all going to need some time to get acclimatized to these altitudes, Susan, but I can promise you Beryl will be my personal responsibility."

"How about letting me speak for myself?" Beryl complained, injecting a light note to cover the irritation she was feeling. "I've never had any trouble adjusting to high altitudes, Susan, and I'm as healthy as I look."

"Great," Susan laughed. "But since you didn't submit to the same checkups as the other team members, I wanted to be certain."

"She's *not* a team member," objected Jane, who was listening from beside Susan.

Susan shrugged indifferently. "When you see Brad again tell him how much I had looked forward to meeting him. Kent does nothing but sing his praises."

"Kent?" Beryl murmured questioningly.

"Susan's the wonderful doctor I told you about. She's been overseeing my brother's illness; my family's all betting on a wedding between those two." Rock inserted the words smoothly, a slight pressure on Beryl's arm indicating she had said something wrong.

"Oh, *that* doctor," mumbled Beryl, trying desperately to remember exactly what Brad had said about a brother of Rock's who had been seriously ill recently. Some sort of heart problem, was all she could remember. Brad had mentioned that Kent's doctor was a beautiful woman and a romance had developed between the two. "Are best wishes in order?" she asked, breaking the awkward silence.

Susan's eyes lowered quickly. "Not yet."

"Time enough for that when we all get back," said Rock, guiding Beryl away to a group of men gathered around the fire. They greeted her in a much friendlier fashion, showing great interest as she explained how surprised she'd been to find the team gone when she arrived in Katmandu.

Beryl tried to sort out all the names but soon gave up, remembering only Fred, a free-lance photographer; Lon Purcell, a short, stocky, red-haired former professional football player; and Reagen Hendriks, whose tall handsome appearance epitomized the ideal of the national park ranger he was.

"Which park do you work in?" asked Beryl, returning Reagen's smile as he grasped her hand in both of his.

"Mount McKinley, in Alaska. I've been there nearly four years now," he replied.

"I've always wanted to see Alaska," Beryl exclaimed.

"We'll have to arrange a visit. Maybe next summer?" His almost perfect features broke into a smile, making it clear his invitation was genuine. His hands tightened over hers, communicating understanding of how alone Beryl must be feeling. This was a gentle sensitive man, a sharp contrast to the domineering Rock Rawlings.

Her muscles tightened abruptly as Rock brushed her hand away from Reagen's. "Don't forget she's my girl, Hendriks." His voice held an unmistakable note of warning.

"Don't tell me you're the jealous type! How flattering...." Beryl feigned surprise and widened her eyes provocatively, only the determined line of her jaw revealing her displeasure.

Reagan laughed heartily, but Beryl noted the silence of the rest of the group. "Let me get you something to eat," Reagen offered. "You must be starving."

"I'd appreciate that." Beryl moved away from

Rock, and one of the men stood up to offer her his folding camp chair. "No, thanks. I'll sit by the fire," she refused with a smile, sinking down on a large stone and holding out her hands to warm them. Rock stalked off into the darkness.

Her sense of triumph died down somewhat and she shivered slightly. How was she going to conceal her antagonism when Rock acted as if he owned her? She'd never cared for the masterful, male-animal types; their egos were too fragile to allow any woman to have a mind of her own. If Rock wanted her to go along with this charade he'd better meet her halfway and treat her with a little respect.

That's what she had noticed first about Paul. He was willing to listen and he seemed to respect women as equals. And they had liked so many of the same things...old movies, eating snow cones in the park, spending an evening talking to friends. Now she wondered if all of that had been only an act. Had he actually been dating her in hopes of blackmailing her father? Or had his wife been lying?

For a moment she closed her eyes and remembered that horrible Friday evening when she'd been waiting for Paul to come by for her. They were driving to the airport and would then take the flight to Mexico; all of her clothes were packed, and a friend had agreed to feed her Siamese kitten, Jade. Then the phone had rung. She had started not to answer it—and she still got chills thinking what a fool she might have made of herself if she hadn't.

The voice on the phone had been a woman's. She sounded young, no older than Beryl herself, and it was obvious she'd been crying...was still crying, in fact. She had sobbed out an incredible story that she was Paul's wife. She lived in Midland, a town in West Texas where Paul frequently went on business trips.

The worst part was when she'd started begging Beryl not to take her husband away from her. She ended by telling her, "Don't you know he's only taking you to Acapulco so he can blackmail your father?"

Beryl's first reaction had been disbelief, but that was quickly followed by white-hot anger at Paul. The next few moments were a blur; she remembered only that she had hung up the phone and the next thing she knew she was talking to her dad.

From her perspective now she wished she could replay that part of her life. She would have stayed calmer, not called in her father, found out the facts and handled the situation herself. But then she had wanted only vengeance, and she knew her dad could wreak that on any of his enemies.

Her family had rallied around her. "Poor Beryl. She's incapable. She must have our help." Oh, they hadn't said those exact words, but that's what it had all meant. And how could she argue after the way she had reacted?

Her dad had convinced her she had to resign from her job immediately and move home while he checked out the facts. She had spent those days secretly hoping that it had all been some monstrous mistake, but her hopes were useless. The woman was Paul's wife. He admitted it himself when she finally took one of his numerous calls. He defended his actions, saying that he was separated and a divorce was imminent, but Beryl didn't believe him. Not then. It was too late; but not too late to lose her naiveté where men were concerned.

Absorbed in her thoughts, Beryl blinked in surprise as Reagen hovered over her, holding a tin plate filled with a thick dark stew. "You can use my plate tonight," he offered, setting a steaming cup of tea on the rock beside her.

"But what will you do?" Beryl smiled up into his smoky gray eyes.

"I've already finished. I assume yours is still packed with the supplies you brought?"

"Yes...." She glanced over to see Rock approaching with a similarly filled plate and asked, "Did the men bring the crates yet?"

"They're stacked with the rest of the equipment," Rock replied, moving deliberately in front of Reagen and settling himself down beside Beryl. He flicked an assessing glance as Reagen moved off before his long muscular thigh pressed closely against hers.

Denying the pulsing knot that suddenly coiled in her stomach, Beryl dipped her fork into the stew and began eating. That intimate gesture of his was no accident. He was clearly marking her out as his territory in everyone else's eyes.

Lon's voice broke into the silence, betraying amusement as he looked at Beryl through the leaping flames of the glowing fire. "When did this significant relationship begin?" he asked.

"Last summer," Rock answered between bites. "Or was it last spring, sweetheart?"

Beryl shrugged indifferently. "More like the cold gray wintertime." Her clipped reply ought to show

him what she thought of his attempt at acting, she
decided. When they were alone she would demand an
explanation of how far he intended to carry out this
pretense.

"Sounds like 'The Newlywed Game,'" laughed
Reagen. "I always enjoy hearing them ask the bride
what her husband's favorite food is—she never gets it
right."

"Maybe that's why it's so hard to find a happy
marriage," Susan responded, her tone surprisingly
bitter.

"Knowing your husband's food preferences
doesn't make for happiness in marriage," Lon inserted.

"What does?" Rock asked casually.

A laugh swept around the camp fire, and Beryl
stiffened in embarrassment, realizing what the others
were thinking. Lon chuckled before asking, "Since
when did that subject interest you?"

Rock leaned deliberately toward Beryl, wrapping
his free arm around her and pulling her against him.
"This conversation's gone far enough," he answered.

Beryl barely controlled herself from speaking, her
cheek brushing against Rock's as she attempted to
twist away from his firm grasp. Why couldn't he
keep their relationship impersonal? *Impersonal!*
She'd only met this man today and already she knew
he'd unfurled a depth of emotional response in her
that threatened to pierce the wall of indifference
she'd been so carefully constructing around herself.

She had no intention of getting her emotions in a
tangle about any man again. At the moment, all at-

tractive men had off-limits signs on them—and that even included someone as devastating as Rock Rawlings!

Not willing to think any further along those lines, Beryl switched her attention to the conversation going on around her. She noticed Susan had moved her chair closer to the fire and was sitting beside Reagen, her curly brown hair swinging against his shoulder as they laughed at something Fred was saying. The two made an attractive couple, Susan's petite darkness contrasting vividly with Reagen's blond good looks.

From what Rock had said, Susan's interests lay with his brother, Kent. That left Reagen free; and Beryl resolved to get to know him better. He was such an obviously attractive man, even if he wasn't quite as impressive as Rock. It would be foolish to let Rock keep her from becoming friendly with the other men on this trek, if only to maintain her own sense of independence.

As she gazed into the fire her eyes grew heavy, and she felt herself slowly relaxing. At first she was hardly aware of the gentle pressure of firm fingers massaging her back. She closed her eyes, leaning forward slightly and enjoying the feeling of the tension draining from her body.

Opening her eyes halfway, she found herself staring directly into a pair of glittering dark eyes only inches from her face. She pulled back abruptly, moving away from the suddenly disturbing warmth of Rock's lean torso. It wouldn't do to have him think she was attracted to him. They were definitely going to have to come to a firm understanding about their relationship—and the sooner, the better.

The need to reach that understanding came even sooner than she'd expected. "Time for bed," Rock announced, standing up and reaching out a hand to help her. She refused churlishly, jumping up without assistance rather than risk a return of the sensations his slightest touch could arouse. The rest of the group rose slowly, folding their chairs in response to his quiet commands.

"Our tent's this way, honey," Rock said in a voice that carried to every member of the group. He grasped her hand and squeezed it in a way that left no doubt of his displeasure over her earlier rebellion.

She ignored the rebuke, removing her hand when they were out of sight of the group. They had reached a squat blue tent, standing a little apart from the other brightly colored ones in a way that marked Rock out as the leader.

Beryl's eyes darkened with awareness as she surveyed the tiny interior of the nylon shelter. "You can't be serious about our sharing this?" she snapped. This wasn't at all what she'd pictured when Rock had discussed the tent situation with her. A vague recollection of the roomy substantial canvas structures she had slept in on childhood camping trips with Brad and her dad had prompted her to agree to sharing a tent. But this was barely large enough to contain the two sleeping bags that were lying in intimate contact in one corner.

"What's the alternative?" Rock's low voice held a decisive finality as he knelt and began to unroll the bags.

"Wait!" Beryl told him in her firmest tones. "Wait just one second."

Rock's forehead creased with concern as he held a finger to his lips. "Shh," he warned. In the sudden quiet Beryl was aware of the voices of the others in their party through the thin walls of the tent.

Kneeling beside him, she whispered in seething protest, "There's not enough room in here for both of us!"

"You and Brad are about the same height, aren't you?" His mocking glance slid over her as he finished, "So we shouldn't have any trouble finding room to stretch out." Then he turned his back on her squarely and decisively.

Beryl's mind swirled with chaotic thoughts as she tried to decide what course of action to take. As far as she could judge, they would be almost touching if they both lay down in the tiny tent. "It's not going to work," she whispered in his ear.

"What's not going to work?" His voice full of irritation, Rock continued spreading out the down-filled sleeping bags.

"This idea of yours to act as if we're lovers. I'm no good at deceit."

"Then you'd damn well better get good at it," he snapped. "Your performance this evening rated a big fat zero."

Beryl seethed with anger; she detested the helpless position in which she found herself. "Just what's the purpose of this pretense? It doesn't make sense to me," she said in an effort to make him discuss the problem with her.

Rock waited a moment before answering. He adjusted the small kerosene lamp he had brought into the tent with him and then turned to address her, his voice offhand and casual.

"No matter what we told them, they'd never believe we didn't have something going between us. This way we'll get the jump on them and forestall the gossip behind our backs. We can't afford to have emotional undercurrents disrupting the team, and you're going to have to learn to live with that."

"Are you implying that it would be impossible for any man and woman to share a tent without being sexually involved?" Beryl demanded.

Rock stared at her carefully, scanning her face with a searching gaze that contained a flicker of speculation. "You're a very attractive woman," he said finally, the harsh note in his voice making the statement sound almost like an accusation. "If the other men on this team thought you were available, they could very well start trouble making a play for you. Reagen's actions tonight are a good example."

"That's ridiculous," Beryl scoffed. "Reagen was only trying to make me feel welcome—which is more than I can say for your reaction this morning."

Ignoring the interruption, Rock continued, "Scaling a mountain is a tremendous team effort, Beryl. The challenge of that is enough without adding any distractions. Besides, Brad would never forgive me if I let one of these guys seduce you."

Indignation surged through Beryl, and her words, when she finally managed to speak, came out in a thin squeak of protest. "I assure you, I have *no* intention of allowing myself to be seduced. Can't you give me credit for having a little common sense?"

A mocking smile briefly curved the corners of his mouth. "I'm not taking any chances."

Before she could form another protest, he pointed at her pack, which was sitting near the doorway of the tent. "Get ready for bed and don't waste any more time worrying. As long as you're willing to cooperate, so that this expedition goes smoothly, you have nothing to fear. Now get undressed and into that sleeping bag."

Frustration over the situation in which she found herself made Beryl pause for a moment before turning her back on Rock. Her fingers trembled with annoyance as she reached into her bag and pulled out the thermal underwear that was to have been Brad's. "How about these?" she asked. "Will it be cold enough to wear them?"

"Not tonight; just wear what's under your clothes."

Beryl glanced up, a vivid picture of her wispy bra and panties filling her mind. "I will not."

"Then wear your birthday suit for all I care. But get in that bag!"

His face was harsh in the flickering light from the lantern, and she turned away from him again, fighting the rage that was threatening to choke her. Rage that was directed not only at his lack of understanding but also at her own inhibitions.

Her life had been sheltered, chaperoned, full of demands that she be conventional and above reproach, so that no scandal would ever mar her father's political career. But just because she had no intention of shedding her clothes in front of a man she'd just met didn't mean she was naive or unsophisticated.

Rummaging deep into her bag, she finally located the large bath towel that was packed at the bottom. She pulled it out thoughtfully, shaking it vigorously and then gazing consideringly around the tent. "Do you have any string?" she asked.

"What on earth for?" Rock replied impatiently. "You're not planning on strangling me, are you?"

"Don't tempt me," she flung out. Her voice sounded grating to her own ears as she explained, "I saw this old movie once about a man and woman who were *forced* to share a motel room. They hung a blanket in the middle of the room. I'm going to use this towel to do the same thing."

Giving a long sigh, Rock raked a hand through his hair and then reached for the towel. "Okay, Miss Puritan. If you think your body is so delightful that I'll leap at you at the first glimpse, I'll help you string up this divider."

He disappeared from the tent and within minutes returned carrying a large ball of twine. They worked in silence, stringing it up from the far end of the tent to the doorway and then throwing the towel over the middle so that it fell between the two sleeping bags. Rock sat back and grinned at the bright orange terry cloth hanging forlornly over the twine, barely dividing the confined space in two. "Does that make you feel any better?" he mocked.

"It marks off our personal space," Beryl replied with satisfaction. "Just don't trespass!" But her angry retort didn't appear to have dented his mockery: his gaze slid over her figure in the shadowy light once again in a manner that left her senses reeling. She turned away swiftly, pretending to smooth the towel into a position where it would cover more.

He moved behind her abruptly, causing a gasp to escape her lips as he shut off the kerosene lantern and cast the small space into sudden darkness. Her eyes adjusted slowly to the dimness, widening as she turned to find him shedding his shirt and then pulling off his boots.

Bronzed skin gleamed in the darkness, shadowed by a mat of thick dark hair that tapered off across his chest. "Why did you turn off that light before I got out my things?" she accused, trying to hide the turmoil she was feeling as she shifted her fascinated gaze from his rugged torso.

"Don't you know how well silhouettes show up on the outside of a lighted tent? Your undressing could have been quite a treat for the rest of the group." He laughed as he observed her. "You've got a lot to learn about camping, Beryl, but I think I'm going to enjoy teaching you."

"Don't think you have a willing pupil!" When she was certain he was inside his bedroll, his back turned to her, she slipped out of her outer clothes and into one of Brad's cotton shirts with feverish movements. Crawling into her sleeping bag, she tossed restlessly, trying to find a comfortable position.

"Settle down and go to sleep," Rock ordered in a low growl. His harsh tone made Beryl's nerves jangle, and she felt like screaming over the contented rhythmical sound of his breathing.

If only she had someone to talk to for a few minutes until this overpowering tension drained from her. She rose on one elbow, saying crossly, "It's not going to work."

"What's not going to work?" Rock sighed in a voice brimming with weary resignation.

"No one's going to think we've been going together. I blew our whole cover story when I didn't know who your brother was. Don't you think you'd better fill me in on your background so I won't make a mess again?"

"I have no intention of telling you a bedtime story tonight. Can't you let me sleep?"

Beryl leaned closer, the towel brushing against her face. "Then what can I tell Susan and Jane if they ask me what I like about you? Women *do* talk about those things, you know."

Rock groaned in exasperation. "Tell them you're attracted by my body, not my mind," he snapped.

Beryl's gasp of anger was muted by his low chuckle as he turned over and fell asleep.

CHAPTER THREE

WHEN SHE AWOKE the next morning Beryl saw sunlight filtering through the tent flap. She stretched out her cramped muscles slowly, smiling ruefully as she realized that she had slept in the same position all night, curled into a tight ball, as far from Rock as their close quarters allowed.

She crawled out of bed, sneaking a quick look first around the towel divider to make sure the other side was empty. After dressing hurriedly she ran a brush through her unruly hair and went outdoors.

A sleepy-eyed Susan was standing near the fire. "I hope I didn't oversleep," said Beryl apologetically.

"Not today," answered Susan. "The Sherpas and porters are all arriving and we'll be sorting through our supplies and filling our backpacks. I guess there's no need asking if you slept well?" Susan emphasized the words in a way that made her meaning obvious.

Beryl colored swiftly but managed a cordial answer. "Anywhere I can brush my teeth and wash up?"

"If you insist on hot water you'll have to heat some. But there's an icy cold stream over there." Susan pointed toward a clump of trees on the far side of the camp before walking off.

Beryl stared after her retreating figure for several

moments, wondering if she had imagined the distinct chill in her voice. Last night Jane had made her disapproval obvious, but Susan's attitude had been more accepting. Had Beryl done something to displease the beautiful young doctor? So far things didn't look too promising for a pleasant trip.

The sting of cold water as Beryl scrubbed herself was intense, but when she finished she felt refreshed and able to face whatever the day brought. When she reentered the tent, Rock followed, carrying a cup of steaming fragrant coffee. "I was going to wake you up with a kiss and a cup of coffee if you'd only waited."

"That's hardly necessary, since no one could see your touching performance." Beryl began applying lip gloss.

"Some things I do to please myself." His broad smile creased his face, crinkling the tanned skin at the corners of his piercing dark eyes.

Beryl fought the temptation to smile back, saying in stubborn tones, "If you don't mind I'd like to be treated exactly like any of the other team members."

"That's a generous attitude to be coming from one who's been waited on hand and foot all her life."

"How would you know?" Beryl snapped.

The line between Rock's eyebrows deepened as he watched her. "We're going to have to do something about that mane of hair," he said abruptly.

"We?" Beryl surveyed him coolly. "If you'll loan me a pair of scissors I'll whack it off."

"Not something that beautiful!" He was still smiling, making Beryl wonder if this was another of his teasing gibes. "Braid it and pile it on top of your head to get it out of the way," he continued.

"Out of the way of what?"

"Wild animals, giant insects, birds who swoop down and try to carry off innocent young maidens. Don't forget this is the enchanted land of Nepal, Big Beryl Bartlett."

Beryl whirled, her luminous green eyes burning fire. "Don't you *ever* call me that again!"

Surprised by her venom, Rock drew back, a frown replacing the smile. "No insult intended. I've heard Brad calling your dad Big John, and the name just slipped into my mind."

Sighing deeply, she told him, "Okay, so I'm a little touchy about that name. I reached this height by the time I was twelve, so some of the kids tagged me by that. The worst part was that I was chubby, so they changed it to sound more like Big Barrel Bartlett."

Rock's laugh rang out rich and deep, filling the confining space. "What did you do, then?"

She smiled at him teasingly. "I got the biggest, thickest board I could find and hid behind some azalea bushes. When they came up I swung out and clobbered them. Two of them wear shiny porcelain bridges in place of their front teeth to this day."

"Thanks for the warning. I'll watch closely to see that you're in front of me when we start through the bushy areas."

"You do that." Beryl's fingers were busily braiding her hair into two plaits, and she fumbled with nervousness as she felt Rock's eyes continuing to watch her. "Don't you have anything to do?" she snapped irritably.

Rock shrugged, smiling broadly. "I'm waiting for everyone to finish breakfast before we start sorting supplies," he explained, his eyes continuing to flick over her deliberately.

Clumsily she wrapped the braids into a coil on her head. Why did she let this man affect her this way? No wonder he thought she was such an innocent maiden.

"Here, I'll take that coffee now," she said in a voice that lacked its customary graciousness.

"If you want any breakfast you better come along before the food's put away," Rock explained before leaving the tent.

Beryl followed soon afterward, wondering how she would ever understand him. He could be thoughtful one moment and then become arrogant and demanding in the space of a second. Worse than that, when he exerted the slightest charm he had a way about him that made her forget her intentions to ignore him.

Susan and Jane were seated in light aluminum chairs near the fire, sipping coffee and talking. Beryl sauntered toward them self-consciously, wondering if she would be greeted with any friendliness. Jane stopped speaking and glanced up when Beryl reached them.

"What's for breakfast?" Beryl asked.

Jane pointed toward a portable table. "Help yourself. It's not much."

After scooping up a helping of scrambled eggs and a chunk of buttered bread, Beryl walked back toward the women and seated herself on the nearest rock.

Susan asked, "How did you find the cold water?"

"Brr...! But it made me feel wide awake. How much colder does it get on this trek?"

"The trek's nothing," Jane said haughtily. "Those of us going up Mount Everest will reach temperatures of minus sixty. If you add in the wind-chill factor it'll be much worse."

"Remind me to start looking for a way back to Katmandu as soon as possible," Beryl answered, sipping her coffee slowly.

"Quit trying to scare Beryl," said Reagen, who had moved toward the women. He flashed a smile in her direction and sank down beside her. "I'm hoping to have her with our team a long time."

Beryl watched as Susan's eyes narrowed slightly, and a thought crossed her mind. Unless she was greatly mistaken, Reagen interested Susan. But how could that be, since she was involved with Rock's brother? On impulse she said, "A lot of you were already acquainted before this expedition. Have you all climbed together before?"

She knew her surmise was accurate when she saw Reagen glance in Susan's direction and then look away swiftly. "I've climbed with everyone on the team before," he told her, "but not under Rock's leadership. Susan and I trained on Mount Rainier. Wasn't that about five years ago?"

Susan shrugged, shaking her brown curls indifferently. "Something like that; it was too long ago for me to remember exactly."

"We'll have to catch up on what's happened in those years," Reagen continued lightly. "I had no idea you were involved with Kent Rawlings until Rock mentioned it last night."

Susan caught her breath sharply and glanced around. "Until Kent recovers I don't think Rock should be discussing it," she replied in a low voice.

"You mean his life's still in danger?" Reagen persisted.

"No, nothing like that!" Susan stood up quickly. "That sounds like a great idea for us to catch up with each other. Maybe we can get together after the work's finished."

"Maybe," Reagen agreed evenly. Turning to Beryl, he asked, "Are you and Rock serious?"

Beryl fought back the heat flushing her cheeks, unsure what her answer should be. Before she had to answer, Reagen added, "Anything less than a resounding yes means there's still hope for the rest of the guys."

Susan's mouth set in taut lines and Jane jumped from her seat. The two women walked toward the tents, every line of their straight backs indicating their disapproval of what they'd witnessed. "Why did you do that?" Beryl accused. "You knew it would make Susan and Jane dislike me."

"That's their problem," Reagen returned bluntly. "As far as I'm concerned, your arrival is the best thing that's happened to me on this expedition."

BERYL was still mulling over the conviction that Susan was more interested in Reagen than she cared for anyone to know when she saw the others gathering around the boxes for the task of sorting the supplies. When she joined them Lon explained, "We're making a division between the supplies that'll be needed as far as base camp and those we have to use on the climb up Mount Everest. You stay here by me to unpack Brad's boxes and I'll help.''

"Thanks," said Beryl. Lon's friendliness was a balm to her ruffled feelings. She watched as Rock strode around the camp, giving his directions in a decisive efficient manner that made his leadership evident.

His strong profile was etched against the towering mountains in the background. Watching him, her eyes caught by his determined jawline and his thick hair ruffled in the cool breeze, she again felt almost awed by him and wondered how she could have dared to argue so much when they were alone.

But why should she take all the blame? Rock took pleasure in needling her, as evidenced by his teasing chuckles when he elicited an angry response. And that was the answer to her dilemma on how to deal with him: she'd have to learn to control her irritation and smile sweetly until he retreated in defeat.

Her resolve was gone within seconds when Rock called out, "Honey, you're not required to carry anything, so don't bother filling Brad's pack. I've arranged for one of the porters to be responsible for your bag."

"I'm perfectly capable of taking my share of the load." Beryl began stuffing clothes into the pack with renewed determination, aware that the look of displeasure that crossed his rugged face was not too encouraging.

Rock strode toward her after watching in silence for several minutes. "Are you trying to say you're capable not only of hiking but also of carrying a pack?"

"That's *exactly* what I'm saying." The air of utter stillness around them as Beryl glared into Rock's angry eyes was proof that everyone on the team was interested in the outcome of this encounter.

"And how many pounds do you propose to carry?" his grim voice continued.

"How many are you carrying, Susan?" asked Beryl.

"Between thirty and forty, but I'm in shape," the doctor answered.

Beryl smiled up at Rock. "That sounds about the right amount for me, too. Where do we weigh these?"

Rock broke in, "I didn't know you were such a stubborn little fool. I'm about to let you learn your lesson the hard way. But tomorrow you're going to have to walk every mile of the way, and no one on this team is allowed to help you. Do you understand?"

Beryl gave him her most regal nod, one that the headmistress of the exclusive finishing school she had attended would have been proud of, before continuing her packing.

Rock towered over her, as if undecided how to end the conversation. Then he swiftly whirled around and strode off. Beryl raised her eyebrows, grimacing at his departing back. As laughter erupted spontaneously Rock turned abruptly, catching her in the act.

For a moment the silence was broken only by choked-back laughter from the other team members. As a slow smile began spreading across Rock's face the tension ebbed from the group.

"Good Lord, how did I ever get myself tangled up

with a handful like her?'' He shook his head ruefully, amazing Beryl by the adroit way he managed to inject a hint of affection into his tone. He should have been an actor, she decided angrily.

The arrival of the Sherpas and porters from their camp made a welcome diversion. Brad had explained that the Sherpas were expert Himalayan mountain men whose physiology made them capable of tremendous exertion at high altitudes. According to him, no expedition could hope to succeed without their help.

"I'd like all of you to meet Mangmu, who will be chief during our trek," Rock began introductions. The diminutive man's weather-beaten face and wiry body exuded energy and enthusiasm.

"What you-a been feeling?" Mangmu greeted the group, a proud radiant smile creasing his face as he displayed his knowledge of English.

"How many Sherpas are there?" Jane called out.

"Nine, besides Mangmu," Rock told her.

"Then this throws everything off," Jane complained crossly. "I suppose you want *her* in your group, Rock?" She glanced at Beryl to emphasize her meaning.

"That's correct. Be flexible and I'm sure you can juggle your list a little to solve the problem." His voice was calm, but there was a hint of authority underlying his cool tone.

Beryl bit her lower lip to keep from snapping back. It was ridiculous the way the other woman resented her presence . . . unless she'd been involved with Rock herself. There was only one way to find that out: she'd have to ask someone, and Susan seemed the most logical choice.

She turned toward Susan to find the attractive doctor eyeing her thoughtfully, as if she had guessed what was bothering Beryl. Before she could lose her nerve Beryl asked in a low voice, "Why does Jane resent me so much? Does it have to do with Rock?"

Susan's laugh was low and musical. "It's common knowledge that Jane worships the ground Rock walks on. But lately she's backed off the chase herself in favor of her best friend, Fran Howard. You were a little of a surprise to the group. Jane had spread the word that Rock was thinking of settling down at long last, but I guess she had her facts wrong."

Completely at a loss for words, Beryl stared into Susan's eyes. She knew she had promised Rock that she would pretend they were lovers to the rest of the group. And if Rock were really her lover, wouldn't this news bother her? But she couldn't pretend to be someone who had casual affairs with a man who was already involved with another woman. Being accused of that once in life was enough.

Susan rescued her, saying, "I hope I haven't upset you with anything I've said. Rock won't tolerate gossip about team members."

Beryl managed a smile. "You haven't told me anything I hadn't already guessed. No one would pick Rock as the marrying kind," she said truthfully, trying to push down the feeling of revulsion she felt over portraying herself as someone with such different standards from her own.

Changing the subject, she asked, "How do you ever learn all of those men's names?" Her hand swept the group of Sherpas and porters who were ranging around the boxes.

"Don't bother with all the porters' names; they probably won't stay with us for more than a week, and then they'll drift off and be replaced by others along the way. They're notorious for giving up at the first sign of trouble."

"Their work seems wretched and not very rewarding to me. No wonder they give up." At Susan's look of surprise, Beryl continued, "Are they Nepalese?"

"They're from every country in this part of the world. Many are refugee Tibetans; others are from India and Pakistan and a few are Nepalese. You can probably distinguish where they're from by their clothes."

Their ragged wide-legged pants, bare feet and old shawls and vests at first appeared more like castoffs from a rummage sale to Beryl. After Susan began pointing out the differences in headgear, her meaning became clearer. The two women watched as the porters talked shrilly, their words growing angrier as the moments went by.

"What's the problem?" Beryl asked.

"No problem. They're bargaining for what they'll carry and how much Mangmu will pay them. They go through this same procedure all over again every day, and that's the sound that wakes us up most mornings."

"It's horrible," agreed Reagen, who had joined them. "What are you going to do about that pack, Beryl? You were only taunting Rock, weren't you?"

"Not in the least. I don't know why all of you have

this idea that I'm some hothouse flower that will wilt in the sunlight.''

Reagen's eyes sparkled with appreciation. "Maybe it's because you're so beautiful," he answered. "Remember, if you can't make it tomorrow, let me know. We'll sneak behind a rock and empty some of your pack into mine."

Susan's gasp of disapproval preceded her walking hurriedly away. Once more Beryl looked after her in distress. "I wish you'd quit trying to get me in trouble with Susan."

"You're not the target," Reagen replied enigmatically.

"Every time I turn my back you're over here playing up to my girl, Hendriks." Rock, accompanied by two Sherpa men and a little girl, continued, "I'd like you two to meet the most important people on our team, the cooks. This is Donglu and Gompa. And here. . . ."

He reached down to pat the small girl on the head, but she had moved behind him and was peeking around his thigh, beautiful brown eyes widened with fear as she stared at Beryl. Rock laughed and began speaking to the child in the Sherpa language. Taking her hand, he coaxed her to move from her hiding place and come with him until they reached Beryl.

"What are you telling her?" Beryl asked, kneeling to smile at the trembling young girl.

"I'm reassuring her that you're a normal, ordinary human being and not some deity from the mountains that's here to do us harm."

"Don't be so sure of that," teased Beryl. "Actually, I'm the legendary yeti.'' Brad had loaned her several books to read about the mysterious Abominable Snowman of the Himalayas, the precursor of Bigfoot of the Cascade Mountains in the States.

Rock's eyes darkened as he looked at her. "That's not funny, Beryl. Quit making fun of yourself." There was no trace of a smile on his rugged features.

Beryl shrugged and turned away, feigning indifference. It seemed that nothing she said or did could please Rock. Couldn't he even understand when she was joking? All morning she had been trying to convince herself that the rush of conflicting emotions he had unleashed in her the day before was only a result of extreme fatigue and confusion over the strange circumstances in which she found herself.

But that didn't explain the way she was so utterly conscious of his nearness—of his powerful masculinity and supreme self-confidence, which always left her floundering after any exchange between them. She angrily pushed aside her thoughts and hurried to join the others, who were drifting toward the tables for lunch.

Rock announced an orientation session just as she was finishing the last bite of a meat-and-cheese sandwich. By the time she had drained the tea from her tin cup, the only seat left in the half circle formed on the grassy meadow was beside Reagen. She settled herself next to him, returning his warm smile of welcome.

As she glanced up her green eyes collided with Rock's frowning dark ones, but she shifted her gaze away quickly. She wasn't going to give in to his petty demands that she steer clear of friendship with the one person who seemed most willing to see that she enjoyed herself on this trip. A little concern for her feelings on Rock's part might make her view matters in a different light.

Rock's explanation of the varying altitudes they would be encountering on their three-week trek soon had her engrossed. "The difficulty of this hike is the fact that we'll be climbing up, then down and sometimes back up again in the course of one day. It would be much easier on our bodies if we had a slow but steady uphill progression," he explained.

"Altitude sickness is something we can all expect in one form or another. I want you to memorize these symptoms and report them promptly to Susan, so we can adjust our progress accordingly."

He named light-headedness, mild headaches, a sense of disorientation to reality followed by feelings of euphoria. "All in all, it's very similar to falling in love," he added, glancing at Beryl with a broad smile.

She lowered her eyes, biting her lip in anger. Did Rock think it necessary to go to such lengths to tease her? "You're blushing," Reagen whispered in her ear.

Beryl stayed away from Rock the rest of the afternoon, reading the trip itinerary and getting better acquainted with some of the other team members. Fred invited her over to have a look at his camera equipment, explaining that he was the official photographer for the trek, but he wanted to see everyone else's prints and slides when they returned. "If we're successful, these photos will make a great book," he told her.

His remarks reminded Beryl of her resolution to keep a record of her experiences on the trek. "Are you a writer?" she asked.

"Unfortunately, no," said Fred. "When we get back I'm going to try to find a travel writer to work with."

For a moment Beryl was tempted to mention her own writing experience, but she decided against it. First she'd better start her journal and see how her impressions flowed on paper.

Evening brought abrupt darkness once more, and the large camp fire was comforting as they gathered around it. The evening meal, the first prepared by the cooks, was a mixture of rice and chicken mingled with spices that were unfamiliar to Beryl. She ate hungrily and drank several cups of strong tea as she sat in a camp chair in front of the fire.

Looking around at the sea of strange faces, she found thoughts of her life at home intruding. What would her family think when she didn't return? Would Rock's message reach them? Monica and Big John, as her dad was affectionately called, would be frantic with worry, but they'd be faced with a difficult decision. The wrong stories leaked to the press might hurt her father's chances in the upcoming election.

"Why the frown, my lovely lady?" Rock leaned over and surprised her by dropping a light kiss on her cheek.

She was suddenly gripped by a burning desire to turn toward him and respond to the aching needs quivering uncontrollably inside of her; the urge shocked her with its strange intensity. But she forced herself to remain outwardly calm, answering slowly, "Was I frowning?"

"Most definitely. Are you regretting your impulsive action?"

"My actions weren't impulsive. I planned on leaving the supplies and flying back to Katmandu. If you hadn't been off your schedule by a day, I'd be on my way to Dallas now."

"Trying to blame me, are you?" he said huskily, running a fingertip lightly down her spine. She was conscious of his compelling masculine scent and the sound of his deep even breathing. Time seemed to stand still as Beryl felt her pulses racing almost as if she were in some immediate danger. Flee, her instincts warned. Stay, her emotions warred.

Rock's hand reached the nape of her neck and began a slow sensual massage that drained her last shred of resistance. She found herself leaning against his solid bulk, warmth seeping through her, erasing her earlier worries and bringing with it a powerful awareness of her vulnerability to Rock's hypnotic appeal.

"Drinks are ready," Lon called out. Rock shifted abruptly away, leaving Beryl swaying as she descended to reality.

She grasped the mug of creamy hot chocolate offered by Lon and held it between her hands, savoring its warmth. Her first sip told her it was liberally laced with rum.

"Here's to the success of our trek," Rock toasted the group, and Beryl thrilled with excitement as she glanced around at the expedition members holding their mugs aloft in the light of the fire.

Tomorrow would be the first official day of the trek. She was determined to set aside her worries over the way Rock affected her and enjoy this adventure. Climbing to the foot of Mount Everest was a challenge worthy of any price it demanded.

CHAPTER FOUR

THE SHRILL SOUND of the bargaining porters was deafening as Beryl opened her eyes the next morning. A faint pink glow shone around the edges of the flap that was secured over the opening to the tent, indicating it must be dawn. A sudden chuckle made her glance over at the towel divider, meeting Rock's piercing regard as he leaned around the edge to observe her.

"Sleep well?" His voice had that low teasing quality that could set her pulses racing so easily.

"Yes, thank you."

"I find that a little hard to believe; no one could sleep well in that cramped little corner. Why don't you break down and relax? If you accidentally touch me in your sleep, I'll try not to take it as an engraved invitation to make love to you." His derisive tone had such a superior air that Beryl longed to think of a fitting retort, something that would leave him speechless for a change.

"That's good thinking; I'm an expert in self-defense," she bluffed.

His amused laughter made her itch to retaliate, but his next words were businesslike. "Dress in layers today so you can strip down during the heat of the day.

And don't forget to keep an extra pair of socks in an accessible place in your pack. Before this day is over you're going to be crying and begging for my mercy, offering me anything I want in return for being carried.''

''Don't hold your breath until that happens,'' she answered. Nothing was going to force a squeak of protest from her today. Rock's delight in proving his superiority was something she wasn't prepared to deal with.

When he left the tent, Beryl crawled out of her bedroll, determined not to be the last one to straggle out for breakfast. She dressed in the layers Rock had ordered and hurried down to the crackling fire, where several people were standing.

Breakfast was a rush job with no one bothering to sit down as they ate their scrambled eggs and bread. There was an air of anticipation all around her that made Beryl long to be included as one of the team. Maybe after she proved that she could keep up with the best of them they'd quit seeing her through Rock's eyes.

All around the group tents were being struck and ponies loaded with the heaviest packs. Beryl watched in amazement as the wiry men strapped loads onto their backs that must have weighed more than they did.

It was a bright sun-filled morning, the air crisp and exhilarating, when they set out shortly after sunrise. The Sherpas led the way, followed by the tattered line of porters. Above the cloud line peeped several snow-covered mountain peaks. The group followed the path along the edge of a green field several hundred feet and then entered a shadowy forest filled with the scent of pines and rhododendrons.

"How's the pack doing?" Rock was following close behind her.

"Great," Beryl cheerfully replied.

"Let me know immediately if it starts bothering you." Beryl glared behind her as he continued, "There's nothing personal in my concern; an injured person delays the whole group."

"That sounds logical," she answered coolly.

Rock's strong hand grasped her waist and pulled her against his side, overbalancing her and making her grab his coat to keep from falling. "You're the most maddening woman I've ever met," he whispered.

Beryl flung herself away, replying in a low voice, "If you expect me to play the great lover, you'd better start treating me with a little respect."

"Would a whole lot of respect have you hanging all over me?" he chuckled.

"Don't count on it," she snapped, increasing the distance between them as she moved ahead briskly. The man was insufferable, stalking her, anticipating her cries for help every moment. She'd show him; he knew nothing about the hours she'd spent jogging, so if all went well, he was in for a surprise. She was adjusting to the weight of the pack quite nicely. And the trail, zigzagging from valley to hill and down again, was not as bad as she had feared.

As the morning progressed Beryl shed her down jacket and then the heavy vest under it. She was beginning to tire when one of the men yelled, "When's that break? I need to check for blisters."

"I've been waiting all morning for our neophyte hiker to call for help," Rock drawled in reply. "Since she's too stubborn to admit she's about to drop in her tracks, I suggest we rest in ten minutes."

Beryl ignored Rock's remarks, rounding a corner in time to see the Nepalese gathering around a small fire they'd built to boil water. She slipped off her pack and sat down on a ledge.

Rock knelt in front of her, unlacing her boots and slipping them off, followed by her socks. "You're the first man I've ever had kneel before me," she teased.

Rock examined her feet noncommittally and then glanced at her, frowning. "No blisters?"

"Was I suppose to grow some?" Her green eyes widened innocently.

"You've probably developed thick skin dancing all night at wild parties," he accused.

"Sounds like you've heard a lot about me," agreed Beryl blandly. She accepted the cup of dark tea Gompa's daughter brought her and took a gulp, carefully avoiding the twigs floating in the top of the mug, enjoying the delicious taste. Wiggling her toes, she glanced up at the azure sky to watch an eagle patrolling above her in stately grace.

"Beautiful country, isn't it?" Rock murmured from beside her.

Turning at the sound of his husky voice, Beryl gazed at his rugged profile, solid and comforting, but at the same time dangerous in a way that doubled her heartbeats. "Well, what do you think of it?" he persisted.

"Lovelier than Brad described it."

"It gets better." Rock was looking at her warmly, his eyes crinkling with a friendliness that held no trace of his usual mockery.

"Impossible; you can't improve on perfection," Beryl responded breathlessly.

When the signal to start was given she quickly replaced her socks and boots and jumped from the ledge. "Walk over here with our group for a few minutes," Reagen called to her.

Beryl glanced at Rock and he nodded tersely. The team had been divided into groups by Jane. Rock and Lon were her team members and Reagen was teamed with Susan and Jane. Eager to be included with the other women, Beryl hurried forward.

"You're having a great time, aren't you?" Reagen commented, making room on the path for her to walk beside him, which left Jane and Susan following.

"I love it!" Beryl told him.

Rock's voice thundered from a distance behind her, "Beryl, you and Reagen slow down. You're not to move out of my sight," he ordered.

"Such devotion," Jane observed sarcastically.

"Devotion or possessiveness?" Beryl tossed over her shoulder, fuming at Rock's insistence on dominating her.

"Possessiveness runs in the Rawlings family." Susan's tones carried a hint of pain.

Reagan turned, his gray eyes cold. "Then why get involved with them?" he asked. Without giving Susan an opportunity to answer he turned his full attention back to Beryl, asking her detailed questions about Brad's illness and her journey to Nepal.

At noon Rock suggested a dip in a nearby stream before they ate. The men began stripping down quickly and Beryl saw that Jane was joining them, leaving on her undergarments before stepping into the icy water. The native porters gathered around the edge to gawk curiously, drawn by the unaccustomed sight of so much pale flesh.

Turning her back on the group, Beryl moved over a ridge and sat down. Was it her strict upbringing that made her cheeks burn at the sight of such casual nudity? Or was it only a result of all the warnings that she never do anything that could be bad press?

What would the gossip columnists make of this trip? A smile crept into her eyes as she pictured the hurried conferences around the breakfast table between her mother and father, with Big John's press agent there to advise them. Rock might not like it so much if his little scheme to keep the team peaceful backfired into a scandal about his private life.

"What's so funny?" Rock crawled over the ledge and towered above her, dripping beads of moisture that clung to the dark mat of hair on his chest. The muscles on his thighs rippled through the corduroy jeans that clung to his damp legs.

Beryl's appealing blush revealed the tension his powerful presence created in her. She fought down a desire to reach out and touch his bronzed skin, tracing the sinewy muscles with feather-light strokes.

The spell was broken by Rock's teasing gibe, "Why did you run and hide?"

"If the Nepalese collapse with fright over how tall I am, think what my pale skin would do to them," she answered with an astringent tone that banished her embarrassment.

"I know what it does to me." His voice was edged with mocking laughter as he slipped on his shirt.

"How would you know?"

The dark eyes glittered with amusement. "I peek when you're getting undressed," he answered.

Beryl's words of indignation stuck in her throat as Fred called out, "Aren't you two hungry?"

"Coming!" Rock pulled Beryl to her feet and squeezed her against him in a quick hug. She sighed inwardly, pulling away. How could you stay angry with someone who turned on the charm so easily?

Lunch was a cold meal of chunks of freshly baked bread and meat and fresh cucumbers. Mangmu, the Sherpa chief, joined Rock and Beryl, eager to practice his English on them. It was all they could do to keep from laughing at some of his mistakes.

Beryl studied the little man's intelligent face, noting his brown skin and coal-black eyes. Mangmu smiled back at her and then began speaking rapidly to Rock in his native tongue. Rock's low chuckles as he answered were infuriating, convincing Beryl she wasn't imagining that she was the topic of conversation.

"What are you two saying?" she interrupted.

Rock shook his head warningly at her, whispering, "Later."

When they were on the trail again she repeated her question. "He said you were. . . ." Rock paused and smiled secretively. "Well, the gist of it was that he thinks I've got quite a woman."

"It certainly took a lot of words to say that," Beryl snapped.

Rock threw back his head, chuckling. "His description of you was a little more graphic," he admitted.

Beryl sighed in exasperation. She focused her attention instead on the surefooted packhorses as they made their way up a steep hill laden with skin bags stuffed with tents, blankets and food. Rock's teasing banter would stop if she could learn to ignore it, she reminded herself.

At the midafternoon break he suggested the group vote to see if they were ready to make camp or could go on for several more hours. When Beryl raised her hand with the ones voting to continue, Rock frowned. "Quit trying to make a martyr out of yourself."

She ignored his censure and was the first to rise when the vote indicated the majority was in favor of moving on. Within a few minutes, however, she was wishing she'd voted differently. The pack had begun gouging into her back, sending sharp jabs of pain jolting through her, but she stubbornly refused to mention it, slogging on determinedly as the trail rose steeply. Her breathing became ragged and she could barely nod when Rock asked, "Doing okay?"

When they started down the trail it was all she could do not to cry out in pain. The downhill portion was much harder on the legs and feet, and her toes felt as if they were jamming against the ends of her boots. Rock gave an order to halt at almost the precise moment she had decided she could go no farther.

"At last," Susan moaned. "I swear I was going to collapse if we hadn't stopped." She sank down on a tuft of grass in the valley to which they'd descended. "We've been walking for ten hours today. I'll probably be dispensing medicine for blisters all evening."

It took the last vestiges of Beryl's strength to remain standing as she removed her pack and leaned it against a tree. "Okay, let's have it." Rock towered over her menacingly.

Beryl blinked with surprise. "Have what?"

"Your story. How long have you been training for this trek?"

"A question that stupid doesn't deserve an answer. How could I guess that Brad would be ill?"

His dark eyes sharpened. "Am I supposed to believe that you managed a ten-hour hike when you've never climbed mountains before?"

"I went to summer camp in the Rockies several times as a teenager. Believe it or not, rich kids don't have servants do our hiking for us. Also, I jog every day in Dallas."

Beryl couldn't prevent a note of superiority from creeping into her voice. It had been fun showing Rock he didn't need to worry about her holding up as long as the rest did. After so many years of being told to hide her athletic abilities, she enjoyed deriving the benefits of her long hours of practice.

"You must run in the Boston Marathon." Rock glared at her through narrowed eyes that displayed his skepticism of her explanation.

"Is it some sort of crime to be healthy?" she countered. Giving him no time to answer, she added,

"And is there a stream near here where I can bathe in *privacy*?"

"I agree," said Susan. "Let's find somewhere to clean up, Beryl."

Beryl followed her out of the group after first pulling a towel and clean clothes from her pack. Why was Rock acting so irritated with her? Had he wanted her to collapse and be carried so he could verify that she was the little fool he'd accused her of being?

Or was it only that he couldn't stand athletic women? Someone soft and clinging who had to be helped up a steep flight of stairs was probably his preference. Well, that was his problem. He wasn't going to have to be around her any more than was absolutely necessary.

The cold water in the stream was numbing, but after soaping all over, rinsing off and briskly toweling dry, Beryl felt almost as good as new. As she started to dress, Susan exclaimed, "What's wrong with your back?"

"My pack must have cut into it," Beryl mumbled, wishing Susan hadn't seen the raw places that were beginning to sting.

"You'd better have Rock take care of them for you," Susan warned her. "Never let any injury go untended when you're this far from civilization."

Beryl nodded quickly, vowing mentally that she'd manage to rub some ointment back there herself without mentioning it to Rock. "What made you decide to be a doctor?" she asked, intent on changing the subject.

Susan settled herself on the ground and began brushing through her brown curls. "Smells," she said. At Beryl's puzzled look she laughed and continued, "I always loved the smell of a doctor's office. My dad was a doctor, so I spent hours with him."

"It takes a lot of dedication to go as far as you have," Beryl commented, dropping beside her on the ground.

Susan stared off into the distance for several moments. "Sometimes I wonder if it takes too much. You have to cut everything else out of your life when you're first starting out. Family, friends, lovers. . . ." Her voice trailed off.

"Was it worth it?" Beryl asked softly.

Susan jumped to her feet, her face set in hard lines. "I came on this trek to figure that one out. It's beginning to look as if I've been worrying about it far too long." She walked away briskly, her head held high with an air of defiance.

When Beryl returned to the campsite the Sherpas had all the tents up and a fire was blazing merrily. The meal was unappetizing; rice and meat, bread, coffee. Not until chocolate bars were brought out for dessert did everyone's spirits brighten.

Rock was conferring with several of the men as Mangmu pointed to a map, while Beryl leaned back against a log, watching the flickering lights and munching on her candy. Reagen dropped to the ground beside her. "You never did call on me for help," he said.

"I didn't need any, but thanks anyway."

Reagen's voice lowered as he went on, "I find you very attractive, Beryl. I've never cared for dependent women, and your spirit is a real turn-on."

Beryl shifted uneasily away from his intent gaze.

"Isn't there someone back home waiting for your return?" she asked.

The light died from Reagen's eyes and his voice was harsh. "I've only been seriously involved with one woman, and she chose her career over me."

"Isn't that a contradiction of what you just said about liking independent women?"

"I didn't think so; at the time I thought compromises could be made," he replied.

"Compromises on both sides?"

Reagen sighed. "We were both young, ambitious, determined to reach our own goals...." His voice died away and he was silent before determinedly changing the subject. "How about you? What do your friends back home think of your hiking through the Himalayas with Rock?"

"They don't know unless the message Rock sent got through."

Jane had moved closer to the fire and seemed to be hovering over them, listening to their conversation. She called out suddenly, "Rock, did you hear what Beryl said? No one knows she's here with us. Does that mean someone will look for her? Any problem like that could cause our climbing permits to be denied when we get to base camp."

Beryl gritted her teeth in anger at the woman's interference, but she answered calmly, "Don't worry about any trouble. A Texas politician would never risk such adverse publicity about a wayward daughter. If my dad doesn't hear where I am he'll go through diplomatic channels and make discreet inquiries."

Susan joined them, saying, "It must get tiresome being the daughter of such famous people."

"It does, but it's not their fault. I only wish I could fit their image of what a Southern girl should be."

Rock's shadow fell over Reagen and Beryl as he moved toward them. "So you express your rebellion by jogging and running off to join a bunch of mountaineers in Nepal?"

Beryl looked up in anger. It was bad enough that he made caustic remarks to her when they were alone, but she wasn't going to ignore public taunts. Jumping to her feet, she said, "I thought that 'Dr.' in front of your name was for physiology, not psychology." Ignoring the laughter around her, she stalked off in the direction of the tent.

She was removing her last garment and reaching for her nightgown when she heard Rock enter the tent. She jerked the cotton gown over her head and began removing the pins from her tangled hair, loosening the braids. The reddish blond wavy strands defied her best efforts to brush them into place.

She heard Rock undressing on the other side of their homemade barrier and kept her back firmly turned in that direction. As she started to crawl into her sleeping bag he said, "Wait one minute; I want to take a look at that back of yours."

"Not on your life!"

"Either you cooperate or I'll hold you down. Susan said you had some raw spots and she gave me ointment to prevent infection."

Beryl dived into her bedroll, refusing to answer him as he continued, "For heaven's sake, can't you get it through your head that I'm not interested in seducing you?"

"Is that all you ever think of?" Beryl retorted

angrily. "I don't particularly relish the idea of having you slap some smelly cream on my back."

"I'm giving you exactly ten seconds before. . . ."

At the grating sound of his order Beryl reluctantly flipped over onto her stomach and pulled her gown from under the top layer of the bedroll. "Go ahead and get it over with."

The thought of Rock's hands on her exposed back made her muscles bunch into tense ridges. His feather-light touch as he began rubbing the salve on surprised her. "You're a game kid, not complaining once all day about these blisters," he murmured comfortingly.

Beryl held herself as still as possible, biting her lower lip as fiery darts of pain spread through her shoulder blades. She managed to stifle a moan, but a tear slipped out of the corner of her eye, tumbling down her cheek in spite of her best effort to hold it back.

Rock's hands finished and then she felt his warm breath fanning her cheek. Time was suspended as she waited in anticipation, her senses longing for something she couldn't describe. He lowered his head until his lips brushed lightly against her skin, wiping off the tear before kissing her softly. "Sleep tight, sweetheart," he whispered, his voice oddly kind.

Beryl kept her face turned from him, not wanting him to see how much his tenderness had affected her. She listened to him as he prepared to crawl into his own bedroll. Outside, the camp had settled down into an eerie silence, broken only by the occasional cry of a bird.

Sleep eluded her as she listened to the quiet sounds

of Rock's breathing. Her heart was thudding, so loudly she was certain he could hear it where he lay. For the first time since sharing the tent she was aware of a feeling of intimacy that frightened her.

Was it because of his unexpected kindness? When he was teasing and taunting her, she was able to feel anger. This aching emptiness that made her quiver with uncontrollable longings was not something she knew how to handle.

Did he feel it, also? Listening carefully, she heard Rock's breathing take on a slow rhythmic pattern that indicated sleep. There was her answer: she was only Brad's sister to him, and if she had an ounce of sense she'd keep reminding herself of that.

During the night Beryl dreamed a huge bird was swooping down, darting toward her head. It came closer and closer and she ran stumbling down the trail, panic-stricken, the bird's claws only inches above her. Just as the first talon touched her she felt strong arms grasping her, pulling her out of the bird's path. Looking at her rescuer's face, she met the disturbing magnetism of Rock's dark eyes in her dream.

His arms surrounded her, pulling her against his chest as his rugged face came toward her, leaning nearer as if to kiss her. She half woke, groaning, filled with a wild desire to turn over and fling herself around the muscular form sleeping beside her.

Turning quietly so as not to awaken him, she rose on one elbow and pulled aside the towel. Rock's face was outlined by the shadowy moonlight filtering through the tent walls. He slumbered deeply and peacefully, his powerful jutting cheekbones and square jawline somehow at odds with his sensuously carved lips and heavy lashes.

Dismay slowly filled her as she realized what she was thinking. To let a nightmare cause her to throw herself at Rock would be disastrous. With a soft sigh she turned back and sank down inside her sleeping bag. She mustn't let her strange surroundings tempt her into turning their relationship into something she would regret later.

It was a long time before she settled back down to sleep.

A NEW SOUND awakened her the next morning. Instead of the shrill bargaining of the day before, she heard mournful cadences chanted in the still morning air. In answer to her whispered inquiry, Rock explained, "It's one of the Buddhist religious holidays, and they're chanting prayers."

"Does that mean they won't carry their loads today?"

"No, they don't have that custom." He pulled aside the barrier between them. "How are you feeling today?"

Beryl answered truthfully, "I ache all over."

"So you *are* human, after all. After that amazing performance yesterday I was beginning to believe you *might* be a yeti."

A sense of recklessness rushed through Beryl; grabbing her pillow, she shoved it down over Rock's head. "Take that back or I'll smother you!"

Joining in her laughter, Rock broke her hold and pushed her back down on the sleeping bag, his bronzed face close above hers. "Oh, no, you don't...." His words died as they stared at each other, a dawning awareness in both pairs of eyes.

It began softly, his warm breath brushing her cheek before firm moist lips touched hers, moving gently, delicately, sensuously tantalizing her senses. She found her lips parting in response and his tongue gradually invaded her mouth, the intoxicating masculine taste of him sending new sensations spiraling through her.

His hand moved to her hair, smoothing it back from her face and bringing her head closer to his as the kiss became increasingly insistent, hungrily demanding more from her. A budding passion was unleashed in her body as he continued his assault on her lips; she was lost in the wonder of the moment, her nerves going wild with pleasure.

Her arms crept up to encircle his neck, her fingers free to explore the texture of his skin and slide into his thick dark hair. His lips trailed down to her throat with light breathy kisses, and a hand insinuated itself into her gown, his fingers lightly moving over one soft breast, his warm fingertips caressing gently, arousingly, as if his actions were the most natural thing in her world.

Nothing that had gone before had prepared her for this assault on her senses. She went limp in his arms, sighing with delight, her lips burning from the demands of his mouth as it returned to hers, his kisses drugging and intoxicating her. Completely caught up in the fire flaring and spreading through her, she was barely aware when his arms lifted her, sliding down her back.

He drew back, a concerned expression creasing his

face. In a husky voice he said, "I'm sorry, Beryl. Did I hurt your back?"

She wasn't capable of responding for a moment; her eyes mirrored her incredulity that he could break off their lovemaking so abruptly. Her senses were still tremblingly aware of him as he pulled her gently to a sitting position and began lifting her gown to look at her back.

Sanity returned and heat rushed into her cheeks, followed quickly by a sense of anger at the ease with which he had turned off his passion. She struggled, fighting off his hands, jerking down her gown. She hadn't wanted him to stop, and he knew it. She had ached to be held in his arms, really held, but it had meant nothing to him. What a low opinion he must have of her now; just some woman ready to throw herself at any man who desired her....

"Beryl, you're going to have to let someone put bandages on those sores today or you'll never be able to carry your pack," Rock explained in irritated tones. "If not me, who do you want to help?"

"Okay," Beryl muttered. "Do it fast and no funny business." She turned once more onto her stomach, pulling her gown above the covering bedroll.

Rock removed the gauze and tape from his first-aid box and deftly placed the bandages. When he'd finished he gently massaged her back for several minutes. "This isn't funny business," he told her, mimicking her earlier tones. "Your muscles are tied in knots."

Her reply was muffled but defiant. "I'll make it just fine."

The pressure of his hands gentled. "You have a

fantastic body, Beryl. Are you a professional swimmer?''

''Don't you remember? I spend all my time dancing at debutante balls!'' She pushed herself over and sat up, green eyes flashing with indignation. ''Would you please leave so I can get dressed?''

Rock looked at her, his smile casual, before turning to dress. Beryl sank back into her bed, her face burning with embarrassment. He took his time, whistling happily as he gathered his things and folded them carefully into his pack.

''How did you find my stubbly chin?'' he asked suddenly.

Beryl whirled over on her side and glared at him. He repeated his question, grinning down at her with a gleam in his eyes that further infuriated her.

''Atrocious,'' she muttered, clenching her fists tightly to keep from grabbing the nearest object to throw at him.

Rock chuckled. ''It'll get worse before it gets better. All the men are growing beards; they offer protection from the bitter cold when we start our ascent.''

''That's absolutely no concern of mine,'' Beryl flung after his departing back.

CHAPTER FIVE

ANOTHER SUNNY DAY greeted Beryl when she stepped outside the tent, brightening her mood and reminding her of the hike that lay ahead. After sloshing cold water on her face and brushing her teeth, she hurried to the morning fire, determined to ignore Rock.

A chorus of friendly voices greeted her, asking about her sore muscles, teasing her about the pack she'd carried the day before. Their acceptance of her as one of the team was apparent, and it left her smiling and content.

Rock was the only one who didn't speak; he stood by the fire eating his breakfast and gave her only a cursory glance with an expression that was unreadable. After filling her plate with several tender fluffy pancakes topped with melted butter and syrup, Beryl chose a spot to sit that was large enough for only one.

Rock started forward with one of the coffeepots, but Reagen stepped in front and poured the fragrant liquid into Beryl's cup. "Still enjoying yourself?" His eyes raked over her with an appreciative gleam.

Beryl nodded. "I love it; everything is so much more alive in these mountains! In Dallas things are so routine, so predictable, on such an even keel that sometimes I feel like screaming."

Susan joined them. "How's the back?"

Beryl grimaced and avoided Rock's eyes. "Better, but that ointment stung."

"I didn't know your back was hurting," said Reagen. "Want me to carry some of the things in your pack today?"

"Before long the men on this team will be taking numbers to see who's next in line to help Beryl," Susan remarked derisively. "I don't recall hearing any offers like that for Jane or me."

Beryl felt herself flushing. "Reagen feels safe offering; he knows I'm not interested in his help." Why was it that Susan always made her feel guilty when she was talking to Reagen? She didn't appear to be petty about anything else.

After finishing her breakfast Beryl slipped off and seated herself some distance away beneath a tall shady tree, pulling a small thin notebook out of her pack. She was determined to start her journal today. The scenes around her were changing so rapidly; already she was having a difficult time remembering her first impressions of Nepal.

She was concentrating on writing on the small pages when a shadow fell across the book. Looking up, she found Rock towering over her. From this position he seemed taller than ever, and for a moment she enjoyed the sensation of getting to look up at someone else.

"Don't tell me you're writing down the innermost secrets of your heart." His mocking laugh was loaded with amusement, a smile lingering on his sensuously molded lips. He dropped down beside her, his shoulder so close it pressed her back against the trunk of the gnarled tree. "Are you recording the details of our kiss in that diary?" he whispered, his breath brushing her cheek.

Beryl stilled her pounding pulses and eyed him coolly. "At the risk of deflating that massive ego of yours, I'll have to admit it was the farthest thing from my mind."

As a broad smile broke across his face she felt a burst of raging anger. It was impossible to ruffle this man's arrogant self-confidence. She jumped up quickly, brushing the twigs off her jeans and reaching to pick up her pack from the ground.

"If I wrote anything at all about you in my journal, it would be an account of how little mountain climbers know about women," she said scathingly. Then, whirling around so quickly she almost lost her balance, she marched toward the camp. His hearty laugh followed her mockingly down the trail.

Most of the equipment had been packed and the cooks were carefully extinguishing the remains of the fire when Beryl reached the campsite. Bright sunlight shone through the forest, reminding the team it was time to begin the day's trek.

Susan gathered up her backpack and walked over to join Beryl. "Don't remove your vest today even if it's sweltering," she advised. "You need that padding over your shoulder blades." Her words were crisp and professional, with no discernible warmth.

Rock returned to the camp a few minutes later and began directing operations as the team moved down the trail. He gave Beryl a broad smile that seemed to echo his earlier amusement. She turned her back on him pointedly, determined not to give him any excuse to laugh at her again.

THE SORENESS OF BERYL'S MUSCLES worked out as her hiking pace developed a rhythm. Mangmu drifted back to walk beside her, eager to describe some of the customs of his country. He showed her the amulet he wore around his neck, explaining that it had been given to him by his lama, who had got it from an old monastery high in the mountains.

Beryl attempted to display the awe that appeared to be expected of her. "What will it protect you from?"

"Demons and darkness," he told her. Then, as if to ward off any evil lurking in the area, he chanted several phrases in a mournful tone.

An arm grasped Beryl firmly around the waist and she looked behind to find that Rock had joined them. "Mangmu is invoking one of the great compassionate ones to add to the success of our venture," he explained.

Beryl tried unsuccessfully to quell the small shiver of delight that rose in response to his nearness; she was disgusted with her weakness where this man was concerned. "Where did you learn to speak Sherpa?" she asked.

His eyebrows quirked upward, indicating that he was aware of the cool politeness of her question. With a shrug of his shoulders he released her, his tone matching hers. "I've been in training for this attempt to climb Mount Everest for more than five years. Two years ago we climbed Annapurna and I had a chance to practice what I'd been learning then."

Their conversation was interrupted as a cry went through the group of porters ahead of them. "What is it?" Beryl exclaimed, sensing the excitement in the men's voices.

"They sighted some langurs. Let's hurry before they frighten them off." Taking Beryl's arm he started off at a trot, half carrying her with him. After rounding a bend in the trail she saw a large group of big, curly-tailed, silver-furred creatures sitting in the thickly wooded area. The scornful expression on their faces as they viewed the onlookers seemed ridiculously out of place.

"Look! Babies!" In her excitement Beryl grabbed Rock's arm.

He patted her hand, covering it with his own broad palm and pressing it into his arm. "The villagers around here consider langurs nothing but pesky nuisances because they eat their gardens. If the Hindus didn't view them as sacred, they'd all be killed off."

"Why are they considered sacred?" questioned Beryl, eager to learn all she could about the fascinating customs of the region.

"They're believed to be living manifestations of their monkey god." Rock lowered his pack and took a camera out of one of the front pockets.

"Darn, I don't have my camera where I can get to it." Beryl was rummaging frantically through her pack.

"I'll share my pictures with you," Rock told her as

he began adjusting his light meter. "Stand over there and I'll take your picture." He pointed to a ledge.

"Not on your life! I look awful." Beryl's reaction was automatic, born of long years of ducking pesky photographers who pursued the Bartlett family.

"Quit being silly. You photograph like a dream and you know it." His voice held a mixture of teasing and mock admiration.

"What flattery! Especially from someone who wouldn't have the slightest idea how I look in photos."

"I've seen pictures of you before. You've got gorgeous bone structure. Those high cheekbones and big green eyes are a photographer's dream."

"When did you ever see a picture of me?" Beryl demanded.

"Dammit, get quiet before you frighten off the langurs. Now give me a dazzling smile."

Beryl struck a model's pose, her hands on her hips, her face contorted into a grimace. "Is this what you had in mind?"

"Am I going to have to come up there and put a smile on your face?" Rock bellowed.

Meeting the eyes of several of the group who had joined them, Beryl relented and tried to assume a relaxed stance, attempting to smile graciously. When Rock indicated he was finished and began replacing his camera she joined him. "Tell me where you've seen a picture of me before," she ordered.

"Ask me nicely," he drawled.

"Oh!" Beryl gasped and spun away from him. But curiosity got the better of her, and after several minutes she tried again. "You've never seen one; that's why you can't answer my question."

"Did anyone ever tell you how attractive you are when you're upset?"

"Back to the pictures," Beryl reminded him crisply. "Since our only mutual acquaintance is Brad, he must have shown them to you. Don't tell me he's been trying to do some matchmaking on my behalf."

"Hardly," Rock returned swiftly. "He knows how touchy you are on that subject."

Beryl pressed her lips together tightly. The thought of her brother discussing her personally with Rock rankled. What had Brad told him?

She cringed inwardly, remembering some of the incidents that Brad considered amusing about her. Like the time when she was seventeen and had slipped out the back of their home, leaving her mother to entertain one of the many eligible young men Monica was always parading before her.

Noting that Rock was glancing toward her with a puzzled frown on his face, she said, "You're still avoiding my question about the photograph you claim to have seen."

"I was with Brad one day last spring when he stopped to pick up a photo from a studio in Los Angeles. After seeing that picture I tried to get him to introduce us, but he refused. I think he called you a stubborn little cuss, and I can well understand what he meant now."

"Remind me never to ask you for a personal reference." Beryl tried to hide the pleasure Rock's words gave her behind a screen of brusqueness. What photo was he referring to? She didn't remember going to a studio in California.

As they continued down the trail she raked her memory and at length remembered. Last year she had attended a charity ball in California. The event had been duly recorded by a leading photographer in the area.

The misty sea-foam tiered dress with a matching emerald necklace and earrings had complimented her natural coloring to the maximum. And the skillful makeup job and professional coiffure had made for as idealized a portrayal of the real Beryl as possible. No wonder Rock had said she photographed like a dream. But why should Rock's approval of her looks mean anything to her, she reminded herself forcibly.

When the signal came for the lunch stop, she sank down gratefully onto a moss-covered rock, rubbing her calves to ease the slight ache in her muscles. The climate had changed dramatically during the morning, from crisp freshness at the higher altitudes to warmth and humidity in the lower areas, making her long to take off the clinging vest.

As she felt the fatigue slowly begin to drain from her, she looked around at her surroundings, reveling in the fresh scent of the thick pines. They had stopped by a small waterfall, and the air was filled with the noisy splashes made by the glistening water as it swept down a pile of jagged rocks. She was sitting a little apart from the rest of the team, content to drift into a dreamy state of pleasant relaxation.

"If you don't hurry, all the food will be gone." Rock's crisp efficient admonition broke through her thoughts with an icy abruptness that matched the cold running water behind her.

His face was dark and impassive, revealing nothing of his teasing earlier in the day. It must be because they were away from the rest of the group and he no longer needed to act a part, she reminded herself ruefully as she hurried over to where the cooks were dispensing cold sandwiches, cheese and fruit.

Rock's attitude remained cool for the rest of the day. He was polite and he showed concern for how she was weathering the hike, but aside from that he was indifferent. At first Beryl felt hurt, but she reminded herself that this was what she wanted. If they were to live closely for the next few weeks, indifference was needed on both their parts.

This second day of hiking seemed much longer than the first, and Beryl sank wearily to the ground when Rock called a halt in the late afternoon. Exhaustion seemed to be blurring her vision as she unfastened the straps on her pack and slipped it off her aching shoulders.

A brilliant sunset over the snow-clad peaks in the distance closed the day with a melting pot of intense colors. The oranges, reds and clear yellows of the fiery ball faded slowly into soft purples and grays against a cloudless sky. As the sun disappeared behind the ridges, gusts of cool evening air drifted down from the high mountains, and Beryl was suddenly grateful for the warmth of her down jacket.

The team had stopped in a grove of tall pine trees whose foliage rustled invitingly in the cool wind. The parched earth underneath was speckled by the charred remains of many fires, indicating that other expeditions had camped here before. As Beryl leaned back against the base of a shadowy tree she could hear the soft musical cadences of the Nepalese porters as they set up the tents and started a fire.

Occasionally Rock's firm measured tones rose above the other voices as he gave directions and answered questions. She allowed her gaze to search for him in the shadowy half-light of dusk. A nearly full moon had appeared over the mountain ridges, shedding a silvery light over the landscape and making it easy for her to pick out Rock's lean figure towering over the porters and cooks.

She wriggled back against the tree and stretched her legs straight out in front of her. The tension seemed to be melting away, leaving a disquieting excitement in its place. She felt a sense of vague restlessness, brought on by the unfamiliar intimacy of the scene before her.

The strange environment and excitement made it difficult to concentrate, and she soon gave up, allowing her gaze to drift back and focus on Rock. His broad shoulders were outlined by a plaid wool shirt in various shades of brown as he leaned over and stirred the camp fire to life. In the first flickering bursts of flame, his features were etched sharply against the darkening sky. Beryl's eyes traced the line of his unyielding jaw, lingering softly, almost caressingly, on his firm lips.

A prickle of excitement kindled deep inside her, and instantly she was reliving the feel of those lips pressed against hers. For a moment she allowed herself to savor the memory of the delightful sensations his kiss had aroused in her. Then, angry with herself for her involuntary physical reaction to him, she turned her head away to blot out the sight of him. She had thought she was immune to men like this. Hadn't her experience with Paul inoculated her against Rock's type? Evidently not; in the future she was going to have to take extra precautions not to let her body betray her like this.

She concentrated on the activity around her, realizing that she was becoming used to the speed at which the small army of tents appeared each evening. It seemed as if the team had stopped only moments before, but already the fire was blazing merrily, casting fascinating giant shadows on the walls of the colorful nylon shelters.

A tantalizing aroma of spices and meat drifted out into the night on the gentle breeze, drawing Beryl to her feet. As she joined the huddle of people around the fire, she was welcomed by the cheerful friendly smiles Lon and Reagen threw in her direction. She sat down carefully on the edge of a large rock between the two men. "Wow, am I ever hungry!" she said.

"You may not be so hungry when you hear we're having chicken again." Reagen's rueful comment had an underlying edge of humor, and Beryl returned his smile as he moved closer. He leaned back and casually draped one arm across her shoulders, making her acutely aware of the fact that the stone wasn't as large as she had thought.

"It still sounds great to me," Beryl laughed lightly as she edged herself slowly away from him. She was about to stand up when she glanced toward the fire and met Rock's burning gaze.

Their eyes locked in mute challenge, dueling with

silent antagonism in the flickering light. Then, when it seemed that she was going to be forced to admit defeat, he shifted away, turning his back on her with cool deliberation.

She bit her lip indecisively for a moment, undecided whether she should move over and sit with him. It wasn't wise to antagonize Rock. A shiver coursed down her spine as she remembered the fury in his eyes.

"Cold, honey?" Reagen's low voice brought her sharply back to the present.

"Just a little," she told him. "I think I'll see if that dinner is ready." Her voice was slightly breathless as she slid gracefully to her feet and smiled back at Reagen. Then she walked quickly over to where Rock was seated alone, staring into the fire.

He didn't look in her direction as she sat down beside him, but she knew he was aware of her presence. A muscle tightened in his jaw and she could see the taut corded muscles of his neck inside the collar of his wool jacket.

They sat without speaking until his low voice broke the chilly silence. "I don't want you encouraging Reagen or any of the other men. You'll only make a fool of yourself if you throw yourself at—"

"Throw myself?" Beryl interrupted, for a moment almost speechless with rage. Then the words began rushing out in angry denial. "For your information, I wasn't throwing myself at Reagen. How dare you say such a thing? Just because I speak to a man doesn't mean I'm trying to get his attention. I—"

Before she could continue, Rock broke in, "Spare me the outraged-innocent act, please. Just get one thing clear: I don't want any man touching you on this trip; do you hear me?''

"Does that include you, Mr. Rawlings?'' She looked pointedly at his hand, which had gripped her shoulder when they began talking. He looked down at her, his gaze penetrating her defenses like a sharp knife. His hand fell away and he turned from her.

They sat rigidly, an almost palpable tension between them. Then Rock said quietly, "How about some dinner?'' His tone had returned to normal, leaving no hint of the rage that had thickened his voice before.

"That would be great.'' Beryl tried to match her voice to his, controlling the shakiness caused by her anger. Without another word Rock unfolded his lean body and strolled over to where the cooks were dishing up the food.

Everyone was quieter this evening, their tired faces reflecting the strain of breaking into the trek. After dinner was eaten and the dishes cleared and packed away, Rock suggested they have an early night.

Beryl went quickly to their shared tent, hoping to be in bed by the time he got there, so they wouldn't have to talk. She turned on her small flashlight and searched through her pack for her pajamas before switching off the tiny beam and undressing quickly.

The crunching of a pair of boots on the soft ground outside lent speed to her fingers as she buttoned up the top and groped for the zipper of her sleeping bag. She was crawling inside when Rock lifted the flap and made his way into the tent.

In the still intimacy of the tiny structure, even her breathing sounded loud. Rock moved around with

surprising lightness for someone so large, and
with each sound that floated through the thin
towel barrier Beryl could guess exactly what he was
doing.

Two muted thumps, indicating that he had removed his boots, were followed by the slight grating
of metal as he unzipped his jeans. Beryl felt a warm
flush mount slowly in her cheeks as a series of rus-
tling noises made it obvious that he had stripped off
the rest of his clothes.

She forced herself to breathe with measured even-
ness so that he would think she was asleep. As she
heard him stretch out in his own sleeping bag, a small
sigh of relief escaped from her lips. A moment later
the towel was whisked aside and she found herself
staring into Rock's mocking eyes.

"You're not fooling me. I know you're not
asleep," he told her, a harsh smile briefly breaking
the forbidding line of his mouth. "I have no intention of leaving our conversation unfinished."

Beryl twisted away from him and rolled over
against the tent wall, but when she heard the zipper
on her bag being unfastened she whirled around to
find that Rock was smiling derisively at her.

"You might as well listen to me now," he told her
calmly. His next words were said with firm emphasis
on every syllable. "Stay away from Reagen. And that
goes for the other men, too. Save your flirting for the
hometown boys in Dallas."

With a surge of sudden wild anger Beryl pushed
him away and tugged furiously at the towel between
them, attempting to block out his grim relentless
gaze. Under her forceful grip the rope that was

strung between the two tent poles jerked downward, bringing the poles and the tent with it.

"Damn!" Rock's muttered oaths mingled with her muffled shrieks as the tent collapsed on top of them.

"I can't breathe." Beryl was clawing at the wall of the tent over her face, struggling to free herself from the sleeping bag so she could sit up.

"Hold still, you little fool, or you'll get us both helplessly tangled up in here." Rock was groping around on his side of the tent, and after what seemed an eternity he switched on a small flashlight.

"Just stay where you are," he ordered, "and I'll try to get this sorted out."

For the next few minutes the silence was broken only by an occasional curse as Rock carefully untangled the rope and searched for the two tent poles. "Hmm, what have we here?" he said softly as his fingers encountered the soft flesh of her ankle.

Beryl jerked her foot away. "It's certainly *not* the tent pole," she told him. His subdued laughter was infuriating, and so was the manner in which his hand groped along her slender leg.

Rock continued his search, pausing an instant later to give her directions. "Hold this pole steady while I go outside and tighten the guy line. Just hold it still and don't move," he warned before maneuvering his way out of the tent.

She could hear him walking around outside, and soon one side of the tent was stretching into place again. Rock instructed her to steady the other pole, and before long the little shelter was upright once more. Beryl reached into her bag and grabbed her flashlight, switching it on to alleviate the trapped feeling she had experienced when the tent collapsed on them.

"Aren't you coming back in?" she called softly.

"As soon as you turn out that damn flashlight," he mumbled. "That is, unless you don't mind the fact that I'm not wearing any clothes."

Beryl hesitated before clicking off the small beam of light. That man was always embarrassing her deliberately. She had half a mind to leave the light on and see if *he* could be embarrassed for a change!

She crept back into her sleeping bag and shut her eyes tightly as he reentered the tent. "I have no intention of stringing that silly towel back up tonight," he told her decisively.

When she didn't answer he turned away with a muttered, "Good night," and lay down.

For a long time Beryl held her rigid body still, scarcely daring to breathe, hoping that he wouldn't take up the subject of their former conversation again. Only when she heard his breathing grow even and quiet, indicating that he was asleep, did she allow herself to relax.

It was awkward sharing a tent with Rock. But, she admitted somewhat wryly, she was also beginning to find it rather comforting to share this small, securely enclosed space with that powerful muscular form.

Could he possibly have been jealous tonight? Was that why he had been so angry when he saw her with Reagen?

Silly, she scoffed. *You're imagining things. He's only concerned that you not upset any of his team members.*

She tried to work up some anger, but none would

surface. The truth was, she had begun to admire the man. The way he directed the operations of the small team without arousing the antagonism of those under his control had impressed her from the beginning. He seemed to have a natural flair for leadership, a dynamic sense of confidence that made others trust his judgment. Yet he didn't dominate the other team members. Instead, he drew them out, treated them with a respect that encouraged them to share their own ideas and thoughts.

But it wasn't merely admiration she was feeling. No, she couldn't deny the intense physical attraction she felt for him. Every time she looked at him, hiking along the trail or sitting around the camp fire, she was filled with longings no other man had ever aroused in her. A dangerous undercurrent was build-ing inside her, drawing her closer to him, filling her with an aching desire to touch him, to feel his arms around her again, to receive his kisses and return them once more.

She tossed and turned, unable to still her dis-quieting thoughts and relax into sleep. There was no way she was going to let herself get involved with Rock. In spite of the fact that Brad talked about him constantly, she really knew very little about his per-sonal life. Susan's revelations had sounded much the same as Brad's.

She remembered her brother's descriptions of the women in Rock's life, his voice admiring as he de-tailed their beauty and accomplishments. Rock's type of woman seemed to be adventurous, always ready to travel with him to some remote spot in the world and as unwilling as he to be tied down by family life. For all she knew, he was seriously involved with Jane's friend Fran back in the States.

Beryl stretched restlessly in her sleeping bag, tensing as her aimless movements caused Rock to open his eyes briefly. She breathed a sigh of relief as he turned over and relaxed into sleep again.

Go to sleep, she ordered herself harshly, and within moments her tired body complied and her thoughts drifted into slumber.

CHAPTER SIX

"BERYL." At first she thought she was imagining that someone was calling her name. Then it came again, "Wake up, Beryl. I need you."

"Is that you, Rock?" Beryl fought her way back through a hazy cloud of jumbled dreams, propping herself on an elbow and blinking her eyes awake as she peered into the dimly lit recesses of the tent.

Moonlight slanted through the partially open tent flap, giving the darkness an eerie quality. The air was cool against her bare skin as the bedroll slipped away from her shoulders. Outside the tent the night was hushed and quiet, the occasional call of a lonely owl and the clatter of insects the only noises that broke the silence.

Then Rock spoke again. "Of course it's me. Come over here." His voice sounded strangely muffled and distressed. "Hurry up...I need your help."

"I don't understand," Beryl began, still trying to wake herself fully. She had no idea how long she'd been asleep, whether it was late night or early morning. She groped for the towel divider and then remembered that it was gone.

"A person could die while you're trying to understand." This time there was no mistaking the irritation in his voice. "It's taken me ages to get you to wake up. I want you to come here and help me."

"But...." Beryl hesitated, suddenly fully alert and remembering how little Rock wore when he slept. A mental picture of his lean muscular body cut across her confused mind with sudden clarity and she sat up straighter, determined to refuse whatever he wanted.

A groan of pain followed by a muffled exclamation forced Beryl to slide out of her bedroll. She peered anxiously over at Rock, smoothing the silky curves of her filmy pajamas. "Are you ill? Do you want me to call Susan for you?"

"No." His growled reply was followed by another muffled groan. "I don't want you waking up the whole camp. Just turn on your flashlight for a second and get the tube of liniment out of my pack. I've got a muscle spasm that's killing me."

Beryl was instantly ashamed of the suspicious thoughts that had been filtering through her mind. For a moment she'd wondered if he was only faking his illness; she should have known Rock wouldn't stoop to such tactics to get her attention. Her fingers rummaged swiftly through the pack, searching each crevice.

"What's the matter?" Rock groaned. "Aren't you going to help me?"

Beryl's voice trembled with frustration. "I'm looking, but there's no tube of liniment in here."

"Try the first-aid box," he ground out between clenched teeth.

It took a few more minutes of careful searching before Beryl turned and held out the tube triumphantly. "I've found it!" Moving toward his side of the tent, she held out the plastic tube, careful to maintain as much distance between them as was possible in their cramped quarters.

"Turn off that flashlight and come here," Rock ordered savagely, making no move to take the tube from her outstretched hand. His body was motionless, a dim outline in the shadowy darkness.

With the flashlight extinguished she had to grope her way across the tent, feeling for Rock's bedroll as her eyes tried to adjust to the lack of light. Her hand touched a substantial lump and she drew back sharply. "Where's your hand?"

"My hand's not hurting!"

Beryl swallowed nervously, the implication of what he was asking beginning to sink in. "I'd better call Susan," she whispered hoarsely.

"Good Lord, it's killing me and you're so helpless you can't even do anything." Rock's voice was harsh and accusing. "Haven't you ever been asked to work out someone's sore muscles before?"

"Not on a—"

"A man?" he finished dryly.

"A nude man!" Making no attempt to hide her anger, she groped in the darkness until she found his hand and pressed the tube against it defiantly.

"Oh, that's great! Just great! I should do it myself—or perhaps if I got dressed you'd be willing to pour the stuff through my clothes?" When no answer came he gave a massive sigh. "Go on back to your warm bed; I'll manage without you." He continued to mutter angrily as he twisted around in his bedroll, apparently making an effort to lessen the pain he was experiencing.

Beryl hesitated, feeling cornered between warring emotions. Reaching out a hand tentatively, she touched his hard rugged shoulders, wincing as she felt how tense and knotted the muscles were.

Rock uttered a harsh oath as she withdrew her hand. "The fact that this is all your fault doesn't bother you at all, I suppose?" His angry comment sounded strangely loud in the quiet stillness of the early-morning hour.

Her eyes opened wide in surprise. Was he serious? "How do you figure that?" she asked evenly.

"If you hadn't got hysterical over my friendly advice, I wouldn't have wrenched my back grabbing for the tent poles."

"You're insufferable," Beryl stormed. He sounded like a petulant boy. "Why is it that the bigger a man is, the more childish he acts when he's ill?"

"I'm lying here in pain and you want a leisurely philosophical discussion about the differences between men and women?" he asked incredulously. "Why don't you crawl back into bed? I wouldn't want to distress you by making you watch me suffer."

A sudden surge of remorse made Beryl grab the tube of ointment from his hand. Perhaps he was right; she might be letting him suffer needlessly. "Turn over and I'll rub your back," she said briskly, eager to get on with the task now that she'd reached a decision.

Rock's voice was weak as he answered, "Thank you, Beryl. Just give me a minute to turn over; I don't want to make it worse."

Beryl winced as she heard his slow movements, low moans giving emphasis to his painful efforts. Was it possible he was more injured than she realized? "Are you ready?" she asked in a soft whisper when the sounds of motion ceased.

"I couldn't turn over by myself; you'll have to help me." His husky murmured reply filled her with sympathy.

"I'll get one of the men...." She turned to leave the tent.

"No!" Rock's voice was suddenly strong as he uttered the command. "Do you think I want everyone worrying about whether or not I'm capable of leading the team? All I need is a little assistance from you."

A sharply expelled breath expressed Beryl's exasperation as she crept closer. "I don't see how I'm going to help you; you must weigh a ton."

"You're no lightweight yourself," he returned. "If you'll just sit still, I'll use your bulk to lever myself over."

Beryl stiffened with rage. While she was searching indignantly for a suitably caustic reply, he added, "Don't let it bother you that I'm not dressed. My mind's not on anything right now except getting some relief from this pain."

Really, was he capable of doing nothing but hurling insults? He had to be the most unbearable man she'd ever met. "It wouldn't do you any good if it were!"

A suspiciously muffled sound came from beneath the bedroll, quickly replaced by a loud groan. Had he been laughing? That would be the last straw. After a few moments of silence she decided she had imagined the sound. "I'm here, so grab hold," she snapped.

With swift sureness a strong arm encircled her waist, and Rock's head lifted from the pillow. At the look of genuine pain in his dark eyes, Beryl once more felt ashamed of her cutting remarks. Refusing to yield to the temptation to brush the thick tousled hair from his forehead, she reached out to grasp his shoulders.

The feel of his sinewy muscled flesh was like an electric shock, reminding her of the difficulty she'd had forgetting his disturbing presence long enough to go to sleep earlier that evening. After this encounter she'd probably be a mass of jangled nerves, tossing and turning until dawn. "Can you raise your body at all?" she asked.

"I'll give it my best." His dark eyes lifted to her face and he moved against her, burying his face in her lap.

Aware of the thin silky fabric of her pajamas, Beryl urged, "Now move back onto the bedroll so I can knead those muscles."

"Give me a moment to rest," returned a muffled voice, his head pressing more closely against her.

"I really think you need Susan." Beryl's voice was persistent, her resolve weakening under the onslaught of warm sensations surging through her body.

"No, I'm okay," he said weakly, raising his head and sliding onto his stomach. "Now I'm ready."

"Where does it hurt?"

"Mostly on my left side. Start over the shoulder blade and then work down."

Beryl knelt over him, hesitating briefly before pulling the sleeping bag down to his waist, unnerved by the sight of so much bare masculine skin gleaming in the moonlight. Her long hair streamed down over her shoulders, falling onto his broad hard back.

When she tried ineffectually to push it back he said, "Forget your hair and start kneading those muscles."

"The liniment is cold. Do you want me to warm it in my hands for several minutes?"

"Go ahead and pour it on. I can stand it," he said between gritted teeth.

She poured out a generous amount of the liniment and he flinched, burying his head in the pillow and muttering fiercely when the cold creamy liquid touched his shoulder blade. Tentatively she massaged the bunched muscles, rubbing carefully and gently. Her breath was slightly erratic, evidence of the effect his nearness was having on her senses. She could feel the warmth of his skin, and the potent male scent of him filled her nostrils. This was a mistake; she should never have agreed to get this close to him. Her fingers rested lightly against his back as she hesitated, unsure of what to do next.

"Rub hard," he ordered harshly.

She increased the pressure of her fingers slightly. "Harder," he growled. "A big girl like you surely has a little muscle of her own."

"Why you ungrateful. . . !" With a fierce jab Beryl began pounding the taut muscles with clenched fists, determined to show him her displeasure. She followed the pummeling of her fists by pressing her palms firmly against his back.

"Mmm, that's good. Marvelous. Fantastic," Rock

sighed intermittently. "Let's arrange to have you do this every night from now on."

Beryl continued her assault without answering, moving over the broad expanse of muscular flesh, her deft fingers reaching the stiff cords of his neck, eliciting sighs of satisfaction from deep within him.

"Lower," he whispered.

Obediently she moved below the shoulder blade and began anew, adjusting the pressure of her hands to the tender areas in long stroking motions. She could feel the bunched knotted muscles begin to relax slowly under her fingertips.

"Better?" she asked suddenly, leaning back on her heels.

"The best massage I've ever had." Rock's voice was languid and relaxed.

"This is a back rub, not a massage," Beryl retorted firmly.

"Whatever you say," Rock agreed easily. "Don't stop, please. I'm still hurting."

"Where?"

"Down here," he said, pointing still lower on his back.

"Sorry, that's as far as I go. I only do shoulders and necks. If you need anything else, you'll have to call in a specialist." Her tone was crisp and firm, leaving no doubt of her meaning.

"If you hadn't taken Brad's place, he would have helped me." Rock's voice held mocking protest.

"I'm not Brad."

"You're only another team member as far as I'm concerned," he returned. "If you insist, at least go back and work on the other side of my back."

Beryl's first suspicions returned with renewed force. "I thought you said it was your left side hurting."

"It was, but you've made it feel so great I realize my right side is affected, as well," he said reproachfully.

Beryl sighed and poured more liniment onto the right side, once more pounding, kneading, stroking until she felt the tight muscles relaxing under her hands.

Rock's breathing became even and peaceful once more, and she slowed her movements, feeling the rhythmic rise and fall of his torso under her fingertips. She had lifted her hands to slip away when Rock whispered, "Please don't leave me, Beryl. It feels too good. . . ."

"But Rock—"

He moved quickly, surprising her as he turned over on one side and encircled her waist with a strong sinewy arm, causing her to tumble against him. "You feel so warm and soft," he murmured against her hair.

Struggling to sit up, she accused, "You've been faking this whole thing!" But her movements were quelled when Rock's other arm wrapped around her and he pulled her closer, cuddling her against him before she could protest.

"Help," she managed to mutter, her mouth pressing against his chest. The silky mat of hair there gently brushed her cheek as he pressed her head into the hollow under his chin.

"Your skin feels cold and you're trembling," he said huskily. "Lift that cover and slide on in here.

There's plenty of room for two in one of these bed-rolls.''

It would be useless, she knew, to pretend she wasn't tempted. The burning warmth from his body was having a heady effect on her; an almost tangible magnetic force was drawing her toward him. It would be all too easy simply to give in to that attraction, to melt against him and relax into the enticing curve of his arms.

Beryl gathered her shattered defenses with an almost frantic attempt at control. "I'm not interested in how much room there is," she managed to say, pulling away from him slightly.

"Your heart's fluttering like an innocent maiden's who's never seen a naked man before," he said laughingly.

"Don't be ridiculous," she retorted in a controlled voice that barely hid her throbbing anger. She raised her head and found herself staring into laughing eyes; mocking eyes that sent renewed surges of fury through her. "Let go of me or you're going to regret it."

His eyes narrowed. "Don't challenge me, Beryl," he warned. "You've done your best to arouse me, and I'm not sure I'm responsible for my actions." When she pounded angrily on his chest he added, "Lie still. Haven't you done enough?"

Not certain whether the implications of his huskily spoken words should be taken seriously, Beryl went defiantly rigid in his arms. Unexpectedly, he abruptly released her, and she slid quickly over to her own side of the tent.

"How dare you accuse me of causing your crude

actions!'' she hissed. ''You're nothing but a male opportunist!''

"If you're waiting for an apology, you may as well
forget it. Little girls need to learn they can't flirt with a
man and then walk off when they tire of the game.''

"Me? Flirt?" Beryl's voice was shrill with disbelief. Surely Rock must be delirious to be throwing
out such accusations without cause!

Rock sighed. "It was your hands. They're so
graceful, so soft, so sensual. A man would have to be
carved out of granite to withstand that kind of touching.''

"I thought you considered me just another team
member,'' she reminded him.

"I tried, Beryl. I really did, but you wouldn't let
me.'' The amusement she'd imagined earlier was coloring his voice again.

Sputtering with rage, Beryl slammed the liniment
tube back into the first-aid box and crawled into her
sleeping bag, turning her back on him pointedly.

There followed a tense period of silence that made
Beryl feel she had to scream to still the furious
pounding in her ears. She couldn't possibly spend
another night in this tent after what had happened
tonight. Did she dare to drag her bedroll outside
now? Anything would be better than the claustro-
phobic feelings smothering her inside this tent with
Rock.

"Beryl."

After several interminable minutes she answered,
"Yes?"

"I'm ready to apologize if you'll admit your part
in this,'' he whispered.

"My part?" Beryl sat up and pushed back her hair impatiently. "Since all I did was try to help you, I'd be interested in knowing what you're accusing me of now."

"Using your charms to allure me. There's a legal term for that, you know." There was no mistaking the note of humor in Rock's voice.

"There'd have to be some motivation on my part," Beryl countered. She suppressed the laughter that bubbled up inside her, releasing the strain that had been building unbearably.

"Hmm, that does present a problem," Rock agreed. "I'll have to think of something else. How about failure to warn of impending danger?" he teased.

Beryl snuggled down into her bedroll, feeling suddenly relaxed and comfortable once more. "Don't forget that I can always claim self-defense," she murmured drowsily.

THE FIRST FAINT RAYS OF LIGHT were creeping through the tent walls when she heard voices inside the tent. Too sleepy to identify them at first, Beryl turned over, pulling her pillow around her head, trying to drown out the irritating sounds.

"Hush, don't wake up Beryl," she heard Rock whisper.

Jane's voice startled Beryl and she became instantly alert, wondering what the woman was doing in their tent this time of the morning.

"Aren't you interested in hearing our problems anymore, Rock?" she heard Jane whisper. Beryl debated briefly whether or not to let Jane know she was awake; perhaps the problem was something personal she wouldn't want to be overheard. But Jane must not mind or she wouldn't have chosen this small enclosed space to discuss it with Rock.

"Of course I'm interested in everyone's problems, but there's a time for that. Early morning isn't one of them," Rock answered.

"But I need to talk to someone."

"How about Susan? She seems a logical choice."

"She's...." Jane hesitated and then continued, "She's too caught up in her own problems right now. Being the team's doctor and also concentrating on the trek is a big responsibility, you know."

"I know," Rock replied. "But I haven't heard Susan complaining. What's your problem, Jane?"

"It's not a personal problem. It's one the whole team shares. There's an undercurrent of unrest here that I can't exactly explain."

"You'll have to be more specific than that." Impatience was evident in Rock's tone.

"We've never had anyone along before who wasn't a team member," Jane said tersely.

Rock sighed. "If you're upset about Beryl, you're wasting your time. She's only going with us as far as base camp, and she can't possibly disrupt the team in that short a time."

"But Fran begged to come as far as Katmandu with us and you told her—"

Rock broke in, "I know what I told Fran. I didn't invite Beryl, but she's here; so I suggest we all make the best of it."

Beryl stiffened with rage at the resignation in his tone. How dared he imply that she was causing him trouble on this trip? She was keeping up with the rest of them.

Or was the trouble something personal for Rock? Was he having second thoughts about his little pretense that they were lovers? Was he worried about Fran's reaction when she heard the news that he was sharing his tent with someone he had claimed to know in the past? Well, that was his problem; he'd caused it all by himself and he would have to face the consequences as best he could.

Jane was continuing, "Perhaps if you'll talk to Beryl and suggest ways she could—"

"I'll handle Beryl," Rock broke in forcefully. "Now how about going back to bed and getting a little sleep. The porters will be up before long."

"I will," Jane murmured. "And thanks for the talk, Rock. I feel much better now that I know you understand the problem." Her voice was low and thick with emotion, and Beryl felt sympathy welling up inside her. Men never considered all the problems they were causing as they went around spreading their smiles so casually.

The tent flap opened noisily and Beryl heard Jane leaving. Almost immediately Rock shifted toward her. "Beryl," he said softly. "Are you awake?"

Beryl forced herself to lie perfectly still, mentally counting as she took deep even breaths; a trick she had perfected as a young girl at boarding school when room checks were made each evening.

"Quit trying to pretend you're asleep," Rock hissed.

Beryl sat up swiftly and leaned toward him. "What did you want me to do? Disappear in a cloud of smoke? If you don't mind, I'd rather you didn't hold any more intimate meetings at my bedside again.''

He laughed. ''Jealous, are you?''

Beryl gave a brief furious stare. ''Don't flatter yourself. Your type sickens me.''

Rock propped himself up on one elbow, his eyes serious as they studied her face. ''And exactly what is that supposed to mean?'' he asked quietly.

''I thought I spelled that out in the middle of last night. You're a male opportunist. The kind who isn't happy until he has every woman around him wanting him. . . .''

She paused and lowered her eyes, unable to continue when faced with the anger she saw building in Rock's. ''Go on,'' he urged after a long silence. ''You were about to tell me how you *think* I treat women.''

''Think?'' Beryl flared. ''Jane is a perfect example. Anyone with half a brain can see she has a terrific crush on you.''

He answered in a voice of steel, ''I've never given Jane an ounce of encouragement.''

''I didn't say you had,'' Beryl countered, wishing she had never started this conversation. It was sounding dangerously close to a jealous outburst, even to her own ears.

''I don't think Jane is the real issue here,'' Rock continued. ''Why don't you admit what's really bothering you about me?''

''I haven't given it enough thought—''

Rock's hand shot out and he grasped her chin tightly, lifting her face until she was forced to stare into his cold dark eyes. ''Let's get one thing straight at the very beginning of our relationship. You'll have to take me exactly as I am.''

Beryl gasped and tried twisting away, but his hand tightened its grip. ''You've told me your opinion about men, so you're going to listen to mine about women. I've never met one yet who wasn't a crusader at heart.''

Seething with anger, Beryl pulled back. But Rock followed, grating out in a harsh raspy tone, ''All women have this idea of a perfect man...some knight in shining armor that they read about in a fairy tale. As soon as they get some poor guy wound around their little finger, they start trying to smooth off his rough edges, change him into something they approve of, stuff him into that suit of armor.''

His voice rose as he continued, ''Well, I don't fit. Do you understand that, Beryl Bartlett?''

He released her abruptly and leaned back into his bedroll, falling silent as Beryl stared at him. What had she done to bring on that outburst, she wondered. All she had intended to do was tell him she was tired of being treated like a burden on this trip.

''Sorry,'' Rock muttered suddenly. ''There's something about you that brings out the worst in me.''

Inspired, Beryl asked, ''Do I remind you of someone else?''

There was a long pause before Rock sighed. ''No, you're totally different from anyone I've ever known. Now let's both see if we can catch another hour's sleep before we have to get up.''

CHAPTER SEVEN

ROCK HAD ALREADY LEFT THE TENT when a strong shaft of sunlight woke Beryl. She saw his sleeping bag rolled neatly in one corner, his pack leaning against it.

In the bright light of day it was hard to believe all that had happened the night before. Even Jane's bitter accusations seemed unimportant. And what had caused Rock's angry outburst? He seemed so even-tempered with every one else on the team.

Disgusted with herself for allowing him to dominate her thoughts, Beryl pulled out her clothes and began dressing slowly, her skin feeling sticky and damp in the heavy stifling air of the tent. It was definitely hotter this morning, and muggy. After running a comb through her hair, she went in search of Susan.

She found her standing near the camp fire. As Beryl approached, Susan looked up, taut lines around her mouth. "How about a swim while the porters are packing things?" she asked tightly.

"That sounds heavenly! It's so hot today!" Beryl attempted to relieve the strain between them. It bothered her that Susan seemed to have built a barrier around herself, making it impossible for Beryl to feel completely at ease with her.

"Rock says we might have rain today," Susan told her as they walked toward the clump of trees at the far side of the camp.

"Have you known Rock long?" Beryl asked lightly.

"Over four years, since I came to the university."

"And he introduced you to Kent?"

Susan sighed, looking around before saying, "Beryl, I need to talk to someone. Let's sit down over there for a few minutes."

"Sure." Beryl brushed off a rock and perched on the edge of it. "Is it about the Rawlingses?"

Susan nodded. "I became acquainted with Rock through a mountaineering club. When his brother became ill with viral myocarditis, Rock called me in for consultation with their family doctor."

"What's viral myocarditis? It sounds dreadful."

"It can be," Susan agreed. "The muscles of the heart become inflamed, and sometimes the condition is disabling or even fatal. Kent's case was touch-and-go for quite a while, so I devoted all the time I could to watching over him. Maybe I overdid things, because Kent, along with his whole family, misunderstood my interest."

She paused and looked down at the ground for several moments, as if groping for her next words. Beryl prompted, "Then you're not really in love with Kent?"

Her face was miserable and drawn, Susan nodded. "I don't have that kind of feeling for Kent at all. He's a great guy; I really wish I could fall for him, but...." She shrugged her shoulders in a gesture of hopelessness.

"How does he feel about you?"

"Who knows? Right now he thinks he's in love with me, but that's a very common occurrence when someone has saved your life."

"Particularly a doctor as beautiful as you," Beryl added. Susan smiled her thanks and Beryl continued, "What usually happens in these cases?"

"Oh, it'll work out. When Kent recovers I predict he'll realize that what he felt for me was gratitude and we'll laugh about it together. I've had it happen before; it's one of the first things we're taught in medical school."

"Then I don't understand; what's your problem?" Beryl's green eyes darkened with bewilderment.

Susan once more looked around her on every side before answering. "No one except Jane knows about this." She lowered her voice to a soft whisper. "My reason for coming on this trip was to renew my acquaintance with Reagen."

"I knew it! I knew you were interested in him." Beryl was triumphant to learn that what she'd been surmising all along was right.

"Shh," Susan warned. "Rock mustn't hear this. He's very close to his brother, and if he thought I didn't care for him he'd be furious. As far as Rock's concerned, the only reason Kent is fighting so hard to regain his strength is that he wants to get well enough to marry me."

"If he's that devoted to his brother, it seems a little heartless to go off and leave him," Beryl declared heatedly.

Susan looked at her speculatively. "He doesn't tell you much, does he? Rock intended to call the expedition off, but Kent pleaded with us to go on. He didn't want to think we might abandon all our plans on his behalf. We had quite a scene around his bedside with him begging us not to quit. Rock finally decided that we'd do more harm by staying, so he gave in.''

"Does Reagen know how you feel about Kent?" Beryl asked, anxious to get the discussion away from Rock. Susan must think it odd that Rock had never discussed something that important with her.

The look of misery returned to Susan's face. "No," she moaned. "I don't know how to handle the whole situation. Who knows how Reagen feels about me anymore? I've got too much pride to tell him what I've just told you. Rock has told everyone the whole story, so Reagen thinks Kent and I are as good as engaged."

"From what I've heard you and Reagen saying, you haven't seen each other for several years." Beryl hesitated, unsure of how much she should question Susan. "You were close friends?" she asked finally.

"We were engaged. Our plans for marriage were all made." Susan's words were faintly bitter. "Then I blew it."

"Your career?" Beryl was remembering Reagen's harsh comments.

"Yes. I got an offer to be a professor at the university. At the time I thought it was the greatest honor of my life. Unfortunately, Reagen couldn't see my side at all; he was furious because he'd just received a transfer to Alaska and expected me to go with him."

A tear rolled down Susan's cheek, and she brushed it off impatiently. "We fought for days. I told him if he loved me he'd manage to get moved nearer Los Angeles. He told me if I loved him I'd be content practicing medicine in the backwoods of Alaska. He kept pointing out all the advantages, how we could climb mountains there...." Her voice trailed off and she reached for a tissue from her pocket, smiling apologetically as the tears streamed down her face.

Beryl patted her arm sympathetically, "It sounds like a mess. Have you thought about telling Reagen exactly what you've told me? It might mean a lot to him to know you're ready to compromise so you can combine marriage with a career."

"How can I?" Susan exclaimed. "I can't let Rock see me with Reagen. At least, not until I've straightened out the situation with Kent." She paused and glanced at Beryl before adding, "But it doesn't matter anymore. I've seen the way Reagen's been looking at you. I've been a fool all these years to keep hoping he might still care for me."

Beryl's eyes sparkled with laughter. "Silly," she scoffed. "He's only flirting with me to make you jealous. It's been puzzling me why he gives me so much attention when you're looking our way, but until now I couldn't decide why."

"Are you serious?" Hope brightened Susan's face, making the worried lines disappear. "You're not just saying this to make me feel better?"

"Reagen is only flirting with me to upset you," Beryl declared firmly.

"And you're playing up to him to make Rock jealous in turn?" Susan probed.

Beryl blushed, floundering for an answer, wishing

she could be as truthful as Susan had been with her. "That's about right," she returned diffidently.

"It's working! Rock positively glowers every time Reagen walks toward you. Would you be willing to help me out by encouraging Reagen even more?"

"I couldn't do that!" Beryl protested. "What would Reagen think?"

"Oh, we'll let him in on it. If you'll do it, it might give me a chance to talk to Reagen alone without Rock's knowing."

"I don't see how it could hurt," Beryl agreed thoughtfully.

"It may not take long to find out Reagen's no longer interested in me. Then I'll swallow my pride and crawl away to suffer, but at least no one else will have to know."

"What did you have in mind?" asked Beryl, mentally regretting her agreement as the thought of Rock intruded.

"Give me time to think it over and we'll talk again. For now we better get in that water before we miss out on breakfast." Susan's blue eyes were clear and untroubled, shining with a happiness that lighted up her dainty features.

The two women entered the shadowy pathway between the trees, both glancing around automatically to make certain none of the other team members were there ahead of them. The bank of the small stream was thick with tangled underbrush and prickly weeds.

Susan stripped quickly down to her panties and bra. After Beryl had done the same they laid their clothes carefully on the ground away from the muddy embankment and headed for the stream.

The water was heavenly, wonderfully cool and refreshing in contrast to the oppressive heat that filled the air. For a few minutes they swam in lazy circles, content to relax in the water. Susan was the first to break the silence. "I've unloaded all my problems on you, Beryl," she said. "Any way I can help?"

"No, thanks. I'm feeling fine today."

"I wasn't referring to your health."

Beryl paused and glanced over at Susan. "Any personal problems, you mean?"

Susan nodded. "I wasn't trying to eavesdrop, but I heard angry voices in the night. They sounded like yours and Rock's, but perhaps I'm wrong."

"Oh, that." Beryl was about to describe Rock's cramped muscle but then stopped herself abruptly. He had made it plain he didn't want his aches discussed with anyone on the team. "It wasn't important," she finished lamely, not meeting Susan's eyes. When there was no answer she added in what she hoped was a casual tone, "How do you think Rock's managed to stay single?"

"Most women consider him a bad risk," Susan laughed. "He likes to live too dangerously. Jane says he was engaged once to a gorgeous model, but nothing came of it. The woman insisted he give up mountain climbing and everything else he loves."

"Oh..." escaped from Beryl's lips. Now she understood his lecture at dawn. But how was she involved? Was this a standard warning he gave all women he had affairs with? Her face burned at the realization that Rock must be planning to start an affair with her. She'd never doubted that he would be willing to have a sexual relationship if she showed any signs of receptiveness, but this sounded much more dangerous.

"It was a long time ago," Susan continued quietly. "Jane thinks he was burned pretty badly by it. He seems determined enough to keep his freedom now. Maybe you'll be the one to change all that." She stopped suddenly and held a warning finger to her lips. "Shh! There's someone over there in the bushes eavesdropping on us."

Indignation was evident in every line of their bodies as both Susan and Beryl tensed and stared at the thick bushes beneath the trees. In the silence they could hear unmistakable crunching and crackling as someone plowed through the thick vegetation.

"I can't believe any of the guys would spy on us," Susan said crossly. "I hope they didn't hear our earlier discussion. Let's find out who it is."

She splashed her way across to the side of the stream and climbed out, with Beryl following closely behind. The sounds had come from the direction where they had left their clothes, and they marched toward that area, fire in their eyes, ready to do battle with anyone who was daring to invade their privacy.

"No one's here now," Susan sighed, putting her hands on her hips in an exasperated gesture. "At least it wasn't some practical joker stealing our clothes." She pointed at the neat piles on the ground.

Suddenly Susan bent nearer the ground and stared intently. "Come here, Beryl!" she motioned frantically.

Beryl dropped to the ground beside her, her eyes following the direction in which Susan's finger was pointing. In the soft, slightly damp black earth was an unmistakable footprint.

"That wasn't made by any human!" Susan whispered, her tone hushed and awed. "This is definitely some kind of animal print."

The print was about five or six inches across, rounded and fairly deep. "We'd better get back and tell Rock about this," Beryl agreed. Without bothering to dry, the women pulled on their jeans and shirts and hurried back to the camp fire.

Rock was busy talking to Mangmu, but he glanced toward them as they came swiftly across the clearing. "Anything wrong?" he asked.

Both women began in a breathless chorus, "We were swimming and we heard something crashing around in the bushes."

"You think we have a peeping Tom?" he mocked, his eyes searching out Beryl's derisively.

Beryl glared back at him defiantly. Obviously he wasn't going to take anything she said seriously.

"Rock, we're not kidding," Susan interrupted. "There's a footprint on the ground behind those bushes. Some kind of animal print. I think you'd better check it out."

Rock sighed impatiently, raking a hand through his hair. After a brief hesitation he strode toward the stream, Mangmu and the women following. Beryl was seething inside. Why was he so willing to believe

Susan when he did nothing but laugh at her? She hoped he would feel foolish when he saw she hadn't been exaggerating.

Both men dropped to the ground and studied the footprint carefully before glancing at each other wordlessly with an oddly intent look.

"Well, what is it?" Susan demanded finally.

Mangmu spoke rapidly to Rock in his own language for several minutes, his hands and arms gesturing wildly.

At length Rock turned to them. "Mangmu thinks there may be a tiger in the area. One of the porters reported seeing prints like this last night."

Susan's eyes widened in alarm, mirroring Beryl's thoughts of how vulnerable they'd been swimming in the stream. "A tiger?" she echoed.

"Don't get excited." Rock's face reflected a stern impatience as he glared at both of the women. "There's lots of wildlife in this area, and it's not unusual to see a few footprints."

Mangmu was talking and gesturing again, holding his arms far apart and waving them in the air.

"What's he saying?" Beryl asked suspiciously.

Rock eyed her consideringly before answering. "He says this is a large tiger; it probably weighs about twice as much as I do. And the fact that the footprint is still muddy indicates the print was made in the past half hour." He pointed to the ground, showing them how the bottom of the depression was filled with muddy water.

He stood up, raking his hand through his hair once more and staring at the ground for a moment. "This means we'll have to take more precautions, but there's no reason to fall apart hysterically. Under normal conditions, humans have nothing to fear from tigers.''

The four of them walked back to the campsite, and Rock called out to the other team members to gather in a circle around him. Susan and Beryl filled their plates with the breakfast leftovers and joined the group.

"We suspect we may have a tiger in the area," Rock explained calmly. "I want all of you to keep your eyes open today, and don't go wandering off into the woods alone." His voice was quietly authoritative, keeping everyone in the group relaxed.

Beryl sipped her coffee, finding it hard to keep her mind on what Rock was saying. It seemed impossible that this competent man with his superb leadership ability could be the same one who had begged for her attention the night before. How dared he accuse her of falling apart over something as serious as a tiger when he couldn't even cope with a simple muscle cramp!

It didn't take the team long to finish packing up the camp, and within a short time they were once more on the trail. No one seemed particularly worried by the thought of a lurking tiger, and soon Lon was leading the group in singing some funny and slightly risqué hiking songs.

Susan moved up beside Beryl and whispered, "Why don't you join our group in a few minutes? Then Jane and I will drift off and leave you and Reagen alone."

"Whatever for?" A frown creased Beryl's brow.

Susan shrugged self-consciously. "I was wondering if you'd mind telling Reagen the truth about Kent and me. Every time I imagine talking to him, I panic. If Reagen isn't interested in me anymore I don't think I can stand it."

"What do I tell him?" Beryl flinched from the thought of being the one to discuss Susan's personal life with Reagen.

"Tell him what I've told you. Ask if he'd like to discuss it with me. If he sees that you're willing to set up a time for us to be together without Rock's knowing about it, it just might work," Susan pleaded.

Remembering Susan's fierce pride, Beryl knew how hard it must be for her to ask this favor. Brushing aside a flicker of apprehension as she thought of the problems she was creating for herself, she said, "Okay, I'll try."

"Thanks," Susan smiled. "Promise you'll level with me if Reagen says anything to indicate he's not interested?"

"You don't have a thing to worry about," Beryl assured her.

"Are you two still whispering over that tiger?" Rock drawled, moving over beside them.

Susan stepped away guiltily and Rock laughed. "I'm asking Beryl to come back to our group for a while," she told him. "It would be nice to get to finish our conversation without being made fun of for a change."

"Later," Rock chuckled. "First I'd like to talk to Beryl myself."

"We'll talk now, Susan," Beryl said firmly, moving away from Rock's side even as she spoke.

Susan maneuvered Beryl back to her group, and all three women made an attempt to look as if they were deeply involved in an absorbing conversation. Finally Jane pretended to need a brief rest. "You and Reagen go on, Beryl," Jane said authoritatively. "I want Susan to check my feet for blisters. We'll catch up in a few minutes."

"I never miss an opportunity to be alone with Beryl," Reagen teased, pulling Beryl's arm through his. Susan shot a last worried look in Reagen's direction as they moved off the trail.

When they were out of earshot Beryl said, "I've got something important to tell you, so quit teasing."

Reagen looked at her searchingly for a moment. "Go on."

"It's about Susan and—"

"Forget it," Reagen cut her off, his mouth twisting into a contemptuous curve. "I'm not interested in hearing about her."

"Not even that she wouldn't have joined this trek if you hadn't been one of the team members?"

"Who told you that?"

Beryl jutted out her jaw. "Susan."

Reagen stopped and faced her, grabbing her by the shoulders roughly. "Look, I can't handle much more where that woman's concerned. I've spent years getting over her and I don't want to get involved again. As far as I'm concerned, she's the same as married to Kent Rawlings." The pain in his voice was evident as he spoke.

Beryl licked her lips nervously, wondering how best to tell him the truth about Kent. "You're all wrong about that. She doesn't care for Kent that way.''

"Poor guy! So she's going to stomp on him the way she did me.''

"You're so caught up in self-pity you won't even listen,'' Beryl exclaimed. "Susan has never said she cares for Kent. His family assumed it when she spent so much time helping him. Haven't you ever heard of that happening between patient and doctor?''

Reagen's hands dropped from her shoulders and he looked away from her for several minutes. "I've heard of that happening,'' he admitted finally. "But what does that have to do with me?''

"Susan would like a chance to talk to you about it. She regrets her decision not to marry you.''

Reagen's hesitation was brief as his gray eyes began sparkling with interest. "Did she really say that to you? I'd like to hear those words from her myself.''

Beryl relaxed as she saw he had no intention of rejecting Susan. "I'll see what I can do about arranging a time for that talk,'' she promised.

Reagen looked happier than she'd seen since joining the trek. "Why not now?'' he persisted. "We've been apart too long already.''

As he turned to walk back toward Susan, Beryl grabbed his arm. "Wait, Reagen. You can't talk to her now.''

With an exasperated sigh Reagen stopped. "What's that supposed to mean?''

"It's Rock,'' Beryl whispered breathlessly. "And Kent's friends on this team. Don't you understand that nothing can be done that would make him have a relapse?''

"How would he know?" Reagen's jawline tightened stubbornly.

"When the mail runners come, someone would be sure to write home and mention your getting together with Susan. Word might get back to Kent. And then Rock is the real problem: he'll be furious if he thinks Susan is double-crossing his brother. We'll have to keep it a secret."

"Nothing's a secret for long in a group like this." Defeat filled Reagen's eyes.

"Susan has a plan. She's asked me to let people think you're with me while you and Susan have a chance to be together."

Reagen hesitated, looking at her oddly. "What about Rock? He'll never stand for that."

"What can he do about it?" Beryl spoke more bravely than she felt.

Reagen hugged her shoulders briefly. "You're a daring woman, Beryl Bartlett. I'm going to practice flexing my muscles, because Rock won't give you up without a fight!" And he strode on ahead of her, a new lightness in his step.

Beryl's brief happiness in helping Susan died quickly as she fought back worries about what she'd agreed to do. Was she being unfair to Rock? Undermining the peace of the expedition as he'd warned? No, she told herself; it seemed more likely that he'd only been exaggerating the dangers in order to keep her meek, submissive and out of what he would consider to be trouble.

Looking up, she found that her own quickened

pace had brought her to Rock's side. She smiled at him brightly to banish the guilt she was feeling.

"Save that radiance for Reagen," he growled. Turning to Fred, he began asking questions about the problems the photographer had been experiencing with some of his cameras.

Beryl stopped to look back toward Susan and Jane. The other women were not far behind, and as Beryl turned, Susan lifted her shoulders in an anxious quizzical motion. Beryl smiled broadly and gave up a thumbs-up signal before hurrying ahead to catch up once more with Rock and Fred.

The weather grew hotter and hotter as the afternoon wore on, reaching as high as one hundred degrees in the bright sunshine of early afternoon. When Rock finally called a halt, the afternoon shadows were lengthening and the sky was thick with gathering storm clouds. Flies buzzed incessantly in the sultry atmosphere and a rust-colored light filtered through the trees. Distant muffled claps of thunder reverberated through the surrounding mountains.

The porters set about the task of pitching the tents as heavy drops of rain began splashing into the forests. Beryl leaned against one of the trees, ignoring the moisture gathering on her hair and shoulders. It wasn't until Rock called for her from the door of their tent that she ran across the meadow. By the time she reached him, small pellets of hail were cascading upon her.

"My pack! I left it outside," she gasped, aware once more of how winded she became at this altitude.

"It's waterproof." Rock pulled her into the tent, brushing raindrops off her cheeks with a stroking motion that left her senses tingling.

Streaks of lightning flashed through the thin walls of the tent and the thunder continued its ominous rumbling. Suddenly a dull roar was heard and a sudden burst of wind struck the camp in wild fury, ripping at the flimsy nylon shelter.

Beryl tried to stop the shudder that swept through her, but it alerted Rock and he pulled her roughly into his arms, cradling her head against his chest, kissing her hair lightly. A wave of contentment washed over her, replacing fear with tranquillity and relaxing her tense body as she wrapped her arms around his waist. Her heart pounded against her rib cage as his hold on her tightened and she heard him softly repeating her name.

Every cell in her body gave itself over to him involuntarily as his arms molded her closely against his hard unmoving length, and her mind blocked out all the reasons why she had no intention of liking this man. Outside, the storm raged around them, but inside the circle of Rock's strong sinewy arms Beryl felt more secure than ever before in her life. What harm could it do to revel in the sensations his nearness aroused, she asked herself.

The rain stopped and the wind died down as suddenly as it had begun. Beryl moved away from Rock reluctantly, not looking at him. "Are you all right?" His voice was slightly husky.

"Fine, thanks." Beryl still found it impossible to meet his eyes, afraid of what he might read in hers. In an effort to pull herself together, she laughed shakily. "I'm amazed our tent's still standing."

"I'd better check to see if any of the others collapsed." Rock moved outside with Beryl following. Only one tent had been damaged, its aluminum poles twisted and the orange cloth lying in a heap on the ground.

"Anyone hurt?" Rock called.

"No, and I think these poles can be straightened out." Lon was gathering up the material, examining the poles.

After urging the cooks to hurry with their preparation of the evening meal, Rock assisted Lon with repairing the damage. "Do you think the storm is over?" Lon asked.

"Not yet." Rock pointed toward the mountains, where the sky was darkening again.

Soon they were eating their hastily prepared meal, watching a brilliant display of lightning crisscrossing the rugged peaks above them. Slowly the lightning grew in intensity and the roar of the accompanying thunder became deafening.

Beryl, Susan and Fred helped the cooks pack away the utensils and douse the small camp fire, which was smoking more than burning. Rock was busy talking to Mangmu, and once everything had been put away they joined him.

"I think we'd better pull down the lighter tents. We can all stay in the dining shelter for this evening at least." Rock's face was slightly tense, his mouth firm and unyielding.

Beryl watched as the porters unpacked a large canvas structure and began setting it up. So far the team hadn't used the canvas dining shelter, preferring to sit outside to eat. The shelter itself consisted of a large canvas roof with netting down the sides. Canvas flaps could be rolled down over the sides, but there was no floor and it was obvious they weren't going to be kept dry.

"Why are you using this?" she asked Rock when he paused to rest beside her for a few minutes.

"Mangmu thinks we should all be together during the storm," he told her. For a moment his penetrating gaze swept over her, and then he added, "I might as well tell you. Mangmu says the porters sighted the tiger again today. And since animals sometimes act differently during a storm like this, it's better that we stay in a group."

Beryl took in this piece of information silently, her gaze never leaving Rock's face. Before she could reply, he swung away from her and went back to work.

Once the dining shelter was up, the group reluctantly packed away the smaller tents and brought their sleeping bags to the larger enclosure. After carrying her gear along with Rock's to the shelter, Beryl went in search of him. She found him near the porters' camp, bending over a large crate in heavy concentration with Mangmu. As she walked toward them, Rock drew out a long gleaming rifle and began inspecting it carefully.

A little ripple of fear mingled with revulsion winged its way along her nerves, and she went up to Rock quickly. "What's that for?"

"This is part superstition and part common sense," Rock told her. "Mangmu wanted us to get the rifle because the porters are still very nervous. He says there's a lot of talk about the legendary yeti tonight and stories of misfortune about to overtake the team. So, just to be on the safe side, he's going to stand watch over the camp.''

Beryl eyed the rifle distastefully. "I still don't see why you need a shotgun.''

"This isn't exactly a shotgun." Rock's voice held a note of dry humor. "It happens to be a Weatherby— a very high-powered rifle." He stared at her intently, taking in the slightly widened eyes and the disapproval mirrored on her face. "Don't worry about it," he said sharply. "Mangmu is a very skilled guide and he knows what he's doing.''

Beryl looked back at him for a moment, matching the intensity of his glinting dark eyes. His calm confidence reassured her, and finally she smiled before walking back to join the others.

Huddled inside with only the brilliance of the lightning illuminating the darkness and casting an eerie glow on their faces, the group attempted light-hearted conversation. "How about some singing?" Susan suggested.

"You sound like a cheerful scout leader I once had," Reagen teased. Beryl noted the look that passed between the two and felt pleased she'd had a part in helping to mend their quarrel.

Rock entered the tent and soon everyone was singing and telling jokes, forgetting the threatening storm. In spite of her intentions, Beryl relaxed against Rock when his arm encircled her waist, drawing her close against him, making her aware once more of the magnetic appeal he held for her.

Within a short time another storm burst through

the camp in an explosion of wind, hail and driving rain, accentuated by blinding lightning and rending, tearing rolls of thunder. The canvas flaps were meager shelter against the force of the rain, and soon the tent became moisture-laden. "No wonder the porters get frightened if they have many storms like this," Beryl whispered into Rock's ear.

His grip tightened. "Stay close to me, honey, and you don't have anything to fear," he returned softly.

The wind died down as suddenly as it had begun, but the heavy rain continued pelting massive drops onto the tent walls. "It looks as if we'll have to plan on spending the whole night in here," Rock told the group. "Try to arrange yourselves as best you can while I check on the others." He pulled on a rain poncho and ducked out of the shelter.

The group good-naturedly arranged their bedrolls in rows on the crowded ground, teasing Beryl about her need to leave room for Rock beside her. She was grateful for the darkness as she felt herself flushing over their teasing innuendos.

But why wasn't she denying them? This was her chance to show the group that she was not as involved with Rock as he had led them to believe. It couldn't be that she wished it were true, could it?

Beryl had drifted off to sleep when Rock returned much later. She heard him removing his boots before stretching out beside her. Opening her eyes, she tentatively reached out and felt his hair in the darkness as several drops of moisture fell on her face.

"You're soaked," she whispered. "Was anyone hurt?"

"One of the porters got a glancing blow from a

falling tree, but Susan doesn't seem to think it's too serious.'' His voice was low and seductive as he adjusted his long frame in the narrow space beside her. The thickness of their clothes was not enough to keep the warmth of his body from reaching hers.

Beryl lay rigidly beside him, fighting off her body's aching response to his nearness, listening to the thudding of his heart as the rain echoed the sound on the walls of the tent. She slowly relaxed against him, and as exhaustion overtook her she finally drifted off into a deep sleep.

CHAPTER EIGHT

HOURS LATER BERYL AWOKE feeling warm and content, completely secure. A prickly sensation on her cheek slowly impinged itself on her foggy consciousness. Edging herself away, she stopped abruptly as strong arms tightened around her like a steel band.

Her heart thudded wildly and her mouth suddenly went dry. Why was she being held by these arms? And whose leg was flung casually across her, pinning her against the ground?

Struggling to free herself, she looked around to meet the scrutiny of Rock's glittering eyes, and realized that she must have snuggled closer to him in her sleep. She lay stiffly next to him, her thoughts chaotic in the still darkness, trying to ignore the soft brush of his warm breath against her cheek. Her body went suddenly limp as strong fingers cupped her chin, turning her face until her lips were only inches apart from Rock's.

A small sigh escaped her lips as his mouth came down on hers, hard and insistent, exerting pressure until she parted her lips. His exploring kiss muffled her weak protest, making a mockery of her half-hearted attempts to resist. Beryl succumbed slowly to a fierce pulsating excitement that her mind couldn't seem to control.

The weight of his body shifted to cover hers, his lips leaving her yielding mouth to trace the vulnerable line of her throat. She twisted restlessly as his breath teased the open collar of her shirt, her arms creeping up to encircle his broad back.

Suddenly she went rigid with protest, her eyes widening in the darkness as she remembered where they were. What if someone else was awake and saw her in Rock's arms? No matter what he had led the others to believe, she didn't want to lose her self-respect; she still knew she wasn't just another one of Rock's lovers.

He lifted his head and stared at her, his eyes black pools of desire as they questioned her withdrawal. He followed her gaze around the tent and then smiled wryly. "Another time...another place?" he whispered seductively, letting the palm of a hand skim over her breasts as he shifted his weight slightly and moved away from her.

Beryl felt panic rising in her. What messages did she give men that they thought she was eager for their lovemaking? Paul hadn't believed her when she said she wanted to wait, that she felt a physical relationship was worthless unless it was in the context of love. And now Rock: he was convinced she wanted to start an affair with him.

She slept fitfully until the others in the tent began slowly awakening. The morning sky was cloudless and the first rays of sunlight dispelled any feelings of gloom that lingered from the night before.

In the harsh light of day Beryl kicked herself mentally for her anguish during the night. Why had she panicked over Rock? He wasn't unreasonable; he wouldn't try force. He only needed to be shown that she wasn't interested in him.

After breakfast Rock instructed the porters to lay out the tents to dry for several hours, forcing a late start for the day's hike. As Beryl straightened up from spreading her damp coat and jeans on a large overhanging ledge, Rock came up behind her and pulled her into his arms, turning her around and kissing her on the mouth.

She spun away hastily, her voice harsh. "No."

"What's the matter?" he asked cheerfully. "My beard bothering you? It'll smooth out in a couple of days."

Beryl willed her voice to remain calm as she answered, "It's not your beard, Rock. I don't feel right about what happened last night. I want you to know I don't usually act that way; it must have been the storm...."

Rock's tone was curt. "It impressed me more as the normal desire of a woman for a man."

"How do men always manage to bring that into every conversation?" Her smile was tight and bitter.

"Don't try that on me again." Rock's eyes raked over her relentlessly. "You damn well wanted me as much as I wanted you last night, and we both know it."

"Why don't you give that a test? Why don't you try keeping your hands off me and see if you're right?"

"There are more than hands involved here," he ground out derisively. "You're signaling me all the time that you're interested."

Beryl lowered her eyes quickly, feeling a surge of guilt. Of course she was interested; she had all the normal urges of a woman, and he was a master at arousing them. "Then we need to be apart," she said quietly. "Shall I ask Jane to change tents with me?"

At the look of dismay that passed across Rock's face, she had to stifle a triumphant laugh. "Don't you dare," he threatened. "You know that would never work."

She had him on the defensive for once, and she felt a reckless urge to follow up her victory. "What's the matter? Don't you trust yourself with her? Afraid of a woman who might take you seriously?"

Rock swore under his breath. "Why do you always pick the wrong moment to start a discussion like this? Can't you see I don't have time to stand here and talk some sense into you? But don't think I'm through."

Her temper rose. "I am." Suddenly sobs welled up in her throat and she tried choking them back. The last thing she needed now was a show of weakness, but she couldn't help it. Anger had a way of bringing out the worst in her.

Her eyes blurred with tears, and she turned to snatch a tissue from the pocket of her jacket. Then she felt Rock's arms encircling her, pulling her against his chest once more with a gentleness that completely unnerved her.

His hands stroked her back gently as his lips grazed her hair. "Don't cry, sweetheart," he murmured.

A torrent of tears coursed down her cheeks, and she burrowed her head into his chest, furious with herself over this emotional display. "It's okay,"

Rock soothed her. "It's normal to be upset over what's happening to you. The strange country... the high altitude. Just cry it out on my shoulder, sweetheart."

For a moment she felt tempted. It had been a long time since she'd given way to her feelings, and he was so strong, so comforting. His hands began to stroke her hair tenderly and the warmth of his body was gently reassuring.

His hands moved down her shoulders and then to her back, pressing her against the hardness of his muscles, and she felt a flicker of desire race through her veins. She flung herself away quickly and Rock dropped his hands to his sides. "Okay?" he said thickly.

"Fine; I need a little time to myself." Beryl rubbed at her cheeks with her tissue, aware that she must look like a grubby flushed child.

"Don't hold your feelings on such a tight rein anymore," he said quietly. "If something's bothering you, I can always find time to talk."

Her temperature rose once more over his bland assumption that her tears were proof she needed him. "I think you're right," she said evenly. "We need to finish that discussion soon."

As the hike began Beryl kept to herself, doggedly marching along the flower-strewn trail without seeing the magnificent scenery on all sides. Mangmu was far out ahead of them today, his long strides making them all hurry to keep up. He carried the gleaming rifle in his hands.

Several times Rock called out for Beryl to slow down and not move ahead of the rest of the group.

"We're moving through some treacherous areas today," he warned.

Beryl smiled grimly. "Treacherous" wasn't a strong enough word for the problems she was encountering. She might as well face what she'd been trying to avoid. It wasn't simply Rock who was causing the trouble by showering unwanted attention on her. He had been right: she was sending out silent but potent signals that she was interested in him.

What was it about him that represented such a threat to her? She'd met other men who were handsome, self-assured, experienced with women, and they hadn't interested her. But this time was different. She felt trapped by his gentleness, his ability to tease and see his own faults, his comforting presence when she needed him. Was that it? Was it his gentle method of seduction that was unnerving her?

She'd been coming up with all types of excuses for her anxiety on this trip, but she knew now what her body had known from that first moment in the hut. Rock inflamed her senses and made her forget everything that was important to her when she was near him.

Since this was her problem she would have to solve it. Running away wouldn't help. She needed to learn to handle Rock's light kisses and caresses without making such a fuss over them or turning them into more than they were meant to be. Then he would get the message that she wasn't available for a casual affair.

Behind her Rock's laughter rang out and she turned quickly, watching with pleasure as he listened attentively to one of the men. It was easy to see her dilemma clearly; somehow she had fallen into the old trap of believing that friendship without sex couldn't exist between a man and a woman. Now it was up to her to prove that was a myth.

If she wanted Rock as a friend... Beryl's fists clenched involuntarily as she realized how much she wanted his friendship, how much she longed to talk with him and share his love for this country with her. She shivered at the thought of the loneliness of the next few weeks if Rock were angry and distant with her.

No, she wasn't going to let that happen. She was going to steel herself to think of his touches and kisses as she would those of any male acquaintance, no matter how treacherously her body responded. She could hide her rapid heartbeat, the blood singing in her ears, the warmth spreading through her each time he was near. She knew she could because she had to.

During the lunch break Rock joined her as she sat on the grassy turf. "How are your shoulders holding up?" he inquired in a calm friendly tone. His firm fingers massaged her neck muscles gently as he spoke.

Beryl smiled brightly. "Great. I'm not half as tired as I was yesterday."

"Things always smooth out after the first few days." Rock's probing gaze sought and held hers, his hand dropping away from her shoulders.

"I'm glad to hear that." Beryl gazed back steadily.

There was a glint in his eyes as he said, "For a

novice climber you're doing fantastic. Don't let my teasing get to you." Her own gaze fell away in awkward silence.

During the afternoon she didn't resist when he reached for her hand and held it firmly in his. There was a feeling of growing companionship between them, their shoulders and thighs making intermittent contact as they hiked along the narrow trail.

Beryl was the first to break the silence. "How long have you been climbing mountains?"

"I started as a teenager. It's a strange sport: while you're torturing yourself in ice storms and freezing rains you swear you're never going to do it again—but within a few months you're busily planning your next trip."

"Have you ever been injured?" A hint of concern crept into her voice.

"Not seriously. But it's definitely a dangerous sport. That's where the challenge lies."

"In defying death?"

"Only a fool defies death, Beryl. The challenge is to live." His face clouded over momentarily before he continued, "Some people would consider the risks I take foolish, but they're important to me. Can you understand that?"

Beryl was nodding when the sound of Susan's voice broke into their conversation. "Rock, how far to the next village?"

"A couple of miles. Why?" Rock turned to face Susan.

"That porter who was hurt in last night's storm should be left there, I think. His shoulder is giving him a lot of pain."

Rock moved alertly ahead with Susan to check on the porter.

Beryl leaned against a tree and was mentally congratulating herself on healing the rift between Rock and herself when she saw Reagen approaching. His cheerful voice greeted her. "Susan and I had a minute together earlier. We're wondering if you'll accompany us out of the camp to take the porter to the village and wait until we get back. That way Susan and I can have a little more time together without Rock knowing we're alone."

Beryl bit back a negative answer, wondering why she'd ever promised to do this for Susan, since it was contrary to everything Rock wanted. But the pleading look in Reagen's eyes made her nod tightly.

He hugged Beryl against him. "You'll never know how grateful I am to you for doing this for Susan and me. I think things are working out great."

Rock's terse voice made Beryl pull back from Reagen guiltily. "We're going to set up camp down the road." He pointedly ignored Beryl as he continued, "Reagen, Susan would like for you to accompany her to the village. She says you've had some experience in carrying injured people on a prior trek."

"My strong back always gets me into trouble," Reagen groaned mockingly, removing his pack. "I'll need someone along to cheer me on. How about you, Beryl?"

"I'd love to," she answered brightly, feeling foolish as she heard the false cheerfulness in her own voice. She began unstrapping her pack.

"That's ridiculous. You're tired, and Reagen and

Susan don't need any help." Rock frowned down at her.

"Who, me? Tired? I'm ready for a good run about now," Beryl joked. "Let's go find Susan, Reagen, and see what she'd like us to do."

Reagen was shaking with laughter as they rounded a bend in the trail, out of Rock's sight. "That was the best performance I've seen. It did me good to see that surprised look on Rock's face."

"You don't like him, do you," Beryl observed, making it more a statement than a question.

"I respect Rock. But I resent his wanting Susan to marry his brother."

The injured porter accepted Reagen's help gratefully, and the four of them were soon on their way. When they were far enough outside the camp, Beryl sat down in a grassy meadow and pulled out her journal. "I'll wait for you here," she offered.

"We won't be too long," Susan promised. "If you hear any strange noises, run for camp and forget all about Reagen and me."

"Don't worry. My generosity only extends so far!" Beryl responded with a laugh.

Once the others had left the meadow and reentered the shadowy forest, quiet descended over the peaceful spot where she sat. Soon she stretched out in the springy grass and opened her small notebook. Her journal entry seemed effortless today and she finished quickly.

Time hung heavy on her hands. After a quick reread of everything she'd written so far, she decided to try writing a poem. All that would come to her mind were descriptions of Rock, comparing him to the formidable mountains and unexpected valleys. Just as she was constantly caught unawares by the sudden revealing of a jewellike meadow or glistening lake, so Rock surprised her with his changes from calm authority to searing anger or thoughtfulness and gentleness.

When her mind began concentrating on his sensual lips she tore out the page where she'd begun writing and flopped over onto her back, scanning the azure sky above her. Absentmindedly she tore the poem to shreds and stuffed it into her pocket. Tonight she intended to throw the pieces into the camp fire and watch them turn into ashes.

When Susan and Reagen returned hand in hand, Beryl ran to meet them, glad to escape from her thoughts. "Am I the first to offer congratulations?" she teased.

Susan answered quickly, "We're not rushing anything; we still have lots of things to work out."

"Nothing that can't be resolved by a little compromise on my part," Reagen inserted quietly.

"And mine," agreed Susan. Her gaze lingered lovingly on Reagen for several moments and then she turned to Beryl. "Thanks for all your help. I hope you're not in too much trouble with Rock."

"I'm not worried," Beryl bluffed.

"Then you won't mind giving us more time to be alone? We promise not to ask too much," Reagen added.

"As long as Rock doesn't threaten to throw me over a ledge, I'll help." Beryl's outward confidence didn't reflect the chaotic thoughts whirling inside her head.

When the three returned Rock was scanning the area, and his penetrating gaze seemed instantly to take in the fact that Susan was between Reagen and Beryl. "I was about to go looking for you," he told them. "Did you have trouble finding a place for the porter to stay?"

"None at all; I'm sure he'll be fine. How long before we eat?" Susan's brisk tone made it plain she didn't have time to spend discussing an accomplished fact.

"You've got time to clean up," Rock answered. Taking Beryl's hand in his, he said, "Come with me, sweetheart. I want to show you something."

He led her to a spot where Fred was crouching on the ground. Beryl knelt beside him, gasping with delight at the sight of a ball of gray fluff with enormous golden eyes fringed by black masks.

"A baby owl," she cooed, touching the soft down with a fingertip.

"We can't decide which tree it fell from," Rock explained, pointing to several tall pines above them. "I'm surprised its parents aren't out searching."

"Probably out grocery shopping," Beryl teased. "May I pick him up?"

"It's better if we don't," Fred told her. "How about you two sitting on that rock and keeping an eye on him for several minutes while I set up my camera? But if his parents come, you'd better make a dash to get out of their way."

Beryl nodded, her eyes shining with pleasure. "What shall we name him?" she asked Rock, who was looking down at her.

"That's your job," he drawled. Dropping onto the

ground beside her, he said, "See what you might have missed going off with Reagen?"

"And Susan," Beryl corrected firmly.

"Just make certain she's always along." His voice was rough as he spoke; clearly he was seething with anger...and some other emotion she couldn't define.

Beryl ignored the fluttering sensations his nearness was causing, concentrating on the tiny bird before them. It was trembling slightly and she was instantly sympathetic. "How old do you think he is?" she asked softly.

"Fred's done a lot of wildlife photography, and he estimates he's about two weeks old. Look how big his eyes are as he watches you."

"You don't have to be afraid of me," Beryl cooed, holding herself still as Rock's thumb outlined the contours of her face with a lightness that robbed her of her breath.

Shifting away from him, she asked, "What happens if his parents don't come back for him?"

"They will," Rock murmured, slowly moving his thumb to stroke her lips softly. "Look at me, Beryl."

Beryl's eyes lifted and she met his, a rich sable with glittering depths that burned into her flesh. "Don't forget our agreement," he said quietly. "You know I don't want you going off with Reagen."

"I wanted to see the village," she stammered, staring at the harsh lines of his face, mesmerized by his eyes, which gleamed hypnotically.

"I'll accept that this time, but no more," he warned. He leaned over and his lips brushed against hers, moving back and forth sensuously, sending darts of flame through her. She fought against a sudden desire to yield to the fierce response growing inside her.

When she could stand it no longer she swayed against him, surrendering to his gentle persuasion, parting her lips and inviting him to plunder. With a shuddering groan he grasped her firmly and began a fierce exploration, his lips crushing hers possessively.

A sound of fluttering wings penetrated Beryl's consciousness and she drew back just as Rock began dragging her after him into a clump of trees. "Good Lord, we forgot about the parents," he rasped.

Peering out of their hiding place, Beryl watched as the two large owls swooped down, flapping furiously. Suddenly one dropped to the ground, fluttering with what looked like a broken wing. Fred's movie camera was whirring in the background, making Beryl wonder how long he'd been watching the scene.

"Let's get out of here," Rock said. "That poor owl's willing to be captured to save its offspring." He pointed at the bird that was obviously pretending to be injured. Motioning Fred away, he then indicated Beryl was to crawl through the cover and leave the birds alone.

"Will they carry the baby back to its nest?" she asked anxiously.

Rock nodded, brushing away the damp earth that clung to his knees. "If you need to clean up before we eat, you'd better run along," he suggested, dismissing her as if she were a recalcitrant child.

LATER THAT EVENING the team members made themselves comfortable around a warming fire of sweet-smelling juniper. Someone threw a branch into the center of the fire, and with a roaring crackle a great gust of flame illuminated the tired faces of the group. Because of their lack of sleep Rock canceled the training session he'd planned and opened the discussion for general comments.

Beryl loved observing the way he made a point of seeing that each one was given a chance to contribute to the conversation, drawing out those, like herself, who were reticent and adroitly cutting off those who tended to talk too much. He sat beside her, one arm around her shoulders, occasionally rubbing the nape of her neck with a thumb.

A sudden, almost overwhelming urge to move into his arms overtook her. She closed her eyes and clenched her fists, trying to still the thud of her heartbeat. Was she out of her mind? She had known Rock only a few days and already she felt as if he were necessary for her happiness. She moved out of his reach, pretending to feel a need to be closer to the warmth emanating from the blazing fire.

Glancing around the circle, she looked at the other team members. In the space of a few short days many had started to become close friends. Perhaps it was the strange surroundings or perhaps it was the shared goal, but for some reason she felt closer to these people than she did to many of the people she had known all her life in Dallas.

Only Jane remained hostile. There had to be some way around that, Beryl decided. Tomorrow she'd talk to Susan and see if she could think of something that could help.

Susan interrupted her thoughts. "I don't know about you, Rock, but I'm tired. How about an early night?"

"Good idea," Rock agreed.

Beryl was undressed and already in her sleeping bag when Rock arrived. She had replaced the terry-cloth barrier between the two sides of the tent, but he swept it aside and asked quietly, "Are you asleep?"

For a moment she debated about ignoring him, but then she sat up, clutching the top of her sleeping bag to her breasts. In the dim light radiating from his flashlight, Rock's eyes appeared darker than ever as they probed her face with disconcerting intensity.

"I just wanted you to know there's nothing to fear from the tiger tonight," he told her. Their gazes seemed to be locked together, and Beryl was more aware than ever of the intimacy of the small shelter.

It seemed inevitable when he leaned over and gently turned her face toward his, tilting it back as his mouth met hers, warmly, naturally, masterfully firm in its possession. She held herself perfectly still, trying to remember how she had decided to act earlier that day. She tried conjuring up pictures of companionable kisses from male acquaintances, but then the images started blurring and she felt oddly weak.

Her lips parted helplessly under the feel of those lips and the way his arms went around her, his lean body pressed tightly against hers, his muscled chest hard against the softness of her breasts. The intimacy of their embrace extinguished her last flicker of resolve, and Beryl's hands slipped to his powerful shoulders, sliding along the muscles that rippled beneath her fingertips. He parted her lips probingly and her body melted against his.

This was madness, but she had lost her power to resist. How could she win a fight against something she wanted this much? Her hands reached his thick hair and her fingers curled around it as her whole body began to burn.

"Dr. Rawlings—come! Quick! Big trouble!" Mangmu's singsong voice sounded through the still night air.

"Damn," Rock groaned with muffled vehemence as he drew away slowly. He was crouched by the tent door when the footsteps reached them.

The guide's mixture of Sherpa and muddled English made it difficult for Beryl to follow their conversation, but she was able to establish that a fight had broken out among some of the porters and that Mangmu needed help in controlling it.

"I'll be back soon," Rock said tersely. "Don't go to sleep."

Beryl shuddered, every nerve ending in her body still tingling with the sensations he had aroused in her. In spite of all her determination she had dissolved in his arms. For a moment she gave in to her feeling of self-loathing, twisting down into the covers as a sense of hopelessness settled over her, remembering her vow never to get involved with someone who could not make a full commitment to her.

Rock would be back soon. He had threatened her with those words. Sooner or later he was going to

make a serious effort to get her into his bedroll, and
now she wasn't certain she could handle it.

Resolutely she sat up in bed and reached for her
flashlight. After flipping it on she found the mirror
in her case and glared into it. One look at her tense
worried face was all the antidote she needed, and she
laughed, releasing the tension she was feeling. She
had been doing it again, making a big fuss over a simple good-night kiss.

Once more in control of her emotions, Beryl fell
asleep within minutes. Sometime later she stirred,
shivers running down her spine. Umm, she was
dreaming that wonderful dream again, the one in
which strong arms were rescuing her.

She eased her position and gave herself over to the
sensual pleasures she was feeling. The hand at the
nape of her neck was stroking it softly. Another hand
moved languorously down her spine, teasing and
stroking her into wild surrender as she arched her
body forward.

Her mouth parted and she met her dream lover's
lips, inviting him to enter and explore deeply. Hands
moved to her pajama top and one slid inside, cupping
a breast tenderly, fingers kneading the soft nipple to
tingling hardness. Twisting and turning with pent-up
longings, she threw her arms around the lean body
over her, gasping a name in her sleeplike state, begging him to make love to her, imploring him to hold
her tighter or she would die.

The husky tones of a voice murmuring in her ear
startled her back to harsh reality. Dreams didn't talk
like this! Her first attempt to pull back was met by

hard resistance as an arm with the strength of a band of steel held her closely.

Kicking and struggling she fought her way free, pushing herself to a sitting position. In the moonlight she stared into Rock's glittering eyes, the fierce arousal in them evidence that this had been no dream.

Her breathing ragged, she was driven to hit out at him. "Damn you! Leave me alone...."

His eyes narrowed as if she had struck him, and a look of bleak indifference shuttered his face. When he didn't speak she said frantically, "I was asleep and didn't even know what was happening!"

"Then how did you know to moan my name over and over?" His angry accusation cut through the tension-filled air like a razor. In the dim light she could see that the powerful muscles of his chest were tensed and he was breathing heavily. He seemed to be controlling his emotions with great difficulty; Beryl was well aware he had not wanted to put a stop to their lovemaking.

Shame flooded through her. Rock would never believe it if she told him she had thought it was all a dream.

They glared at each other in the moonlight for several tense moments. Rock was the first to speak, saying bitterly, "At least you're not trying to deny that. But let me warn you: I won't stop the next time you hand me an invitation—and you'd better be prepared to face the consequences." He looked at her coldly, his eyes glinting like pieces of obsidian.

Beryl's head shot up from her pillow. She clutched

her unbuttoned top together as best she could. "You are the rudest, most insulting man I've ever met," she told him, her voice low and breathless. "You accuse me of all kinds of things and you don't know the first thing about me."

"I know a damn sight more about you than you do about me."

"What do you know?" Beryl demanded, her jaw jutting out at a dangerous angle.

The shuttered look still on his face, Rock moved back, revealing more of his broad tanned chest in the silvery moonlight. Beryl's eyes were drawn to it as a slow realization came to her that he had removed his clothes before crossing to her side of the tent.

Forcibly moving her gaze up, she brought her thoughts back to their argument. "If you know so much about me, why can't you say it?" she managed.

With a sudden movement he leaned against her. "Beryl," he whispered, his breath hot against her cheek, "let's stop this fighting."

"No," she choked out, terrified of the feelings he was causing in her.

"I want you," he whispered. "But you know that, don't you? You've known that since we first met. Quit confusing me with Paul."

Paul. The name hit Beryl like a bombshell and she pushed Rock away, struggling out of the bedroll and shoving her feet into her boots. Without bothering to tie them, she grabbed her jacket and started toward the tent flap.

All she could think of was a need for some air. A

need to get out of this confined space, to get away from Rock. She needed to think.

Her rapid movements startled Rock. "Stop," he grated. "Where in hell do you think you're going?" Beryl heard him reaching for his clothes as she moved through the opening.

Her first thought was to hurry toward the fire, but it gave off only a faint glow and was too centrally located. She needed to be far away; she needed to think about Brad's betrayal of her. Why had he told Rock the story of her stupidity with Paul?

Had it been told as a joke? "You won't believe this one, Rock, but that dumb sister of mine thought this guy really cared for her, and he turned out to be married. His wife said he intended to blackmail Big John...."

Sobs were welling up in Beryl's throat as she stumbled along, stopping only long enough to tie her bootlaces and do up her jacket against the cool night air. No wonder Rock had no respect for her. No wonder he considered her ripe for an affair with anyone. That was probably why he had warned her against being friendly with any of the other men.

She circled the tent area several times, walking rapidly to work out the pain. A gust of cold blustery wind caught her by surprise and she snuggled deeper into the jacket, looking for a sheltered place to sit.

She found a smooth stone in a clump of trees and sank down on it, letting the hurt wash over her until it began receding, leaving her feeling limp and drained and more than a little foolish for her dramatic departure from the tent. Then a sudden movement made her turn and she saw Rock glide easily out from the shadows of the trees. He settled himself onto the ledge beside her.

"How long have you been standing there?" she asked sharply. She didn't like the feeling that he'd been there without her knowing it; it seemed an intrusion on her privacy, almost as if he had been reading her thoughts.

"I've had my eye on you since the moment you left that tent. Have you forgotten the tiger?" A thick dark brow was lifted in mockery.

Beryl shivered. "I stayed near the tents," she said defensively, feeling incapable of sparring any more with him. She wanted only to be left alone, to stay out longer and soak up the peace and quiet. Glancing upward, she saw a warm smile on Rock's face.

"I'm not going to apologize for mentioning Paul, but I will admit to poor timing," he said in a low voice.

"Why did Brad tell you about him?" The hurt was still raw inside of her.

"He wanted revenge. We spent a long evening over some drinks plotting ways to do it best."

A smile hovered on Beryl's lips as she pictured Rock taking on Paul. It wouldn't have been a fair contest.

Rock's next words surprised her. "Did he hurt you terribly?"

The smile on her face froze. Should she tell Rock that she had never loved Paul, that he had only reinforced her determination not to fall in love with any man until she was certain they shared the same dreams in life?

No, she couldn't say that. She couldn't talk to him about her desire for trust between a man and a woman that could lead to a lasting relationship. He wouldn't understand. In his own way he seemed to be like Paul, wanting a physical relationship with a woman but no commitment on either side.

"I'll survive," she said huskily.

"I don't doubt that." His tone was abrasive. "Let's go back to the tent now. We've got a long day ahead of us tomorrow...."

CHAPTER NINE

BERYL AWOKE to the sound of gentle rain falling on the taut nylon tent. There was no sign of Rock. When she finished dressing and stepped outside, the rain had stopped but the sky was overcast and dismal, matching her troubled mood. During breakfast she stayed across the fire from Rock, acutely aware of his voice when she heard him talking to the others.

The tents were struck and packs loaded more slowly because of the mud and numbing cold. Lon expressed the way she was feeling when she heard him asking, "Hey, Rock. How come we're moving out in this mess today?"

"It's our fifth day out and we haven't made enough progress. Anyway, it's too near monsoon season to delay longer. This will probably pass in a few hours," he answered.

Beryl wore Brad's thermal underwear for the first time, tucking it around her waist with safety pins to take up the difference in their sizes. Even then the chill permeated every layer on her body.

There seemed to be no trail, but the Sherpas led the way as if they knew where they were headed in the monotonously gray valley. Several hours dragged by with Rock calling out whenever Beryl would stray out of his sight. She answered him with a wave, not looking behind her.

Reagen filled the void by moving to her side. His anecdotes about the animals and tourists he dealt with in the national park where he worked gradually lightened her mood. She was laughing good-naturedly at one of his tall tales when they came without warning to a chasm with a waterfall cascading at one end; a deep dark ravine separating them from their destination.

No wonder Rock had warned her not to wander off; in the fog she'd been in earlier she might have stepped over the edge. She stared down the steep, heavily vined sides: a ragged rope bridge swayed precariously across the gap. Surely that wasn't the only way across?

A shot rang out suddenly through the still air, startling the whole group into stunned silence. Rock hurried ahead in the direction the sound had come from while the rest of the team huddled together without speaking. He returned a few minutes later, Mangmu walking beside him, talking and gesturing loudly.

"What happened?" Reagen demanded.

"One of the porters spotted the tiger, and Mangmu took a shot at him. Evidently he missed the animal completely, so at least we're fortunate not to have a wounded tiger on our trail."

Beryl breathed a sigh of relief as she heard his words, grateful that the animal hadn't been hurt. Even though she knew how dangerous a tiger could be, she was glad that she hadn't been forced to stand by and see one killed.

"What are we going to do now?" Susan asked, her usually calm voice revealing strain and uncertainty.

Rock took in the look of apprehension on her face and spoke decisively. "There's nothing to worry about. As soon as we get across to the other side of the ravine, we shouldn't have anything more to fear from the tiger."

"I'd say we have more problems with that bridge than any tiger," Lon interjected, eyeing the flimsy swaying structure. "What does Mangmu say about that?"

"He thinks it's safe enough," Rock replied in clipped tones.

"What about the packhorses?" Beryl asked. "Surely they can't cross that?"

"The porters are going farther downstream with them. They'll find a place to wade across and join us on the other side." He finished his curt explanation and strode off again to direct the movements of the porters.

Jane was standing near Beryl, her eyes fixed on the swaying bridge before them. "I'd rather take my chances with the horses than that bridge," she muttered.

"Maybe it's time we asked Rock for another vote," Reagen joined in. "As far as I'm concerned, that bridge isn't safe."

Lon interrupted, "It would take us hours to climb down into that ravine and back out again. Since when are mountain climbers afraid of a little height?"

"I hate bridges like that," Jane complained angrily. "Why is Rock making us cross here?"

In an attempt to reassure her, Beryl said, "If Mangmu thinks it's safe, then that's good enough for me."

Jane's eyes narrowed for a moment, then she turned her back and stalked away. Beryl attempted to shrug indifferently, feeling at a loss when it came to dealing with the woman's hostility. Shouldn't the reassurances have been coming from the opposite side? Jane was the experienced mountain climber.

Lon moved beside her. "Don't let Jane upset you. She's been a terror on this whole trip."

"Then it's not just me?"

Lon shook his head. "Something is obviously bothering her. And I think it's more than looking out for Fran's best interest. Your best bet is just to ignore her." He smiled cheerfully, erasing the memory of Jane's unfriendly behavior. "Ready to cross that bridge?"

"If you go first," laughed Beryl.

"I think I will; my graceful agility will make all of you cowards ashamed of yourselves," he teased, his short, powerfully built body attempting a dainty pirouette.

Beryl convulsed with laughter as Reagen intoned, "Hear, hear! Come and see the greatest tightrope artist in Nepal!"

Grasping the rope handrail, Lon stepped onto the narrow span with a flourish, but his movements slowed to a tortured deliberateness that made Beryl's heart lodge in her throat. Up to this point the trek had made its demands on her physical strength, but now she felt as if every nerve in her body were being tested to its limit.

Tears of relief sprang to her eyes when Lon finally reached the other side and stepped onto firm ground. "Okay, you guys," he called. "All of you who didn't think I'd make it, show me your stuff now."

Rock had returned and was standing by Beryl. "Are you frightened?" he asked in a low voice.

"Of course. But I'd like to go next if I may." If she had to wait too long she was afraid she might develop an immobilizing fear, making her incapable of crossing the ravine. "Anything's better than suspense."

Rock's arm grasped hers, holding her back. "No, we'll go last. I'm staying here until everyone else gets across, and I want you where I can watch you."

Beryl frowned and withdrew her arm. "I'm perfectly capable of taking care of myself," she retorted, angry at Rock's insistence on treating her as if she couldn't function without his superior help.

"That's a decision I'll make," was his exasperated reply.

Rock directed the team members in the order they would go, his encouragement mingling with Lon's from the other side of the ravine. More than half the group had crossed when Jane's turn came.

"No," she gulped. "I want to go last."

"Move it, Jane," Rock said decisively.

"Please. . . if I could go directly in front of you I'd feel safer." Her long straight black hair was streaming over her face and there was a wild frightened look in her dark eyes that worried Beryl.

"That's Beryl's place," Rock told her. "Now it's your turn." His eyes were hard, brooking no disobedience to his orders, but his voice softened as he added, "I won't take my eyes off you. Now go!"

Her face a pale shade of green, Jane clutched the rope convulsively with her left hand and started across. For a mountaineer she seemed to be acting extremely strange. As Beryl watched the other woman's awkward movements a vague premonition of danger filled her.

When Jane reached the halfway mark Beryl felt some of the tension draining from her; relieved, she told herself that her apprehensions had only been the result of an overwrought imagination. Suddenly the air was rent by a scream as Jane's foot slipped from the rope, causing the bridge to sway precariously. The entire group tensed, expelling their breath with long sighs when she righted herself and stood looking down at the rushing stream below her for long moments.

"Way to go!" shouted Susan, who had crossed with little difficulty earlier.

Jane remained rooted to the spot, her body frozen still as she clutched the rope and continued to stare downward. The pallor of her skin was frightening to those who watched.

"Come on—start moving, honey," Lon called in a reassuring voice.

There was still no answer; Jane continued to stand as if paralyzed.

"Jane," Rock urged softly. "Watch Lon over there and move toward him. One step at a time. Make your foot move."

"No, I can't." Her eyes closed tightly as she moaned her answer in an unnaturally hoarse voice.

The minutes ticked by slowly and there was complete silence from both sides of the ravine. When Beryl felt she could stand it no longer she turned to Rock. "I'm going to help her—someone's got to walk with her."

"No," Rock objected. "I'll go and then come back for you." He grasped her arm, his voice low and menacing.

"You weigh too much, you big oaf," Beryl protested, fear tinging her voice with palpable anger. Before he could react she brushed his arm off and walked to the rope, moving silently onto the bridge, not wanting to alarm Jane before she could reach her. There was no time to be frightened. For the moment Beryl's whole attention was fixed on helping Jane cross that bridge.

Beryl had almost reached her when Jane suddenly turned. Her abrupt movement sent the rope swaying as she screamed at Beryl, "Get away from me! You're going to make the bridge break!"

Beryl kept moving slowly as the bridge swayed precariously beneath them. After one dizzying glance at the ravine yawning dangerously below, she forced herself to look only at Jane. Her mind reeled as she was assailed by visions of the bridge snapping suddenly and dashing them against the jagged rocks.

Pushing aside her thoughts roughly, she edged closer to Jane. In a gentle voice, and with more assurance than she was feeling, she said, "That's okay, Jane. We'll make it together." Patting Jane's rigid shoulder lightly she coaxed her to take one step at a time, and after several excruciating minutes they slowly crossed to the other side.

Lon was waiting for them, and his muscular arms

reached out to grasp Jane when she neared his side, pulling her to safety. Clapping burst out spontaneously from both sides of the chasm as Beryl set foot on the ground.

Her knees buckled under her and she collapsed, sinking fluidly to the ground, too spent with nervous exhaustion even to respond to the praise the team was heaping on her. The sight of Rock starting across the bridge made her squeeze her eyes shut, her fists clenching into tight balls in her lap as visions of him hurtling to the chasm below caused her to feel faint with fear.

"Wake up. Time to get moving." Rock's low husky voice in her ear sent a sharp spurt of joy singing through her veins.

Beryl accepted his outstretched hand and rose beside him. "Do we have many more challenges like that?"

His arm draped casually over her shoulder, he answered, "Not unless the monsoons come early and wash out the bridges."

The other team members had clustered around Jane, who was sitting huddled on a rock, her slim shoulders still shaking in the aftermath of what had happened. "Move back," Susan ordered them. In her hand she held a small tumbler of amber liquid, which she handed to Jane. "Drink this—it'll help you."

"Thanks for what you've done," Rock whispered to Beryl, his arm tightening around her shoulders. Then his fingers bit into the soft skin of her upper arm as he raised his voice to say clearly, "I should lecture you, Beryl. You could have been killed back there, and it would have been all your fault because you disobeyed one of my orders.''

For a moment Beryl was confused, unable to grasp the swift change he had made from admiration to admonition. ''Someone had to help Jane,'' she protested.

''Don't you think we were all aware of that fact?'' Rock eyed her harshly, his irritation apparent in the grim lines of his face. ''When I give an order, I expect it to be obeyed. The safety of every one of the members of this team lies in recognizing that.''

Beryl fought back angry tears as she pulled her arm away. ''Yes, sir,'' she snapped furiously, hissing her words out in an effort to keep to a whisper. There was no way she was letting the others see her humiliation. They had made it plain they appreciated her efforts.

She strode off quickly when they were back on the trail, eager to get as much distance as possible between Rock and herself.

When they reached an easy trail, Rock suggested they break for the day. ''According to my map there are some stone shelters we can use in case it rains again. This group deserves a rest this afternoon.'' No one disagreed.

The sun was peeping out from behind the clouds, warming the temperature to a pleasant degree of comfort. Susan and Beryl claimed a secluded part of the nearby stream for themselves, leaving the cleared area to those who bathed in the nude.

''How are things between you and Reagen?'' Beryl asked Susan.

''Great! But it's awful to see each other and not be able to be alone when you want to.''

"It shouldn't be too hard to arrange a way."

Susan frowned. "From my perspective it seems impossible. How did Rock react to that trip to the village?"

Beryl shrugged. "He warned me not to throw myself at Reagen."

Susan's laugh showed her surprise. "That doesn't sound like Rock. Maybe it's doing him good to think he has competition for a change. Most women find him irresistible."

"You're referring to Fran?" Inside, Beryl's heart was starting to pound furiously.

Susan glanced over at her. "So that does bother you a little?"

"I only hope she doesn't take Rock too seriously. I don't like being cast as the 'other woman.' That happened to me once, and believe me, once is too much."

"You? The other woman? You look more like the girl next door to me, Beryl," Susan teased, splashing water at her.

Beryl joined in the laughter and returned the splash. "Now that you've spoiled my elaborate hairdo, how about loaning me some shampoo? This stuff of Brad's is ruining my hair," she responded lightly. Susan's interest was making it increasingly difficult not to confess her ambivalent feelings where Rock was concerned. But such confidences would be disastrous, so she steered the conversation back to safer ground.

The cool water was wonderful, invigorating Beryl as she dipped under the rippling surface repeatedly. "How about washing some clothes today?"

"Only those that dry quickly. Nothing's worse than having to tote along a bunch of soggy garments that weigh a ton," Susan told her.

"What about our heavier garments?"

"They never get washed," came Susan's laughing reply. "Our next full rest day it would be a good idea to air all of them."

Rock joined Beryl when she returned to the tent area. "I think it's time we had a little talk," he ordered, his eyes on her damp hair waving softly down her back.

"What's there to talk about? I thought you settled everything back at the ravine."

"Come with me," he insisted. He took her arm and strode purposefully toward a grove of trees.

"Don't manhandle me!" Beryl flared as he pushed her to a seat on the ground and towered over her.

"Manhandle?" He grinned mockingly. "If that's all you know about it, the men in your past must not have been much."

Beryl itched to slap the mocking smile off his face. "And I suppose you think you're the answer to every woman's prayer?"

His arms shot out and he grabbed her by the shoulders, pulling her hard against his chest. For a moment her luminous green eyes met his glittering black gaze before his mouth closed over hers in a plundering kiss. His lips, hard with anger, forced hers apart, his tongue probing the sensitive inner recesses of her mouth.

At first she struggled, refusing the response he was trying to force from her. She fought to remain passive under his kiss, but the erotic demands of his mouth gradually aroused a flicker of submission. The soft strands of his beard brushed her skin as of their own will her lips began to answer his.

Beryl swayed against him, her defenses weakened, crumbling beneath the onslaught of his masterful seduction, helplessly melting under his fiery touch. She arched closer, giving in to the unwanted curl of excitement flaring through her.

Abruptly he jerked away from her, leaving her drained body swaying without support. She groped for a nearby tree, shuddering and gasping for air, staring at him with smoldering eyes.

"Don't throw out any more challenges at me," he ordered harshly.

Pride came to her rescue. "Is that all women are to you? A challenge to be conquered like some mountain?" she countered, anger surging through her.

He threw back his head and laughed. "How do you manage to do it?" he asked. "Every time I try to start a rational discussion with you, it ends up in a blazing row."

He turned in irritation as he heard his name being called. Jane was emerging from the woods, walking toward them.

"I'm sorry if I'm interrupting anything." Her voice held no trace of regret as she glanced at Beryl.

"We're not through talking." Rock was frowning at Jane.

"Perhaps I should make an appointment," Jane responded angrily.

"Is it something important?" Rock returned stonily, his displeasure obvious.

"Only to me. I need to talk to you about what happened to me out there today. You know how long I've been climbing mountains, and I've never panicked before. I don't know what it means.'' She looked distraught as she stared at him.

''That sounds very important to me,'' Beryl said firmly. As she walked away she heard Jane's voice break and stifled sobs.

A volleyball net had been set up, and after checking to see if her clothes were drying she joined the players. She found it difficult to concentrate, however, her thoughts whirling constantly as she relived the past few moments.

Why did she melt so spinelessly every time Rock touched her? No wonder he was laughing at her. She had never been vulnerable this way before, but Rock couldn't know that.

''Hey, watch out! That's the second ball you've let get past you, Beryl,'' one of the men on her side of the net scolded her crossly. She turned her attention to the game with an apologetic smile, banishing thoughts of Rock from her mind.

The evening meal was an unexpected treat. Rock had ordered the unpacking of a crate of freeze-dried food, and soon the savory smells of thyme, basil and oregano simmering in a thick tomato sauce filled the air, luring all the campers to the serenity of the blazing fire.

''I can't believe it: my favorite meal, spaghetti and meatballs!'' Lon exclaimed.

''I hope there's some garlic toast, and I wouldn't mind a good red wine, either,'' added Fred.

''Sorry about that,'' Rock cut in, emerging from the woods. ''But Susan might be persuaded to cough up a little medicinal spirits to brighten up our coffee."

"Is it a celebration?" asked Susan.

"It's only three weeks before my birthday. Does that qualify?" Reagen offered, grinning at the laughs his remarks brought.

"You convinced me," Susan agreed, leaving the warm circle to go to her tent. When she emerged she handed a bottle of spirits to Rock. "You can pour."

As he reached Jane she held out her cup with a smile, saying, "This reminds me of that last night before we left Los Angeles, Rock. That little Italian restaurant. . . do you remember?"

"Let's save our reminiscences for another time," Rock answered. "Time for us to sample this good food."

Jealousy flared deep inside Beryl, shocking her at the depth of pain it caused. If Rock hadn't intervened so adroitly she was certain Jane would have mentioned Fran or some other woman who had shared his last evening. But why was she letting it hurt her like this?

"Hold out your cup," Rock ordered, smiling down at Beryl's eyes. "A little something to cheer you up. It's been a hard day for everyone."

After the plates were washed Rock suggested they gather around the fire for a gripe session. "Now's the time to say what you've been thinking and bring everything out into the open. You know I don't tolerate people talking about other team members behind their backs. As we continue gaining altitude each day, our tempers seem to be getting shorter and shorter. If you have a valid complaint against anyone, feel free to express it now.''

Several joined in expressing a problem that they felt another member of the group was causing. The member singled out was then asked to explain his side. Rock took suggestions from the others on how to resolve the issue; as a final measure, he made a decision based on their suggestions and asked for a follow-up report at the next session.

Beryl watched Rock's rugged face illuminated in the flickering firelight. It was impossible for her to quell the surge of admiration she felt as she observed his calm leadership. He would make a superb father, one who would take the time to listen to his children and help them learn how to resolve problems.

Big John's method had been to encourage Brad and Beryl to stand up for themselves, while Monica had stressed politeness and reserve. That often left Beryl floundering without any real guidelines when in a difficult situation.

Rock always seemed so sure of himself, so in control. The few times when he had seemed doubtful of a course of action, his indecision had lasted only for seconds and then his leadership had exerted itself again, more self-confident than ever.

Susan began to speak, mentioning Jane's name, and Beryl switched her attention. She was worried about how Jane would react to criticism after her harrowing experience earlier in the day.

''Since Jane and I are going to be team members when we begin the ascent I'm concerned over what happened today. A partner who panics can be extremely dangerous,'' Susan pointed out.

"Why don't you tell the group what you told me today?" Rock nodded toward Jane, who was sitting with downcast eyes, her body hunched in a defensive ball.

"I'm horribly ashamed of my actions," she began hesitantly. "I'm sure it has nothing to do with mountain climbing. Once, as a child, I was pushed off a narrow bridge by some kids, and I fell and hurt myself. I suppose that memory must have come back to haunt me today."

She paused and glanced toward Susan before continuing. "I promise that when we get to base camp I'll try several practice climbs. If I find that feeling returning I'll go back to Katmandu. I'd never think of endangering anyone's life or hurting the team's efforts in any way."

"Are you willing to accept her promise, Susan?" Rock stared at each woman in turn.

"Yes, that's all I wanted to hear," Susan replied.

"Then that's settled. Any other problems?" The grooves in Rock's face deepened and his shoulders sagged with exhaustion. He must not have slept any better than she had after their quarrel the night before, Beryl decided.

As if he felt her intense scrutiny, he turned and met her gaze. For a moment that same fiery surge of awareness flared between them with frightening intensity, and both seemed oblivious to the others around the camp fire.

"Well, there is one thing." Jane's voice broke the spell between them. "I hate to mention it, but since it's bothering me I suppose I should."

"Then mention it; we want everything out in the

open." Rock pulled his gaze away from Beryl and looked at Jane.

"It's you, Rock," Jane began. Ignoring the hard looks being given her by the others, she rushed on, "This year you're too...too preoccupied to notice the rest of us. This is my third trip with you, and I can see a difference."

"The only difference between this and any previous trip is Beryl's presence," Rock said quietly. "Is that what you're referring to?"

The silence was taut for several moments. "Yes, that's it," Jane responded. "You're so interested in her that you look cross anytime the rest of us try talking to you. Has anyone else noticed it?"

"That's stupid," Lon put in bluntly. "Anytime I've needed to talk to Rock he's been available. He spends every evening talking to all of us. Why don't you admit that your problem is really jealousy of Beryl?"

"No labeling," Rock interrupted. "Jane's criticism has validity." He ran a hand through his hair and glanced toward Beryl. "I have been paying a lot of attention to Beryl. She's a big responsibility. Anyone have any suggestions on how to handle her?"

"How about giving Beryl to me?" Reagen joked. General laughter followed his remark. Beryl sat staring at the ground, her cheeks flaming, her fists clenched tightly. Jane's antagonism was beginning to irritate her; and even more, she was furious with Rock for saying he found her a nuisance.

When the laughter stopped Rock said, "Sorry, Reagen, but I have the option on her, so that one's out. Any other suggestions?"

"Why not rotate the groups you're with on our daily hikes?" Fred suggested. "That way everyone would have more access to you."

Rock's frown deepened and he stared at his hands for a few moments. "You must remember that Beryl hasn't attended any of our training sessions and is completely unfamiliar with this country. I feel it's necessary to keep an eye on her every minute."

"Don't you trust the rest of us?" Jane asked eagerly. "As far as I'm concerned, when I'm in her group I'll take the responsibility for watching after her."

"Dammit!" Beryl stood up so quickly she upset her half-filled coffee cup onto the ground. "I've had all of this group's insufferable superiority I can stand. I can take care of myself!"

"Please..." Reagen's voice pleaded as he picked up Beryl's cup and placed an arm around her shoulder. "I don't blame you for being angry. After you saved Jane's life today it's going a little too far for her to promise to watch you."

"What melodramatic rot!" Jane exclaimed. "Is Beryl running around telling everyone she saved my life today?"

"Sit down, all of you," Rock ordered. When they obeyed, he continued, "Let's sort this out. To answer your charge, Jane: no, Beryl hasn't mentioned what she did for you today, but it was brave of her. I assume you've thanked her properly." He stared intently at Jane, his frown deepening.

"Thanks," Jane mumbled.

"That's not necessary." How had all this started, Beryl wondered. Nothing made her more miserable than to be the center of attention this way.

Rock ignored their interchange. "As for you, Beryl: everyone is amazed at your performance on the trail. You're out ahead of most of us every day, and no one doubts your ability to take care of yourself—least of all me! But Jane's offer to watch you should be accepted as the genuine gesture of friendship it was."

Beryl bit her lip to keep a sarcastic retort from slipping out. Was he so naive where women were concerned? Surely he didn't believe Jane wanted to be her friend? But there was no need for her to be rude in return. "I accept your offer, Jane," she said clearly.

"I'm glad," Jane replied in a saccharine-sweet voice.

"Then it's decided that beginning tomorrow I'll rotate groups. The person taking my place each day will be responsible to see that nothing happens to Beryl," Rock stated.

There were nodded assents before the group started breaking up. The talk was relaxed as the chairs were folded and the cups rinsed out in readiness for the next morning.

Rock was behind Beryl when she entered the tent. He knelt and spread out the two sleeping bags, giving her an oddly questioning look before stringing up the towel divider.

Taking her chin in his hand, Rock gazed at her thoughtfully, his eyes glittering. "You're doing a great job, Beryl. I have to admit I never thought you'd make it. You've surprised all of us."

He dropped his hand and moved to his own side of the tent, flicking off the flashlight and plunging them into shadowy darkness. Beryl gazed after him in surprise. She hadn't expected that praise, least of all from Rock. Undressing quickly, she pulled the top of her sleeping bag securely around her. It was getting more and more difficult to understand him.

Across the room she could hear him breathing. She punched down the small pillow and buried her face in it. Did he really admire her ability to keep up on the trail, or was there some other meaning to his words?

Her own inconsistency angered her. Just a day or two earlier she had longed for Rock to respect her stamina and ability to function as one of the team. And now that she had what she wanted, it made her angry. Sheer exhaustion overtook her finally, and she fell asleep.

CHAPTER TEN

IT WAS ROCK who awoke first, and his restless movements roused Beryl. "Is something the matter?" she asked, surfacing from a dream in which he had been taunting her for refusing to crawl through an overgrown swamp.

"Can't you hear that rain?" He groaned and reached for his clothes. "We're falling behind schedule, but I don't think we can start out in this."

"Then why are you getting dressed?" Beryl lay back on her pillow, glad of the prospect of a little more sleep.

Rock grimaced. "I'm going to let the others know they can sleep later. I didn't intend to wake you."

"Mmm, that's considerate of you," Beryl murmured. She heard Rock chuckle as he left the tent.

When she next awoke she opened her eyes to the sight of Rock resting his chin on his elbow just beside her head. "You look about ten years old when you're asleep," he said.

"I feel a hundred," she grumbled. "Is it time to get up?"

"No hurry. It's still raining." The nearness of his face only inches away was causing her heart to thud loudly, and she turned over on her side to escape his unnerving gaze. "What are we going to do?" she asked.

"I can think of lots of good things to do on a rainy day. If you're lonely, I'll be glad to keep you company." Amusement spilled out of his voice.

"I'm sure you would," Beryl responded dryly, huddling defensively under the cocoon of the covers, unwilling to spar with him at the moment.

Rock sighed contentedly, leaning back on his own pillow. "I'm waiting for the smell of fresh coffee before I go outside." His voice was low and husky, his tall body stretched out beside her in companionable intimacy.

"How long will that be?" Beryl inquired. It wasn't fair for him to be that devastatingly attractive this early in the morning. She must look a mess, with her tousled hair and colorless face.

"Not long. Gompa's got the stove going. Would you like to help me with something today?" His warm vibrant tone made it obvious that he didn't expect her to refuse anything he asked of her.

Beryl's answer was shaded with doubt. "If it's something I know how to do."

"That answer's worthy of a politician's daughter," he chuckled. "I'm sure you can do this. It involves a little writing."

"Correspondence? Secretarial work?"

"No, writing. Since you seem to enjoy keeping that diary of yours, I was wondering if you would edit some notes of mine on how the trek is going."

"That sounds easy. I write speeches and press releases for my dad's campaign. And before that I worked for a while editing Lone Star Oil's company newsletter."

Rock raised one eyebrow inquiringly. "Why did you leave that job?"

"I wasn't fired, if that's what you're thinking," Beryl flared. Under his steady scrutiny she continued, "My dad needed me and it seemed best at the time...."

"And you wouldn't have to see Paul anymore?" he probed in gentle tones.

"That Brad!" Beryl flung out her brother's name. "Wait until I get back to Dallas and tell him what I think of his big mouth!"

A disarming smile lit Rock's eyes. "He cares for you, Beryl. He was worried about you."

Her voice was thin and dry. "He didn't need to be; I can take care of myself."

"All of us can do with a little help at times."

Rock's caressing tone made Beryl look away hurriedly, shakily. "If we're going to get this work done, maybe we'd better start. Where are your notes?"

Rock chuckled. "There's plenty of time. On past trips I've forwarded these notes to Kent, and he's sent them to the backup team in Los Angeles after checking them over. Kent and I may not be twins, but we've always been close friends."

"It must have been awful when he was so ill." Beryl turned to watch Rock as she spoke.

His voice floated warmly and intimately across the space between them. "Things looked pretty bleak there for a while. The doctors in San Diego didn't give us much hope, so the family had Kent flown to the university hospital in Los Angeles. That's where Susan took over his case.''

"She must be an excellent doctor.''

"The best. You can't believe the individual attention she gave Kent. At the time we didn't know they were falling for each other.''

Beryl noted how he avoided saying "love.'' "Kent fell in love with her right away?'' she pressed.

Rock shrugged and turned to face her more fully. "He claims it was a case of love at first sight.'' His faintly derisive tones hung in the air, making anger flare in Beryl.

"And you doubt it?''

A taut silence stretched between them for several moments, then Rock continued, "I'm different from Kent. He's a romantic.''

"You say that as if it's a crime!''

"No, merely a matter of perspective.''

"That's a dry academic answer, professor,'' Beryl chided, the smile on her lips not reaching as far as her eyes. "Are you trying to say you're a little skeptical of love's sweet dreams?''

"Something like that.'' Rock was serious. "I think I've already expounded on my philosophy about women. Today's woman doesn't want a man in her life; she wants a project, someone to remold into a manipulable puppet.''

Beryl was enjoying being the one to probe for a change. It was time he got a dose of his own medicine. "Is this a true confession I'm hearing?''

He shot her a grinning glance. "You're getting better at these sparring matches.''

"I'm learning from an expert,'' she agreed smugly.

"Has any woman tried to make a saint out of you?"

"God help her if she did," Rock sighed. "But if you seriously want to hear about my past, I'll tell you. I was engaged once. She demanded that I give up anything more dangerous than a dip in a hot tub."

Beryl spoke without warmth. "And you wouldn't consider giving in an inch, would you? Everything has to go your way or you'll look for greener pastures?"

He ignored her gibe. "I thought it was wrong to pretend to be something I wasn't. We would have been miserable together."

"Then she's a fortunate woman that things worked out so well," said Beryl, her teeth clenched together.

Rock nodded. "That's what she thinks. She married a friend of mine and they asked me to be godfather to their first child."

"How nice for you," Beryl responded, seething inside, avoiding the mocking glances being thrown her way. Somehow she'd been hoping Rock had been more wounded by his broken engagement. Instead, he considered it a lucky escape.

"I'm not the cynic, Beryl," he pointed out quietly. "You're letting yourself wallow in your grief. This may sound trite, but you're going to get over those wounds soon. Why don't you help the healing process along?"

"Will you be sending a bill for this counseling session?" she snapped irritably. Wasn't it just like him to try to turn this conversation into a discussion of her failings?

He leaned over and touched her cheek with one finger, sending a tingling sensation down her spine that radiated to her whole body. "Only if I can have an active part in making you forget Paul," he murmured.

Beryl pushed his hand back. "If Kent's like you, I hope Susan can handle him."

The amusement lingered on Rock's lips, but he moved away. "He's not like me at all. And he's not much like Susan, either. While I was out playing as a kid, he was always indoors reading books. Susan's so energetic and active—sometimes I wonder what they see in each other."

Aware that this might be her chance to make him understand the truth about Susan's feelings for Kent, she spoke eagerly. "Maybe it was only a case of their being thrown together so much during a trying time. When Kent gets better, he probably won't feel the same way."

"Susan doesn't have to worry about that," Rock said flatly. "He would never let her down."

"That's nice," Beryl mumbled, beginning to understand the magnitude of Susan's problem.

The cook's gong sounded outside, and Rock sat up. "Time for that coffee."

"My turn this time." Beryl yanked the towel divider back into place and scrambled into her clothes. "I'll bring you some coffee after I wash up, okay?" she told him as she moved to the doorway of the tent.

"Black," he agreed.

Beryl paused by the bubbling pot of coffee on the camp stove under the dining awning and then wandered off in the direction of the mountain stream, shivering as the drops of rain pelted against her. The rushing waters of the clear cold stream were invigorating, and she felt better for having washed her face and brushed her teeth before making a dash back to the shelter.

"So you're up," Susan exclaimed when she returned.

"Rock's still in bed, is he?" asked Fred. "I can't blame him, considering the company he's keeping."

"Say, that's an idea," Lon teased. "Why don't we split up and team with these women? That would make my tent an attractive place to be."

Beryl felt herself flushing with a mixture of embarrassment and annoyance; but it was difficult to react to such innocent teasing. Susan rescued her, saying, "Ignore these men; they're only jealous. What are you going to do this morning?"

"Rock wants me to help him with his reports," she stammered.

"Likely story," Lon put in.

Beryl ignored him. "What are you and Jane doing?"

"I'm working on the medical reports the government here requires, and if you weren't busy I was going to ask for some help. Maybe another time?" Susan suggested.

"As soon as I'm free."

"I'll remember your offer," Susan answered. She made a dash then for her tent, and Beryl watched her, puzzled by something she had sensed in her tone. Then she understood: Susan had hoped for some time alone with Reagen.

Pouring out two cups of coffee as full as she

thought she could carry them, she decided to hurry through with Rock's work and see if she could help out Susan. It must be wonderful to know someone loved you, but the torture of not being given a chance to be alone together would be intense.

When she returned, Rock took the cup of coffee from her hand, motioning for her to sit on the only space not covered with his notes. "What a mess," Beryl remarked, glaring around the tent.

"Mess? You are looking at the most organized section of chaos in all of Nepal," he responded. Handing her one of the papers, he said, "Skim through this and see what you think about it as a general introduction describing the team members."

"What's it going to be used for?" Beryl asked.

"A short newspaper blurb. Then we'll include it in a longer newsletter for the sponsors of the expedition."

"Who's sending out the newsletters? Fran?"

Rock brushed the hair from his forehead impatiently. "I don't have time to explain the entire operation to you this morning. Read the paper, please."

Beryl forced herself to read it quickly. "There's a lot more to a trek like this than meets the eye, isn't there?"

Rock nodded. "Years of planning go into it, and then so many little unexpected things can disrupt the whole thing."

"Like a woman showing up in place of one of the climbers?" she snapped.

"Some things have their compensations," he replied, a devilish grin in his eyes.

Beryl flung her head back, causing her wavy hair to stream over one shoulder. "Don't be too certain of that!"

"Is that a challenge, young lady?" Rock grabbed her arm playfully, pulling her against him so close that the heat of his body permeated the chilly air.

Beryl fought back the fire flaring inside of her. Turning away, she avoided his seeking mouth, her hands striking out and raking down his cheek.

"Dammit, sheathe those claws," Rock growled, drawing back abruptly.

Beryl leaned over and gingerly inspected his cheek, fearing she'd cut the skin. When nothing but a faint red glow was visible, she tilted her chin defiantly. "Leave me alone if you don't want me to fight back."

"Lesson learned," he replied grimly. "Now how about doing that work you promised, so I can finish what I need to do today?"

Beryl bit back the answer bubbling on the tip of her tongue and concentrated once more on the report in front of her. "The information is here all right, but it's not well organized," she conceded at length.

Rock groaned. "I'm going to remember that caustic remark the next time I'm grading student papers. Do you think you're capable of fixing it?"

"No problem, if you'll quit distracting me."

He favored her with a chilly stare. "Strange, I was about to say the same to you."

Beryl retreated against her bedroll and was soon absorbed in the rewrite. Several times she saw Rock frowning at her as she marked out whole sentences and scribbled notes to herself in the margin. When she'd finished she took out a clean sheet of paper and carefully rewrote the report, adding and deleting to produce a crisp, tightly worded copy.

When she finished she handed it to him, suddenly feeling less certain of his approval than she had while working on it. He grabbed it from her, his forehead creasing with concentration as he read it, no sign of what he was thinking on his rugged face.

Beryl felt her heart pounding as if his words were of life-or-death importance. When they came, the unexpectedness of the praise left her feeling almost dizzy. "Damn, if you haven't been holding out on me! This is tremendous, Beryl. From now on you're in charge of everything in the literary department."

"Won't that change my status to a full-fledged team member?" she asked, happiness flooding through her.

"Only as far as base camp, Miss Bartlett. But if Brad had ever mentioned it, I'd have seen about making use of your talent."

"It's really more of a skill...something I've learned on the job."

"And something not everyone can learn, no matter how hard they try. It's a good thing Kent's already involved with Susan or he'd be making a play for you. He likes women with a literary bent."

His words chilled Beryl. Did he move to make it so apparent that her attributes weren't the type that appealed to him? "Give me that paper you've just finished and I'll see if I can clean it up," she offered briskly.

With heads bent, they passed the morning engrossed in work. Beryl interrupted at times, asking for clarification of something Rock had written or commenting on information new to her. "I didn't know that until 1951 there was no way into Nepal except by narrow bridle paths, often too steep for horses," she said.

Rock stopped writing. "It's a tremendously interesting country, Beryl. We're seeing only one aspect of it, the high Himalayan country. The foothills with the Katmandu Valley are entirely different. They remind me of Switzerland or northern Italy."

"I know; it's unreal. When my plane touched down I felt as if I were landing in the middle of a Hollywood set of Shangri-la," Beryl told him.

"And you didn't have any chance to go sightseeing?"

She shook her head. "That will have to wait until my return. Even then I probably won't have much chance, because Big John and Monica will be expecting me to fly straight home."

A frown drew Rock's brows together. "You can't miss seeing Katmandu," he said. "It's a city of flashing gold spires and jeweled roofs. And the temples—there are hundreds of them!"

"Time for lunch—or rather, brunch." Rock and Beryl glanced up as Reagen's head came through the flap.

"And about time, too!" Beryl joked, warmed as always by Reagen's friendly appraisal of her. Her stomach was already grumbling; with the rain there had been no proper breakfast.

"Why don't you try knocking?" Rock growled.

"Did I interrupt something?" Reagen arched his eyebrows expressively.

"Work! Now, if you'll leave, we'll try to get this finished before we eat."

After Reagen had backed out, Beryl whirled on Rock. "Your manners are atrocious sometimes."

Rock's eyes lit up with amusement. "I thought it was my beard you found atrocious."

"And a lot of other things about you, too. Would you care for a detailed list?"

"Spare me. After being treated to a sampling of your skill with words this morning, I'm afraid it might crush my fragile ego," he said.

"A bulldozer couldn't do that," she stormed. "I think I'm ready for some fresh air."

The rain had stopped and the sky was lighter when she came outside. The team members were standing around Gompa's fire, eating thick brown stew over mounds of white rice. Cups of hot tea and chunks of heavy peasant bread rounded out the meal.

Rock came out soon afterward and filled his plate before sitting down beside Beryl. Fred joined them, moving his camp chair so that he faced them. "What's this about your being a writer, Beryl?"

Beryl flushed and cast accusing eyes at Rock. He shrugged and continued eating a flaky potato. "I have been thinking about writing a travel article about Nepal. Not using the team's name, of course," she added hastily.

"Why not?" asked Rock.

"Don't you have someone who's doing that officially? Back in Los Angeles?"

"No, we don't. Fred is planning on getting a ghost writer to help with the trek's chronicle."

"How much experience does the writer have to

194 A QUESTING HEART

have?'' Beryl inquired, leaning forward interestedly.
"I'd like a crack at that myself.''

"I was hoping you'd say that,'' Fred responded.
"Every time I've seen you get out that journal and
start writing I've been tempted to mention it,
but...."

"I'd understand if you didn't think my writing was
professional enough.''

"It's not that,'' Fred explained. "It's only that I
thought you didn't have time for it. From what
everyone says, you're not in need of money, and this
will take a lot of hard work.''

Beryl sighed. "You may find this hard to believe,
but people with money like to be useful, too. Why do
you think everyone who inherits wealth isn't automatically happy?''

"Poor little rich girl?'' teased Rock.

"Don't laugh. I come across people with Fred's attitude all the time. But it's usually worse. I hate that
old line about how could I take a job from someone
who really needs it.''

Rock's eyes darkened and he spoke huskily. "I've
never given that much thought. I think it would make
me damn mad.''

Beryl shrugged, feeling ridiculously pleased at his
ability to empathize. "Then would you consider me
for this project?''

"Absolutely,'' Fred assured her.

Susan motioned for her then, and Beryl set her
plate down and excused herself. "Be back in a moment. I'd like to talk about this some more,'' she told
Fred before making her way over to Susan.

"Are you busy this afternoon?'' Susan spoke in a

low voice, one that couldn't be overheard by Rock.

"What did you have in mind?"

"Reagen's got a plan. Just go along with what he suggests." Susan was almost pleading.

Beryl nodded and took a gulp of her tea, meeting Susan's eyes warily. She'd never been good at pretense and now she was caught up in it, pretending first to be Rock's lover and now Reagen's. Sometimes she thought she was actually suffering from altitude sickness and that lack of oxygen was making her consent to all these schemes.

As the group began breaking up, Rock announced, "Time for us to get back to work, Beryl."

She was putting down her cup after rinsing it off when she heard Reagen say, "Beryl, you promised to come to my tent this afternoon and look at my pictures of Alaska."

Suddenly the area fell silent, and everyone seemed to be turning and staring. Beryl glanced guiltily at Rock, wetting her lips nervously as she noted the dark color rising in his face. "I almost forgot. I'll be there in a few minutes," she answered shakily.

"Like hell you will!" Rock interrupted. "You have a job to do and you're not shirking it." He turned and strode toward the tent. Beryl hesitated momentarily before smiling apologetically at Reagen and following Rock.

When she entered the tent, Rock was waiting for her. "Have you forgotten your promise not to start anything with the men on this team?" he asked, his voice barely above a whisper but deadly nonetheless.

"I'm not," she said coldly. "Where's all that work I'm supposed to be doing?"

"It's canceled; we're moving on. The sun's about out, so I'm going to round up the porters and we'll get started. Too much idleness breeds trouble with some people."

"It's too late," Beryl exclaimed. "We'll only be able to hike a few hours."

"That's a few hours nearer to our destination...." He didn't need to finish his sentence; the implication was plain.

He pushed past Beryl, turning when he reached the tent flap. "Gather up those papers and put them back in my case for me, Miss Bartlett," he ordered sarcastically.

Beryl's fingers were trembling as she scooped up the papers, placing them inside the case she'd seen Rock using. How was she going to face the rest of the team after this? They'd probably resent being forced to leave because she had made Rock angry.

She stayed inside the tent until Mangmu came to dismantle it. The shrewd almond-shaped brown eyes in his cheerful face made her feel uncomfortable. "This is a lot of work for just a short hike," she said apologetically.

"No trouble. Dr. Rawlings in hurry to reach camp before monsoons," he explained. "He good man. You lucky woman."

Lucky? The very thought made Beryl want to laugh hysterically. Right now she felt thoroughly miserable, and Mangmu was calling her lucky!

No one seemed unduly upset by Rock's surprise announcement. As they strapped on their packs and prepared to start hiking, Jane read out the names of the groups for the day. She emphasized to Fred that he was responsible for watching after Beryl, since Rock would not be with her.

"Let's talk about our book," Fred suggested.

"What do you have planned?"

"One of those big picture books people buy to give each other at Christmas."

"So they can display them on their coffee tables to impress their friends," Beryl added knowingly.

Fred laughed. "That's it. It's going to be a chronicle of our trek: mainly photos, but some narrative accompanying each one."

"It sounds wonderful but a little overwhelming." Beryl spoke hesitantly.

"If Rock's keen on your writing, that's good enough for me. Are you keeping a record of everything?"

"Not as much as I should. I'll be more faithful from now on." Beryl felt her heart begin to pound with excitement. The whole idea sounded fantastic, a dream come true. Her first big chance to establish a real writing career. "Maybe you can let me know what scenes and events you're photographing, so I can make extra notes on them."

"I'll do better than that: I'll give you a list of everything I'd done so far, and you can work on that, too."

Fred's enthusiasm made Beryl forget her troubles with Rock, and the afternoon passed quickly. The clouds had parted, drifting into mounds of spun sugar that hung over the distant mountain peaks, obscuring the snow. Birds were singing noisily and the air was light and as delicate as a bubble, heady with the scent of mountain flowers. Far ahead of her

Beryl could see Rock towering over those around him, leading the group with long sure strides, making her wonder if she had only imagined the angry sparks in his eyes.

They stopped for the night just as the sun was falling behind some distant hills, the light draining out of the sky and the cold air creeping in. Their evening meal was a hurried affair, eaten standing up. They made their way to the tents wearily.

"Good night, Beryl." Rock entered the tent long after she was in bed, speaking softly.

"Good night," she murmured, contentment stealing over her at the sound of his voice.

CHAPTER ELEVEN

BREAKFAST WAS ALMOST FINISHED when Beryl joined the group the next morning. She shot an accusing look at Rock. "Why did you let me oversleep?"

"Don't blame me for your lazy ways." His eyes roved over her in casual amusement, noting the disheveled state of her pants and shirt. Nothing escaped him; he was obviously aware that she'd dressed in a hurry.

Beryl took the plate the cook handed her and sank down crossly on the ground. Rock's enjoyment over her oversleeping rankled; he knew how important it was to her to be on schedule. Before she managed to eat more than a few bites, he was giving directions for the team to move out.

They were back on the trail by six. Beryl was in the same group as Susan, and she saw Jane joining Rock. The other woman apparently had something interesting to say, because Rock was leaning over to listen, laughing frequently.

"Reagen made a mess of things yesterday," Susan said grimly.

"I'd say it was more Rock's fault."

"What did he say about it?"

Beryl kept her eyes on the path in front of her. "Nothing; that's not his style. He'd rather throw his weight around with the whole team."

"Not a word? Good Lord, he must walk on eggs where you're concerned. Everyone assumed he must have kept you up half the night screaming at you, especially when you dragged out looking so miserable this morning."

Beryl's long slim legs halted and she turned to face Susan, rigid with irritation. "I was angry because I overslept. Rock had nothing to do with it." Her annoyance deepened when she saw the skeptical look in Susan's eyes.

"But don't you think you're overplaying your hand with him?" Susan persisted. Beryl arched her eyebrows expressively and Susan explained, "Reagen and I know you're playing hard to get, and it's certainly whetted Rock's interest. Those worshipful female undergrads who gather around him after each lecture have made him wary around women."

"Wary? His ego's so massive he's convinced no woman can resist him!" Beryl answered.

Susan's blue eyes flamed with disapproval. "You're wrong there. Rock is a great guy; he doesn't do anything to encourage those girls."

Beryl answered in a brittle tone, "He doesn't have to. Just being Rock Rawlings, the intrepid mountaineer of rugged features and bulging muscles, does the trick nicely."

Susan's laugh rang out in the clear mountain air. "Then you're not as immune to his charms as you pretend?"

"It takes more than sex appeal in a man to interest me," Beryl declared firmly.

"I'm convinced," Susan teased. She shook her head at Beryl in amusement. "But I really don't

think Reagen and I should ask for your help anymore.''

A wave of heat rose to Beryl's cheeks and her
temper rose with it. ''That's nonsense. I said I'd help
you have time alone and I meant it. I don't understand what the fuss is all about.''

''Are you sure? Promise you'll mention it if you
want us to stop asking for your help?''

Beryl sighed with exasperation. ''I've never meant
anything more in my life. Now can we please change
the subject to something more interesting?''

The early-morning hours sped by and they reached
a small village by midmorning. Several large menacing dogs watched their arrival with bored indifference, while a group of children stopped playing
long enough to shout greetings and wave.

''Look, a store,'' shouted one voice. ''A real
store!''

''Come on,'' Beryl urged. ''Let's have a look inside.'' She and Susan hurried with the others,
crowding into the dim interior, fingering the brightly
colored wares. Reagen joined them and Beryl could
see Susan whispering a hurried message in his ear.

Reagen turned and put his arm through Beryl's.
''I'm in the mood to buy you something today,'' he
announced.

Beryl smiled back and began holding up cooking
pots and carved figurines. ''What are you buying
me?'' she asked.

Picking up a pointed straw hat that had multicolored ribbons plaited into it at irregular intervals,
he slipped it over her hair and stood back to admire
her. ''Perfect. This is what I'm buying for you.''

Beryl was laughing appreciatively, tying the
streamers under her chin, when she felt hands grasping her chin and removing the hat. She looked up
into Rock's face, startled by the depth of anger she
saw there.

"That's my privilege and don't you forget it
again," he warned, handing the hat back to Reagen.
Then he reached for an identical one hanging on the
wall.

"Don't I have some say in the matter?" Beryl shot
back.

"Did Reagen forget to mention that this is a bridal
hat?" Rock's calm voice was at odds with the pain
his strong fingers were inflicting as they dug into her
arm.

Aware that they were making another scene in
front of the group, Beryl felt sickened by the whole
situation. "Put the hat back," she said. "It would
only be something extra to carry, and I can get one
on my way out." She turned and pushed her way out
of the store.

Outside she had to endure the agony of being
stared at by the villagers. Every time these people saw
her they were fascinated by her height. Even though
Beryl sensed their interest was friendly, she found it a
bit tiring after a while.

She sighed angrily and sat down on her pack. Why
was it that every time she talked herself into a good
mood Rock seemed determined to spoil it? Anyone
who could handle all the admiring females Susan had
described must surely know that the best way to control this situation would be to ignore it. His approach
was directly opposite to that; he seemed to relish

public confrontations when she was with Reagen, causing the whole group to speculate on what was happening: something he'd vowed to go to any lengths to prevent.

She felt the warmth of a small body leaning against her knee and glanced down to find a young boy slipping his hand into hers. She smiled at him and reached into her pack, bringing out some coins to put into his palm. His softly spoken words of gratitude embarrassed her. After all, she had always had so much in life!

Instantly she was besieged by swarms of children clinging to her, begging, pulling, grabbing at her pack. Rock's sudden appearance calmed the situation immediately, and his firm voice ordered them to leave her alone. "Don't tell me you gave money to one of these children?" he said crossly.

"Yes, I did." Beryl tilted her chin defiantly, waiting for his next sarcastic comment.

"Unless you have enough coins for all of them you shouldn't do that." He turned away from her then and directed the last of the stragglers out of the store.

The sight of his broad impassive back irritated her beyond reason. She was tired of having the arrogant Dr. Rawlings order her around and try to ruin her trip. Shouldering her pack, she greeted Reagen with an unnatural gush of friendliness as they started down the trail again.

Her act obviously didn't fool him. The first question he asked was, "Certain I'm not causing too much trouble between you and Rock?"

"Not really."

"I've never seen him so damned possessive before, not with any other woman."

Beryl shrugged indifferently. Her feelings about Rock were too ambivalent to discuss with anyone right now.

"Susan and I are determined not to make things awkward for you," he persisted.

Forcing a smile to her lips, Beryl brushed aside his concern and asked a question about the trees lining the path.

For some reason the rest of the day seemed to pass by slower than any other day she had spent hiking. Perhaps it was her awareness of Rock's easy manner as he once more joked and talked with Jane, not bothering to turn and check on Beryl all afternoon.

By the time he finally called a halt for the day, she felt more than ready to set up camp. Her misery seemed destined to increase later that evening, however, as Rock stayed out by the camp fire laughing and talking long after she had gone to their tent.

As Beryl stretched out in her sleeping bag that night she made a determined effort to think about something besides Rock. *Forget him,* she ordered herself. Didn't she know she had to get a good night's rest so she could cope with his disturbing presence the next day?

THE NEXT TWO DAYS were spent slogging steadily upward. Rock continued to ignore Beryl on the trail, assigning her to various other members of the team on their daily treks. Grudgingly she admitted to herself that much of her enjoyment was gone without his constant companionship.

By the third day Beryl felt she had to make an attempt to break the barrier between them. It was ridiculous for him not to realize that they could be civil to each other, and there was no reason for him to lose sleep in order to avoid talking to her. She deliberately stayed awake that night, sitting up the moment he entered the tent.

His eyebrows shot upward in surprise, but he said nothing, moving quietly to his own side of the tent. "I'd like to talk, Rock," she told him, her voice husky.

She was intensely aware of him, conscious of his long lean body bared to the waist, deeply tanned skin stretching over hard chest muscles. His powerful appeal infused a slow warmth through her, conjuring up images of his disturbing caresses and passionate kisses.

"Is something wrong?"

His cold formal tone almost stopped her, but she continued bravely, "You seem to find plenty to talk about with everyone else."

He was surveying her thoughtfully. "Is that an accusation?"

"No," Beryl said, determined not to let this become another of their senseless fights. "I was wondering why we no longer had anything to say to each other."

She could hear him removing the rest of his clothes and crawling into his bedroll as she waited for his answer. Suddenly he swept aside the terry-cloth barrier and leaned forward, eyeing her appraisingly. "Okay. You choose the subject and we'll talk."

For a moment all thought fled from her mind; his

piercing regard increased the size of the lump in her throat until she found it almost impossible to squeeze any words out. "Well, most people start talking about themselves. Where they're from...you know the sort of thing."

He laughed shortly, his glance raking over her in surprise. "I never was too good at making light conversation," he told her, "but if you don't mind being bored, I'll be happy to share the details of my life." He paused and leaned back thoughtfully. "I was born in San Diego. My dad's a high-school principal, not exactly a tycoon like yours."

Beryl sat forward eagerly, relieved that Rock hadn't refused her request even if he wasn't discussing quite what she'd planned. "How many sisters and brothers?"

"One of each. My sister lives in Southern California."

"Are your parents or sister mountain climbers?" Rock was making her pull the words out of him.

"Not on your life." His husky laughter filled the small tent, drawing them closer together in the moonlight. "They've always thought me crazy for taking all the risks I do. I joined a mountain-climbing club in high school and I've been involved in its challenges ever since."

"You like that word 'challenge,' don't you?"

"I must, or I wouldn't have taken you on, would I?" His rich voice held traces of indulgent amusement, and Beryl felt some of her old irritation returning. There was his attitude toward women again: mere sexual playthings, and if one didn't cooperate he could always look for someone more accommodating. "Was that all you wanted to talk about?" he quizzed her.

"Yes," she replied coolly, disappointed by the turn their conversation had taken.

"How about you, Beryl?"

"Me? I thought Brad had told you all about me," was her tart reply.

Rock chuckled. "I'm asking you to tell me. What do you want out of life?"

"It's been fairly well mapped out for me," she said indifferently.

"Biology is destiny?" he taunted.

"No! You know I don't believe that. I was referring to being a part of the Bartlett family. I'm not a rebel in life. I can't be happy going around embarrassing my family, and since the press always sticks its nose into what we do, my life will have to be fairly routine. I think writing will fit into that picture better than most careers."

"But you won't always be a part of the Bartlett family. What then? What do you want?"

A thought flashed through her mind unbidden, searing in its intensity, making her realize she had been secretly harboring a wish that she could win Rock's love, that she could.... "I've been too busy to give that a lot of thought, but I'm sure I'll never lack for things to do," she answered vaguely.

"At the risk of being told I sound like a nosy professor, may I point out that your heightened respiration rate and the color in those beautiful cheeks tell me you're upset by my questions?"

"You may not! I'm not an experimental subject submitting to your scientific scrutiny, Dr. Rawlings.

Anyway, even noted professors aren't always right."
She adjusted her position in her sleeping bag and
wished him a curt good-night, ignoring his laughter.

After a few minutes he spoke softly. "I've been
missing our fights, too, Beryl."

ANOTHER DAY OF HIKING passed uneventfully,
marked only by the ever increasing crispness in the
air that indicated they were climbing higher and
higher.

The usual crop of sore feet, blisters and colds was
taking its toll on the group, but so far no one had
been injured or become seriously ill. Beryl was having less difficulty adjusting to the thin atmosphere,
but she still had days when each step seemed to be
torture.

Rock's announcement that the next day would be
spent in camp resting and catching up on chores was
greeted with cheers by the weary hikers. "It will be an
opportunity for you to write letters to the folks back
home. I'm going to dispatch a runner back to Katmandu to carry them," he said.

Dinner that evening was a quiet meal; everyone
was tired and sore, and for the first time some of the
group's enthusiasm seemed to be slipping away. As
Beryl stared into the crackling fire she reflected on
the days that had passed. Rock was keeping up the
friendly companionable relationship that had developed between them since their conversation. He
seemed as eager as she was to end the icy silence that
had put such a strain on them both.

Susan dropped to the ground beside her, slanting a
rueful smile in Beryl's direction as she rubbed her

feet. "You'd think a doctor could practice a little of the medicine she prescribes for others," she said laughingly. "My feet are killing me, and I can't even ask for sympathy because I've been advising everyone to avoid this type of mishap with a little careful prevention."

Beryl agreed with her sympathetically. Although she had been holding up fairly well thus far on the trek, she had to admit that the endless miles of hiking were taking a toll on her own muscles and tenderfoot skin.

When Lon brought around mugs of steaming chocolate, both of the women accepted a cup gratefully, chatting idly as they sipped the soothing hot drink. It was very late before all of the team members stumbled to their tents, and as Beryl crawled wearily into her own sleeping bag her last thought was that she hadn't had a chance to say good-night to Rock. As far as she knew, he was still deep in conversation with Mangmu, engrossed in studying the piles of maps that guided the team on their quest to scale Mount Everest.

Daybreak brought a pink glow to the sky that was visible through the tent flap. Beryl sat up and crept out of bed quietly, not wanting to disturb Rock's sleeping form.

The cooks were adding wood to the fire when she greeted them. "Up early," said Gompa, his toothless mouth forming a welcoming grin. His young daughter hugged Beryl; her earlier fears had been forgotten as the two had come to know each other.

Beryl accepted a cup of weak tea and a packet of biscuits from Gompa's outstretched hand, happy for the solitude around her when she realized she was the first team member outside. Contentment flowed through her as she looked toward the mountain peaks.

When would she get her first glimpse of Mount Everest? Its elusive peak had been veiled by haze and clouds, and daily the team waited to see who would be the first to sight it.

After a quick wash in the stream she heated water over the fire and shampooed her hair. As the cooks began clanging pots together in preparation for breakfast, more and more of the others straggled out of their tents.

Susan joined Beryl and the women took turns rinsing their hair by pouring pans of warm water over each other's head. Jane was as withdrawn as usual, her few words of conversation biting and sarcastic.

By the time Beryl finished washing some clothes, the rest of the group were up and milling around, enjoying the sun's rays in the chilly morning air.

"I want you to write Big John and assure him you're safe and sound," Rock told her. He surprised her by dropping a quick kiss on the top of her damp hair—causing a leaping sensation in her chest that caught her off guard as usual.

"Why? Are you getting worried about those legendary fists of his?" she asked lightly, covering up her intense reaction to his tender gesture.

"How big did you say he was?" Rock teased.

"He's monstrous—makes you look like a dwarf."

"Be sure to tell him I haven't laid a hand on you," Rock advised her, pulling her against him to kiss her again.

"Love before breakfast. It must be the real thing," Lon observed, humor in his grouchy tone, as he passed them on his way to the camp fire.

Beryl drew away from Rock. "I'll need to borrow some paper before I can write any letters. I've used most of Brad's on my notes."

"Look in my pack in the tent. You ought to find plenty there." Rock seemed oddly reluctant to loosen his hold on her, but Beryl jerked herself away from him and hurried toward the tent.

She searched through his pack carefully and was pulling out some thin aerograms when a picture fell out. It was of a woman, one who appeared to be in her early thirties, extremely attractive and stylishly dressed. Her short brown hair framed a round face, her wide mouth curving upward in a smile that suggested she knew some pleasant secret.

Was this Fran? Beryl stared at the picture clutched in her hand and then turned it over slowly to look for a clue on the back; but there was nothing. Hearing footsteps approaching, she shoved the picture into the pack and turned hastily when Rock entered.

"Did you find the paper?"

Her heart was thudding painfully as she answered, "Yes. Yes, I did."

His eyebrows arched as if he were puzzled by her response, and he gazed at her intently. "What's the matter?"

Darn, how did this man have the ability to read people's reactions so accurately? "Nothing's the matter," she insisted, edging her way out of the tent as rapidly as possible.

Why was she letting that picture bother her so

much? From the beginning she'd gathered that Rock was involved with Fran, at least before he left for the trip. Maybe she hadn't seemed real before; that must be it. Now she had a face, and Beryl could no longer pretend she didn't matter.

She suddenly felt a desperate need to be alone. Hurrying across the meadow, she searched until she found a rock ledge to hide behind. She needed privacy to sort out her thoughts, her feelings.

Leaning against the ledge, she let her mind whirl in miserable confusion as she stared out over the valley below. She stretched out her legs and sat back, dry-eyed, as the pain seared through her. What was it Rock had said the first day she met him? "When things get too much for you over here, look up." Little had she dreamed then that her worst problem would be her growing attraction to a man who was totally outside her realm.

She lifted her head and gazed around her. A person could see for miles here: the forests, the paths, the streams and the barren peaks above the tree line. The gleam of the glacier fields was blinding.

Serenity flowed through her as she became lost in the timeless scene before her. This winding land of calm emerald valleys nestling between forbidding towers of snow-covered rock was the fabled Shangri-la. And in Shangri-la anything was possible, or so the legends said.

Her spirits calmed and she began writing her letters. Her parents needed an apology for any worry she had caused them. She explained how her plans to return had been thwarted by a day's delay in the group's itinerary, expressing her hope that someone had reached them with the news.

Knowing how eagerly her brother would read her letter, she gave a day-by-day detailed account of what the group had seen and done. She mentioned each person in the team but was careful to make only a cursory reference to Rock.

Her letters completed, she reached into her pack and took out her small journal. She had spent all her time recently writing notes for Fred and had been neglecting her personal record; but what could she say about this period in her life? That it was half miserable and half ecstatic? After staring at the blank pages for an indeterminate period of time, she closed the book without writing anything. Her thoughts were too painful and confused; they certainly weren't worth recording.

Picking up her letters, she sealed them and walked back to the campsite, adding her mail to the pile that was collecting in the rush basket provided.

Rock was sitting at a folding table, his head bent over the page on which he was writing. The memory of the picture she had seen burned in Beryl's mind. Was he writing to Fran now?

Furious with herself for slipping back into her negative thoughts, she called to Reagen, who was pitching a ball to one of the other men. "Mind if I join the game?"

"You can join all my games," Reagen replied suggestively. Out of the corner of her eye she saw Rock glance up and glare at his rival. Her spirits lifted and she ran to catch the ball thrown at her.

After the game Susan and Beryl gathered up their

laundry and folded it away, leaving the heavier items, which were still damp, spread out over some low bushes to finish drying.

"What's this I hear about your teaming up with Fred on his book project?" Susan asked.

"I'm giving it a try," Beryl told her.

"That's great. I had no idea you were a writer. You ought to brag about your accomplishments sometimes, the way the rest of us do."

"Are you two through writing letters?" Jane's biting tones intruded on the pleasant conversation.

"It didn't take me long," said Susan. "How about you?"

"I've been keeping a running letter going for my friends since the first day," Jane replied. "How about you, Beryl? Do you have a lot of male admirers to write to at home?"

A look of displeasure crossed Susan's face and she started away, leaving Beryl to answer. "I wrote to my parents and my brother."

"Rock's enjoying his letter writing." Jane pointed to where he was still bent over the table, engrossed in his task.

"He probably has dozens to write," Beryl agreed in an even tone. She knew she had an opportunity to find out more about Rock, but she couldn't bring herself to give Jane the satisfaction of telling her.

"Doesn't that bother you?" Jane eyed her deliberately, a cool smile barely lifting the corners of her lips.

Beryl shrugged indifferently, hoping the sound of her quickened heartbeat didn't reveal her agitation.

Jane refused to let up on the attack. "I suppose

you're pretty sure of yourself with men. After all, you can dangle out your fortune and make it hard for any man to resist.''

"They've managed so far: I'm still single!'' Beryl laughed, attempting to lighten the conversation. She looked desperately in the direction Susan had gone. Why had the other woman left her alone with Jane? And why was Jane so intent on getting in her barbed remarks?

Jane's eyes narrowed and a look of distaste crossed her features. "You enjoy playing the part of an ordinary girl, pretending you're no different from the rest of us, don't you?''

"For heaven's sake, Jane! The fact that my parents are relatively well known and wealthy doesn't mean I don't have the same problems as anyone else,'' she snapped irritably. This conversation was infuriating, and she wondered why she was sitting here allowing the woman to insult her. Perhaps it was because Jane was so edgy these days that no one else seemed willing to spend any time with her, and all her life Beryl had tended to sympathize with the underdog.

"And what problems are those?'' Rock sauntered up to the ledge where they were seated, looking at the two women with a slightly puzzled frown. He seemed to sense that their conversation was not a pleasant one.

"Beryl's trying to convince me that having a fortune doesn't make her attractive to the opposite sex.'' Jane's whole expression had changed, an almost friendly smile crossing her face as she looked up at Rock. Beryl groaned inwardly as she realized that the other woman had no intention of letting Rock see the anger underlying her remarks.

Rock's eyes raked lazily down Beryl's length, causing color to mount in her cheeks. Only his slightly clenched fists revealed that he was displeased with Jane as he remarked lightly, "Beryl's attractiveness is evident to any man long before he knows who she is."

Beryl gaped at him in surprise as he turned to address her. "How about going to a village with me this afternoon?" He took her hand and pulled her up beside him.

"Any reason why I can't go, too?" Jane asked, her jawline rigid with anger. She eyed Beryl now with open hostility.

"Sorry, but this village doesn't want the expeditions trooping through without an invitation. Mangmu says I'm allowed to visit, but I can't take a crowd." Rock's arm encircled Beryl's waist and he drew her against him possessively.

"Then perhaps I shouldn't go...." Beryl's voice was slightly shaky. She hated this constant push-pull between Jane and Rock. Especially since they insisted on using her for the rope.

Rock glanced down at her, his gaze oddly dark. "Mangmu told me to take my woman with me."

Jane whirled around and stalked off. "You shouldn't say things like that to irritate her," Beryl chided him.

"I'd forgotten she was here," he replied quietly.

CHAPTER TWELVE

FOR ONCE lunch was a leisurely meal, with hot food instead of the usual hurried sandwiches and cheese. Gompa was presiding over the fire when Rock and Beryl returned to the main area of camp, and he looked up with a friendly smile. His daughter was busily chopping potatoes and other vegetables, and Beryl hurried to help.

Rock engaged in a lengthy conversation with Gompa, punctuated with laughs and amused glances in Beryl's direction. Finally he looked up and called, "Hey, Beryl! How would you like a cooking lesson?"

"What makes you think I need one?" she retorted flippantly.

"Don't tell me you know anything about cooking!" Rock mocked her gently. He came over to stand beside her, kneading her shoulder with firm strokes of his fingers while he smiled down at her.

"You might be surprised if you knew a little more about me," she responded.

"Give me more time and I'll find out as much as I can about you." His low murmured reply was for her ears only, and the intense scrutiny of his dark eyes made her pulses race sharply.

Beryl fought to steady herself, fighting against the sudden devastating effect he had on her as the warm, faintly musky odor of his skin and the feel of the rough tweedy texture of his shirt against her cheek blotted out everything else. For a moment she allowed herself to relax in his grasp, to enjoy the heady sensations caused by the intimate press of his undeniably masculine legs against her own soft curves through the barrier of their jeans.

She was dangerously close to falling prey to Rock's disturbing masculinity, his lean sexuality. Never before had she been so tempted by a man, and she had to admit that, quite frankly, she enjoyed her responses to him. Enjoyed them, that is, as long as she refused to heed the small warning voice in her head reminding her that she didn't want to be one of those foolish girls who sat in his classes watching him with adoring eyes while nursing a secret passion for him.

With a faint sense of relief she realized Reagen had come up behind them, and she turned eagerly to greet him. "If there's going to be a cooking class I want to be in on it," he announced.

She felt, rather than saw, Rock's immediate reaction, the sudden tensing of his muscles, the clenching of his jaw. Deliberately she tucked her arm through Reagen's in a friendly gesture and pulled him over to the makeshift table where Gompa and his daughter were busy at work.

For the next half hour Reagen and Beryl laughed good-naturedly as Gompa kept up a steady stream of conversation in his singsong voice, directing them in preparing a hot spicy Indian-style curry filled with all types of chopped vegetables and fruits and the ubiquitous chicken. It didn't seem important that they couldn't understand a single word of what he was saying. His natural friendliness and their obvious interest transcended the boundaries of culture and language.

Gompa's daughter succumbed to several fits of giggles as she tried to teach Reagen to pronounce the names of the foods they were handling. "I never did have a flair for languages," he said finally, shrugging his shoulders as he smiled over at Beryl.

"My Texas drawl isn't too compatible with Sherpa, either," Beryl agreed.

"If you need any help, I'll be happy to translate." Rock's words came suddenly from over her shoulder, his tone coldly formal and rather distant. How long had he been standing there?

Irritation made her voice sharp as she replied, "We're doing quite well, thank you." She gave him a lofty nod of her head and turned back to the table, catching her elbow against one of the pots and knocking it to the ground.

"I'd hate to see you in a regular kitchen if you're this clumsy outdoors!" Rock teased. He was clearly enjoying her discomfiture at appearing in such a bad light.

Lunch was finally ready and everyone attacked it happily, heaping lavish compliments on their efforts. Gompa and his daughter appeared pleased to be included in the friendly camaraderie of the group.

"What's your interest in cooking?" Lon asked Reagen, looking up after dishing spoonfuls of spicy chutney and golden raisins over his stew.

"I'm a modern man; I'm planning on doing half the cooking when I marry," he said.

"That'll be the day," laughed Fred.

Reagen carefully spooned a pile of freshly grated coconut on Beryl's plate, saying, "I'll be married before this year is over."

Beryl bent over her plate, wondering if Reagen had reached the end of his rope and was going to use this opportunity to tell the truth about Susan and himself. She placed a forkful in her mouth and the fiery spices burned, choking her. Sputtering helplessly, she grabbed for her cup of tea just as Rock's broad palm struck her between the shoulder blades, jarring her almost off of her precarious perch and spilling the tea down her blouse. Amber droplets slid off her hands and tears welled in the corners of her eyes.

"Stop," gasped Beryl.

Instantly Rock whipped out a tissue and knelt before her, mopping up the spilled tea on her jeans and then moving to the front of her blouse. With a practiced touch he stroked the liquid from her breasts until she pushed his hand away with an embarrassed gesture.

"Please, I'm fine," she breathed. "All I need is something to drink."

Without replying, Rock leaned closer and gently wiped the tears from her cheeks before picking up her cup from the ground and handing it to Susan, who had moved beside them. "Make yourself useful, doctor," he said, a hint of censure in his tone.

Susan giggled. "You almost killed Beryl with that blow on her back and you're trying to accuse me of not being helpful?'' She poured out a cup of tea and handed it to Beryl. "It was probably the curry," she added.

Beryl nodded and gulped down the liquid. "You were about to tell us about your marriage, Reagen?" Lon probed, smiling broadly at Beryl.

Gompa turned and spoke rapidly to Rock, who listened carefully before translating to the group. "Gompa says that he enjoyed giving the cooking lesson today. However, he feels that Beryl was the better pupil. Reagen should stick to mountain climbing and forget about becoming a chef."

Everyone began laughing, and Reagen made a great show of pretending to be crushed and insulted, saving him from having to answer Lon.

Rock leaned over, whispering in Beryl's ear, "Still want to go with me to the village this afternoon?" His voice was rather harsh, but for an instant she glimpsed an elusive quality in his eyes that made her answer quickly.

"I've been looking forward to it! When do we leave?"

"Right away." Rock gave her an answering smile and suddenly placed an arm around her shoulder, hugging her to him briefly and then releasing her.

Their path led through a bushy area and then they stepped out into a clearing. All around them were hills and ridges. The trail curved and twisted, strewn with loose stones, and Beryl found herself clinging unselfconsciously to Rock's arm.

She felt almost a part of him as they jostled against each other, aware of his hard lean thigh brushing against hers, depending on his compact strength to steer her across the rugged terrain. There was a oneness to them that they'd never known before. Was it because it was their first time alone together— really alone, with no worry about keeping their voices low enough not to be overheard?

On turning a corner they came upon slopes covered with great masses of reddish flowers on green-leafed rhododendrons. Here and there, far in the distance, Beryl could see women and children, their heads burdened with baskets filled with the wood they were cutting.

"Are they Sherpas?" she asked, stopping to catch her breath.

Rock answered with a nod of his head. "The Sherpas are an amazing people. Because they're born at these high altitudes, their physiology is adapted to breathing the thin air. They're a peaceful, intelligent, hardworking people, perpetually cheerful. Some researchers believe their happy-go-lucky way of always laughing and singing is due to the altitude, but I prefer to think it's based on their serene outlook on life."

"Why do the men travel around so much?" she asked, finding it easy to imagine Rock giving a lecture in the same way he was talking to her.

"Money. It's impossible for them to stay put in the mountains of Nepal; there's not enough tillable land or sunshine to raise food for everyone. So the men take turns herding or trading for six months or more each year. Guiding groups like ours also adds to their income." His grip tightened on her hand.

"Theirs sounds like a difficult life—having to

travel so far from home to earn a livelihood,'' Beryl
reflected. ''Is money really that important?''

''The less you have, the more it is, I guess.''
Rock's answer was spoken lightly, his tone teasing, so that Beryl couldn't guess what he was thinking.

''It's a strange thing,'' Beryl observed. ''When you
have plenty of money, you never give it a thought.''
Her eyes clouded over with worry. ''Jane seems
angry with me because my parents are wealthy.''

He frowned. ''You said you've met with that attitude before. Why should you be bothered by
Jane?''

''I don't know; somehow her anger is...dif-
ferent,'' Beryl persisted. ''Oh, I know she's annoyed
that I've come along on the trek, but there's more to
it than that. I wish I knew what was wrong. Do you
have any ideas?''

Rock laughed lazily. ''Didn't you remind me not
to try analyzing people? The only thing I know is
that Jane's background is very different from yours.
She's a self-made person all the way, like your dad.''

''Big John?'' Beryl scoffed. ''That's the official
line for press releases, but he's from a ranching family that never wanted for a thing.''

''And your mother?''

''Monica's rattles came from Neiman's. Her father
was one of the old-line oil tycoons.''

Rock grimaced. ''That sounds more like a merger
than a marriage. Do they care for each other?''

Beryl lifted her eyebrows in surprise at the personal
nature of his question, eyeing him thoughtfully.
''I've never given it much thought. The Bartletts

aren't given to public displays of emotion, much less private discussions.''

"That must have been hard on you," he murmured softly, his eyes moving down to her mouth and lingering there. "You're a very loving woman, Beryl."

Her face registered shock and she gave a nervous laugh. "Me? Loving? What makes you say that?"

He shot her a strangely disturbing look. "There are lots of ways to show love, Beryl. What did you think I meant?"

"I never try outguessing experts," she replied coolly, refusing to let his remark ruffle her.

His laughter rang out as he pulled her against him, giving her a brief hug. "Typical female response: if you don't want to discuss something, change the subject."

"Is there such a thing as a female response?" Beryl slanted her green eyes obliquely at him.

"Yes." His voice made it plain he didn't expect disagreement.

"Then you'll agree that your answer sounded like the typical male response? When you don't understand a woman, accuse her of being vague."

"You win this round." Rock's voice was husky with amusement. He bent and dropped a brief kiss on her forehead, running his fingers lightly through her thick hair.

Beryl hesitated before pulling back, a part of her mind warning her that she mustn't let the situation get out of control. The sight of a small furry black animal diverted her attention. Pointing excitedly, she exclaimed, "Look, there's a baby yak! He's so wobbly on his feet—do you think he's just been born?''

Rock turned to see, his face creasing into a smile. ''I believe so.''

''And there's the mother yak.'' They had seen yaks before on their trek, but never this close.

''I think the mothers are called naks,'' Rock explained seriously. He gripped her arm when she started to move forward. ''No, don't try going any nearer. That mother looks nervous to me.'' He reached for the small camera slung casually around his neck and snapped several pictures.

''Don't forget you've promised to share your photos with me,'' Beryl reminded him. ''If you'll mail the negatives I can have prints made.''

''Why can't I deliver them personally?''

''Will you be coming to see Brad when you return?'' she asked, carefully keeping any hint of eagerness out of her voice. ''He'll appreciate that.''

Rock's eyes narrowed. ''Sometimes I don't know how to take you, Beryl. I hope you were only joking.''

And I certainly don't know how to take you, Beryl protested silently, seething with a million unanswered questions.

Rock drew a strange repressed breath, but he seemed lost for words. With a light touch he guided her back onto the trail, and she had to hurry to keep up with his long stride, glancing up at his impassive face from time to time in an attempt to assess his thoughts.

Suddenly the village lay nestled before them, hidden in a valley that was lushly green. Neat fields of wheat, barley, maize and potatoes surrounded the small town, laid out in geometric blocks and small plots of minute precision.

Steep streets with a group of rough-stone houses, most of them two-storied with narrow windows, were clustered together at one end. At the other were mud-and-twig huts, long-haired goats grazing in stony walled-in patches of ground at their sides.

Rock pointed out a large metallic cylinder with writing engraved on it, explaining, "This is a prayer wheel. The Sherpas never pass one without turning it around; it's the same as saying their prayers."

Beryl regarded the wheel thoughtfully, tempted to go over and turn it around herself. What would she pray for? She wasn't even willing to admit to herself what it was she wanted. Indulging in useless fantasies about Rock wasn't going to change anything.

Shaking off her tormenting thoughts, she asked, "And that?" She pointed to a turreted thick-walled building clinging to the side of a mountain above the village. It was a massive fortress with watch-towers on the corners and heavy gates that seemed to warn against trespassing. Swarms of men clothed in dark brown robes appeared to be massed outside the gates.

"A monastery; the men are Buddhist monks. I believe a famous lama is in residence there. Several of our guides are going to make a pilgrimage there this afternoon."

"Is a lama something like a priest?"

"More a living deity, they believe. His word becomes a part of their religious thought." Ruffling her hair, Rock added, "You're really interested in learning all about this country, aren't you?"

Beryl nodded. "I wish I'd known I was going to be here so I could have read more about it."

"Before your next trip you'll have lots of opportunity to read up on Nepal."

"Sure," Beryl scoffed. "I know how much chance I'd have of being chosen for one of your teams. I don't possess all the academic and physical qualifications."

"You possess every necessary qualification as far as I'm concerned." His eyes glinted down at her.

Beryl glanced away, becoming increasingly confused by his enigmatic comments. One minute he was cold and remote; the next, his every word was like a caress, his touch searing her with tormenting sweetness.

A swarm of children came rushing down the path toward them. They took Rock's and Beryl's hands in theirs and began talking rapidly. Rock dug into his pocket with a broad smile and gave each child a small coin.

"I see you came prepared," Beryl observed, helping to distribute the coins to the smallest of the naked children.

A welcoming committee greeted them, women with square burnished faces and men with fierce features and weapons hanging from their waistbands. An old woman held out a bright scarf and a cup of thick liquid for each, speaking rapidly.

"Chang," Rock explained, accepting a mug. "It's Sherpa beer, usually made from potatoes. You're

supposed to accept three cups and drain them off if you wish to be their friend.''

Beryl dreaded taking her first sip and was grateful that its taste was bearable; something like a sweetish beer. After her third cup she felt distinctly light-headed, but Rock appeared none the worse for wear as he talked with the Sherpas who had surrounded them.

The villagers gave them seats close together, obviously viewing them as more than friends. Beryl remembered Rock's description in one of the training sessions of how natural the man-woman relationship was here in Nepal. Little girls were betrothed as early as eight years of age, and marriage always took place by the time they were twelve. It would have been beyond their comprehension that Beryl was unmarried at her age.

The strange language swirled around her and she sat entranced with the unreality of it all, enjoying the warmth of Rock's body against hers. What would it be like to be Rock's woman, Rock's wife? She let herself drift into a dreamworld, remembering the feel of his mouth, his firm lips, his invading tongue and his muscular hands, exploring and teasing, bringing almost unbearable pleasure.

She pulled herself upright, common sense warning her not to become enmeshed in hopeless dreams. What was wrong with her today!

Rock glanced down at her. ''Would you like to visit one of their homes?''

''I'd love it,'' Beryl agreed quickly, hoping the shakiness of her voice didn't reveal any of her secret thoughts. One of the women, dressed in a sturdy wraparound garment with a bright-colored striped apron over it, took her by the hand and began speaking rapidly. Her broad flat face was creased with a welcoming smile.

"Go with her," Rock urged. "She's asking to show you her home."

Beryl followed the short woman down a narrow street until they reached one of the larger stone two-story houses. The ground floor was made of dirt and appeared to be used as a storage place for the red rhododendron firewood. A ferocious dog, short and squat with bristly whiskers, barked menacingly.

A Tibetan mastiff, thought Beryl in alarm. Rock had warned the group about the viciousness of the animals. But at a word from the woman the dog lay down, putting his head between his giant paws and closing his eyes.

They climbed the stairs and entered a large room dominated by an open fireplace. A pile of handmade rugs on the floor seemed to comprise the only beds for the family. Copper and brass pots were on wooden shelves at the rear of the room. In one corner sat a large wooden loom with crude foot pedals; an ancient woman worked industriously at it, seemingly indifferent to the fact that a visitor was in her home.

The hostess indicated Beryl was to sit on a rug that she spread out on the floor. After quickly preparing a cup of tea, she offered it to her with another broad smile. Although there was no attempt at conversation, their exchanged smiles made the visit seem normal. When Beryl left she felt as if she'd made a friend.

Rock was waiting for her when she returned. "We'll have to start back to camp now. Enjoyed yourself?"

"I loved it. It's hard for me to believe I'm really here, doing all this." *And with no one watching over me, directing my every move,* she added silently. She was only beginning to realize how restricted her life had been in the past.

The trail back was steep, and Beryl had to rest several times on the ragged stone walls that lined the path. Looking up, she sighed with pleasure at the beauty that lay before them, the magnificent snow peaks in an immense arc bounding the world. Rock murmured some of their enchanted names—Manislu, Annapurna, Nanda Devi—in a hushed reverent voice.

"And Mount Everest?" Beryl whispered. "When will we see her?"

Rock used the Tibetan name. "Chomolungma is still hiding from us, like a shy maiden waiting to be convinced that she's ready for love." Dropping down beside her, he wrapped his arm around her shoulder. "Are you sorry you were forced to come on this trip?"

"You know better than that. I wonder now why I've been wasting so much time in Dallas." She spoke in a cool tone, trying to ignore the glint in Rock's eyes.

"What do you do that wastes your time?" he asked.

"Besides jogging?"

He grinned, his arm pulling her closer into the mold of his body. "Yes, after jogging, what then?"

"I've already told you. I go to Junior League luncheons and have fittings for clothes to wear to dinners and dances. It's very important that I be seen at all the right places, you know."

"I should hope so," Rock murmured, his lips nuzzling her cheek.

Beryl pulled herself away from him slightly. "I don't think you're listening, Rock," she accused.

"I'm trying." Rock had pulled her back against him, brushing aside her thick wavy hair to kiss the nape of her neck lightly.

The masculine smell of his leather jacket, scented with woodsmoke, filled her senses, sending chills down her spine. What were those reasons why she wasn't going to let him kiss her again? She couldn't remember a one; that was so natural, so right. She wanted his kisses, and everything else was blotted from her mind as she turned to him instinctively, burying her head against his broad chest.

She heard his sharply indrawn breath and a hand lifted her chin, his dark gaze burning into her eyes, asking a question. What did he want her to say? She couldn't think, not when she was this close to him, wanting him this much. She moistened her lips and stared mutely at him.

His lips met hers and the kiss was warm, gentle, undemanding, his soft beard rubbing against her chin sensuously. Her traitorous mouth responded eagerly and the kiss deepened, changing to one of total mastery, his mouth plundering hers hungrily, drawing from her a response she had never known she was capable of as a curling flame of desire licked through her body.

A hand moved into her blouse, finding a breast and cupping it. His fingers brushed like fire against her nipple, circling it gently, causing a knot to form in the pit of her stomach as she fought the urge to beg him to make love to her. He knew exactly how to arouse her, and she was no match for his sensual movements, the touch of his fingers on her breasts, the taste of his tongue in her mouth.

His lips left hers to trail down her soft throat and back again as one of his legs moved against hers, its pressure filling some of the aching void she was feeling. "Beryl. . ." he rasped. "Do you know what you do to me? How much I want you?"

She dug her hands into his hair, arching her body against his, giving herself over to the urgency of her need as a slow warmth crept through her limbs. His mouth moved back to hers, teasing and playing with her lips for long agonizing seconds until she felt she would die from the exquisite torture. When she parted her lips once more he took swift advantage of the pleasure she was offering, and his tongue ravaged her until her desire rose to a fever pitch.

"Yoo-hoo! Rock! Rock Rawlings!" A shrill yodeling sound swept through the mountain pass, echoing in rippling circles until it penetrated the sensual haze that engulfed them. They drew apart reluctantly.

With a pained smile Rock rose and circled his mouth with his hand, yelling his reply. Taking Beryl's hand, he pulled her to her feet as she finished buttoning her blouse. "How about voting for only the two of us on our next trip?" he said, brushing the strands of hair back from her face and tucking her arm into the crook of his as they started up the path toward the tents.

Beryl's senses were still reeling. She remained silent in a sort of dazed confusion, fighting against the response his lovemaking had aroused in her. His compelling lips, his plundering tongue. . . .

Stop it this minute, she warned herself harshly, stumbling over a stone on the path. Rock tightened his grip on her arm and hurried her along.

CHAPTER THIRTEEN

"HOW'S THE DIARY COMING?" Rock asked before they reached the camp.

"Journal," Beryl corrected brusquely.

He quirked an eyebrow, grinning at her. "Sorry—*journal*. But there's no need to be defensive, you know. I'm duly impressed with your talent in that area."

Beryl slanted her green eyes at him, mollified by his words. It was good to be recognized finally as more than her father's daughter, a name in the society pages.

"You didn't answer me about your journal," Rock reminded her quietly.

"I write in it every time I get a chance," Beryl told him.

"I hope so; Fred's depending on you now."

"I'm keeping thorough general notes on the trek for Fred," she explained. "But part of my journal is private, as well."

"I wonder what's in it..." Rock teased her, amusement crinkling the corners of his eyes.

"Wouldn't you like to know!" Beryl responded tartly. She stopped, placing her hands on her hips. "I'll bet you're certain it's filled with descriptions of the great Rock Rawlings, the dauntless and brave mountaineer!''

Rock's loud chuckles were infectious, and Beryl found herself joining in helplessly as they neared the campsite. How could you handle someone who found your worst insults humorous?

"I'm back," Rock shouted. "What was the call for?"

"Call?" Lon came out of his tent, rubbing his eyes sleepily. "The only call I've heard is yours, and it woke me out of a beautiful nap."

"Sorry," Rock said curtly. "Someone called my name and I hurried back."

"Oh, no." Jane put down the book she was reading and looked contritely at Rock. "Mangmu was practicing his English and I had him work on pronouncing your name. Did he get a little loud?"

With an exasperated mutter Rock strode off in the direction of the Sherpa's tent. "Did I interrupt anything?" asked Jane, her voice as thick as molasses.

"Not that I know of," Beryl replied nonchalantly. "But it looks as if you irritated Rock all right."

The sun had dried her clothes, leaving them fresh and smelling of the flower-strewn meadow. She shook the grass from them and busied herself packing them in readiness for the next day's trek.

Seeing Rock's pack sitting in a corner of the tent, she felt a surge of uncontrollable curiosity. She peeked awkwardly out of the tent and then shifted over to the pack, pausing before it in a state of indecision.

Her hand reached out as one part of her mind fought the suddenly overwhelming desire to see that picture again. Perhaps if she could be sure it was Fran it would help her remember why she had to guard herself against Rock. Maybe then she'd have the strength to resist his devastating male seductions.

No, she told herself fiercely, it was unforgivable to pry like that. She had too much honor; the first time had been an accident, but there was no excuse now. Or was there? She had never made any inquiries about Paul, and that had been a mistake.

Without giving herself time to think about it longer, she began impulsively searching through the pack until she sighted the photo where she'd carefully replaced it. Directly beneath was a small envelope, and as if of its own volition her hand snatched it out greedily. The return address caught her eye immediately. It was from Fran.

Beryl's hands were trembling as she carried the letter over to the tent flap and stationed herself beside it. The letter was brief, little more than a note that must have been tucked inside Rock's pocket at the airport to be read on the plane.

Her eyes skimmed past the words:

Please carry this picture with you to the summit of Mount Everest. And remember that my prayers and hopes are with you and your team all the way. I'll never forget the wonderful times we spent together this past year....

A movement outside caught Beryl's attention and she almost fell over in her haste to get the picture and letter back into the pack. Now she knew: Rock had left Fran pining for him at home while he was taking every opportunity to make love to another woman on this trek.

She should have known he wasn't interested in a long-term relationship with her. She couldn't compete with Fran. Fran was already a part of Rock's world. Her brief note alone was proof that she and Rock had already shared more than Beryl could ever hope for. . . .

She supposed it was jealousy that was bothering her the most. She hadn't felt jealous of Paul's wife, only sympathetic toward her and outraged at having been an unwitting party to his deceit. But this was much worse, to feel sorry for another woman and almost hate her at the same moment.

What was even more terrible was that there was a part of her still wanting to fight for Rock's attentions. Still whispering to her that Rock was beginning to care for her. She must be mad even to think such a thought.

Get hold of yourself, reason warned her as she moved outside the tent into the brightness to join the others sitting around the newly laid camp fire. Some were writing letters and others simply relaxing. Beryl took out her notebook and began writing, disciplining her numb mind to concentrate on the pages before her. Soon her pen was fairly flying as she described her visit to the Sherpa woman's home, and on reading it over she felt a glow of satisfaction at her first serious literary effort.

When she finished she moved to sit closer to the fire, her eyes straying obsessively to Rock, who was now talking to two of the men. Their heads were bent close; sketchy phrases of conversation punctuated with bursts of laughter carried across to her as they relived a prior trip they'd taken together. Beryl looked around desperately for Susan, anything to divert her attention from Rock's long lean body, which fairly reeked with masculine power.

Mangmu's arrival interrupted the scene; he hurried to Rock's side, excitedly conferring with him. After several moments Rock stood. "How many of you feel like attending a dinner theater tonight? Mangmu says we're invited to a feast at the monastery."

"Anything to get away from rice," Reagen shouted. "I hope there's some gorgeous blond star singing and dancing at the theater."

"Fierce dragons and warlike snakes will be more like it," replied Rock with a grin.

Everyone else endorsed the suggestion enthusiastically, pulling on warm coats and following Mangmu out of the camp. The way to the monastery was steep and rocky, and they were all breathing raggedly by the time they reached the arched stone entrance. Outside the gates, merchants had stretched canvas tents; on the ground before them lay their colorful wares—sweaters, socks, mirrors, balloons. Others were hawking prayer beads, incense and amulets.

Inside the courtyard Beryl stopped to watch the crowds milling around, making a mental note of the sumptuous satins and brocades worn by some of the locals, in sharp contrast to the ragged peasant dress on others. Rich words of description filled her mind, and she longed to have paper to start recording the scene before a single shred of the visual impact was lost.

Blasts on a pair of trumpets from the battlemented walls opened the festivities, and everyone made a chaotic scramble for seats on the mossy ground, pushing aside bleating goats and whinnying ponies. A group of monks motioned to Rock, leading the team past the villagers seated on the ground. Red and yellow cushions were scattered in one area, and the monks indicated they were to sit on them.

"No less than the best seats in the house," Susan whispered.

Beryl sank down beside her with Reagen on her other side. "We had so hoped for some time alone today, but you were gone...." Susan's voice trailed off.

Remorse struck Beryl. She had promised to help them have a chance to be together. "I'm sorry," she whispered. "Some other time."

A large canopied stage was directly in front of them. Dancers in silk robes burst out waving wands covered with streamers, accompanied by the sounds of brass horns, shrill oboes and tinkling bells.

The women dancers' faces were powdered, their shiny black hair arranged in smooth rolls and adorned with jasmines and camellias. Their almond-shaped slanting eyes were outlined in black under beautifully arched eyebrows, and their lips were red and smiling. The male dancers, dressed in black silk robes, had their faces brightly painted. On their feet they wore silk slippers with pointed toes curving upward.

Mangmu whispered excitedly to Rock, who in turn translated his words to the group. No one in the audience seemed to mind the noise their conversation made. Several young boys circulated among the honored guests, offering trays laden with sugary dates, cashew nuts, cardamom seeds and coconut chips.

Drums covered with yak skin accompanied the frenzied movements of the dancers and actors who wandered on and off stage, their exotic costumes and headdresses transporting the viewers into an enchanted world. Some of the villagers in the audience joined in the dancing sporadically.

The drama concerned religious themes, but its complicated plot involved daring rescue attempts from dragons and warring kings. The dancers and actors sang much of the narrative in a plaintive minor key.

When a loud gong sounded, Mangmu led the group to a large room inside the stone monastery where an array of food had been laid out on a long wooden table. The team groaned with anticipation as they saw bowls of fresh vegetables along with yak cheese, coarse bread, hard-boiled eggs and various sweet puddings.

After the meal the gong sounded once more, and Beryl felt she would drop with exhaustion. She joined the group as they made their way back to the cushions and the play resumed. The music became wilder and wilder, the dancers blurring in front of her eyes as she grew more tired. Glancing around, she saw that several of her friends' heads were nodding as a drowsy stupor overtook them all.

"Time for us to be getting back," Rock announced. He thanked the monks for their hospitality and left an offering in the earthenware pot at the door.

"How did you like that?" he asked Beryl as they descended the trail, the star-filled sky glittering above them.

"I loved it at first," she responded truthfully, "but when you can't understand what's being said it begins to all blend together. Do they have extravaganzas like that often?"

"One that elaborate is held only once a year. But on every religious holiday they have a celebration of sorts."

Beryl tried to match her mood to his, relaxed and easy. She wasn't fooling herself any longer: knowing about Fran wasn't enough to make her ignore this man. But soon she intended to discuss what was bothering her with him. She owed herself at least that much.

When they returned to the campsite, Susan called for Rock and he headed with her in the direction where the porters were camped. Someone must be ill or injured, Beryl decided, so it seemed unlikely Susan would want her to help her be with Reagen tonight. She hurried toward the tent, eager to be undressed and asleep before Rock returned. She needed a little rest; maybe then she would have the courage to confront him.

What would she do if he blew up at her? Some men were like little boys who reacted furiously when they were thwarted. She'd seen Rock's anger; it could be fierce where she was concerned. If it was more than she could handle, she'd carry out her threat: she'd ask Jane to exchange tents with her for the rest of the trek to base camp.

Rock poked his head into the tent, calling cheerfully, "Get one of my sweat shirts out of my pack for me, sweetheart. I'll be back in a minute to change clothes."

Beryl nodded dully and went over to his pack. She was pulling out the shirt when Rock entered the tent, and she kept her back to him. He came up behind her and put his strong arms around her, fitting himself against the curves of her back and leaning forward to plant kisses on her head.

"Damn," he muttered, "why does Susan need help tonight?"

"What's the problem?" Beryl's throat felt tight with misery.

Rock shifted away and began unbuttoning his shirt. "We need to give tetanus injections to the porters. One of the packhorses is sick, and Susan suspects lockjaw."

Beryl whirled around, grabbing his arm. "What will happen to it?" Each morning she made a point of petting the wiry little horses, feeling sadness over their difficult life of carrying burdens in these awesome mountains.

"This is nothing for you to be involved in." Rock stripped off his shirt quickly.

"Don't treat me like a child, Rock. Will the horse live?"

He dropped his shirt onto his pack and reached over, cupping her face in his hand. "I'm not the doctor, darling."

Beryl wrenched her head away, but he pulled her roughly into his arms and held her against his bare chest. The staccato beating of his heart sounded in her head, and she felt the tension in the taut length of his body. "Don't fight me, Beryl," he murmured, letting his hands roam knowingly over her back until they molded her into his hips.

She acquiesced, feeling numb and dispirited, too drained of feeling to make any response. Then, unexpectedly, he flung her from him as quickly as he had pulled her into his arms. "Okay, let's have it. My guess is that you've decided to spend a little more time grieving over that bastard in Dallas."

She stood staring at him, attempting to think of a fitting retort. Rock took her silence as agreement. "You were damn willing to have me make love to you this afternoon."

Beryl gazed at her feet indecisively, licking her lips nervously as she mentally tried to form a reply. "Damn, Beryl," he continued. "You have to know that if Mangmu hadn't called, I would have carried you under those trees—"

Beryl was breathing raggedly. "Stop!"

His mouth stretched into a grim line. "You can't admit that you want me to make love to you? You want to go on pretending that another man can never mean anything to you when all the time—"

She covered his mouth with a hand, desperate to stop the vivid pictures he was conjuring in her mind.

"I'm not saying I don't want you, Rock," she whispered.

His arms enveloped her, his mouth moist as it traveled across her cheek to her ear. "God, I've been wanting to hear you say that," he said fiercely.

His lips covered hers and she felt his need, a need so great that it crumbled the strength of resolve she'd been building against him all day, carrying her along on its tide mindlessly, without fear, without reservation. Beryl could feel a difference in Rock's hands as they caressed her back, stroking, teasing, sliding lower to press her fully against him. His kiss was insistent with a burning urgency, conquering her, consuming her. Their bodies moved in total harmony, a symphony of mutual passion and naked desire.

Rock's mouth moved burningly to her throat, his voice murmuring her name over and over. She dug her fingers into his arms, holding onto him breathlessly, intense pleasure pulsing inside her. She didn't want to think, she didn't want to remember; she wanted only to swirl endlessly inside this savage kaleidoscope of joy.

Rock drew back from her and she stared into his triumphant eyes. His next words chilled her. "I knew you wanted me. I knew you wouldn't hold out forever. I'll go see if Lon will help Susan tonight."

Beryl's breath came out in a long sigh that left her trembling. "Please don't. All I want is to be left alone."

The smile died from his eyes. "Don't act like that," he snapped. "I'm sorry if I can't devote my full attention to you. Don't you understand that I have some duties I can't ignore? Haven't you already caused enough problems on this trek without making demands I can't meet?''

His savage movements as he jerked up the fleecy gray shirt and pulled it over his head left no doubt of his repressed fury. "Don't bother to wait up for me. This may take hours," he ground out before departing.

Beryl threw herself down onto her bedroll, pounding the pillow with frustration and longing, shaken by a raging tumult of emotions as she tried vainly to stop the flow of tears. She was tired, not only physically but emotionally. She was tired of fighting her desire for Rock, tired of these raging torments he started within her, tired of allowing Rock to think she didn't care that he wanted only one thing from her.

"Beryl." Jane's voice was hesitant, and Beryl flipped over and stared up at her as she poked her head through the tent flap.

"Did you need something?" Beryl asked curtly, but as soon as the words were out she regretted them. There was no reason to vent her anger on someone else.

"What's the matter? You've been crying." The warmth in Jane's voice surprised Beryl.

She sat up and brushed the tears from her face hastily. "Come on in," she mumbled. "Give me a moment to calm down."

Jane sat cross-legged beside her. "If there's anything I can do to help...."

Beryl forced a smile. "I'll be fine. Is there something you wanted?"

"It's strange, but I felt like talking to you all of a sudden. We've never given ourselves a chance to know each other."

Had Jane overheard any of their quarrel? It was an odd time for her to decide to be friendly, after all her days of rudeness and sarcastic remarks. "I've had the feeling you dislike me," Beryl said bluntly, deciding to confront her directly.

Jane bit her lower lip and glanced away. "I've never cared for people who go through life riding on their money or looks or family. All the rest of us had to go through an application process. Even your brother had a hard time getting chosen for this expedition. Except for you, all of us were selected purely on the strength of our qualifications."

"I'm only going as far as base camp," Beryl pointed out.

Jane nodded. "Right now you look as if you could catch a fast plane back to the States." Leaning over, she patted Beryl awkwardly. "I never expected to feel sorry for you, but I do. I've cried a lot of tears over Rock myself."

Her kindness unnerved Beryl momentarily, and she felt another tear threatening to form. With a decided effort she smiled. "I'll be fine. I think it's because I'm so tired. Maybe this trek is too hard for me after all."

"You're holding up just great," Jane said brusquely. "It's hard becoming a member of the R.R.R. club."

"What's that?"

Jane smiled grimly. "The Rock Rawlings Rejects. I'm a charter member."

Beryl shrugged. "We don't have to let ourselves be victims."

Jane's dark eyes gleamed. "You're right there. We can fight back. That's what I tried telling Fran, but she wouldn't listen. None of us do at first."

Her bitterness shot like an arrow through Beryl. "How serious are Fran and Rock?"

"What did he tell you?" Jane flung back her hair; some of her taunting spirit had returned.

"We've never discussed Fran. Susan said you thought it was serious between them."

"Fran worships Rock. She came to work in his department over a year ago. When I saw her volunteering for hours of extra work to help on research projects, I tried warning her. But she wouldn't listen; she invited him over for dinner so they could discuss the work and she joined every committee in the backup team for this expedition."

"What was Rock's attitude?" Beryl was relentless in her probing. She wanted to hear everything, even if it hurt so terribly she couldn't bear it.

Jane appeared puzzled. "The same as usual. He's always nice to everyone."

"But when did their affair begin?"

"There's no affair; Rock has a strict rule against any sexual involvement between members of his department. Personally I think it's an excuse, but he insists it prevents problems."

Beryl attempted to readjust her thinking quickly. What was Jane saying? That there had never been anything serious between Rock and Fran? That it was only another woman with a crush on him? "But isn't Rock a womanizer?" she asked.

Jane laughed. "Not Rock! He dates some, and I don't doubt he's experienced enough. But he's too busy to let any woman have much importance in his life. When he wants a woman, he always chooses one of the glamorous career woman around Los Angeles who have no intention of settling down."

Beryl felt a pulse pounding in her temple. "You've been a big help, Jane," she said sincerely.

"I'm glad. I knew it would make you feel better to know you're not alone. To tell you the truth, I've been trying to get over being mad at you ever since I saw how much you were helping Susan and Reagen. But it's not easy when you think someone has it too good in life."

Only a part of Beryl's mind was listening to Jane. She was feeling almost light-headed with relief, dizzy with happiness that Rock wasn't like Paul after all. Why hadn't she listened when he told her not to confuse him with the man who had used her so?

With a start, Beryl tried to imagine what Jane was expecting her to say. "I didn't choose my parents any more than you did yours," she answered quickly, hoping it was an appropriate response.

Jane tensed. "I certainly didn't choose mine. They didn't even want me; I spent most of my life in foster homes."

"I'm sorry."

"Don't feel sorry for me! I can't stand pity. I've conquered all of that a long time ago. It doesn't pay not to be strong, Beryl."

"I envy you, Jane. My life has been too easy and I've had to fight for the chance to stand on my own two feet."

Her frank revelation seemed to please Jane. She rose, apparently satisfied with the new tone of their relationship. "Let me know if I can help you as far as Rock's concerned," she insisted.

Beryl shook her head. "Really, I'm fine. But I appreciate the offer."

A surge of happiness coursed through Beryl as soon as Jane left her. She wanted to dance and sing; she wanted to run out and find Rock and tell him how sorry she was to have misjudged him; she wanted to admit to him that Paul meant nothing to her.

She was leaning over washing her face with the water Mangmu brought her each evening when Rock entered the tent.

"Did you promise Susan you'd help her this evening?"

Susan's voice sounded behind him. "Rock doesn't believe me when I say you're willing to help tonight, Beryl."

Beryl reached for a towel, wondering what the other woman was referring to. Susan persisted, "Tell Rock I'm not just imagining your offer."

Beryl swung around to face them and saw the tenseness in Rock's features, the taut lines around his mouth. She longed to reach out and touch his arm, communicate some of the things she was feeling for him. "Well?" he said harshly.

She glanced at Susan and met the plea in her eyes. "I remember now," she managed. "I promised you at the festival tonight."

Rock shifted away angrily. "This is against my better judgment, but since it's a rush job I won't say no. But I'm warning you: don't keep Beryl up too late, Susan. She's exhausted.''

"With two of us it shouldn't take too long," Susan assured him.

Rock moved aside, ignoring Beryl's goodbye as she brushed past him to leave the tent. Once outside, Susan made a mock-shivering motion and pointed back toward Rock. "What's his problem? He's been like a volcano about to erupt all evening."

Beryl shrugged. Jane would probably fill Susan's ears soon enough with the story of how she had found Beryl in tears over Rock, but for now she didn't want to discuss it. "What did you want me to do this evening?"

"Reagen and I are desperate to be together for a little while, Beryl. Come over to the medical shelter and I'll show you something that needs to be done."

When they reached the canvas shelter, Susan pointed to a portable table and took a sheet from a stack of papers.

"These are immunization certificates for the porters we gave injections to this evening,'' she explained. "I've got a list of their names here and I want you to make out one for each. Use your fanciest handwriting, because some of the men will treasure these slips of paper the rest of their lives."

Beryl smiled at the thought of the simple things that brought pleasure to their austere lives. "What do I say if Rock comes to investigate where I am?"

Susan stopped packing away her supplies and frowned thoughtfully. "I told him how much I need-ed your help, so he probably won't. But this is a messy situation; I've never been involved in such deceit before.''

''I know.'' Beryl nodded sympathetically. ''Did you write Kent today and tell him about Reagen?''

''I tried to,'' Susan moaned. ''But I'm not certain how his recovery's coming along. What if something I said made him give up trying? The Rawlingses would never forgive me, and I couldn't forgive myself.''

''I'm sure it'll work out. Go on and see Reagen.''

Susan's red thermos was filled with hot coffee, and Beryl poured herself a cup. Anything to keep her eyes open. As she scanned the list of long strange names she realized what an exacting task this was.

The coffee revived her momentarily and she started writing. When she held up the last certificate, admiring the fancy curlicues she'd made, the small kerosene stove at her feet sputtered and died.

Leaning back to stretch her tired muscles, she glanced around in the darkness. Had Susan expected her to stay until they returned? Cross with herself for not having asked, she huddled into the protective cocoon of her thick down jacket, resting her head on the aluminum table and longing for the warm bedroll in the tent where Rock lay sleeping.

A hand on her shoulder jerked her into wakefulness, and she looked up to see Reagen's shadow over her. ''Damn, I forgot all about you. Why didn't you go on to bed?''

Beryl blinked, trying to focus on her surroundings and the sharp tone in Reagen's voice. ''Where's Susan?''

Reagen pointed toward a tent, laying a finger across his mouth in a warning gesture. Helping her to her feet, he added, "Thanks, Beryl."

She nodded sleepily and stumbled toward her own tent, determined not to awaken Rock when she arrived. She removed her shoes and then slipped off her coat and jeans before creeping inside, crawling over to her bedroll with slow cautious movements.

She had reached it when Rock sat up abruptly. "Is that you, Beryl?"

Breathing shallowly, she answered, "Shh, you'll wake up the others."

"How late is it?" he asked, becoming more alert as he reached for his flashlight.

"Not too late," she mumbled, shoving the flashlight out of his reach with her toe in a way that was meant to seem accidental. "We finished all the certificates."

Rock leaned out of his bedroll and picked up his thin watch with its luminous dial. "Like hell it's not late!" he growled. "It's nearly three o'clock. What have you been doing?"

Beryl's heart thudded painfully as she attempted to quell his anger. "Working. And now I'm going to sleep. Will you please be quiet?"

"I'm going to have a word with Susan tomorrow and tell her what I think of her keeping you up so late."

"Quit treating me like a child who's stayed up past her bedtime," Beryl complained.

"Come over here and let's kiss and make up," Rock chuckled. "That'll show you how little I think of you as a child."

Relief soared through Beryl as Rock's familiar teasing convinced her he was regretting his earlier outburst. "Still certain you're irresistible?" she countered laughingly before turning her face to the opposite tent wall.

When she awoke she was alone in the tent, and the deluge of sounds outside convinced her she'd overslept. Dressing hastily, she frowned at the dark circles shadowing her eyes and applied a bright lip gloss in an attempt to divert attention from her pallor.

"Here comes Beryl," Rock shouted. "Pitch me that last biscuit so she'll learn not to sleep so late anymore."

"Don't you dare," Beryl returned, hurrying over to the table as the smell of the fragrant bread reached her.

"Don't worry; I saved you plenty," Susan assured her. "Anyone who'll help me do my work is never going to go hungry." She poured Beryl a cup of coffee and made room beside her. "I hope you're not too tired."

"She ought to be," Rock growled. "No more staying up until three o'clock, Susan, unless it's a life-or-death emergency."

"What's this about three o'clock?" asked Lon, who had just reached the group. "I hope you're asking Reagen where he spent his night. Was it a Sherpa girl he met at the monastery?"

Reagen's stricken expression revealed his guilt as he attempted a laugh. Beryl glanced at Rock and met his cold black eyes burning into her. "That *is* interesting," he observed casually. "What were you doing, Reagen?"

"Just out for a walk. What is this; do we have a curfew?"

"As leader of this expedition, I've made it plain I expect everyone to stay as rested as possible before we start up Everest."

Jane sauntered up, warming her hands by the fire. "What's all the fuss about, Rock?"

"We've got some team members staying up too late," he replied tersely.

"Who?" Jane probed relentlessly.

Rock hesitated a moment before saying, "Reagen. Susan. Beryl."

"Not Susan; she was in bed by midnight." Jane's announcement sent shock waves through Beryl. It took her several minutes to realize that Susan was not correcting Jane as sounds of teasing laughter floated around the camp.

"Try getting yourself out of this one, Reagen," Fred teased. "I wish I'd had my camera ready so I could have caught the guilty looks on your face and Beryl's."

"That's enough," Susan cut him off. "Beryl was helping me and she finished up after I left. What are you—a bunch of gossips trying to make something out of nothing?"

"Yeah," said Reagen. "The next time I take a walk to get away from Lon's snoring, I'll be sure to ask Rock's permission."

"Okay, let's get packed and ready to move out," Rock interrupted.

Beryl remained seated, forcing herself to eat the dry morsels of biscuit she'd found so appetizing at first. After several moments Susan returned, dropping down beside her.

"I'm sorry about what happened," she said softly. "Reagen and I both went to our tents and forgot all about you. I guess we assumed you'd gone on to bed, since the lantern was off. If Rock's too angry, I can tell him the truth." Her blue eyes clouded over.

At the sight of her friend's misery, stubbornness stiffened Beryl's backbone. "You don't have to do that. Rock doesn't own me. He can't tell me who to see or when."

"Jane mentioned to me how upset you were last night," Susan continued sympathetically.

Beryl shrugged, fighting down the feeling of hopelessness Susan's words caused. "Let's forget it," she said, setting her cup down and standing up. "How are things going with you and Reagen?"

"Wonderful! We found out so many things when we talked last night. Do you know, we compared what's been happening these past few years and it's uncanny how we've been thinking the same thing at the same time? Last Valentine's Day I sat by the phone all day trying to get up the nerve to call him, and he says he did the same."

As they walked toward the area where the tents were being struck, her animated voice continued filling Beryl in on all the coincidences. Beryl slipped into her tent to get her pack before the tent was dismantled and was confronted by Rock's fierce gaze.

"What are you doing here?" she stammered.

"Waiting for you. I told Mangmu to finish up here last."

She attempted to move past him, but he caught her wrist, wrenching her down beside him. "Why did you do it, Beryl?" he spat out, his angry voice bouncing off the flimsy walls of the tent and echoing through her weary mind.

CHAPTER FOURTEEN

BERYL FORCED HERSELF to break the hostile silence lengthening between them, alarmed by the violence lurking in Rock's eyes. "I haven't done anything that's going to hurt your precious expedition," she answered stonily. Her eyes stung with unshed tears as she remembered her pleasant thoughts the evening before. All she had wanted today was to enjoy being with Rock, letting him see that all the imaginary roadblocks she'd been putting between them were no longer there.

Rock cast a contemptuous glance her way. "The expedition's not on my mind and you know it." He turned away for a moment, breathing deeply, as if struggling to gain control of himself. Beryl reached out a hand and placed it on his arm tentatively, and he whirled around, grabbing her arms, pulling her to him so that she fell against his chest. She stared into the angry dark pools that were his eyes, listening to the furious pounding of his heart beating against hers.

"What are you trying to do to me?" he ground out harshly. "Drive me out of my mind?"

"I was working—"

"Don't lie to me," he flung back thickly. "Did you let him make love to you?"

Beryl jerked away, impelled by sudden fury over his accusation, and he quickly moved on top of her, pinning her body down with his. "Is that what I've been doing wrong—backing off every time you've given me one of those wide-eyed innocent looks when all the while you've been going behind my back with another man?"

Before she could answer his lips ground down over hers, holding hers captive with the violent force of frustration and thwarted desire. She struggled to free herself, twisting and turning under him, but her efforts only served to inflame him, and his hands roved under her writhing body to press her against the lean hardness of his own.

When her movements stilled, his kiss became gentle, a languorous exploration that ignited a fire within her. Her arms crept around him, moving over his powerful body and coming to rest at the nape of his neck as her fingers curled into his thick hair.

He drew back, breathing raggedly, and fell away from her. "You haven't answered my question," he rasped. "Is he your lover?"

Beryl turned swiftly to face him, and the utter contempt in his eyes chilled her. How could she ever convince him of her innocence without hurting Susan? "No man on this team has made love to me," she said in a low voice.

"Then you did this to me deliberately? To get even because I had to leave you last night?"

"No, Rock. You don't understand." Beryl shifted away from his scornful regard, all too aware of the

tiny explosions sent tingling down her limbs by the
very sight of his sprawling form.

He lifted her face with his hard smooth palm, cradling the back of her head, and bent to meet her parted
lips. His mouth was warm and gentle, masterfully
firm, as it covered hers, his free hand moving down
to the base of her spine.

Beryl whimpered softly, attempting to twist away.
But her actions didn't fool Rock, she knew. She was
all flames and melting fast. He raised his head, hovering close above her. "Help me, Beryl," he whispered, his dark eyes glazed with passion.

With one fingertip she traced the line of his lips. "I
want to help you," she murmured.

"Then take your hands off me and listen carefully.
Don't answer until I'm through."

Beryl dropped her hand with a swift angry movement. "Don't get in a huff," Rock told her. "You've
got to stop distracting me. You've got to help me put
the group's interests first again. Do you realize how
close I came to hitting Reagen out there this morning? My God, I wanted to *kill* him, Beryl."

Her eyes widened, but she clamped her lips together as he continued, "Think how you'd feel if that had
been Brad. Would you want his team leader to let
personal interests cloud his judgment? To cause a
lapse of attention that might result in injury to a team
member?"

Beryl shook her head. She realized the enormity of
what Rock was saying and wondered what he wanted
from her, how he intended to change his own actions.

"Good," Rock continued, acknowledging her understanding and moving away from her slightly. "Then we're together on this. We're both going to concentrate on the team's needs and forget our personal feelings."

"Do you want me to share someone else's tent?" she asked.

"Good Lord, no. How would that help me? We're going to be nothing but friends to each other from now on. Can you handle that?"

Beryl nodded briefly. "How about you?"

"I think I can manage as long as you don't deliberately provoke me in any way," Rock answered with a heavy sigh.

"I don't start all our fights," Beryl said defensively.

Rock's grim face broke into a smile. "There you go again, making something out of everything I say. I'm not accusing you of anything, Beryl. All I want is your help and cooperation."

"Right," Beryl responded briskly. "Does this mean I can't speak to Reagen or any of the other men again?"

With a sudden movement Rock grasped her hands and gazed at her in silence, only the slight throb of a muscle in his jaw revealing his tension. "It's your decision from now on whom you choose for friends," he said at length.

He dropped her hands then and made his way swiftly out of the tent, leaving Beryl to stuff her pajamas into her pack before hurrying outside. All around her the tents were down, already packed on the horses, and the team looked ready to move out.

They started the trek across the sun-drenched meadows with eagles patrolling the turquoise sky above them. Surrounded by towering mountains, the high pasture seemed an oasis with its thick barley fields and clumps of wild flowers. Susan walked beside Beryl, not speaking. Jane soon joined them.

"Gosh, it's beautiful here," she said. "I dread moving into those hills today." Her eyes scanned the forbidding terrain with a worried look.

"It'll be okay," Susan comforted her. "This is your chance to show the team you're not developing a fear of heights."

"How about you, Beryl? Are you afraid of anything?" Jane asked.

"Lots of things. Why?" Beryl was still seething inwardly over Jane's remarks at breakfast, finding it impossible to believe she had spoken in innocence.

Jane grabbed her arm. "What's the matter? I thought we'd sorted out things last night."

Beryl's lack of sleep plus the emotional turmoil inside her made her want to scream, but she answered calmly, "Then why did you say Susan was in bed by midnight?"

Susan intervened, "I was, Beryl. I thought you understood that Reagen and I forgot all about you. Then later in the night Reagen woke up and remembered."

"Was that what all the trouble was about?" said Jane. "Is Rock very mad at you?" Her interest was obviously laced with sympathy.

"Yes. I was worried when you two stayed in that

tent so long this morning, but he didn't seem too upset when he came out," Susan added. "Of course, you never can tell with Rock. When he's concentrating on leading this team he can set everything else aside."

"We...worked it out," Beryl told them, reluctant to discuss the situation further. "Now, why don't we forget everything except this beautiful scenery for a while?"

Their path began to lead upward, and soon they were hiking single file as it narrowed treacherously. On one side was nothing but jagged rocks, on the other the world fell away abruptly.

The precariousness of the steep narrow track kept Beryl's mind off of her troubles, for she had to concentrate on each step she took. Behind her Fred kept up a steady stream of conversation about the panorama that lay below them. "I've got to get some shots of this," he exclaimed. "Think you'll be able to describe it?"

Beryl nodded. "What chances do we have of a publisher's being interested in this book?"

She glanced over her shoulder at him. Fred was the youngest team member, only a year older than herself; he was the type most of her friends considered handsome with his mass of curly hair and even features. He always seemed to be at a fever pitch of excitement about the shots he was taking, and she enjoyed listening to him declare confidently, "If the expedition's a success the book is already sold."

Beryl clutched at the jagged rocks that bordered

the trail on one side. "It will be a success, won't it?" she asked anxiously. "What can happen now?"

"The main challenge hasn't even started. Once we reach base camp and start up, you'll see what I mean."

"You'll have to tell me about it," she mumbled.

Fred looked genuinely sad. "I keep forgetting you're not going on with us. You'll be missed, Beryl."

The sincerity of his compliment eased some of the aching caused by Rock's anger, and she flashed him a grateful smile.

When they reached the summit, Rock called a halt for a rest break. "The descent's going to be twice as treacherous, so we'll want to be rested before we start. I'm considering roping us together in teams of two. What do you think, Mangmu?"

"No need," Mangmu answered. "Good team. Good climbers. If horses can do it, so can you."

"Thanks," laughed Rock. "Does everyone agree to going it alone?" His eyes sought Beryl's intent gaze, and she nodded. She wasn't afraid to give it a try, and if the others felt capable she'd watch to see where they stepped before making a move.

After cups of tea, the order was given to move out. Rock motioned for Beryl and she joined him. "I want you beside me," he said. "We'll go first, with Jane directly behind us."

They watched as the packhorses, loaded with the precious supplies, made their long descent down the slippery trail, their hooves sending rocks tumbling to the chasm below. Next came the porters, and when they had cleared the trail Rock started down. "Grab my pack if you start to slip, Beryl. I can hold you up without any difficulty."

"I'm fine," Beryl breathed, keeping her eyes glued to the trail beneath her feet. The bulk of Rock's broad back was a welcome sight as she placed her feet gingerly on the loose stones, testing the ground for firmness before putting down her full weight.

Behind her she could hear Jane's labored breathing, much too loud to be accounted for by the altitude they had reached. Why was the woman so unwilling to admit her fears? By isolating herself, refusing to speak frankly with the others about her dread of heights, she was shutting off any help or assurance the others could offer.

Mangmu greeted them when they reached the valley below, congratulating them effusively and offering them hunks of sweet bread from the cooks' packs while they watched the others struggling down the treacherous trail. More than half of the group had arrived and all of them were laughing and joking, voices tinged with relief, when a shout went up from one of the Sherpas. "Rock falling!"

Beryl turned her head and stared in horror as a dark speck grew larger and larger before her eyes, bounding right for the team members still left on the trail.

She saw it strike another rock, exploding into a fusillade of sharp fragments as Rock leaped to his feet and started up the trail, literally clawing his way up. Beryl shuddered, closing her eyes as Jane screamed, "He's falling! Help! He's falling!"

The silence was as sudden as the screams when she

saw Lon grabbing Jane and clamping his hand over her mouth. Beryl buried her head in her lap, clenching her fists and praying for Rock's safety.

He couldn't die like this; not before her very eyes; not when she loved him so much. She lifted her head and saw only a blur of brightly colored jackets leaning over the trail above. Hurriedly she closed her eyes again, certain she would soon know the full extent of the tragedy.

The sound of the team returning minutes later made her lift her head, and she felt strong hands pressing into her shoulders. "It's okay. Reagen was hurt, but Susan thinks it's only a bruise."

Beryl lifted her eyes, unable to believe that Rock was standing in front of her. The sight made her dizzy with relief and happiness. "That's wonderful," she murmured, luminous green eyes melting with dazed happiness. "I was so afraid something had happened to—"

"I know," Rock cut in curtly. "Why don't you go see if you can make yourself useful to Susan? She was right behind Reagen, so it shook her up pretty badly, too."

After an hour's rest Reagen was able to move on. He leaned on a staff with both Susan and Beryl staying by him, assisting him when he needed help and encouraging him to ignore the pain and keep going to work out the soreness. The others on the team adjusted their pace to that of their injured teammate.

Rock stayed far behind, and Beryl struggled against her desire to cast glances over her shoulder and reassure herself he was there. She relived that horrible moment when she had thought he was the one falling, that moment when her last doubt about being in love with him had vanished.

It was a frightening knowledge, she realized. She had always viewed falling in love as a dreamy haze in which everything would be perfect, in which all mis-understandings could be cleared up with a little tolerance on each side. But now she could see that had been only an illusion. Loving a man meant giving him power over you. Without him you knew only emptiness and misery, and a longing to be with him.

Scenes of her encounter with Rock in the tent that morning played in her mind like something from an old movie, reminding her that she had made a prom-ise to him. She had vowed not to do anything to stand in the way of this expedition's success, this team's necessary unity.

But there were no guidelines, no new behavior she was supposed to adopt, no way of knowing when she was causing trouble or not. Anger threatened to spark, but she shrugged it off; making an issue out of the situation wasn't going to change any-thing.

They made camp by a gurgling stream in the foot-hills of the next cluster of high mountains they would cross. "Sometimes I don't feel as if we're getting anywhere," Beryl moaned, removing her pack and sinking onto the grass. "Everywhere we stop the mountains are right in front of us, waiting to be climbed all over again the next day."

"Say, that'll make a great line for our book," Fred responded. "I'll take a picture of you sitting here all forlorn and grubby, and that's the caption we can put under it."

"You can label me as the team's biggest complainer," she laughed. "Were you able to get any pictures today?"

"Some superb shots. I even got one of you when you were falling apart because you thought Rock was plunging to his death. He'll enjoy seeing you cared that much."

"You wouldn't dare!" Beryl's eyes widened and then she sank back down, feeling foolish as she saw the gleam of amusement in Fred's eyes. "Did you expect me to be laughing over a rock hurtling down toward people?"

"Not when you think it's hurting your man! Why do you try pretending you're not too interested in Rock? Are you trying to drive him crazy?"

"That's not my purpose," Beryl sighed before changing the subject.

"Time for a swim," Rock shouted. "Cutoffs are the uniform."

Within minutes most of the group had grabbed what they needed from their packs and were splashing around in the clear chilly water. Lon improvised a float from canvas and pack frames and soon shouts could be heard from those who were riding the foamy rapids downstream.

"Not you," Susan ordered when Reagen hobbled to the bank. "Too much danger of getting hurt again. I asked Gompa to boil some water so we can alternate hot and cold compresses on that bruise."

"Slave driver," Reagen moaned. "Guess I'll have to content myself with sitting onshore and watching all those wet clothes clinging to you women.''

Rock acknowledged his remark with a grim smile. "Are you going to join the rafters?'' he asked Beryl.

"I'd love to,'' she said, shaking the water from her streaming hair and catching hold of the hand he offered.

"Those wet clothes do cling nicely,'' he whispered as they climbed onto shore and made their way along the grassy bank. "This may be the first test of my new policy.''

You're not bad yourself, thought Beryl, every nerve ending in her aware of Rock's powerful shoulder muscles, the sinewy lines of his legs, the flat waist and damp hair darkening his chest.

"Have you ever gone rafting before?'' Rock asked.

His words forced her eyes up. "On the Guadalupe in central Texas. That's probably tame by your standards.''

"No,'' he disagreed. "I've heard some great things about that river; maybe you can show me what the natives do there soon.''

His words made her ridiculously happy. Pulling his hand forward, she broke into a run, laughing at his surprised look. "Sometimes I can't believe your stamina,'' he said.

Rafting turned out to be an optimistic way to describe what the others were doing. Beryl joined them and attempted to stay afloat, clinging to Lon's contraption in the midst of the rushing white waters. "I give up,'' she cried at length, stretching herself out on her back on some grass.

Rock flopped down beside her, propping himself up on one elbow to brush the drops of water from her face. His eyes outlined the contours of her oval face, lingering on the softly curving mouth in a way that left no doubt about his interest in it.

He lay close to her, so close she felt the tenseness of his muscles against her side. Intoxicated by her awareness of the power she held over him, she smiled lazily into his eyes and heard him catch his breath. "You little temptress," he whispered, his mouth nuzzling her shoulder. "Don't you remember your promise?"

"Do you?" she murmured, looking into eyes glazed with smoldering desire.

His eyes dropped down to her breasts molded by the wet fabric in a way that emphasized their rounded firmness. "Stop it, Beryl. Stop provoking me."

With a deep groan he leaned back and then sat up. "It's time to see how dinner's coming. Go put some dry clothes on so I can get my mind on something else."

Before she could make a move, Susan called out, "Hey, Beryl!" She made her way over to where Beryl was still lying and flopped down beside her as Rock strode off.

"What is it?" Beryl asked, sitting up to brush the water off her shoulders.

Susan lowered her voice. "I just remembered it's Jane's birthday today. Would you help me plan a celebration?"

Beryl nodded her agreement. "Any ideas?"

"I'll check with Gompa and see if he can whip up one of his cakes. Then why don't you ask Rock if the men can think of a gift for her? Some memento of the trip?''

"Sounds like fun. And I'll let Fred know so he can record the celebration for our book."

Susan gave her a sharp look. "Then you really have forgiven Jane for all the trouble she's been causing you? I didn't know whether to believe her or not when she said you two had straightened everything out."

Beryl managed a wry smile. "I hope so. She's decided I'm having troubles with Rock, so she feels sorry for me."

Susan laughed. "From Rock's face this morning it looked as if all the trouble was on the other side." Both pairs of eyes glanced over at Rock. He was standing in the middle of the stream, helping Jane hold onto the raft. "She keeps telling me that she's over her crush on Rock, that she's missing Calvin."

"Who's Calvin?"

"A librarian at the university. He's a dear; Jane would be smart to turn her attentions on him."

"Does he like her?"

Susan nodded. "They've been dating for more than three years now, but Jane can't stop comparing him to Rock. Maybe this trek will help."

"I hope so," said Beryl with fervor, flushing as Susan began laughing. "Stop it," she snapped irritably, but then grinned to soften her words.

After changing from her wet clothes into a clean pair of jeans and an emerald green silky shirt in honor of the birthday celebration, Beryl went in search of Rock. He was still in the water, and she hesitated momentarily before motioning for him to join her.

His eyebrows rose and he whistled his appreciation. "Were you planning an evening out?" he teased. "You're looking very classy."

Beryl frowned her disapproval. "Susan and I are planning a birthday celebration for Jane. How about your making something for her, some kind of souvenir of the trek?"

"That's very thoughtful of you, considering how poorly she's treated you."

An impish grin lit up her eyes, but she bit back the words on the tip of her tongue. It wouldn't do to tell him that Jane thought he had been picking on her. "We smoothed out our differences last night," she said at length.

"Interesting," Rock replied noncommittally. "I'll see what I can do about that gift. Someone's sure to have an idea."

Fred located some candles and began planning his camera shots as soon as Beryl told him. Susan reported back that Gompa was making a cake, and soon Beryl saw that Rock and several of the men were gathered at one of the tables, poring over their maps with a sketch pad at hand. With only a short time left before dinner, Beryl hurried back to the tent. Pulling out her journal, she began writing. When the dinner gong sounded she tore out one sheet and folded it into a small square.

Dinner time was unbelievably dull and lonely without Rock beside her, Beryl decided as she tried to join in Fred's and Reagen's conversation. Even the cheerful flickering light of the camp fire only emphasized the fact that she had come to depend on the warmth of Rock's shoulder touching her and the feel of his leg brushing against hers as she ate.

The rest of the group seemed more boisterous than usual. Rock circulated among them, laughing, teasing, encouraging, and for the first time she realized what he had been trying to tell her that morning. Their confrontations had been making him less attentive to the rest of the team. But that knowledge did nothing to lessen the aching void she was feeling.

Near the end of the meal, Susan slipped away. Within seconds she and Gompa returned with the candle-covered cake, and soon everyone was singing a rousing rendition of "Happy Birthday."

Jane's usual reserve fled; her face was wreathed in smiles. She stood up and took a quick bow as Fred issued orders on where he wanted everyone to stand.

After Jane blew out the candles and the cake was cut, Beryl slipped over to sit beside her, handing her the square of paper from her pocket.

"What's this?" Jane asked.

"Read it."

Jane unfolded the paper and began reading. She glanced up when she was finished, whispering, "Thank you, Beryl. I don't think I've ever had anyone write a poem for me before. I'll put this among my trip souvenirs; it's truly beautiful."

"Secret?" Rock was towering over them, holding a scroll tied with a heavy twine bow.

"It's one of Beryl's poems, Rock. She wrote it personally for me."

"Poems? Are you a poet, Beryl?" he asked quietly.

Reagen interrupted, "Beryl's always full of surprises. Read it to all of us, Jane."

Jane glanced at Beryl and saw the stricken look on her face. "Not on your life," she said belligerently. "Ask her to write one for you."

Reagen laughed. "I may just do that," he said softly.

Beryl watched as a flicker of anger shone in Rock's eyes, but he recovered quickly. "After a poem, I'm afraid this gift may not be much, Jane. But from the whole team, we'd like to wish you a happy birthday with many more in the years to come." He handed her the scroll and then took his seat.

Jane began exclaiming with pleasure as she unrolled the long piece of paper. It was a quaint handdrawn map of their trail, filled with humorous signs that were reminders of the events along the way.

"I love it," she said. "I think I'll have Calvin frame it so I can put it in my office at school and share it with the students."

As the group began breaking up, Beryl lingered by the fire, helping to clear up the remains of the cake and dreading going to their tent. She glanced around and saw that Rock had disappeared; maybe if she sat here longer he would be asleep by the time she got to bed.

Jane came over and sat down beside her. "I don't know how to thank you and Susan for planning this party. When's your birthday?"

"Not for months," laughed Beryl.

"Rock giving you any more trouble?"

"No," Beryl answered. "Don't get mad at Rock; most of my problems are my own fault."

Jane sighed. "I never could get really mad at Rock—I've had him on a pedestal too long. Has he ever told you all he's done for me?"

Beryl shook her head. Jane continued, "I was a student in one of his classes. At first I made excellent grades, and then I had to take a night job to pay my expenses. Soon I didn't have any time to study and my grades started slipping. He called me into his office and in that understanding way of his soon had me spilling my whole story."

"Yes, he has quite a way," Beryl remarked wryly.

"He even arranged for me to get a job in the geography department and encouraged me to take up something that would give me more self-confidence in life. I chose mountaineering because he was the leader of the local organization."

"Did he know you were afraid of heights?"

Jane's lips thinned into a tight line. "I'm not really all that afraid...." Her shoulders sagged in defeat. "Yes, I am, too. But it's getting worse. I've always been able to hide it before now. It really bothers me."

"Why don't you give up mountain climbing?" pressed Beryl.

"That's what Calvin says. His hobby is golf, and he's trying to get me to learn so we can play together."

"He sounds nice," Beryl commented. Her eyelids were growing heavy and she was fighting to stay awake.

"He's not as glamorous as Rock, but then who is?" Jane responded.

Beryl smiled. "I think I'd better get a little sleep, Jane. Good night."

"Good night," Jane answered.

She had settled down in her bedroll and was fluffing her pillow, congratulating herself on not awakening Rock, when he spoke in a fully alert voice. "Have you been with Reagen?" His quiet low tone flustered her more than any tirade he'd launched into in the past.

"No," she said. "There's nothing between Reagen and me. We're friends, simply friends. Can you understand that?"

"Not really. What is it you like about him?"

Beryl fished for an answer. Reagen's charms were obvious, but none of them were especially appealing to her. At length she answered, "He's funny, always telling jokes. He makes me. . . laugh."

Rock's chuckle surprised her. "I wasn't aware you wanted to be amused. Shall I try putting on a clown act for your benefit?"

"That's hardly necessary," Beryl snapped.

Lean muscular arms snaked out, wrapping themselves around her.

Expecting an assault on her mouth, Beryl attempted to swivel her head away. She was totally unprepared when Rock's muscular fingers began moving down her ribs, sending bursts of laughter bubbling out of her and convulsing her into a limp rag.

"This isn't fair," she shrieked as he continued his tickling assault. "Brad must have told you how ticklish I am."

"You're laughing," Rock pointed out, his fingers gentling as Beryl's laughter neared hysteria and tears welled in her eyes.

"Hey, quiet down, you two!" A bellow from a neighboring tent made Rock stop his attack, and for a moment Beryl lay motionless in his arms, a wave of red suffusing her already flushed cheeks. Then, firmly pushing aside his arms, she moved back to her own bedroll and crawled inside.

As she settled the covers around her shaking figure, she thought she heard Rock give a low chuckle from the other side of the tent. Damn the man!

CHAPTER FIFTEEN

DURING THE DAYS FOLLOWING, Beryl discovered a new Rock. He was courteous, thoughtful, friendly; his behavior couldn't be faulted in any way. But he was so remote, so impersonal, that at times she felt like starting an argument, disagreeing with him—anything to break out of the stalemate that existed between them.

There were no more problems where Reagen was concerned. Like everyone else, he and Susan fell into their sleeping bags at the end of each day, exhausted from the long hikes Rock was demanding.

Beryl turned her attention to this exotic country through which they traveled. Enchanted Nepal. Every day the fascination grew as the mountaineering team trudged on. The lush valleys gave way to harsher terrain as they neared the tree line, but the peace and beauty of the snow-covered peaks lured them onward. It was easy to understand why the devout Buddhists worshiped these mountains, considering them deities.

Beryl listened enviously as the team discussed their preparations for the assault on Mount Everest—magnificent Chomolungma, goddess mother of the world. She felt she was beginning to understand the thrill they were anticipating now. It wasn't that they took foolish chances, as she had once imagined; rather, they accepted that the challenge of their planned climb lay in the risk inherent in it.

As the group gained new altitudes the weather became chillier, with only brief periods of sunshine and warmth when their path descended into the valleys. The rain came and went intermittently until the morning they awoke to a dazzling world of white outside their tents.

"Come here," Rock called to her as he peered through the tent flap.

Beryl joined him, staring out at the white expanse. "It's beautiful," she whispered, surprised when his arm moved around her, holding her shivering body close to his.

He kissed her on the forehead and then patted her playfully. "Get dressed before I forget my resolve," he warned.

Beryl was reluctant to move outside the warm circle of his arm. She wished she could deny her longing for him, the urge to have him pull her closer and kiss her again, to melt into his embrace.

As she dressed moments later in her warmest layers of clothes, she found herself sighing heavily. There was no excuse for the way she was missing the intimacy she'd shared with Rock; she should never have let him become that important to her. She tried being objective, but despite all the cool reasoning in her mind, nothing had changed for her. No doubts had crept in to disclaim the intensity of the love she felt for him.

She loved him deeply . . . and wanted to be loved by him in return. She longed for him in a way that bordered on desperation, knowing she would never meet another man she could want so completely. She ached to share his life, to be a part of his adventures, to be the one he turned to when in need.

But there was more to her feelings than that. She wanted his exquisite lovemaking, his tender kisses and firm caresses, his molten passion. She closed her eyes, remembering their intimate moments together, wanting more. . . .

Out by the fire, Rock came over and sat down beside Beryl as she warmed her hands in front of the flames. "Will this be your first time hiking in the snow?" he asked.

"Yes, is it difficult?"

"Not with the small amount on the ground now. But before we make it to base camp we'll go through some hard crusty snow that'll try your endurance to the limit." He patted her on the shoulder, adding, "I have no doubt you'll make it."

Beryl felt a ripple of exhilaration that banished all her gloominess. She looked toward the peaks above her, where a dusting of fresh powdery snow lay glistening in the sun. She was slowly realizing that as they moved nearer to their goal, leaving civilization behind, the things that had once seemed important were beginning to be outweighed by the sheer enjoyment of being alive, of experiencing this unique challenge and commitment.

By midmorning the trail ahead became obscured by dark clouds. Light snow began drifting downward, melting on the hikers' flushed faces as it reached them. The break for tea was brief and they stamped their feet and clapped their hands in an attempt to keep warm in the chilly air.

"Ready for a halt?" Rock asked.

The consensus of the group was to try to make more progress. "I agree," Rock told them. "We're two days behind schedule already." He came over to Beryl. "Are you warm enough?"

"I'm fine."

"You stubborn little mule. You'd tell me that if all your toes were frostbitten, wouldn't you?" The smile in his eyes took any sting out of his words. He kissed her on the nose and pulled her knitted cap down over her ears. "Promise me you'll let me know if it's too much for you?"

Beryl nodded, grateful for the thaw in their relationship. As she moved out to join her group, she heard the Sherpas beginning to sing. These mountain people amazed her: generous, kind, merry, they were able to take any misfortune that came their way with a patience that stiffened her own backbone when the going got rough.

The porters, on the other hand, complained unceasingly, muttering and cursing over each obstacle they encountered. When Beryl asked about this startling difference in the two groups, Reagen explained, "The porters do that to increase their bargaining power. They're convinced that they'll be paid less if they smile or look too comfortable."

One of the team members started a rousing marching song when the Sherpas ceased singing. Soon the others were joining in, choosing their own favorites in turn. The morning passed so quickly that Beryl had difficulty believing it was lunchtime when Rock gave the signal to stop.

In the afternoon the morning snow retreated under the onslaught of bright sunshine and the trail dipped downward, revealing a grassy meadow far below. The change in one day from numbing cold and swirling snowflakes to bright sunshine and green fields covered with wild flowers seemed unreal. The hikers shed their heavy coats and stepped up their pace, eager to reach the verdant meadow in the valley.

The discussion around the camp fire that evening was lively, for the team sensed that they probably had few evenings left before their trail would lead into the mountains above the tree line, a land of ice and snow filled with dangerous risks. "Any chance I can climb Mount Everest with you?" Beryl asked as she felt Rock's body leaning against hers.

"I'm afraid not. As you know, probably only two or three of us will actually reach the summit. And only those who have been training rigorously have a chance." Smiling down into her eyes, he added, "Maybe we can go mountain climbing together sometime. I'd be happy to start you off on an easy ascent somewhere."

What could it hurt to dream a little, Beryl wondered. She never expected to hear from him again after they separated, but for now she'd go along with his idea. "Sure," she murmured.

"Don't you agree, Rock?" Jane's voice was insistent, making them both aware that she must have been trying to get their attention for some time.

"I'm sorry. I didn't hear your comment," Rock answered calmly, but Beryl felt his body tighten with irritation.

"I suggested that we'd better get some extra sleep tonight. The map shows we'll start a long climb tomorrow."

"Excellent suggestion," Rock agreed, rising to his feet and pulling Beryl with him.

Snow fell again during the night, a soft light snow that melted as soon as it touched the ground. Beryl woke up several times, glancing over at Rock's side of the tent, wondering if he was asleep.

His breathing was even and regular, mingling with the soft fall of the snowflakes against the side of the tent. The thought that these nights would soon be over brought tears to Beryl's eyes, and sleep was slow in coming.

Teamed with Jane and Lon the next morning, she started off in high spirits, happy and excited at the prospect of climbing to an altitude where few people had ever been. Jane pointed out the tree line to her. "Those scrubby little bushes are all we'll see today, and soon even those will be gone. It's a desolate, forbidding country."

The fierce note in her voice bothered Beryl. Jane was an intense, enigmatic woman, and Beryl was determined to draw her out. "Do you enjoy your work at the university?" she asked lightly.

Jane smiled. "I love it. I teach geography, one of the most demanding subjects in the curriculum. Knowing I've traveled a lot, the students seem to listen more carefully. If you're not careful, geography can be a dull subject."

"I always found it so," Beryl admitted. "Now I can see what I've been missing."

"That'll all be changing now, I predict. Rock thrives on outdoor adventures, so you two will probably be traveling anytime he's not involved in teaching."

Fred had joined them, and he quickly picked up on Jane's last remark. "Are you planning on moving to Los Angeles, Beryl?"

Beryl attempted an indifferent shrug. "I don't have any plans in that direction," she hedged.

"What direction?" Rock's voice sounded behind them, and all three turned.

Beryl felt herself flushing and saw that Fred appeared to be embarrassed, also. "Mind your own business," Jane told him with a forced laugh. "Beryl is my partner today."

"Aren't you supposed to be with your group?" Beryl pointed out.

"You three looked more interesting." A broad smile filtered across Rock's features. Beryl's eyes traveled over his powerful frame and rested on his strong face, his eyes as black as pieces of coal and as piercing as a panther's. He reached out and pulled her onto the path beside him. "How about walking with me a few minutes?"

"Come on, Fred, let's move ahead," said Jane, her tone almost indulgent as she grasped Fred's arm.

"Aren't you forgetting something?" Beryl glanced obliquely at Rock.

"Friends can spend some time together. Sometimes I think you're overdoing my suggestions."

"They sounded more like orders to me," Beryl retorted.

"Do you have any idea how alluring you are when you open those green eyes so wide?" Rock spoke huskily, one hand moving to massage the nape of her neck.

The warmth of his hand on her skin melted Beryl.

She had been aching for his touch, throbbing with unsatisfied longings and desires. But he had asked for her help; he had made it plain he didn't want to let any emotions stand in the way of duty.

Reluctantly she shrugged, pulling away. "I don't think that's wise," she told him shakily.

"I doubt that a mere touch from me is that devastating," he said dryly. "Is something the matter, Beryl?"

"Only that I think you're right."

"Now, that's a change," was his mocking reply. As Beryl stopped on the trail and crossed her arms defiantly, he turned to face her. "Before you sound off, try telling me what I'm right about." His eyes held a look of grim amusement.

Beryl sighed and started down the path. "I've noticed that everyone on the team is much happier now that we're not fighting anymore."

"Except me?" he asked quietly.

"Especially you!" Beryl flared. "You're always whistling and smiling and joking."

"That's good," he responded. "I'll keep reminding myself of that." Then he glanced away from her quickly. "Good Lord, we're getting separated from the rest of the group. After all my warnings to everyone else!"

Beryl rejoined Jane, her mind filled with her interchange with Rock. It had been strangely satisfying, and she wasn't certain why. One thing she knew: Rock was missing her; he wasn't tired of her, as she sometimes worried.

As the morning lengthened everyone began groaning. Beryl pressed her hand against her forehead to ward off the throbbing ache that was building inside her head, no doubt a reaction to the light, oxygen-depleted air. Her arms and legs began aching and with each moment the pack became heavier. Worst of all was a sharp pain in the sole of her right foot.

Unwilling to admit how she was feeling, she plowed onward, a determined smile on her face. She wasn't a quitter, someone who had to call a halt to the rest of the team over a little pain. She wouldn't give up without attempting to make more of an effort than this!

The pain in her foot continued to increase in intensity until at last Jane asked, "What's the matter, Beryl? Are you having trouble breathing?"

Beryl nodded. "And my foot hurts."

"What's wrong with it?"

The note of concern in Jane's voice surprised Beryl, melting her resolve to be brave. "It's absolutely killing me. If I didn't know better, I'd say I must have cut it."

"Let me check for you." Jane found a large flat rock and motioned for Beryl to sit. Kneeling, she began to remove the heavy boot.

Rock's group arrived and he stopped. "What's wrong, Beryl?"

She fought down a mad desire to throw herself into his arms as his tone of sympathy sank into her tired brain.

"Go on with your group and leave us alone," Jane told him. "I'm capable of helping Beryl. It's probably only a pebble in her boot."

Rock hesitated, but Beryl forced herself to add,

"For heaven's sake, Rock, I'm fine. Jane is my team-mate today."

He left but turned back when he reached a bend and stood watching for several minutes, a worried frown on his face. Beryl waved at him impatiently, indicating he was to move on. It wouldn't do to fall apart at the seams over a little pain. What would the rest of them think of her?

When Jane removed her boot, she shrieked in alarm, "There's blood in here, Beryl!"

Beryl peered down and saw the red stains on her sock. She jerked it off and began rubbing a hand over her foot.

"Look, it's a pebble, just as I thought." Jane held up a small, sharply jagged rock triumphantly. "That ought to solve the problem. You'll be fine now." Using her canteen, she wet a handkerchief and washed Beryl's foot before applying gauze and tape from her pack.

"Umm, that feels much better," Beryl sighed. "Thanks for all your help."

"Anytime," Jane answered brusquely, reminding Beryl that it was hard to understand this woman. "Rock will be worried about you," she continued. "Why don't I run ahead and let him know you're fine? When you get your boot back on, you can catch up with us."

Beryl nodded and bent over to retrieve her boot. Jane turned to ask, "Are you certain you can find us?"

"This trail looks pretty well marked to me," Beryl laughed. "I'll be there in a minute." She slipped on a clean sock and carefully laced up her boot.

Restrapping her pack on her back proved to be more difficult than she had thought. It kept slipping to one side, and after several exasperating attempts she sat down to catch her breath. Everything seemed ten times harder at this altitude.

After several minutes she made another attempt and succeeded in doing a halfway-decent job. She set off determinedly, rounding a crest and then taking a sharp veer to the right to follow the well-trampled path.

Around the bend she was met by a long line of Nepalese men and their heavily laden woolly yaks. They crowded her onto a narrow ledge, where she was forced to wait until they passed. How had the rest of the group gone past them? Was there any chance she wasn't on the right trail? As the worries assailed her she checked her watch and found, to her alarm, that nearly an hour had passed since Jane had left her.

Once the trail was clear she walked as rapidly as her unevenly balanced pack and sore foot would allow, until she reached a crossroads. All around her the mountains rose higher and higher and the stunted gnarled trees leaned over the glaring white precipices with grotesquely shaped limbs.

Beryl stopped, her breathing labored, and tried to decide what to do. Both trails looked equally well traveled. She glanced at the trees around her to see if Rock might have left some sign or marker telling her the way to go.

Cupping her hands around her mouth, she began yelling for him. The sounds echoed back with no returning answer. There seemed to be no course left but to choose one of the trails. She decided to pick the one that appeared to lead more uphill than the other. Wasn't that what she had heard the group discussing the night before?

After climbing for what seemed an endless amount of time and having to make several more decisions at places where the trail branched off, Beryl acknowledged to herself that she was thoroughly lost. Standing at a river crossing, she stared unseeingly before her. What should she do now? Rock had warned her repeatedly that the most disastrous thing that could happen was to become separated from the group.

Should she sit and wait to be found or should she try to find the others? The decision seemed impossible to make, and for the first time she conceded that Rock had been right in telling her that only trained climbers belonged in these mountains.

An incredible silence closed around her as the full awareness of her predicament sank in. What if she weren't found by her group? Was there a Sherpa village nearby where she could get food?

But her knowledge of the language consisted only of a few phrases Mangmu had taught her, and he usually ended up laughing over her attempts to say them. And what if she wandered into one of the superstitious villages where people were afraid of her strangely colored hair and unusual height?

Panic rose in her, and she fought down the trembling sensation in her knees. She couldn't allow herself to lose control; this was her first real test in life. Now she would find out if she was as capable of taking care of herself as she had bragged about to Rock.

Beryl rose to her feet, refusing to give in to the

clouds of panic threatening her. Rock was looking for her at this moment; she had to believe that! She wasn't stranded in this strange enchanted country. The answer lay in action, and so she started across the river, not allowing her imagination to run riot again.

The day went by in a haze as Beryl continued climbing over ledges and crevasses, through a bamboo forest, over small gurgling streams and above roaring rivers until she stepped out onto a ridge from which she could see for miles around her. Leaning against a rock, she managed to remove some food from her pack. While she was munching on the hard cookies and dried fruit that Rock insisted each person carry at all times, she was suddenly gripped by a feeling of exhilaration. Everything became colorful, significant, charged with vitality. She felt she was in the midst of some tremendous experience, a watershed after which nothing would ever be the same.

All her reasons for fighting Rock, for doubting he was really interested in her, for not allowing herself to show him how much she cared for him, seemed so foolish. If she saw him again—she stopped and corrected herself—*when* she saw him again she would be honest, trust her own instincts, enjoy the time he wanted to share with her to the fullest. What did her fierce pride matter? She was ready to accept whatever part of himself Rock was willing to give.

Her heart was beating erratically and she had to control her impulse to shout and sing. Sobering after a few minutes, she remembered Rock's descriptions of altitude sickness. That probably accounted for some of the euphoria she was feeling...but not where her love for him was concerned.

Beryl took a few sips from her canteen and started climbing again, hurrying this time. She had to stop a moment later, pressing a hand against her reeling head and swaying unsteadily as black dots swam before her eyes. She attempted to calm her breathing as her vision cleared.

Glancing at her watch, she decided to time herself, sporadically tying scraps of cloth from her backpack to bushes in case she was being followed. She talked to herself in low tones, reminding herself that if she remained cool and composed, using her mind to guide her instead of allowing wild imagination and fears to gain control, she would be found.

The afternoon sky grew bleak and the sun scudded behind some clouds as a chill icy wind cut harshly through the mountain passes. After dressing in the warmest clothes from her pack, Beryl forced herself to slog upward on the steep stony path until she reached an extremely treacherous section coated by a thin sheet of glassy ice. On one side lay an awesome drop to the floor of a canyon.

Her head throbbing and her face painfully red and windburned, Beryl stopped to consider her best course of action. Then she heard a faint sound. Had she imagined it? Could the eerie wail of the wind be playing tricks on her?

The sound came again, and this time there was no mistaking it. Someone was calling her name! It echoed through the mountain pass, sending happiness and hope singing through her veins. Rock had found her, just as she'd known he would!

"I'm here!" she called, smiling as her words came echoing back to her. Down below, across a crevasse, she saw something waving, something red. She grabbed her knitted cap and began waving it in return.

"How in hell did you get there?" Rock's words were garbled, but Beryl hugged herself with excitement as she recognized his voice.

"I flew! I'm the fabled snow leopard with wings!" she shouted back.

"Wait there! Don't move—I'm coming!" With Rock's last words still echoing around her, Beryl removed her pack and sank down into a sheltered nook, answering his calls as they came nearer and nearer.

Mangmu was the first to reach her, his broad smile the most welcome sight she could imagine. Without thinking she jumped up to hug him and almost lifted the wiry little man off the ground in her gratitude.

Rock rounded the corner and stopped, watching the scene through darkened eyes. He held out his arms and she ran to fling herself into them, instinctively seeking the consolation of his flat muscled chest and the reassuring beat of his heart.

"Beryl," he murmured. He wrapped his arms around her and then slid a hand under her jacket, moving his fingers comfortingly down her spine. "There, it's all right now. I've found you." Gently his hands soothed her, stroking her hair as her lips began pressing kisses against the solid wall of his chest.

She looked up and met his dark burning gaze. Relief mingled with desperation in his voice. "I thought I'd never get to see you again!"

"Hold me tight, Rock. Please hold me. I can't stop

shaking...." Beryl nuzzled against him, seeking his warmth. His arms tightened convulsively and his mouth descended to meet her parted lips. Beryl returned the kiss, arching back as a wave of bliss washed over her and her fears and discomfort were all forgotten.

Her body had stopped shaking when he finally drew back. Taking her face between his hands, he tilted it up. "How did you ever get this far today? We've been on your trail for hours, but even Mangmu had a hard time keeping up." His thumbs teased her earlobes abstractedly as the comforting bulk of his body pressed against hers.

"When I realized I was lost I kept pressing on, hoping to catch up with you."

"But how did you get lost? If Jane's responsible for this in any way, I swear she's going to pay heavily."

"No," Beryl declared. "It was all my fault. Some herders and their yaks delayed me. Then I must have taken a wrong turn. But it was wonderful at times."

"Wonderful?" Rock looked dazed. "Don't you know you put me through the worst moments of my life today?" He rubbed his bearded jaw against her hair. She could feel his heart, thudding raggedly beneath her cheek.

She snuggled deeper into his embrace. "I think I'm talking nonsense," she mumbled. "For a few minutes this afternoon I felt totally happy and free, as if everything were perfect in life."

"That's the way I felt when you answered my call," he said huskily, his lips brushing her temple. "Promise me you'll never wander off again. I don't think I could ever go through another experience like this and keep my sanity.''

"I promise, Rock," she murmured. "I know I caused you a lot of trouble.''

"More than you'll ever know." There was a trace of grim humor in his voice. Then his eyes softened. "Beryl, I know what we agreed. I know I promised to treat you only as a friend. But I can't keep that promise. I want you too much, darling," he muttered. "Please let me hold you in my arms and make love to you tonight.''

Beryl trembled with a piercing sexual awareness. Words stuck in her throat, and she could only nod her assent.

He gathered up her pack, strapping it onto his back, and carefully replaced her cap, his hands stroking her cheeks before lightly, tenderly, tracing her lips. Beryl watched him with shining eyes that reflected the overwhelming love she was feeling for him.

CHAPTER SIXTEEN

THOSE OF THE TEAM who were left in camp ran out to greet Beryl. Jane was the first to reach her, and Beryl noted that her eyes were red rimmed and puffy. "Oh, Beryl, you're safe!" she exclaimed. "Please tell Rock it wasn't my fault. He's been so mad at me...."

Rock's voice was apologetic. "She's already told me that, Jane. Why don't you show Beryl that stream so she can wash up?"

After the evening meal Rock had the cooks prepare hot chocolate, and he poured rum in each mug in honor of Beryl's safe return. The group sipped companionably as they munched on fried yak cheese and popcorn, quizzing Beryl about her frightening experience. In the circle of warm firelight she realized there had been a change in her relationship with the others: they seemed to have accepted her totally, and there was even a hint of admiration in their attitude toward her.

Lon teased, "If it had been anyone else lost, we'd all be getting a sound lecture on delaying the expedition." His eyes twinkled, challenging Rock to answer. Laughter floated around the group.

"You're right, but it wasn't anyone else," Rock responded, pulling Beryl against him and kissing her cheek.

Beryl circled his waist with her arm, feeling a slow warmth creeping through her as she remembered what he'd said on the trail. For a moment a pang of apprehension assailed her. Should she tell Rock that no man had ever made love to her before?

It would surprise him, she knew. She had guessed that he believed she'd been involved in a sexual affair with Paul, and she had never tried to set the record straight. But explaining it was too difficult. Tonight she wanted only to have her years of innocence come to an end, to be guided tenderly and expertly into womanhood by the man she loved.

She stirred, snuggling closer against Rock, and listened as one of the team members started singing a plaintive French love song. Soon the others joined in, their voices blending sweetly with the night sounds drifting on the air.

When the song ended the team began gathering up their cups and breaking into small groups as they made their way toward their tents. Beryl started to rise, but Rock's hold on her tightened. "Let's stay here a few minutes," he murmured in her ear, his lips tracing feather-light patterns on her cheek.

Beryl sank down, relaxing against Rock, glad for a few more minutes to rest in the circle of his arms. "If you've changed your mind since this afternoon, I'll try to understand," he whispered, his teeth nibbling delicately on her earlobe.

"I want you, too," she returned softly.

Rock's arms tightened convulsively around her and then he rose, pulling her with him. "I'll join you in the tent in a moment," he said. "First, I'll go make certain everyone else has settled down."

Beryl slipped into the tent, stripping off her clothes and washing with the bucket of warm water Mangmu had thoughtfully provided. She was pulling on her nightgown when Rock entered the tent.

The moonlight floated in, outlining his lean figure, not hiding the way his gaze roamed over her body, a way that made his intentions plain. Beryl laid down her brush and faced him, her breath catching in her throat. A violent shiver darted down her spine.

Grasping her arms, Rock said, "Do you have any idea how I felt when I thought I might never hold you like this again?" Pulling her into the safekeeping of his embrace, cradling her head on his chest, he stroked her silky hair, whispering endearments in her ear. His burning words of desire sent delicious waves of response shuddering through her.

Beryl raised her head to look up into his eyes, and her throat tightened at the hunger in them. She wanted his touch so much, wanted his kiss, the sensuous feel of his smooth skin against hers; she wanted him to hold her until the outside world was blocked out and it was only the two of them, fulfilling the primitive needs they aroused in each other.

What if Rock hadn't found her? Her arms curved around his neck, her hands caressing and kneading the taut muscles there as the thought of the danger she had faced that day mingled with the passion he ignited in her. Soon they would be separated again; this time he would be the one facing a constant challenge for survival. How she would regret it if something happened and she was never able to share her love with this man who held her heart!

Moistening her lips, she offered them provocatively, pushing aside the last doubts that remained, disregarding any signals in her brain to be cautious. His mouth came down on hers, parting her lips hungrily, his tongue demanding a response with a sweet urgency that filled her with the need to be possessed by him completely.

Tantalizing fingers slipped inside her gown, engulfing her with a fire that nothing could extinguish as they cupped her breast and with slow deliberateness began teasing the nipple gently. She dug her hands into his thick hair, holding his face against hers as his kisses took on a savage intensity. His hands and lips became wild and uncontrollable as they roamed over her soft curves, kindling a desire within her that raged out of bounds.

With her body arching against his, she sensed he was reaching the limit of his patience. Through the haze of her passion she helped him to undress, her fingers curling into the rough hairs on his chest, until at last she watched unashamedly as his muscular brown frame in all its masculinity was revealed before her. His strong arms moved quickly, lifting her gently, moving her to the sleeping bag.

Her body was more alive than it had ever been, her senses heightened to a fever pitch that made her aware of the scent of pine trees, the gurgling of the nearby brook, the faint aroma of woodsmoke. But all these sweet impressions were intertwined with an all-consuming need to give herself over to the urgency of Rock's hands, which caressed her slender naked body with familiar intimacy as he removed the last barriers between them.

His lips moved down to explore the hollow of her

throat and then continued on a tantalizing trail, burning a path of desire into her already sensitized skin. His hands molded her body against his in a sensual rhythm that was pushing her past the point of no return as she whispered his name incoherently, the whole world a blur and only this moment a reality.

"Don't be afraid of me, darling," he murmured, drawing back to gaze at her, breathing like a drowning man. In answer she pulled him against her, her body consumed with need, nothing else in the world mattering to her now as he molded her softness to his hard desire. Her eyes closed in rapture as she gave herself up to new sensations and ancient rhythms, lost in the mists of bliss and wonder.

THE SOFT WHISPERING SOUNDS of the wilderness night mingled with Rock's even breathing as Beryl lay curled in his arms. Thinking he was asleep, she shifted away from him, but his hold tightened. Pulling her to him, he murmured, "Don't you dare leave." His mouth moved against her cheek, his fingers taking her chin and turning her face to his, his lips touching hers warmly and gently.

A loud insistent whisper sounded outside the tent, breaking the dark stillness with sharp clarity. "I don't think you should bother them this late." Beryl identified the voice as Lon's.

Jane's tone was equally determined. "Rock needs to know how sick Susan is."

Rock's features molded themselves into grim lines as he pulled away from Beryl. "What's the problem?" he called huskily.

"It's Susan." Lon hesitated before continuing, "I hate to bother you, but Jane says Susan's temperature is soaring and she seems to be delirious."

Rock poked his head through the tent flap. "What do you think's wrong?"

"That's the problem: we're not sure. Several others have upset stomachs and I'm wondering if it's something we ate," Lon answered.

"Give me a few minutes to get dressed and I'll be there." Resignation was evident in Rock's features as he smiled over at Beryl. "I hope this won't take long, darling."

She flushed, pulling the bedroll top over her hastily, watching amusement lighting up his eyes as he reached for his clothes. "If you're asleep when I return, do I have your permission to wake you up with kisses?" he asked when he'd finished lacing his boots.

"Do I have a choice?" Beryl countered lightly, trying to force down the lingering traces of self-consciousness she felt at the newness of their intimacy.

Rock whirled and knelt beside her, reaching for her chin. His abrupt movement startled her and she twisted away, but his hand followed, gently swiveling her face back to meet his. "We both wanted everything that happened tonight, didn't we?" His dark eyes burned into hers with a fierceness that was frightening.

"Yes," Beryl whispered, her voice low but firm.

The tension drained from his hold and he lowered his head to meet hers, his lips grazing hers tantalizingly with increasing pressure, his body trembling with arousal as he pulled her against him. He released her slowly, reluctantly. "I better check on what's happening, but I'll be back soon," he promised.

Beryl shifted into a comfortable position in the sleeping bag. She was certain Rock's presence would be required for longer than he thought, and she hoped Lon would be proved wrong in his suspicion that food poisoning was causing the illness.

Her mind drifted back over the events of the day, which had been filled with such conflicting emotions. Fear, panic, exhilaration and then. . .love. Her mind stumbled over the word. Did Rock return the love she felt for him, or was it possible she only wanted to believe that so much that she'd deluded herself? The thought made her shudder.

Please let it be more than a sexual attraction for him, she prayed. Yet she remembered his concern that she might have felt forced into submitting to his caresses. His supreme tenderness and his confession that he'd nearly panicked when she was missing did suggest that he cared for her.

Rock's return was much sooner than Beryl had expected. "Beryl," he began instantly, "I know how exhausted you are, but I need you. Susan isn't the only one who's ill. At least half the Sherpas and porters are groaning in agony, and several others in the team are sick, as well. We've set up a tent and Lon's in charge, so go and tell him exactly what you ate for supper before reporting back to me."

"Let me get dressed," Beryl responded, happy to be needed even though every muscle in her body groaned at the thought of leaving the warm softness of her bed.

Lon's pale face greeted her when she arrived at the makeshift clinic he'd set up. "How are you feeling?" he asked.

"I'm fine. What seems to be the problem?"

"That's what we're trying to determine. Tell me what you ate today."

Beryl listed what she could remember, and when she'd finished Lon announced, "Then that just about proves it. Only those who ate the soup for lunch appear to be ill. The ones who were out searching for you are fine; they had a cold lunch."

"Is it very serious?" Beryl asked anxiously.

"It could be. Susan and several of the porters seem to be the hardest hit, but with luck they'll all pull through." His weary voice revealed his own lack of strength.

"What can I do to help?"

"Rock is coordinating everything, so check with him." He pointed across the campsite, and Beryl walked to where a lantern was burning brightly.

Rock greeted her with a smile. "Maybe you can convince those who need it to drink this foul-tasting stuff," he said. "It's an emetic."

It was nearly dawn before Lon announced that the situation was under control. "Susan is still the most serious case, but barring any complications she ought to come out of it soon. I suggest we crawl into our sleeping bags and not get out until we're rested."

"Agreed," Rock responded. "Come on, Beryl."

Reagen joined the group, saying, "Susan needs your help, Beryl. Jane isn't too well herself, and I don't want to leave our sickest patient without someone to watch over her." His voice was apologetic.

Rock nodded, his strong fingers intertwining with Beryl's as he took her hand. "Let's go get your sleeping bag and move it to Susan's tent."

They walked together silently toward the tent; Rock bent down and pulled out the necessary items. "Are you too tired to do this?" he asked as they made their way to the women's tent. "I can sit with Susan and let you get some rest."

"No, I can do it," she protested.

His arm circled her waist and he stopped, pulling her against his chest. "You're pretty wonderful, Miss Bartlett," he told her, his lips pressing against her temple.

Pleasure flooded through her at his words of praise. Pulling away, she answered, "You're not half bad yourself, Dr. Rawlings."

Susan's eyes were closed, her skin still hot and flushed. Her voice sounded strained and hoarse as she tossed restlessly in her bedroll, mumbling incoherently. Beryl pushed Reagen out of the crowded tent with an order that he get some sleep, since he'd felt the effects of the food poisoning himself.

She gave Susan a sponge bath and made her as comfortable as possible before curling up against the far wall of the tent and pulling her sleeping bag over her legs. She'd been sleeping only a short time, however, when she heard the other woman stirring and thrashing around. One touch of Susan's burning forehead frightened her. The sleeping-bag liner was drenched; it wouldn't do to have her lie in that dampness.

She hurried back to her tent to get a dry liner out

of her pack. Rock was sleeping peacefully, the lines in his face relaxed and serene. Bending over, Beryl kissed him lightly and tucked the bag around his bare shoulders. It frightened her how much she cared for him. How could she have allowed anyone to become this important to her?

Remembering Susan, she broke into a swift run. She awakened Jane and asked her to help move the sick woman and change the liner. Another temperature check revealed that Susan wasn't getting any better. Jane returned to her bed and fell asleep immediately.

Beryl knelt beside Susan indecisively. Should she rouse Reagen? He had been sick, too, and he needed his rest. She sponged Susan again and then sat beside her, drowsing restlessly.

The next time she touched Susan's forehead, her skin felt normal, and her breathing appeared to be getting easier, as well. Relieved, Beryl attempted to find a relaxed half-sitting position between the two sleeping women. It was difficult to get comfortable in the confined space of the tent, but at last she propped herself up against Susan's pack and fell asleep almost instantly.

When she awoke it was warm inside the tent. The realization where she was flooded through her, and she turned toward the woman beside her. To her surprise, Susan was sitting up brushing her hair. "Wake up, sleepyhead," she said.

"No need to ask how you're feeling," Beryl responded, trying to smother a yawn.

"Except for being a little weak, I'm fine. My

worst problem is that I'm starving, but I know better than to have anything but liquids for a while. How are you doing?''

"Every muscle in me is sore from all that climbing in circles I did yesterday, but nothing else is wrong. Any idea what time it is?"

"Nearly noon. Let's go see if we can find a place to wash up; I feel as if I've been without a bath for days," Susan replied.

Susan was weaker than she had thought, but the invigorating splash helped and the two women returned to the tent area. Beryl saw the broad expanse of Rock's back as he stood talking to Lon. As if he sensed her approach he turned and held out an arm, pulling her against him when she reached him and kissing her lightly on the cheek. "I hope you feel as good as you look," he murmured.

Beryl flushed and pulled back slightly. "I'm fine and Susan's much better, too."

Rock turned to acknowledge Susan's presence, his smile deepening as he surveyed the other woman. "It's nice to see you up and around. You had us all a little scared last night."

"Makes all of you appreciate me more," she returned lightly. "Now how about serving me a big juicy broiled steak?"

"It's liquids for you, the same as for everyone else who's been sick," Lon said firmly.

Susan sighed and sank onto one of the camp chairs, accepting the glass of juice Lon offered her. "When are we pulling out, Rock?"

"Not until morning. I think everyone needs to get rested for the last few miles of our trek. Maybe the runner will catch up with us today and deliver some mail. I've never seen so many homesick faces in one place," he answered.

"Does that include you?" Beryl asked lightly.

"Not on your life," he replied, leaning over to face her, their knees touching. "I like it here."

Beryl closed her eyes, allowing herself to savor the low timbre of his voice as his strong fingers held hers. "How about you? Expecting any mail from Dallas?"

"I doubt it," Beryl told him. "Even if my family got my letters I doubt if they've had a chance to answer."

"The mail's strange around here. Sometimes it takes months and other times it catches the first plane out and arrives almost overnight." Rock leaned back, smiling at her. "If you don't get any letters I'll write you one so you won't feel left out."

"I'd like that," she agreed, no longer embarrassed to reveal the love she felt for Rock.

Throughout the afternoon Rock stayed near her, warmth and tenderness in every glance he gave her. They talked and strolled companionably around the area, their hands linked.

Dusk was falling when Rock pulled her down on a rock beside him, saying huskily, "Tonight we're not going to be separated, Beryl."

She lifted her lashes, catching the look of hunger in his eyes and feeling a quickening response coiling through her. She lowered her eyes swiftly, not willing to let him see how much she wanted him to hold her in his arms; but his head descended quickly, his lips molding themselves against hers, his arms pulling her pliant body into the contours of his own muscular one.

"Not here," she murmured, pushing back slightly.

"I'll settle for that. As long as I know you're going to be beside me all night." He moved away from her, still holding her hand in his. "Beryl..." he began hesitantly.

She looked toward him expectantly; surely now was the time for him to mention love, to tell her how much he cared for her.

A shout sounded throughout the camp. "Mail! The runner's here!"

Rock jumped to his feet, pulling Beryl with him. "You can help me distribute the mail," he told her as they hurried back to the group.

Rock patted the runner on the back as he took the bag from him, thanking him in his own language and offering him a meal. "This feels heavy," he said as he held the bag aloft for the eager group to view. Handing it to Beryl, he went on, "How about calling out the names while I talk to the runner and get the news?"

Everyone grew silent and fell back, giving Beryl room as she started calling out each name. She handed the letters to Fred, who had volunteered to distribute them to speed up the process. Rock's name appeared frequently, and his mail she laid beside her on the table, refusing to allow her eyes to linger over the return addresses when stylized handwriting appeared on the envelopes. Wasn't it being terribly sexist, anyway, to think you could tell a woman's handwriting from a man's? And Rock was certain to have family members writing to him.

Near the bottom of the stack she sighted her own name, and a thrill of excitement ran through her as she recognized Brad's firm scrawl. A small pink envelope with scallops around the flaps followed; Monica's dainty feminine imprint was obvious to Beryl even before she saw the return address.

For the first time since her trek had begun she felt the pangs of homesickness. It would be wonderful to see her family and friends again, to tell them about Rock, to share the excitement of all she had seen and done on this journey.

As she sorted the last of the mail she glanced over and met Rock's scrutinizing gaze. He grinned and moved toward her, and she handed him the large stack of letters. "You win; the majority of the mail is addressed to you."

"That's only natural, since I'm the team leader," he drawled, glancing at the letters indifferently. "Did you get anything?"

Beryl held up her two letters, nodding. "My mail must have been among those that arrive in a hurry."

"Great! If you didn't have any I was going to suggest you read mine along with me."

"Your women friends might not appreciate that," she teased.

Rock chuckled. "I'm afraid most of them are from well-wishers, so I doubt if they'd mind." Settling down on a nearby rock, he motioned for her to join him, but a sudden reluctance overtook her.

"I think I'll sit over here where the light is better."

She indicated a rock across the campsite from him where the rays from the setting sun would reach her from behind.

It was obvious the team members were content as quiet descended over the camp and they buried their heads in the mail. As far as Beryl could determine, everyone seemed to have received something. Soon a general bantering conversation began as people called out their news. Although Rock glanced up and smiled each time, Beryl noted that he shared nothing from his letters.

Reluctantly she opened her mother's letter, unwilling to stop watching the others long enough to read her own mail. As usual, Monica began with a recital of everything she had been doing for the past few weeks, ending with a paragraph in which she said she hoped none of the young men in the area heard about this latest escapade of Beryl's. "How will you ever live down a story like this, I wonder?" her letter ended.

To her surprise, Beryl's usual agitation over displeasing Monica was absent. A feeling of amusement at her mother's narrow view of a woman's role had replaced her more usual self-doubt.

"That must be a good letter," Rock called out to her.

"It's from my mother. What makes you think it's good?"

"Your satisfied smile."

"It is nice to hear from her," Beryl agreed, pleased that for once in her life she meant it.

Slowly she opened the letter from Brad, delaying the moment when she would read what he thought of her getting to take his place for part of the expedition. They had always been so close: Brad consoling her when she wasn't allowed to play Little League ball or join his boys' clubs; she practicing with him, rooting on the sidelines, being introduced to his friends.

But now the tables were turned and she was the participant, he the spectator. Glancing down at his first words, she was happy to see he shared her joy; he expressed regret that he couldn't have been the one to go but told her that he hoped she was enjoying every minute of the trip. "Don't forget to keep your journal current. I want to experience everything through your eyes when you return."

Her eyes sped down to the last paragraph, where she saw Rock's name, and then slowed to a painful crawl as she read:

I noticed you didn't mention much about Rock. I hope that means you're hanging loose where he's concerned. While I consider him to be my best friend and have nothing but admiration and respect for him, I don't think he'll ever be one to settle down and live a normal life. In other words, he's not the kind of man I'd want to see my sister fall for. Not that I think there's much danger, remembering how wary you always are. But if you find yourself getting overwhelmed, remember that the kindness he's showing you might be related to the fact that Big John is a major sponsor of this trip. In fact, it's doubtful that without dad there would have been an expedition this summer.

The letter slipped from Beryl's hand as the blood drained from her face, leaving her feeling numb and cold. Nothing Brad could have said about Rock would have bothered her more, confirming her worst doubts, the unspeakable fear of a wealthy woman. Why hadn't she thought to ask who was sponsoring the trip?

All her life she'd been nurtured on warnings about fortune hunters. The very words were spoken in hushed tones, and even now they conjured up searing memories of worried family conferences concerning one of her aunts. Beryl had been seven or eight at the time and had possessed a vivid imagination. In her mind's eye she'd pictured her new uncle as a barbaric half-clothed man standing with a poison-tipped arrow in the jungle. The devastation he'd caused in her aunt's life had confirmed that viewpoint.

When she'd reached her teens she'd watched as some of her well-off friends had defied their families to marry men who cared nothing for them. Already many of them had been unhappily divorced.

Beryl had felt she was too wary, too cautious, too alert ever to allow herself to fall in love with someone false and ruthless. Then why had she lowered her guard where Rock was concerned? Why had she buried her usual caution and never once examined his motives in pursuing her? He must have been pleased that things had worked out so well: first to have her father contribute untold sums of money to finance his dream, and then to have the innocent daughter sent along to amuse him on the trail.

At that thought the pain was replaced by a wild surge of anger, and with it came a firm resolution to bluff her way through this nightmare. She wouldn't let anyone see that tears were threatening to spill from her eyes; she'd have to wait until she could get away, all by herself, before she allowed her emotions to surface. Because the way she was feeling right now she might explode. Or was she more in danger of dying from having her wildest dreams crushed before her eyes?

CHAPTER SEVENTEEN

"BERYL!" Rock's hand gripped her shoulder, shaking her slightly. Startled, she glanced up, wondering when he had crossed over to her. He reached down and picked up Brad's letter, handing it to her.

"What did Brad say that upset you so much?" he asked quietly, kneeling beside her.

She clutched the letter convulsively, frightened at the possibility that Rock had read the last paragraph, determined never to let him know the despair she was feeling.

Laughing shakily, she replied, "It's not the letter. I'm afraid all of the events of the past twenty-four hours have caught up with me and I almost fell asleep." The moment the words had popped out she was furious with herself. Why on earth had she allowed herself to mention what had happened between them? Glancing up to see if amusement was crinkling the corners of his dark eyes, she met a puzzled frown instead.

"You don't look sleepy to me. Your pulse is racing, your face is pale, your—"

"Stop it," Beryl hissed. "Haven't I told you to keep your half-baked observations of my reactions to yourself?"

Rock's features became shuttered; leaning back,

he sat down on the grass in front of her. "Why don't you let me see that letter so I can find out what Brad said to bother you so much? Is it Paul? Did Brad tell you he's divorced now?"

"No," she said, and it took all her strength to get the one word out. If only she could show him the excerpt from the letter and they could laugh together at the idea that he was interested in her because of Big John's money!

But what if they did laugh? Would that prove anything? What could Rock say that would be proof he felt any differently about her? Weariness washed over her and she stood up, glancing around to see if anyone else was watching.

"Don't leave," Rock ordered firmly. "Something is bothering you. If it's not Brad's letter, then what in hell is it?"

"Quit being so melodramatic, Rock," Beryl managed to say with a half laugh. "You're acting as if you own me all of a sudden."

"Things have changed between us." His voice was low and forceful, his gaze piercing and direct.

"Really?" She deliberately faked a huge yawn, stretching her tensed muscles as if what he said was boring her. For a moment she enjoyed the incredulous look that widened his eyes, followed by a bitter twist of his mouth. Even the fierce pangs of love she still felt for him were not enough to make her stubborn resolve weaken.

"You're not trying to convince me that what happened between us wasn't real?" Rock exclaimed, his fists clenching angrily as he faced her.

"Hush," she whispered. "You'll have everyone watching us in a moment."

"I couldn't care less." His eyes were hard and cold.

"But I do, so if you don't mind, I think I'll go join the others in the food line." Congratulating herself mentally on the indifference coloring her voice, she rose and stepped around his rigid body.

As she filled her plate with rice and chicken she listened to the excited conversations flowing around her, trying her best to show sufficient interest when remarks were directed at her. She moved over to sit between Susan and Lon and hunched over her plate, keeping her eyes away from the spot where she had left Rock.

How much longer could she hold out against his hurt looks, his dangerous anger? Until bedtime? But what then? When he touched her all her firm resolutions would probably weaken and she would melt into a mass of responses, making her little more than his pawn, to be enjoyed and charmed until he returned to California.

Then he would put his bigger, more ambitious plans into action. She would be useful on a long-term basis; marriage to someone with her wealth would fit his plans nicely, no doubt. While she financed his trips and stayed home, he could roam around the world, meeting his daring challenges, winning glory for himself, pretending to love her when they were together. Pain seared a path through her, and she realized she had bitten her lower lip.

Turning quickly to Susan, she said in a soft voice, "Can I ask a favor of you?"

"You know you can."

"Will you tell Rock that you need me to sleep in your tent again tonight?"

Susan's eyes widened and she glanced toward the part of the circle where Rock sat. "You'd better paste a smile on your face, because we're being watched right now."

Beryl forced a slight laugh from her throat and continued in a less confidential tone, "How about my request?"

"What excuse can I give? I feel fine now. And besides, there is no way three of us can stretch out in that tent. You and I would have to sit up, because Jane still doesn't feel too strong."

Beryl stared at the ground unseeingly. "I don't mind. You tell Rock you need someone with you in case you get sick again. He'll have to believe you; you're the doctor."

"Maybe if you'll tell me what's bothering you I can think of a better solution," Susan pointed out dryly.

"No." Beryl's voice fluttered with panic. "Please, Susan. Please help me; just for tonight."

Susan patted Beryl's arm, staring at her worriedly. "You know I'll help you; after all you've done for me I could never refuse. Sure you don't want to talk to me about something?"

"No," Beryl repeated. Her denial was abrupt, but she couldn't help it. Even speaking was an effort tonight.

After rinsing her cup and plate she hurried to the tent and dragged out her sleeping bag, which Mang-mu had returned to its place earlier that day. As she reached the other women's tent, Jane peered out.

"Whatever are you doing with that?" Jane asked, frowning at the jumbled roll in Beryl's arm.

Beryl flung down her bag and the change of clothes she'd dug out of her pack, praying that Jane wouldn't demand too much explanation. "Please, Jane, I'd like to sleep here tonight. I don't want to talk about it."

Jane's eyebrows rose. "It's Rock, isn't it?" she said bitterly. "He's tired of you and he's throwing you out of his tent."

"It's not that," Beryl protested wearily, a little frightened by Jane's hostility toward Rock.

"You don't have to pretend with me. Just settle down here while I go tell Rock what I think of him."

"No, don't say anything to Rock." Beryl began backing out of the tent and felt herself bump into someone. She knew it was Rock the moment strong arms encircled her, steadying her, cradling her against him.

"What's the problem here?" he asked quietly.

Jane stuck her head out of the tent flap. "I've got a few things to tell you, Rock Rawlings. It's about time you started—"

"Calm down, Jane," Rock said firmly. "We don't allow fighting among team members. If you have a complaint against me, make it before the group tonight."

Beryl slipped from his hold while he was talking, hurrying off down the trail without looking back. When she met Susan on the trail she told her what had happened. "Please tell Rock you asked me to stay with you tonight," she begged.

"Why go to such elaborate pretenses to get away from me?" Rock's voice sounded grim as he emerged from the darkness and caught up with them. Susan gave him one swift look and hurried away, leaving Beryl to face him alone.

"Well?" Rock demanded. "Are you going to at least let me know why you don't want to spend any more time in my tent?"

Beryl shrugged, her voice refusing to cooperate as she searched wildly for an answer that would satisfy him. At length she said, "Can't a woman regret something she's done without making a big fuss about it? I think it would be better if we stayed apart these last few days of the trek."

"Why?" His voice sounded cold and tired.

"Do you always demand explanations from your women?"

Rock tensed; he spoke between clenched teeth, his nostrils flaring suspiciously. "What's that remark supposed to mean?"

"Take it any way you like." A feeling of triumph crept over Beryl at his shock and rage; her attitude was most certainly something other than he was used to!

"Quit trying to pull that sophisticated act on me," he ground out. He lowered his voice. "You should have told me you were a virgin, Beryl. If what happened between us is bothering you, I think you'd better talk it out with me. It's normal to have mixed feelings."

"You sound as if you've used that line before." Beryl held her head high and smiled slightly to emphasize the tone of amusement she wanted to inject into her voice.

"So that's what's bothering you." Rock's muscular body relaxed, and he chuckled softly. "If you're worrying about my being involved with some other woman, you can forget it. While I don't claim to be inexperienced, I can tell you that no one but you means anything to me, Beryl."

"Guess again, professor." Beryl forced a laugh. "I care nothing about the details of your private life, and I'd appreciate it if you'd adopt the same attitude toward me."

Rock moved closer to her and eyed her carefully. "I do believe you're cracking up. Why didn't I think of it before? You're in the throes of altitude sickness and it's making you light-headed and irrational. Look, I promise not to touch you tonight. Just sleep all this off and tomorrow you'll be back to normal."

"Normal?" Rage surged through Beryl at his arrogant self-confident manner. "*Now* I'm normal. Last night was when I acted irrationally."

Rock continued to eye her thoughtfully for a moment, the planes of his face harshly etched in the faint moonlight filtering through the dense trees. "I think perhaps it is best for you to sleep with the other women tonight. When you get over this little mood you're in, we'll talk like adults." He turned and walked back toward the camp fire.

Beryl leaned against a tree, filled with misery as she stared dry-eyed into the darkness around her, vowing to remain strong in her battle with Rock. Only a few more days and they would reach their destination; then she could return to Dallas and never see him again. At that thought a sob caught in her throat, but she stifled it.

It was foolish to try deluding herself into thinking that she was enjoying this conflict, reveling in hurting Rock, when all she really wanted was to spend the night in his arms, listening to his words of love, feeling his urgent need for her before dissolving into the mists of desire. If only she could forget.... But she couldn't; she wasn't made that way. Her only path lay in rejecting him firmly without ever letting him know he had hurt her, marked her indelibly in a way she could never forget.

She walked around the area restlessly until she heard Reagen calling her name. "Everyone's waiting for you," he said. "We're ready to begin our gripe session."

Beryl joined the group reluctantly, aware that agitated voices were rising as two members of the group expressed discontent. What was it Rock had said—that the Himalayas seemed to breed contentions the same way they fed the moist air passing over them, causing violent massive mountain storms? Tonight everyone was at each other's throat; the haranguing over trivialities seemed almost unsolvable.

Rock gave her only a cursory glance when she joined the group. The line of his jaw was rigid, his rugged features highlighted by the leaping flames of the camp fire, whose warmth did little to banish the chill that permeated Beryl. Did Rock suspect she had learned of his dependence on Big John to finance the expedition, she wondered. And if so, was he aware that had been the cause of her deep hurt? Perhaps only someone in her position could understand how it felt to wonder if people would care for you if they knew nothing about your background.

It wasn't in her to pretend indifference the way she had tonight, but she had no other choice. She couldn't let Rock know how much he meant to her; that would be all the incentive he needed to pursue her relentlessly, breaking down her resolve to end their encounter with her self-respect intact.

Was it foolish to allow this to upset her? Maybe Rock did love her a little for herself. As the wistful thought crept into her mind she shook back her long reddish blond hair and clenched her teeth together tightly. She couldn't allow her foolish dreams to start all over again, making her vulnerable to his persuasions.

No, he had just been using her the same as Paul had done. While she couldn't deny that he must have felt a real physical attraction for her, he had allowed it to flare out of control only because she was a Bartlett. If not, why hadn't he made even a casual reference to her father's part in this trek?

New voices were being raised, and she switched her mind back to the group. Rock's usual low voice thundered into the air. "I've had it with all of you tonight. If this expedition is to have even the slightest chance of success, we've got to forget our petty differences and pull together. As for me, I've heard as much of this as I can stand! Why don't we all get some sleep and see if our moods improve by morning? If not, we may vote to see how many are ready to call the expedition off and return home.''

He punctuated his outburst by standing up and striding toward his tent without a backward glance.

A stunned silence fell over the group. Susan was the first to speak, her voice trembling slightly. ''I've never seen Rock in such a terrible mood before.''

''Do you think he meant it about calling the whole expedition off?'' Reagen asked worriedly.

''It's not like Rock to say something he doesn't mean. What do you think is bothering him?'' Lon wondered aloud.

No one answered him, but one by one heads turned and everyone stared at Beryl. She found herself flushing as disapproving looks settled on her.

''Did you quarrel?'' Reagen probed softly.

Beryl closed her eyes and fought back an urge to cry. It would be closer to the truth if she called Rock's temper a result of thwarted ambition. But she wanted the respect of this group; she didn't want to place a schism between them and their leader just for the sake of a little sympathy on her behalf.

''You might call it that,'' she said stiffly, keeping her eyes averted as she rose.

Susan joined her. ''Rock's right, you know. We're all exhausted from last night and we're at a pretty fantastic altitude here, too. Let's call it a day and see if we can't settle things in the morning when everything looks a little brighter.''

IT WAS A BRILLIANT MORNING, chilly and crystal clear, when Beryl emerged from the tent, blinking from the glare of the sun's rays. She was stiff and cramped from having been squeezed into the small tent another night with Susan and Jane. Hurrying over to a secluded area, she ran through some stretching exercises to loosen up her taut muscles and then jogged in place for several minutes.

The absolute despair of the evening before was replaced by some budding feelings of hope and happiness. She had to be proud of herself; she hadn't fallen apart and cried or begged Rock to reassure her that his interest in her was genuine. And even though some of her remarks to him had sprung more from anger than from the calm reasonableness she'd affected, at least he didn't suspect how much he meant to her.

Only a few more days before they reached base camp, she encouraged herself. If she could hold out until then she'd be able to walk out of the whole situation with some dignity and certainly the respect of the group.

The first sight of Rock when she joined the others for a hasty breakfast almost crumbled her elation into bits. He turned around and looked at her searchingly, and she forced a broad smile, calling cheerfully, "Hey, don't eat all that food. I'm starving!"

"That's good." His voice was low and formal.

She took the roll that Gompa had filled with pieces of ham and scrambled eggs and held out her cup, giving her undivided attention to the fragrant brown stream of coffee being poured into it. "How many days to base camp?" she asked.

"It depends on the group. Two, maybe three. Why?"

Beryl bit her lip in exasperation. Why was he deliberately making it so hard for her in front of the group? "I'm interested, that's all."

"Interested in getting there so you can find a group to return to Katmandu?" he persisted.

"For heaven's sake, Rock," Susan interrupted. "For all you know, Beryl may have decided to stay and help the team out."

"How could she possibly help?" His derogatory tone made Beryl's fists clench involuntarily.

"She could run the radio at camp one. Didn't you mention you're concerned about who's going to be willing to lose the chance to reach the summit? Someone's got to do that job," Susan answered sharply.

"What does she know about radios?" he scoffed.

"Lots!" Beryl couldn't resist cutting in. "You know that Brad is a ham radio fan. For as long as I can remember he's roped me into acting as his assistant, so I know a lot about their operation." She spoke quietly, holding her fury in check.

"Then you and Susan have gone behind my back and arranged all this?" Rock's voice was dangerously controlled.

Reagen broke into the conversation, "I think it would be great for Beryl to help out. That way, if anyone gets sick or hurt and has to descend from one of the higher camps, Beryl can hold his hand and put cool cloths on his fevered brow."

"Yeah, and she can cook for us so we'll have something to look forward to between ferrying supplies up the mountain. How about it, Beryl?" Lon put in.

"Beryl? Cook? Beryl is used to having maids wait on her." Before anyone could answer his sarcastic comment, Rock continued, "Anyway, this nonsense has gone far enough. I'm the leader of this team, and I say Beryl is not setting one foot on that mountain."

He managed a semblance of a smile to soften his words before adding, "I thought today was when we were going to decide if this group is back on the track and able to cooperate enough to go on. How about it? Everyone recovered from last night's bout with the blues?"

Murmurs of agreement swept the group, and Beryl turned her back on Rock. Hastily she forced herself to eat the last bites of her breakfast so that she'd have enough energy for the arduous climb ahead of them that day.

Beryl's group was behind Rock's, and she noted that he made few attempts to check on her progress during the morning, giving her only quick assessing glances from time to time. The frozen slippery ground became more and more difficult to navigate as the day wore on, until one of the Sherpas made a walking stick for her out of a branch from the firewood pack. He showed her how to break the crust of snow and thin ice to stabilize herself.

Above were the glacier-covered mountains, looming ever nearer as they continued their ascent. When they stopped for lunch Rock told the group they had passed the fifteen-thousand-feet mark. Distinctly light-headed, Beryl leaned against a rock and watched as several Primus stoves were brought from the packs and lighted to provide enough heat for the tea.

"When do you think we'll see Mount Everest?" Susan asked.

"It's right up there." Rock pointed to an area covered by clouds. "When those clouds drift away we'll get our first glimpse. They say it's an experience you never forget, like the first time you fall in love." He cut his glance toward Beryl and gave her a piercing stare.

When she saw the others attempting to suppress amused grins, she flared at him. "First time, Rock? You're disillusioning me. I thought it was like the fairy tales, where you only love once."

"Maybe it's time you grew up," he countered. "Life isn't always perfect."

Beryl made a face and shrugged indifferently. Impulsively she added, "Your fairy tales come true, don't they? You dream about something like this expedition for years and years and then you really get to do it."

"More hard work than dreams."

His intent gaze almost unnerved her, but she continued, "I've been meaning to ask—how do you finance something like this? It must be terribly expensive." She glanced around her, including everyone within sight in her question, noting Rock's eyes narrowing in displeasure.

"We get sponsors," Jane explained. "At first it was really hard going. After all, unless you're going to do something that's never been done before, you can't get anyone interested in you. Then Rock came up with this great idea of being the first Americans to reach the top without oxygen."

"Without oxygen?" Beryl felt the blood draining out of her face. "Isn't that terribly dangerous?"

Rock answered in a low voice, "Everything has a

price, Beryl. Maybe that's what I meant by saying you needed to grow up."

"Who would sponsor something like that?" she demanded, horrified. "Isn't it nothing but a suicide mission?"

"Your dad is one of our sponsors, but it isn't suicide, I assure you. An Italian climber has done it, twice. But, no North American has ever *attempted* to reach the summit without oxygen."

"And you're the one, I suppose?" Icy fingers of fear were clutching at her heart as she stared at him; oddly, his remark about her father had barely seeped into her mind.

"I'm usually the last on any climb to require oxygen. But I'm no martyr; if I need it, I'll use it." Rising to his feet, he said, "Better get a move on if we're going to meet our goals for today."

As Beryl plodded on during the long afternoon, her mind kept going back to Rock's matter-of-fact statement of his willingness to try reaching the summit of the world's highest mountain without using oxygen. Surely he wouldn't take too many risks? But she knew he was a man who wouldn't back away from a challenge. Now every day she waited she'd suffer the torture of wondering if he was pushing himself that extra mile beyond his endurance.

Suddenly she made her decision. She wasn't going to return with an outgoing party to Katmandu; she would go on to camp one and stay there so that word would reach her sooner. Remembering Susan's suggestion that she man the radio, she felt a renewed surge of excitement.

Perhaps she could persuade Rock to at least give

her a chance. Camp one wouldn't be too difficult a climb, and she had enough experience so far to get there. That way she could be a part of the expedition and perhaps even be able to help Rock if something went wrong.

Lost in her thoughts, she rounded a curve and found the others standing as still as statues in the middle of the trail. She worked her way up to the front, near Rock and Reagen. "Look, there's Everest," Rock murmured.

Like a fairy-tale palace, an enormous fortress with gigantic steps and buttresses all crowned by a majestic dome of ice, the magic mountain of Shangri-la rose out of the swirling mists before them. Vast pyramids of ice surrounded the mountain peak, glaciers radiating in many directions and making the climb look impossible for any human creature who dared to venture there.

"Think we'll make the top?" Lon asked in a whisper.

"We're going to give it our best," Rock told him.

"That piece of forbidding granite and ice is going to be our home soon." The slight tremble in Susan's voice revealed a hint of the emotion affecting all the team members.

"How about you, Beryl? What do you think of it?" Rock asked huskily, his mask of indifference momentarily discarded in the face of this magnificent vista.

Words failed her. How could she express the awe this mountain inspired? At length she whispered, "Unforgettable. Incredible."

"That's what I thought the first time I saw you," he murmured.

Beryl drew back stiffly, her friendliness forgotten. Did he think all he had to do was charm her, flatter her, utter a few words and she'd melt in his arms? No, she had no intention of succumbing to him again no matter how much it hurt to resist. Love was what she wanted, and Rock offered only passion.

Their path led downhill for several miles, and to Beryl's surprise they entered a Sherpa village, the last outpost before base camp. Hordes of friendly villagers greeted them, and Rock communicated the group's desire to spend the night in homes functioning as inns.

Soon they were being led down the street until they stopped before one of the largest homes. A smiling family greeted them, offering them rugs to sit on and plates full of rice and lentils with cups of *chang*.

After the evening meal was finished, crowds of people filed up the narrow steps and entered the smoke-filled room. Soon the Sherpas were dancing in a single file, arms locked, providing their own music by singing as they stamped their feet in a primitive rhythm. Reagen pulled Beryl to her feet and they joined in, caught up in the holiday spirit that prevailed among these hospitable people.

The women were dressed in Chinese-style damask clothes adorned with heavy, crudely made jewelry and the multicolored, striped aprons Beryl had seen before. The men wore their long black hair braided with ribbons and wrapped neatly around their heads.

Susan had already fallen asleep, her head against the wall, by the time the last guest left. Their host spread out piles of coarsely woven rugs on the floor, indicating the team was to sleep on them.

Aware that Rock was watching her every move, Beryl woke Susan and helped smooth out the rugs, turning her back on the others when she lay down. For a while she could hear activity behind her, then at last the lanterns were turned off and moonlight shone through the only open window in the smoky room.

The long day's march caught up with her and she fell asleep almost instantly. When she turned, later in the night, she found herself staring into Rock's dark eyes. Moving quickly to escape his burning scrutiny, his disturbing closeness, she felt herself being grasped firmly by his hands.

"Lie still," he whispered. "You'll wake Susan up." As he spoke his fingers stroked her shoulders.

"Stop it," she hissed.

Harsh lines appeared in his face. "Sorry; I'd forgotten that you can't stand to have me touch you anymore. Mind telling me why?"

Beryl wished he would quit looking at her like that. His eyes were piercing the thin shell she'd managed to erect between her fierce desire for him and certain knowledge that loving him would lead only to disaster. "It's not very private here," she managed to whisper.

"Everyone's out like a light and you know it."

"You weren't," she pointed out.

"No. I haven't been able to sleep since you decided to cut me off."

Remorse mingled with sympathy threatened to swamp her, and she ground out, "Can't you stand to have someone reject you, Rock? Or do you find it impossible to believe that every woman doesn't think you're irresistible?''

Rock muttered a stifled oath as his fingers pressed into her flesh. Pulling her against him, he covered her mouth with his, his kiss prolonged and deep. She attempted to pull back, but as the kiss deepened persuasively she gave in to her growing need, returning pressure for pressure.

His arms moved around her, his hands gently roaming over her body, and his lean frame pressed against her curves. A hard muscular leg imprisoned her, making it impossible for her to resist him. To her disgust, she found she no longer wanted to push him away; even as her mind was rejecting him her arms were drawing him closer, seeking his warmth.

He drew back finally, resting on an elbow and staring down at her, his breath coming in ragged gasps, a look of raw desire etching his features. "Please, Beryl. Tell me what I've done to make you angry. I can't stand much more of this...."

If only he would speak of love, thought Beryl. *Then I would try to believe him, believe that he cares for me, that he wants me for myself.* As he continued his relentless staring, she closed her eyes and whispered, "Leave me alone, Rock."

"That's not easy." The words came out in a groan.

His undisguised arousal brought a thought to her mind. Why not use this need of his to get something she wanted? He'd been using her, hadn't he? "May I please man the radio for the team in camp one?" she asked tremulously, moistening her lips.

He stared down at her, surprise slowly being replaced by disgust. "Am I to take it that you're offering yourself to me if I'll let you do what you want?"

Forcing a light laugh, she answered, "You know I didn't mean it that way." Her voice was slightly teasing, and she saw him flinch as if he'd been struck.

"I'll put the suggestion to a vote before the group when we reach there. My vote will be no!"

Moving quickly, as if driven to escape from her, he turned away and left her staring after him, feeling thoroughly ashamed of herself.

CHAPTER EIGHTEEN

BASE CAMP AT LAST! Beryl felt fatigue and a strange sense of letdown as she looked around at the barren area dotted here and there with several primitive stone structures. What had she expected? Modern hotels? Hot and cold running water? A plush restaurant with a roaring fire in its fireplace? Laughing inwardly at such preposterous dreams, she lowered her backpack and listened as Rock gave instructions to the group.

"I'll check with the authorities to see that there are no problems with our permit and then find out if we can have the use of one of the shelters for tonight," he told them. "That ought to save a lot of valuable time. I'm hoping to move out and establish camp one first thing in the morning."

Rock's vibrant tone held no trace of the weariness evident in most of the group's reddened faces, and Beryl marveled once again at his stamina and determination. Without his unwavering drive and strong leadership ability it was doubtful if the group would have even held together during the initial trek. But it was going to take every ounce of spirit he possessed to lead them up the awesome slopes of Mount Everest.

If only she could be included in this venture! Surely Rock hadn't meant it last night when he said he would vote against her being allowed to go as far as camp one. She'd been a fool to mention it at such an awkward time. How could she bear leaving him and returning to Katmandu with a group of strangers, wondering every step of the way what he was doing, how he was feeling, whether he was going to fulfill his dream of reaching the summit? No, somehow she had to stay and contribute in some small measure to the success of the expedition, no matter what Rock thought of her motives.

He returned a short time later, his face wreathed in smiles. "We're on," he exclaimed. "Tonight we'll bed down in shelter two and then push out in the morning, ahead of the Japanese group that's due to arrive in a few days."

He glanced over at Beryl and continued, "I think I've found a way for you to get back. There's a group of British hikers here making the return trip to Katmandu within a couple of days. After I check them out, I'll make arrangements and see what supplies you'll need to go with them."

Beryl felt her stomach knot with anger over his casual dismissal of her. "What happened to the vote you said the group would be allowed to take?"

"You know I can't allow you up that mountain. What would your family think if something happened to you?"

"The same as all your families." Taking a deep breath, Beryl faced the others, gathering her courage. "I'd like very much to man the radio and assist in any way I can at camp one. If you think I've earned the right to do that with this group, I'm asking you to vote for me."

The silence was oppressive. Some of her friends lowered their eyes and looked down at the ground while others glanced at Rock, who was coolly assessing Beryl. Lon was the first to speak.

"I think the word 'earn' is important here," he said. "In my opinion Beryl has done quite a job on this trek. She's been helpful, cheerful and as hardworking as any other member. As far as I'm concerned, she's on."

"Me, too," Reagen added. "I think Rock may be letting personal feelings enter into this. If you hadn't had a quarrel, would you be against it?"

"Personal feelings have nothing to do with this," Rock insisted. "My objection is based on the fact that Beryl has no prior experience at these altitudes and did not train with us." His voice was low and calm, but the rigid set of his jawline expressed his disapproval.

"If your objections are along that line, I can report that Beryl is strong physically and shows no signs of problems with breathing," Susan cut in. "I vote we let her go with us. She has some nursing ability and that may prove very helpful."

"Frankly, I'm dying to get in that shelter. Let's take a vote and get this over with." Jane's body was trembling from the cold wind, as if in emphasis of her point.

"All those in favor of Beryl's being allowed to go as far as camp one?" Rock said tersely.

Every hand except his was raised, but Beryl felt a sense of desolation even as she savored her victory. Why hadn't Rock relented and admitted she was capable of helping the team? Was it only anger that

the group had not listened to him, or was he eager to
see the last of her?

"It's obvious I've been outvoted, and while I hope
I'm proven wrong I think we're making a mistake.
Once we get up there, if Beryl falls apart we're stuck
with our choice." Pointing toward the shelter, he
went on, "Let's get set up for tonight and pay off the
porters. We've got a lot of work ahead of us before
we can pull out in the morning." He avoided looking
at Beryl as he led the way inside.

After a hasty meal Beryl watched as Rock counted
out rupees and paid the porters. He shook their
hands and congratulated them on their part in making the trek a success. "Remember," he said, "you
can tell your children and grandchildren someday
that without your help this group could never have
climbed the tallest mountain in the world."

As the last of the porters left the shelter, Beryl was
finally gripped by the realization that she was going
to be allowed to continue with the expedition. Rock
didn't need to worry that she would become a burden
on the team, she reflected. She had to make good—
not only for the sake of the others but for herself.
This was her chance to prove that she was as capable
as the rest of them. And perhaps at the same time she
could make Rock look beyond the fact that she was
the daughter of the largest contributor to this expedition; make him actually fall in love with her.

But why torture herself with thoughts like that?
No, Rock's opinion of her no longer mattered. What
she did on this mountain had to be for herself, even if
she came away with a store of painful memories to
last a lifetime. . . .

"Strategy meeting," Susan whispered softly, startling her into alertness. "You're a part of everything from now on, partner."

Rock was speaking to the hushed group. "Many of us here in this shelter tonight have been dreaming about the struggle ahead for more than five years; some as long as ten or fifteen. I think we owe it to ourselves to work together, to forget any differences that may have surfaced as a natural result of being in such close company these past few weeks, and to operate as a team. That way we can get at least one of us—any one of us—to the top of this mountain. But it will take all of us to do that; each will have to do his part or we will accomplish nothing."

"How will you choose the summit team?" asked Jane, voicing the question in everyone's mind.

"Everyone except Beryl has a chance. We'll all be given opportunities to lead as we set up camps. I believe the selection will be a natural one, resulting from the ones having the most stamina left by the time we establish camp six."

He pulled a chart out of his pack and held it up, showing them a sketch of the mountain with the proposed campsites marked out clearly. Watching the lantern lights flickering over his familiar profile, his strong chin and firm mouth, Beryl felt a sharp sense of loss.

He turned slowly, sensing her scrutiny of him, and they looked into each other's eyes across the shadowy room. Rock smiled briefly, his eyes softening, and Beryl trembled, looking away, unwilling to let him see the love she knew must be visible on her face.

The discussion ended with cups of hot chocolate

being served and toasts proposed. When success for Beryl was mentioned by one team member she felt a sharp sense of pleasure, pushing out the thoughts that tormented her as she met Rock's eyes over the rims of their cups.

At four-thirty the next morning, Beryl felt herself being shaken awake by Susan. "Time to fall out. We're going to get our supplies sorted out and do some real mountain climbing today."

Her nerves tingling with excitement and anticipation, Beryl jumped up and followed Susan out of the shelter. The air was bone-chilling cold, but the morning star shining overhead proclaimed good weather ahead.

By the time a hasty breakfast was over Rock had outlined everyone's job, including Beryl's. Evidently he was going along with the group's decision; there was no further reference to the matter of her status.

After directing two of the men, along with several of the Sherpas who had remained to assist, to scout the route to camp one, Rock told the others to relax in the shelter until they returned. "I'd like to speak with you a moment, Beryl," he added, his eyes searching her face impersonally.

Beryl moved toward him, matching his faint frown with one of her own. Rock waited until the last straggler had entered the shelter before speaking.

"I think we need to get a few things straight," he said harshly. "From now on you're one of the team, and as such, all special privileges you've had in the past are canceled."

The force of the anger that surged through Beryl made her feel almost light-headed. "Special privileges, Dr. Rawlings? Are you referring to sharing your tent?''

''You know I wasn't, but if you want to discuss that I'm willing.'' He glared down at her with a menacing look.

Momentarily chagrined as she realized that she'd misunderstood Rock's words, Beryl stumbled over her next sentence. ''That's the last topic in the world I want to discuss with you. What were you referring to?''

His body relaxed as the tension visibly drained from him. ''Your insolent disobedience of my orders. On the rest of this expedition you are to obey every word I say, no exceptions; the success and well-being of the whole team depend on that, not to mention your own life. Is that understood?''

''Yes, sir,'' Beryl snapped before turning to go inside the shelter.

Rock's hands grasped her and whirled her around to face him. ''Then show it by waiting until I'm through speaking before turning your back on me. You and I have to put aside any personal differences and work together from now on. I've already lost sleep over you, snapped at the team and generally fallen apart—''

''You're blaming me for your actions?'' She cut him off sharply.

''My *reaction* to you would be more accurate; but call it anything you like. As far as I'm concerned, until I stand on top of that peak up there—'' he paused and pointed up to the top of the snow-clad mountain, bathed in pink hues from the rising sun ''—until I reach that peak, you're nothing to me but another team member. And I'm going to feel free to eat you alive if you don't pull your weight or try using your feminine charms on me to overrule some of my decisions. Is that understood, Miss Bartlett?''

''You left out that I might try using my father's name as bargaining power with you.''

''Your father is only a name to me,'' he spat out contemptuously.

''Nothing more?''

''Nothing!'' From the deep lines furrowing his brow Beryl could see that her insinuation had been lost on Rock. Shrugging, she asked sarcastically, ''Would you like me to kneel before you and offer my vow of allegiance, Sir Rawlings?''

''If I thought it would help us get up that mountain, I'd make you crawl to camp one.''

''I think you would.'' Beryl felt sobs of frustration building in her throat as she added quietly, ''I promise to obey your every command. May I go now?''

His hold slackened and a hand moved across her cheek, the grazing knuckles sending ripples of sensation through her, undoing all her good intentions not to let him see how much his merest touch affected her. ''When we get back to Katmandu and this is all behind us, we'll celebrate, Beryl. Just the two of us,'' he said huskily.

She moved away quickly and entered the shelter without answering. Another moment and she would burst into tears on the spot. She was undecided which was harder to bear—his autocratic manner or the sensual implication of his last statement. She intended to celebrate the team's victory all right, but that didn't mean she was willing to take up her relation-

ship with Rock on the old basis again, on his unstated
terms.

By the time the scouts returned it was midmorning
and a few clouds had formed in the sky. The men accepted cups of hot tea and reported that the climb to
the site selected for camp one was less difficult than
had been feared. "Then let's prepare to leave," Rock
decided, naming off the order they were to take.

The strongest climbers were positioned in front,
with the task of stretching out a rope for those following them. Then came the Sherpas and Beryl, using the
rope as a hand line. The team members shouldered
their packs and started out in good spirits.

Within ten minutes it began snowing lightly, the
soft moist flakes falling on Beryl's nose, dampening
her wool cap and even threatening to soak the yellow
nylon Windbreaker she wore over her heavy outer
clothes. She watched as the climbers ahead fixed their
lengths of rope, using ice screws and picks, cutting
steps into the steeper ice with their axes.

Rock directed the operations, his voice ringing out
cheerfully in the icy stillness. "If we can get these
loads up and our tents set up, some of us can start
toward camp two in the morning," he encouraged
them.

As the day wore on the snow turned to a bleak
drizzle of rain and slush, but Beryl pushed ahead.
She wondered how the small Sherpas, clad in their
dark clothing with heavy loads on their backs, could
walk so nimbly in front of her. Shouts and cheering
alerted her to excitement ahead and she quickened
her pace, the feel of the rough rope on her hand suddenly becoming bearable.

"Camp one!" she heard Susan calling over her shoulder. "We're almost there. How are you making out?"

"Wonderful! I don't know how I ever survived without this experience in life," Beryl answered teasingly.

When she arrived where the group had stopped, she saw Rock and several others shoveling out bases to erect the tents. From several of the Sherpas' loads came heavy red canvas and shiny poles—the components of the two large tents that would be set up for camp-one headquarters and the storage of supplies.

Several of the team preferred their own two-man nylon tents and were scouting around for the best location for them. The Sherpas chose to stack boxes and cover them with plastic tarps; but Rock, knowing what a cold night lay ahead, issued kerosene stoves so that they could brew tea.

"That seems cruel," Beryl remarked to Reagen. "We'll be sleeping in down bags in fancy tents while they shiver in those shabby shelters."

"They seem to prefer them to our modern equipment. At least, Rock offered them the use of the tents, and they refused."

His answer mollified Beryl, and she wandered around reading the labels on the boxes until she found the ones designating food.

"Ready to cook?" Lon teased her.

"You don't think I can without Gompa's help, do you?"

"To be honest, I doubt it."

"Since it's mainly a matter of pouring hot water

over the freeze-dried stuff, I'll probably manage. But I will admit I have a lot to learn in that area.''

Lon glanced over at Rock. ''Does Rock know that?''

''It's none of his business,'' Beryl returned tartly.

Camp one was fully established before sunset. Rock opened a couple of food boxes, passing out cookies and candy to the Sherpas, while Lon aided Beryl in melting snow to heat water for their evening meal.

A Frisbee game was in progress outside the tent on the slippery surface, and good-natured yells could be heard cheering on the participants. Any rancor left over from quarrels along the trail seemed to have been forgotten in the excitement of camping along the slopes of Mount Everest itself.

When dinner was ready, everyone trooped indoors to sit on the crates lining the sides of the tent, and Beryl accepted the gentle teasing that accompanied the meal she had prepared. The thought that she might have been spending the night at base camp with a group of strangers, unable to steal glimpses of Rock as he leaned back talking to several of the men, seemed unbearable.

They stayed up late that night, joking, laughing, reading, writing letters. Beryl bent over her journal, determined to record everything that happened for when she returned to Dallas and began working with Fred on his book.

She was absorbed in writing a detailed description of the climb when she felt movement beside her. Turning, she saw that Rock had wedged himself into a small space next to her.

"Writing in your diary?" he asked softly.

"I told you this is a journal. I've been keeping an account of every day's events."

"Very good. And since you'll be manning the radio you'll soon be the most knowledgeable person on the team about everyone's activities."

Beryl felt immediate pleasure at his comment. "How about recording the radio messages? Is there any equipment for that?"

"Yes, the radio's already equipped for that, but we'll probably want to edit it. At this altitude, tempers sometimes flare, and people say things they later regret." His eyes probed hers.

"How about you? Are you regretting something?" Beryl's green eyes met his unflinchingly.

"You could say that." He bit his lower lip thoughtfully, a muscle twitching in his jaw, revealing his tension. "I'm letting all that slide until later."

Silence stretched between them tautly before Rock spoke again. His voice was low, his words barely above a whisper. "Forget everything that's happened between us for a minute, Beryl. I need your advice on something important."

Beryl stared at him in confusion for a second. What could Rock possibly want to ask her advice about? He certainly needed no help in directing the actions of the team, and she couldn't imagine he'd want her opinion on his personal life. She hesitated before nodding briefly. "Okay, what is it?"

Rock looked around at the other people in the tent and then stood up, motioning for her to follow him as he led the way to a more secluded corner behind some of the supplies. It was much darker there, and

Beryl had trouble seeing Rock even though they were crowded intimately, disturbingly, against each other.

She forced a brisk tone into her voice. "What's the problem?"

Rock pulled a tiny flashlight out of his pocket and a crumpled envelope, as well. "It's a letter from Kent," he said crisply, imitating her businesslike manner. "I'd like you to read it."

"Me? But wouldn't your brother object?"

"Go on, read it," he ordered harshly. "Don't worry; it isn't anything concerning you. I just need your advice."

Beryl slid the crumpled pages out of the envelope and smoothed them on her lap before taking the small flashlight from Rock's hand. "When did you get this letter?" she asked, eager for something impersonal to say, some comment that would cover her trembling awareness of his closeness.

"In the last batch of mail," Rock said softly, and Beryl flinched as she remembered what that lot of mail had brought her.

It was several moments before her eyes focused on the page before her, and then what she saw almost forced an exclamation out of her tense throat. Kent had discovered he wasn't in love with Susan! The woman he'd been dating before his illness had visited him and he realized that she was the one he still cared for. He was asking Rock to break the news to Susan gently.

"You tried to warn me that romances between doctors and their patients aren't always the real thing," Rock sighed, running a hand through his hair. "Do you think Susan's going to be too upset?

Maybe I shouldn't tell her until after the expedition.''

"Oh, you should. . . . ''

Rock suddenly cracked one fist against the base of the nearest crate, his angry outburst making Beryl jump in surprise. "I can't believe my brother's going to let Susan down like this." His words fairly tumbled out. "She's a fine girl and I don't want to see her hurt.''

"But she won't be hurt; she'll be relieved!" Beryl's words burst out, causing Rock to stop his sentence midway.

Surprise held him in check for endless seconds. "What do you mean?" he asked finally.

Beryl hesitated, feeling caught in a muddle, wishing that Susan were there beside her to explain. Then sudden decision made her spine stiffen with resolve. Rock would have to be told the truth, and now was as good a time as any. "Susan's in love with Reagen. And he loves her, too.''

Rock's sharply indrawn breath was followed by a muttered oath. "I haven't seen anything to indicate that," he bit out angrily. "Reagen seems to be directing most of his attention to you.''

"Reagen was just pretending to like me," she corrected softly, carefully. "They used to be engaged, and Susan asked me to help—''

"Deceive me?''

"That's not fair. You wouldn't have understood.''

"Understood how much you were enjoying driving me wild by pretending you were interested in Reagen?" Rock's mouth twisted into a bitter line.

Beryl grabbed his arm. "Not that! You didn't

want to believe that Kent was only feeling gratitude or admiration for Susan. She really loves Reagen and she asked me to give her this chance to see if he cared for her. Please don't be angry with Susan."

Rock glanced down at her hand and she withdrew it. "I'm not angry with Susan; I'm relieved that Kent's change of mind won't hurt her. But how could you have agreed, Beryl?" His voice trailed off into silence.

"I gave my word, Rock. But it all worked out for the best; Susan and Reagen are so happy together."

"I seem to have been fooled rather badly," Rock said flatly. "I guess my judgment of character isn't as good as I thought."

Beryl tensed in angry reaction. "Everyone makes mistakes," she reminded him.

"It would have saved all of us a lot of trouble if we'd been honest right from the start." The finality of his remark left no room for Beryl to answer, and he stood up, obviously waiting for her to follow. "I'll leave you to tell Susan, then," he added. "And at least I can rule out Reagen from my list of worries."

When they returned to the area where the others were sitting, Rock announced, "I think bed's in order for everyone. We've got a lot to do tomorrow."

"What are our plans?" asked Jane.

"Rest day for all of you. Mangmu and I are scouting out the site for camp two."

"I don't think that's wise." Susan spoke authoritatively. "Mangmu's probably in shape, but this altitude is a little high for you to have adjusted to it yet. I recommend a rest day for you, as well."

"If I wake up with any problems I'll call it off, doc." Rock moved toward the tent opening. "Those of you going over to the supply tent to sleep had better come with me. We can't waste too much kerosene."

As soon as he left, Beryl motioned to Susan. "I've got some fantastic news for you."

Susan listened attentively as Beryl explained about Kent's letter, smiling and nodding. "It happened just as I predicted. And now I suppose this means you and Rock have patched up your differences?"

Without giving Beryl time to reply, she hurried over to Reagen's side.

THE SKY WAS CLEAR the next morning, and Rock wasted no time lingering over the pancakes Beryl cooked for breakfast before setting off with Mangmu to climb higher. Armed with mountain-climbing and ski equipment, cameras, binoculars, two-way radios and a backpack filled with a lightweight tent and enough food for several days, he and Mangmu trudged off.

Beryl stood watching the departing figures, bright-colored specks on the vast snowfield, until they disappeared from sight. It was uncertain when she would see Rock again, and there was still so much unsaid between them. . . .

The sight of the peaks above reminded her of the dangers he faced. Would he take the precautions he always reminded the others about: drinking plenty of fluids, stopping to acclimatize at the higher altitudes, watching his step in precarious places? At the thought of him rapeling—descending the mountain by means of a rope passed under one thigh, across the body and over the opposite shoulder—a shiver of fear ran down her spine. But in the next instant she chided herself for her concern. Rock Rawlings had managed to survive for many years before he met her!

The Sherpas spent the day ferrying supplies from base camp to camp one until the supply tent was nearly filled. Even though there seemed to be enough for everyone, Beryl knew that more than one expedition had been forced to give up after running out of supplies. She was going to do her part to see that nothing under her supervision was ruined or wasted.

One of the men spent several hours familiarizing her with the radio, and she found herself looking forward to the time Rock had set to call in. At least she'd hear his voice every day, even if the messages were for the others on the team.

Spirits were high that night in the big canvas tent. A huge pot of tea brewed on the stove. The group dined appreciatively on spaghetti and meatballs with cookies for dessert, while a battery-operated cassette player blasted out a string of fairly current hit tunes.

"Do we have plenty of batteries?" Beryl asked.

"Several hundred," Susan told her, leaning back drowsily. "Are you glad you got to come up here?"

"It's wonderful! But without training I don't think I'd like to risk much more. How about you? A little nervous?"

"Not about the climb; only about my chances to reach the summit. I'm not sure what my endurance level will be at that altitude, but I'm not going to stop trying until Rock chooses the assault team."

"Do you think Rock is being foolish in trying to climb to the top without oxygen?" Beryl was unable to keep the anxiety she was feeling out of her voice.

"Rock isn't foolish or impulsive; his every move is carefully thought out, so you don't need to be concerned."

The radio crackled and Beryl jumped to her feet. She crossed the room quickly, clicking on all the appropriate switches as Rock's first communication was received at camp one.

His voice was clear and vibrant; she could almost see him. "Things are great up here," he informed the group. "We've set up the tents and need two volunteers to bring the Sherpas up with some loads tomorrow before we can push on to camp three. One of the volunteers will get a chance to lead."

Several men spoke up at once, drowning out Susan's and Jane's voices. "It sounds as if you've got an army volunteering," Beryl observed dryly.

"Then I'll have to choose. I'd like Reagen to come because he's good at tying those knots in the rope. He can choose his own partner to accompany him."

After giving several more instructions Rock lowered his voice, and its timbre changed subtly as he asked, "Before I sign off, how are you, Beryl?"

Quiet descended over the noisy tent at the sound of his words, and Beryl felt herself flushing, grateful that her back was to the others. "I'm fine. No problems here at camp one."

"Then take care," came Rock's low chuckle. "I'll call back in at six in the morning."

Later that night as she lay in her sleeping bag, listening to the labored breathing that was common in the thin air, Beryl tried to keep from remembering the surge of desire she had instinctively felt upon hearing Rock's voice. He was only having fun at her expense, she reminded herself, no doubt making certain the dumb little Bartlett kid was happy so that future expeditions could be financed. But why couldn't she replace her loneliness with contempt for him? Why did she long to feel his arms around her right now, his mouth pressed against hers in an endless kiss?

Those who were left behind the next morning became restless, and it was with a sense of relief that Beryl heard Rock announce that all except three were to start forward the following day. Rock himself had reached the location for camp three and along with Reagen had set up several more tents brought up by the Sherpas. Everything seemed to be going according to schedule, and anticipation was evident on every face as the group crawled into their sleeping bags that night.

They were becoming accustomed to the numbing cold, so that only the task of getting up each morning remained a torture. When the main group left on the third day, Beryl waved them off excitedly. Lon and Jane stayed behind, and Jane was inconsolable, claiming that Rock was deliberately discriminating against her.

Lon managed to quiet her down; he reminded her that this was a team effort and everyone shared the glory. "If Rock feels we belong here, we do," he stated unequivocally. "You've been on climbs before; he always pulls a surprise near the end and picks someone who's been the best at backing the others. For the moment we have to do our part here.''

The day dragged by until the radio calls started coming in later that evening. The teasing and bragging that came from the various camps indicated a healthy competitive spirit, mingled with a strong sense of team unity.

Rock ended the air time once again by talking personally to Beryl for a few minutes, his voice still as intimate and coaxing as the first time. She was beginning to treasure these few moments, no longer caring what the others might think. Even if he was only making certain things were running smoothly at camp one, these would be the memories she would cherish when back in Dallas.

The next day started out with more work as the first of the sick cases straggled into camp. Susan, who was at camp three, discussed the illnesses on the radio, diagnosing and prescribing the medicines she had left with Beryl. Mostly sore throats, coughs and muscle injuries filled up the sick bay, but Beryl was kept busy making the patients comfortable and administering their medications.

On the fifth day Reagen returned from camp five with a hoarse voice and a case of sniffles. When Rock radioed in that night, he grumbled, ''I'm beginning to wonder whether we'd have such a lot of illness if there weren't a beautiful nurse holding everyone's hand.''

''Jealous?'' Reagen asked, leaning over Beryl and taking the mike from her hand.

''You're right about that!'' Rock returned. ''Just remember that I still don't trust you completely.''

Beryl jerked the mike back, sputtering, "I'm perfectly capable of taking care of myself! You tend to your ropes and ice picks and I'll take temps and give out the capsules down here."

"That's the way," joined in Susan, who was listening from camp three.

After Rock had signed off, Beryl realized that she was finding it harder and harder to remember why she'd felt such anger over Brad's remarks in his letter. Could it have been a case of overreaction on her part? She could have given Rock a chance to explain. If he had to descend to camp one, maybe they could discuss it.

Sitting up in the dark in her sleeping bag, she felt a blast of cold air, reminding her that it might be a long time before she saw Rock again in this icy barren wilderness.

CHAPTER NINETEEN

TWENTY-FOUR DAYS they had spent on the mountain now, and morale had dropped almost as low as the subzero temperatures. After the first few halcyon days of sunny weather and bright skies, the demons of the mountain had vented their furies with severe storms that lasted two or three days, followed only by brief respites when little or no progress could be made by the team.

On day twenty-five, things were no better. At camp five Rock reported that his altimeter registered a dramatic gain as the barometric pressure dropped. Powerful gusts had hit his tent and pressed the walls down, bending the fiberglass poles almost to the breaking point. His voice was muffled by the howling of the wind as Beryl attempted to put him in contact with the other camps strung along the mountainside.

"Think your tent will go?" she heard one of the men asking him.

"If it does, we're in big trouble," he replied wearily.

"What will you do?" Beryl broke in.

"Dig a snow cave; I've done it before." Rock's voice was hoarse, his breathing raspy.

Concern for him flooded through her, and she

blurted out impulsively, "Do you have enough food up there? Are you sure you're warm enough?"

"Are you volunteering to climb up here and take care of me?" Rock's amusement spilled into the tent.

So much for her worry, Beryl thought, disgusted with herself for revealing how much she cared for him.

"I'm only checking in order to write up your experiences. In the future your fans might be interested," she replied tartly.

"I'd almost forgotten my legion of fans. Instead of spending your time writing in your diary, why don't you write me a letter and send it up with the next person coming this way?"

"That won't be necessary," Beryl answered in a crisp voice. "One of the Sherpas brought a bag of mail from base camp yesterday, and as usual most of it was for you. Would you like to hear one of them?"

Ruffling through pages of her journal loudly, she improvised, "My darling Rock. I dream of you night and day and long for your return. All my love—"

Rock interrupted. "That sounds like a beautiful woman from Texas I know. The one who's six foot three—"

"Five feet eleven and nine-tenths in my stocking feet, thank you," Beryl sputtered. "But your guess is wrong. This one is signed Suzy Sweet Lips."

Rock's chuckle was rich and warm. "Now how could I ever have forgotten old Suzy?"

"Say, if there's any mail in camp, how about checking to see if I got one from my wife," said a voice from camp two, and soon Beryl was busy calling out the names of everyone with mail, somehow feeling better for her frivolous exchange with Rock.

It seemed more like their early days together; days she remembered now as being filled with teasing and laughing and touching. All of her anger was gone, melted like snow, and only the good memories remained to haunt her.

When the latest storm had still not abated the next day, tempers reached the explosion level and Rock spent his radio time quelling arguments and rumbles of discontent as the climbers disagreed over future strategy. Jane was particularly bad-tempered, having been forced to retreat as far as camp two after falling on the slippery hard-packed ice and sustaining a nasty cut, which Susan had stitched up. Beryl had noticed there were no letters for Jane among those delivered the day before, and she wondered if that might be what was bothering her.

In a mild diplomatic voice Rock reminded Jane that when the weather cleared she would be able to resume her climb. "But I have something to say to you, Jane, and to everyone else listening. Whoever reaches the summit will be carrying the hopes and aspirations of the whole team. Any glory earned will be shared by all of us."

That night Beryl wrote in her journal:

The furies have stopped us, in the form of violent weather, and I can sense a real worry that our supplies might run out before we get enough clear weather to see one of our teammates reach the top.

Illness is stalking the group and spirits are low. Several have even discussed leaving the mountain. Rock was displeased, but he didn't try persuading them to remain. Only determination and strong motivation can carry anyone to the top of this awesome mountain.

Laying down her pen, she stared around the tent, the other two team members with her already asleep. Was climbing a mountain really any different from loving a man as unattainable as Rock Rawlings? Both were adventures filled with pain and uncertainty. But still they were capable of holding you in their thrall, enmeshed in dreams and desires that were impossible to resist.

The next day dawned clear and a reshuffling took place: Susan ordered anyone sick to come down the mountain, and the climbers who had recovered began making preparations to return up. Rock radioed in that evening with the jubilant news that four had reached the site for camp six and were poised for the final assault.

"Those of you strong enough to carry survival equipment and enough food for a minimum of three days may join us tomorrow if the weather holds out. The summit team will be chosen then," he explained.

Loud cheers accompanied his announcement from every camp except the one presided over by Beryl. Only Jane remained with her.

"I knew it!" Jane stormed. "I knew from the beginning that I'd be stuck here."

"Hold on, Jane," Rock's voice broke in. "Susan says your cut won't be sufficiently healed; I understand you're still having a mild rise in temperature."

"I'm better; Beryl will verify that," Jane returned eagerly.

"Let's stick with the thermometer reading," Rock said gently. His voice took on a harsher note as he added, "It's the doctor's orders for you to remain at camp one. Under no circumstances do I want Beryl left alone. Is that understood?"

"What choice do I have?" Jane moaned before stretching out in her sleeping bag.

Morning brought little relief from the miserable weather. The snow that had begun falling the night before had stopped, but the sky was dismally gray and overcast. Jane chafed and fretted all morning and at noon began dressing for the outdoors.

"Where are you going?" Beryl inquired, eyeing the woman's heavy outer suit and the supplies she was stuffing into her pack.

"I'm going to join the ones at the top," she muttered, pushing her fingers into thick gloves and slamming a cap on her head. With her snow goggles strapped around her forehead she started through the tent opening.

"Jane, please don't. Remember Rock's orders. He'll never choose you to be on another team if you disobey," Beryl pleaded, concerned at the wild look in the other woman's eyes.

"It's more important that I prove to myself that I'm not afraid," she muttered. "I came on this trek to do that and I've got to keep trying. I'll never forgive myself if I don't make one last effort."

Beryl reached for the other woman, desperately trying to think of some way to stop her, but Jane brushed her off and strode out of the tent. Soon she became a mere speck on the horizon, almost stumbling several times as she poked her ski poles into the ice and clung to the ropes left by the previous climbers.

Running worriedly inside, Beryl attempted to reach Rock at camp six, but there was no response. At last she roused Lon in camp three.

"Jane headed out toward camp two claiming she was going to join those ready to reach the summit. I tried to stop her, but she was too determined," she told him breathlessly.

"I knew she was close to the breaking point. But don't you worry about her: she's got a lot of experience and determination. I'll call the others in camp two to watch out for her. It's not too far, and they'll know how to calm her down when she reaches them."

It was several hours later when Rock's voice crackled through the air. Beryl hurried to the radio and answered.

"I hear Jane left," he said without any preliminaries. "Are you there all alone?"

"Yes. Any word of Jane?"

"No one's answering from camp two, but I'm sure she's okay. It's you I'm worried about. I'll send someone down to stay with you."

"Don't you dare!" Beryl protested. "Anyone who has to return here will resent it. I'm safe."

"Then I'll come myself. I'll try to make it as soon as possible."

Shock flooded through Beryl as she realized the enormous sacrifice Rock was offering to make for her. "No, no," she insisted. "I don't want you coming. Promise me you won't?"

There was a long hesitation on the radio before Rock agreed, "If you're sure you're fine we'll let it ride until morning, then. But take care, Beryl. Call me immediately if anything bothers you."

"What can bother me up here?" Beryl scoffed.

"Around three in the morning you'll probably change your mind. Promise you won't hesitate to call?"

Embarrassed and a little angry that his solicitude might have been heard by the others, Beryl signed off. She turned on the cassette player and picked up one of the worn tattered paperback novels that had been left behind. The afternoon loomed before her, lonely and quiet.

When radio time came around that evening, she learned that Jane had arrived safely at camp two, hours after she left. She was in a dazed condition with her fingers and toes almost frostbitten. "As soon as she's stronger, I'm ordering her back down to your tent so that you can nurse her," Susan informed Beryl.

All the other team members teased Beryl about having a chance to be alone, something that was considered a luxury after so many days of sharing cramped close quarters. Rock repeated his instructions for Beryl to call him immediately if she needed him.

"I'm sure I'll be fine," she answered stiffly, wishing he wouldn't persist in emphasizing her dependency on others.

"Give the guy a break," Reagen chimed in. "He really just wants to hear you say you need him."

"That'll be the day," Rock answered coolly. "We'll sign off for now, Beryl. Take care."

Snuggled down in the soft bedroll, Beryl relaxed into its warmth, pleased that she felt no anxiety over being left alone in such an alien environment. She felt certain some of the team members would descend the next day; there were those who were weary and homesick, wishing they'd never started on this expedition. They would use the excuse that she needed their company to give up the struggle.

She awoke just before dawn and sensed that something was wrong. *No, not now; not another storm when I'm all alone,* she pleaded silently. But there was no doubt, she realized when she lifted the tent flap to see a black starless sky. Big cold snowflakes were silently falling and building into drifts along the walls of the tent.

For her it meant being alone for a longer period than she'd anticipated. But for those up the mountain it was the worst possible news. At best, it meant another delay at a time when everything had seemed to be going right at last. But worse than that, the climbers might have to give up their quest entirely.

She slipped back into her bedroll after lighting the small stove and placing a large pan of freshly fallen snow on it to melt. When she awoke again, hot tea or coffee would be welcome.

It was after six when the radio crackled, and she clicked the volume up. "How are you?" Rock asked.

"I'm fine. The yetis stayed away. How's the weather up there?"

"Horrible. Reagen and I are just about at our limit with all this togetherness."

"Sounds like a bad case of cabin fever to me. It's snowing heavily here, too."

"Well, stick inside that tent and don't forget to call me if anything goes wrong, darling."

His use of the endearment sent a spark of pleasure flickering through her, and she drank her cup of tea thoughtfully. There was no question that she longed to see Rock, to be alone with him, to talk intimately and attempt to straighten out their misunderstanding. But first she needed to sort out her own feelings. Enough time had passed since she'd received her brother's letter to allow her to think more clearly. Hadn't Brad always warned her against falling for any of his friends, worried that she'd be hurt by taking their friendly flirtations seriously? Perhaps that was all his warning had meant.

She retraced the moments she'd spent with Rock. When had he done anything to make her think he was self-centered, ruthless, greedy? Instead he had been loving and kind, considerate of everyone else's feelings at the expense of his own. There was no doubt in her mind now; she'd overreacted. She had let the paranoia that infects the superrich color her thinking and cloud her judgment. But was it too late to straighten things out?

As the long day dragged on she began to have hopes. Tonight when Rock called she was going to urge him not to attempt the summit without oxygen. Perhaps in that way she could let him see how important he was to her, let him know that the glory he could win meant nothing compared to his safety.

It seemed as if the last half hour before radio time would never pass, but at last Beryl picked up the mike and eagerly turned to the frequency for camp six. No static greeted her ears. She fiddled with the dials impatiently, realizing there had been none of the usual intermittent garbled transmission for several hours and that never once had she heard the faintest sound from the equipment. After several futile attempts she stared in horror at the machine.

Surely she wasn't cut off from contact with her teammates, alone in the middle of a swirling snowstorm? *Don't panic,* she warned herself, taking several deep gulps of the thin air. *If you can only remember all you've been told about how this monster works, everything will be okay.*

Batteries! Of course, all she needed do was change the batteries. She dug into the supply box eagerly and pulled out what she needed, upsetting several other things in her frenzied hurry.

After removing the old batteries and inserting the new, she tried again. Still no sound. Several hours later, after running through the instruction books and trying each dial, she admitted defeat. The radio was out and she was alone in a raging blizzard!

The long night was pure torture. It seemed as if the deities' fury over the team's invasion of the mountain had deepened, and they spit out vicious howling winds and swirling snow. Several times Beryl peered out the tent flap, frightened by the accumulated snow, worried that she might be buried alive.

At last sleep claimed her—but with it came a terrible dream. She and Rock were seated at a huge table laden with food: luscious fresh tomatoes, crisp cucumbers and tangy broiled grapefruit halves. Beryl reached eagerly for the grapefruit in front of her, but without warning long fingers jerked her plate from her; and fiendish laughs echoed around her as all the food was snatched away, leaving her sobbing in frustration.

She sat up and stared around her, feeling the numbing coldness of the air outside her sleeping bag as it shocked her into wakefulness. She stopped the sobs choking up her throat, knowing it was important to conserve her breath, and then lay back down wearily.

She spent the rest of the night trying to shut out the sound of the howling wind and to quell the fear rising inside of her.

THE NEXT DAY brought an end to the wind, but the snow held Beryl inside the tent like a relentless jailer. Deep lethargy overtook her and she found it hard to force herself to melt enough snow for tea and to rehydrate the unappetizing freeze-dried food. Even the sight of a box of cookies reserved for celebrating when the team returned held no appeal.

Another sleepless night! Near dawn, Beryl drifted off into a fitful sleep, only to be awakened by the sound of a voice calling, "Are you in there, Beryl?"

Jumping up, she pushed open the top of the flap and saw Lon working his way toward her, shoveling out a path. "I'm here," she shouted. "You're the best thing I've seen in days!"

"I'd be more flattered if I didn't know I was the only thing," he answered dryly. "How are you making out?"

"Fine. How's Jane? I've been so worried about her."

"She suffered a little frostbite, but it's not too serious. And she's calmer; making that last effort seems to have wiped away the doubts that were upsetting her."

"I'm glad, Lon." Beryl leaned gratefully against him.

"Why did you turn off your radio?" Lon asked, patting her awkwardly.

"It's broken!"

"That's what the rest of us surmised, but Rock couldn't be convinced something hadn't happened to you. It looked as if all hopes for this expedition were over." He began removing his heavy outer clothes.

"What do you mean?" Beryl demanded, automatically brushing off the snow clinging to him.

"Rock was frantic; he insisted on starting out in the storm to try to get to you. The ultimate sacrifice for a woman, I'd call it. I've never met the woman who would make me willing to give up everything for her!"

Beryl's eyes widened. Was that how Lon saw Rock's concern? "Maybe it's because Rock doesn't seem to think I have any common sense, Lon. I don't know why he can't respect me even a little...."

"Love's funny that way, I guess. It makes you so concerned about someone's well-being that you don't see them clearly." Lon had settled down in front of the radio, and now he began to remove its front cover while Beryl prepared him a cup of tea at the stove.

Her hands were shaking as she held out the mug. "Love, Lon? Do you really think that's what Rock feels for me?"

He wrapped his reddened hands around the mug to warm them. "What else would explain his actions?"

"Are you forgetting I'm the daughter of John Bartlett?"

"So?" He eyed her speculatively, his eyes urging her to explain her statement.

With impatience in her voice she continued, "Don't act so dense. I'm aware that my father is a major sponsor to this expedition."

"Contributor, not sponsor. Rock is very firm about that policy. He doesn't allow others to have too much say in the expeditions he runs, so he limits the amount a person can contribute. There are lots of others who gave the same amount as your family. In fact, the list of people who made contributions is so long that Rock had it microfilmed so he can bury it on the summit in their honor. Your dad's just one of hundreds."

"But my brother implied...."

"Oh, Brad," Lon chuckled. "I've got a sister, Beryl, so I can imagine that he was trying to protect you from getting hurt. You see, Rock's been interested in dating you for several years, but Brad always held out. That's why I was so intrigued when you showed up and Rock introduced you as someone special to him. It didn't take me long to figure out that he was only making sure none of the rest of the guys got any ideas."

Beryl sat staring at him, her eyes wide, as the implication of his words sank in. Did she dare to believe that Rock loved her? But what other motivation could make him even consider giving up his chance of scaling Mount Everest to check on her safety? Suddenly she felt an overwhelming urge to hear his voice. "Hurry, Lon. Please fix the radio so we can let Rock know I'm fine."

"Now you're talking. If I don't fix it soon I'll have to hurry back to camp two and let him know before he comes swooping down this mountain to rescue you." As he fiddled with the wires, he continued, "Do you somehow have the idea that Rock is short of money?"

Beryl flushed with embarrassment. "Not exactly short of money," she admitted. "But these expeditions cost a lot, and a professor's salary...."

Lon swung around and picked up a backpack frame from beside one wall of the tent, sticking it under her nose. "Read that," he ordered.

"Rawlings Mountaineering Equipment." She read the finely etched letters slowly.

"That represents only one of the many items manufactured by Rock's and Kent's company. He's wealthy in his own right, Beryl, so you can relax on that score."

"I'm not interested in his financial status," Beryl snapped, still staring at the name imprinted on the chrome frame. "It's only—"

"I get the picture," Lon interrupted. "You've had some trouble with fortune seekers in life. Let me assure you, Rock's not one of them."

The first static crackled out from the radio, and Beryl clutched the mike, trying to rouse camp six. "Hold on," Lon told her. "Let me get the cover back on this baby."

"Camp six speaking. Is this Beryl?" Rock's voice sounded infinitely weary and almost indifferent, and for a moment Beryl faltered. Had she only been allowing herself to dream that Rock might love her?

"Camp one reporting in. Lon has repaired the radio and we're ready to resume transmission."

"Is that all you can say to me? Don't you know you've had me worried half out of my mind, making a fool of myself in front of all these poor long-suffering teammates of mine? And you have the nerve to act as if nothing's even happened!"

Beryl let a small laugh slip out in spite of her intentions to remain cool. "Nothing's happened, Rock. I got snowed in; the radio quit working, but everything was fine. How are things at camp six?"

"Great now! But you've put me through a terrible forty-eight hours. I had visions of you with the tent blown down, wandering around in the snow, getting frostbitten, hallucinating...."

"I did hallucinate a little," she admitted.

"About me?" came Rock's husky whisper.

"No, I dreamed about fresh grapefruit and tomatoes." Laughter in the background indicated others were avidly listening to their conversation.

"How flattering," Rock responded. "My dreams about you were more along the line of where we're going to spend our honeymoon."

Beryl felt her body tremble, overwhelmed by the emotion sweeping through her. There were no words for the happiness that filled her; she longed to be with Rock so that she could throw her arms around him and feed the inner hunger she felt for him.

"Beryl, are you there?" Rock's voice insistently reminded her that this conversation was being held over an open radio line. The thought of the inevitable amusement on those other faces was like a cold spray, and she replied, "Honeymoon, Dr. Rawlings? Haven't you left out something?"

"Good Lord, Beryl! Are you trying to make me propose to you in front of all these other people?"

"You introduced the topic," she sputtered.

"Well, if you insist, I'll get it over with," he drawled. "May I have your hand in marriage, Miss Bartlett?"

"If you were here in person you'd have my fist right in the center of your nose. You...." At the sound of laughter ringing out, she cringed. Then came the congratulations accompanied by cheers and a big hug from Lon.

"Now that sounds more like my spitfire," Rock chuckled. "I'll have to wait for that until after we climb this mountain. Do you want to wish me luck?"

All anger and embarrassment drained from her, replaced by a searing fear for his safety. "Oh, Rock, please be careful and don't try anything foolish. The mountain's not half as important as your getting back safely so we can have that honeymoon."

"I won't do anything to risk missing it, darling," Rock said huskily before signing off.

CHAPTER TWENTY

BERYL STOOD on the shadow-filled balcony, her filmy gown billowing softly around her tall slender body as the cool late-night ocean breezes washed over her. The scent of lush tropical vegetation, dominated by the sweet fragrance of gardenias, floated from the terrace below, filling her with a feeling of sadness that in the morning she and Rock would be leaving this small island in the Caribbean where they had spent their honeymoon.

Leaning against the wrought-iron railing, she let her thoughts drift lazily back over the past few days. Their time there had been so wonderful, a time of happiness and shared dreams, passionate lovemaking and long hours spent together with no interruptions, no responsibilities, no other people demanding Rock's attention or intruding between them.

An uncontrollable shudder shook Beryl's frame as she remembered that frightening day when she had waited for news of Rock's arrival at the crest of Mount Everest. The lonely tent and silent radio had held her a prisoner, helplessly awaiting the news that would either shatter her life or thrill her with the knowledge that Rock had safely accomplished his mission.

The hours had stretched endlessly; neither the

books nor the games with which she had tried divert-
ing herself had helped to pass the time. Finally the
news had come: Susan had been the first to radio her
that Rock had been sighted on the summit, with
Reagen close behind him. A thrill of joy had surged
through Beryl and she had grabbed her journal to
record all the exultant comments of the other team
members as they radioed in their reports.

Then had come the even more terrible hours; the
hours in which Rock had fought his way back down
the dangerous sheer cliffs of ice, step by step, inch by
inch. Beryl had prayed desperately for his safe return, her only comfort the reassuring comments of
her more experienced companions.

Their reunion had been too public; Beryl's only
desire had been to be held in Rock's arms, to have
him to herself for even a few minutes. She had been
forced to stay in the background, to share him with
all those who wanted to hear the details of his experience on the challenging mountain.

The return trek, being met at the airport in Los
Angeles by the television reporters and cameras,
Monica's and Big John's surprise and pleasure over
her engagement and the frantic preparations for the
wedding in Dallas—all these were little more than a
blur to her now. Monica had insisted on a huge society wedding; and Beryl, with newfound understanding
born of her love for Rock, had given in gracefully to
her mother's wishes. The large church had been filled
with people on the morning of their wedding, and a
sea of faces both strange and familiar had greeted her
as she walked to meet Rock.

Beryl had moved past the people without noticing

them, intent only on Rock's tall lean figure waiting for her in front, the half smile in his dark eyes as his gaze swept over her in admiration and desire. Later that evening they had laughed together as Rock told her how surprised he'd been when he saw her walking down the aisle.

"Somehow I'd become used to seeing you in those jeans and wool shirts," he'd teased her softly. "You really knocked me speechless there for a moment." After a pause in which he kissed her thoroughly, he slid the gown off her shoulders and, gathering her firmly against him, murmured, "Still, I think I like you best wearing nothing at all...."

Music drifted up from the terrace below, a romantic melody popular earlier in the year in the States. A sigh escaped Beryl's lips and then she trembled at the feel of Rock's hands encircling her waist, his head nuzzling the nape of her neck. "Why the sigh, darling?" he whispered.

Turning to face him, Beryl threw her arms around his neck. "I don't want us to leave here ever," she responded.

"Okay," he laughed huskily. "Your wish is my command. We'll become beachcombers and broil fish over our driftwood fires each evening."

"Is that *all* we'll do?" she asked, gazing into his eyes provocatively.

"You're not the innocent little girl I found in that hut in Nepal," Rock answered, his eyes smiling into hers.

"Whose fault is that?"

"I'm willing to take full responsibility for turning you into such a delightful wicked creature." Swooping her up in his arms, he carried her into the bedroom, his eyes glinting passionately down at her, telling her without words how much he wanted her, how much he needed her.

In the soft pool of light from the lamp Rock's tall lithe frame glistened with drops of moisture from the shower he had just taken, his broad chest filled out again after recovering from the rigors of the climb. Her heart bursting with love, Beryl ran her hands hungrily over the ridged muscles, traveling down to his bare lean hips.

"I do love you so much, Rock," she told him softly.

"Show me," he demanded, his lips tantalizing a hairbreadth above hers.

She raised herself and their lips met with a gentle persuasiveness that set her on fire as she returned pressure for pressure. His arms were hard against her body, and she curved sinuously against him, enjoying the feel of his rough chest hair against her soft breasts, her hands stroking the nape of his neck.

His lips moved to her throat, and she gasped with pleasure as his hand gently caressed her breast with a tenderness that aroused her to a fever pitch of excitement, so that she moaned his name over and over. Then, as he bent to kiss her breast, she buried her face in his throat, feeling a coil of need building inside her, and kissed the throbbing pulse she found there, pleased at the growing urgency she sensed in him. Falling back on the pillow and drawing him with her, she watched Rock's face as he moved over her, dark eyes flaming with desire.

One look at her and he pulled her to him, murmuring his love for her, as he claimed her molten body, sharing with her the ultimate joy of both giving and receiving. . . .

Later she lay silently, peacefully, drained of everything but contentment as she heard Rock's heartbeat slow to a soft regular thud that matched her own, his hands gently stroking her. A disquieting thought crept into her mind. Did this wonderful period of happiness really have to end? A slight tremor ran through her languid body, and Rock raised his head to gaze at her inquiringly. "Cold, darling?"

"No, I was thinking about what we have to do tomorrow."

"We're just flying to Los Angeles so that I can resume teaching. Why would you dread that?"

"I don't dread it; I'm only worried. Do you think I'll be able to fit into your life there, Rock?" She stroked the back of his neck thoughtfully.

Rock turned her face toward him, and his fathomless eyes penetrated the doubt that lurked in hers. "Beryl, you belong with me wherever I am—whether it's on top of a mountain or in the heart of Los Angeles. And you're not to forget it—ever!"

He leaned back then against the pillow, his tanned skin gleaming against the pale sheets. Beryl settled her head on his shoulder, curling her slender curves against his lean hardness.

"There's something else—something I was saving for when we got back to L.A.," he went on. "Fred told me at the wedding that he's found a publisher who's definitely interested in your book. He's very impressed with Fred's photographs, and from your writing samples he's convinced you've done a fine account of our expedition.''

The news was thrilling; but it was Rock's emphasis on the last two words, ''our expedition,'' that made Beryl shiver with happiness. He truly had accepted her as one of the team, an important part of the expedition. ''Did you really mean that?'' she asked. ''The part about it being ours?''

Rock pulled away from her suddenly, rolling her over and grasping her shoulders firmly. His face was serious, no trace of mockery evident as he told her, ''Of course I mean it! The only reason I didn't want you going up on that mountain was that I was afraid, Beryl. Afraid of losing you; afraid something would happen and I wouldn't be there to help.'' His voice was slightly husky as he continued, ''You did a great job, Beryl. No one could have run camp one any better.''

Beryl tried to quell her sense of pride at his words, still wanting reassurance from him. ''Then you'd let me go along again sometime? As a real team member? Right from the start?''

''Just try to stay at home,'' he warned her, pulling her back against him. ''However, I've a feeling we'll be staying at home more now. That is, unless you're planning on training all our children to be mountain climbers at a very young age. . . .''

Beryl pressed her lips lightly against his shoulder, trailing her fingers languidly along his muscular chest. ''Sounds like a good idea to me. Maybe Susan and Reagen and their children can come along, too, to keep ours company. But not Jane and her Calvin.

I couldn't bear to see her suffer that much again.''

"I'm not sure I've forgiven Reagen," Rock growled. "After all, for a long time I thought you couldn't choose between the two of us."

Beryl snuggled closer to him. "Don't tell me you were jealous!''

Rock's answer left her shaken and breathless, his passionate kiss making her fully aware of how deeply worried he had been.

After a few minutes of silence his next comment caught her by surprise. "Your record of the trip *is* excellent, but I still wish you'd let me read your secret diary.''

Laughter bubbled out of Beryl. "You would like to read all about how I fell for you, wouldn't you?'' she teased, stroking his cheek with one hand before outlining his firmly molded lips with the tip of a finger.

"If you want us to talk, you're going to have to stop that," Rock groaned, shifting out of her way.

"Stop what?" Beryl asked innocently, her other hand stroking his back as she moved her mouth against his cheek.

"Enough," he laughed. "You distract me from what I was saying. Your diary, wasn't it?''

For answer Beryl pulled his head down and nibbled on an ear, watching his eyes darken, pleased by his blatant need for her.

"Oh, you're nothing but a wicked little vixen,'' Rock murmured. "One touch from you and I can't even remember what day it is.''

Her lashes lowered and she gazed through them at

the hard masculine body, surprised at the way she could never get enough of his passionate lovemaking. "Hold me, Rock. Love me," she whispered.

"I'm going to do that forever, darling," he answered, his mouth covering hers in a possessive kiss that fulfilled her wildest dreams.

Harlequin Presents

ALL-TIME FAVORITE BESTSELLERS
...love stories that grow
more beautiful with time!

Now's your chance to discover the earlier great books in Harlequin Presents, the world's most popular romance-fiction series.

Choose from the following list.

ALL-TIME FAVORITE BESTSELLERS

Complete and mail this coupon today!

Harlequin Reader Service

In the U.S.A.
1440 South Priest Drive
Tempe, AZ 85281

In Canada
649 Ontario Street
Stratford, Ontario N5A 6W2

Please send me the following Presents **ALL-TIME FAVORITE BESTSELLERS.** I am enclosing my check or money order for $1.75 for each copy ordered, plus 75¢ to cover postage and handling.

☐ #17	☐ #35	☐ #41	☐ #66	☐ #73
☐ #20	☐ #36	☐ #42	☐ #67	☐ #75
☐ #29	☐ #38	☐ #50	☐ #70	☐ #78
☐ #32	☐ #39	☐ #62	☐ #71	

Number of copies checked @ $1.75 each =	$ _____
N.Y. and Ariz. residents add appropriate sales tax	$ _____
Postage and handling	$ ____.75
TOTAL	$ _____

I enclose _____
(Please send check or money order. We cannot be responsible for cash sent through the mail.)
Prices subject to change without notice.

NAME _____
(Please Print)

ADDRESS _____ APT. NO. _____

CITY _____

STATE/PROV. _____

ZIP/POSTAL CODE _____

Offer expires August 31, 1983   30456000000

Now's your chance to discover the earlier books in this exciting series.

Choose from this list of great

SUPERROMANCES!

SUPERROMANCE

Complete and mail this coupon today!

- - - - - - - - - - - - - - - - - - - -